INTO A HEARKENING SKY

THE HYPERBOLIA SERIES

UNDER A DARKENING MOON

WITHIN A WAKENING EARTH

INTO A HEARKENING SKY

INTO A HEARKENING SKY

HYPERBOLIA, BOOK THREE

PETER A. HEASLEY

First paperback edition April 2023

The cover is a composite of two altered images:
   "Hubble Sees Anemic Spiral NGC 4921" by Hubble Legacy Archive, ESA, NASA;
   Image of Antarctica provided courtesy of Satellite Imaging Corporation and NASA/USGS.

ISBN 979-8-9867574-4-5 (hardcover)
ISBN 979-8-9867574-8-3 (paperback)
ISBN 979-8-9867574-5-2 (ebook)

peteraheasley.com

For +Charles Louis Heasley

PART ONE

LADYMOUSE

GE+19

A sagging spiral of razor wire sliced the bare blue sky. Lance Corporal Hudson Bridgewater MacDuff was an hour into his watch at the eastern gate of New Norfolk Section A-III, which encompassed one hundred and sixty acres of Quonset huts and 3D-printed, concrete houses planted on Mammoth Tooth Hill, a muddy mound of the recently exposed continental shelf. Old worlders, the people of his mother's generation, had once found a mammoth tooth here, on this knuckle of a hill within a finger of land pointing from the continental slope toward the abyssal plain. The archaeologists of her generation had somehow found that tooth when the mud, into which Hudson was slowly sinking, had been covered by the black sea.

Hudson could find no reason for the razor wire. The only thing that was imprisoning the residents of this outpost on the ocean's new edge was a pioneering sense of reward for their efforts. In other words, the gambler's paradox. Specters, on the rare occasion that they did emerge directly from the Atlantic Ocean, never climbed the Faraday fence that surrounded the town. They simply tore into it as violently as they tore into living things, bursting like flowers in brief blossoms of color and light before decaying into the primordial chaos from which they had emerged.

"If you pull back any farther, another head's going to grow out of that Adam's apple," Benny said. Lance Corporal Hector Benitez was often on watch with Hudson. His company was the only thing that made it bearable.

Hudson tried to swallow, but the angle of his neck would not allow it, and he turned his eyes back toward the ocean, where he was supposed to be watching, anyway.

"What are you staring at up there?" Benny said.

"It helps me see. I always sense the specters coming before I actually see them."

"This is a no-woo-woo zone. Put your head down. You're gonna get us in trouble."

Benny had brought Hudson into this trouble in the first place. They had graduated a few months ago from Norfolk Canyon High School. It was not a high school like Hudson had heard about from the old worlders, with classrooms and bells and backpacks, but one with a few hours of daily tutoring from whatever non-essential personnel the Navy could scrape off its ships. Hudson's mother, Lucy, taught Earth science. Only the best and brightest went on to college these days. Benny was not one of them, at least not when it came to books and tests. Hudson might have been. He might have done better on the college entrance exams if he had not been studying with Benny, who had never had any real hope of passing, but who had aspired toward college so he could go to flight school and live like the guys in *Top Gun*. Instead, Hudson and Benny were serving in the Virginia Naval Militia, a once-independent organization now fully funded and controlled by the US Navy.

The USS *Dwight D. Eisenhower* and much of Carrier Strike Group 2, out to sea during the Great Eclipse nineteen years ago, were currently serving as a base at the mouth of the Chesapeake River while engineers built a series of locks from old Norfolk to the coast. Sea level had fallen nearly six hundred feet—four hundred during the Eclipse itself and ten feet per year since then. The fleet in Norfolk waited behind the only set of locks they had built so far, ninety miles away, before the James River met the Chesapeake. That shallow river had found its way to sea through Norfolk Canyon, the canyon it had carved during the last ice age before the seas had risen and the same canyon that, for the past ten years, the MacDuffs had called home.

Benny bent over to wipe a spot of mud off his boots and said, "You gonna retake the exams?"

Hudson hammered the end of his long Dreamcaster rifle into the ground. "Maybe."

"Don't do that," Benny said. "You're gonna set it off again."

Benny was right, but it was hard to take somebody with permanent dimples seriously. Hudson looked at the midnight-blue tip of his Dreamcaster's devonium bayonet through its metallic cage. He tried to catch glints of copper color in the mid-morning sun.

"What do you mean, 'maybe'?" Benny continued. "All you have to do is tell them you're Lucy MacDuff's son. College is a done deal."

Hudson looked out toward the sea. "My mother is Lucy

MacDuff, which means I have to make sure my little brother, Owen, is fed and clothed for the next few years."

When Hudson looked at Benny again, Benny turned away.

"You're just bored," Benny said. "The old worlders always complain that the apocalypse is way more boring than they thought it would be."

"Well, maybe it's not the apocalypse, then. In the real apocalypse, we wouldn't have to wait so long," Hudson said.

"Wait for what? Death? Not all of us stop aging."

"My mom's not one of the un-aging ones. She's not like Father Joseph."

"You sound like you're dying already."

Hudson looked out at the world available to him: a muddy continental shelf that always smelled like rotting seaweed and a steel-blue ocean that sent out agents of death at irregular intervals.

A garden trolley rounded the hill leading from the shore in electric silence. Benny's dimples deepened. Hudson would let him handle this one.

Benny stood his short, stocky frame squarely in front of the open gate, feet slightly spread, chest high, shoulders back, and Dreamcaster planted vertically before him in both hands. When the garden trolley drew near, he raised the palm of his right hand, forcing it to stop. Two young women they both knew, with looks of resignation on their faces, sat in the cab. Benny gave Hudson a slight smirk, inviting him to take his post in front of the trolley.

"Alright," Benny said with playacted severity. "What have we here?"

The woman driving, Hazel, sighed and said, "You know what it is, Benny."

Benny, pretending to inspect the front fender of the miniature truck, jerked his head back in feigned outrage. "That's Lance Corporal Benitez, ma'am."

Hazel sighed again. "Whatever, Lance Corporal Benitez. It's exactly what you think it is. Baskets of shellfish."

"I'm afraid we're going to have to take a look inside," Benny said. He walked along Hazel's side of the car and sniffed a little.

Hudson knew, and would never say, that Hazel wore perfume only on days she would have to pass through the gates on Benny's shift. Hudson looked at Hope in the passenger seat. When she finally returned his gaze, he lifted his eyebrows. Hope jerked her head to the side. Hudson could never figure out what about him had always repulsed her.

Benny tried to lift the tarp off a woven basket, but Hazel had tied it too tightly. He set his spear against the side of the truck and lifted the basket to see where she had knotted it. Seeing this, she released the brake ever so slightly and slammed it again, sending the Dreamcaster to the ground.

"Whoa there, young lady!" Benny almost shouted.

"Oops. Sor-ry," Hazel sang.

"You could have set that weapon off. You would have made Lance Corporal MacDuff here into a phantom. And he's skinny enough as it is. What's in this basket, anyway? You said shellfish. These are clams."

Hazel, recovering from the real danger of almost having blasted Hudson, replied, "Clams are shellfish, Lance Corporal Benitez."

"Sir is fine, ma'am."

"Okay, Lance Corporal Benitez, sir."

"Alright, then. But we have a problem. Clams are clearly mollusks."

The same Benny who could not pass a test to save his life was recalling details from bio 1 four years ago. Hudson looked at Hope to try to share some sympathy for Hazel, but Hope was drilling her eyes through the fence to her right. Sometimes she was friendly with Hudson, sometimes not. Hudson never knew which version of Hope he was going to find.

Hazel sighed a third time. "What is the difference, Sir Benny?"

Benny leaned his hip against the front of the truck. "Alright. I'm going to let you go, just this once. But no more claiming that clams are shellfish." He slapped the fender of the trolley twice and turned to let them pass. The two men watched the truck turn a corner inside the drab city streets. Benny gazed a little longer.

"Why don't you just have a normal date with her?" Hudson asked.

"With who?" Benny feigned surprise.

"With who? Are you kidding?"

"I don't know what you're talking about," Benny said and walked away from the gate.

"Do it," Hudson said, "so I can have a shot with Hope."

Benny did not answer. Instead, he made sucking sounds with his boots in the mud.

Hudson craned his neck backward again. Beyond the blue veil of the sky was an abyss more impenetrable than the deep ocean. Before he could will it, his head jerked forward again, toward the sea. "Close the gates."

Closing the gates automatically sent the alarm to Marines on the watchtower. Hudson waited with Benny behind the closed gates while confirmation came of spectral emergence. Hudson could already see a slinking worm of bent light crawling over the hill on nearly the same path Hazel and Hope had taken. The alarm blared in bursts of three. This was a fast mover.

It took six more seconds for the specter to find the Faraday fence, and when it did, its bright burst faded quickly, leaving a smell of burnt wool and a humanoid lurching toward the fence.

"It's one of the dumb ones," Benny said. "He's gonna fry himself on the fence."

"Let him," Hudson said but put up his hand anyway. The humanoid kept walking toward the gate.

Benny put up his hand. The humanoid stopped.

"How is it he obeys you?" Hudson said.

Four Marines arrived, roped the machine-man, and carried it away without a struggle.

"I possess a certain *je ne sais quoi*," Benny said. "Meaning I'm at more of his intellectual level."

"I'm not far ahead of you, Benny. I got a B-minus in Earth science. The class my mother teaches."

"Yeah, how do you not get an A in your mom's class, anyway?"

"I guess we both assumed the knowledge would come automatically from living together."

Lucy was always saying that the words "Earth science"

had become an oxymoron. The receding sea should have been revealing more of the Earth, but with every foot it fell, humankind could fathom less and less about what lay underneath. Above, one thing was certain: no known science would bring a human body beyond the moonshock, the hard barrier between the Earth and the rest of the universe. The only thing the moonshock let pass was light. Hudson had once heard his friend Claire say that a photon never experienced time. The eight-minute journey it took from the sun to the Earth was felt instantaneously by the photon. Photons were the happy children of this universe, asleep at a party, waking up for the brief moment when they were passed from one set of arms to another, when they turned from light into heat.

Hudson looked down and saw Benny leaning against a concrete pillar, eyes closed, mouth agape. Benny was not suddenly bored. As much as the man had wanted excitement in his life, coming down from an event like this spectral emergence was more than his central nervous system would allow.

Benny barely opened his eyes and said, "That thing was right behind Hazel."

It almost got us, too, Hudson thought. He drew a spiral in the mud with his boot while he waited for the command to reopen the gate. He could retake the college exam and go where Benny and these people could not—into the sky, away from this place. When someone invented a way through the moonshock, he would go there. But the higher he went, the more useless and alone he would be, like the razor wire on this fence.

2

It was summertime and, so, not much of a dare, but Lucy
called the other students' bluff and led them all out from the
station at a sprint, all of them naked but for insulated boots.
They circled the South Pole in a screaming frenzy. They
would not qualify for the 300 Club, made up of those men
and women who had, during Antarctica's deadly winters,
run from a two-hundred-degree sauna into minus-one-hun-
dred-degree air and back again. That was not the prize for
which Lucy was running this morning.

As she rounded her way back to the station door, she saw
Declan and the truth in his eyes, that a thirty-foot radius of
frozen tundra would be the closest anyone but him would
come to her naked body. He held up a coat, but his eyes had
already wrapped around her. No one else she knew could at
once light flames of warmth and reproach. She stopped in
front of the coat and blew a raspberry at him.

Once back inside the sauna, she and the others reveled
in their adventure while Declan, team leader, remained silent. Lucy held her head cocked back and looked down at
him through shielded eyes. Even with a towel covering her,

she had brought the long copper curtain of her hair over her breasts. Lost in the garden of his blue eyes, dark curls, and nappy beard, she forgot to return some lewd joke from one of the other men. One by one, the heat in the sauna became too much for the others, and they left. Declan stayed behind.

Without taking his eyes off her, he said, "Professor Burns hates this kind of thing, you know."

She shrugged.

A smile snuck onto his face. "Your work can make up for this kind of behavior only so much. Besides, the guys who winter here are not impressed by your little run."

Lucy crossed her arms. She could outlast him in the sauna's heat. It was not a matter of putting up with Declan. He had fought for her many times in front of Burns. It was not a matter of enduring Declan's little lectures, like this one, for she could spend the time watching his blue eyes blaze with stellar light.

"What's the tattoo on your hip?" he asked.

"It's a mouse," she said.

"Why a mouse?"

"Ladymouse. It was the name of my band in high school."

"What instrument did you play?"

"All of them. I'm a one-man band."

Declan turned away and grinned. She felt her shield begin to falter but held her head back. He returned his eyes to her.

"What were some of your songs?"

"My biggest hit was called 'Dirty Band-Aid on the Floor.'"

Declan laughed.

Lucy felt a smile of her own slip through. She had taken that song so seriously when she had been sixteen. It rang ridiculous now. No one but her parents had ever heard it. But it made this man smile. It really was her biggest hit.

"Why Ladymouse?" he asked.

"Because I'm a lady."

"And also a mouse?"

"A mouse can go places no one else can. A mouse lives in the walls, in a world that slips between what we know, in the cracks of our reality."

"And you go to these places, Lucy Ladymouse?"

Mom? came a voice.

Lucy pulled her head forward. "It's been too long in this heat. I've got to go."

***

"Mom?" Hudson repeated. He knocked and opened the door to Lucy's bedroom. His mother was lying in bed, still in her nightgown. "Mom, it's almost noon. Come on. Where's Owen?"

Lucy did not respond.

Hudson walked forward into the tiny bedroom, guided by a thin slit of sunlight. His mother was running her thumb along a framed picture tucked under her cheek. It was of her and Declan, his father. Hudson leaned forward, and his shadow covered Declan's face.

Lucy jerked her head toward Hudson, startled. Her cheek was imprinted with the carved corner of the picture frame. "Why don't you knock?"

"I did, Mom. And I've been calling you several times. Where's Owen?"

"How should I know?"

"Has he eaten yet?"

"He's nine years old. He knows his way around." Lucy sat up. Her dried-up broom of red hair fell forward, hiding her face. She stretched her arms and fingers along her thin legs.

"Alright, well, I'm on watch again, from noon to four. Double-duty day."

"Did you eat?" she asked.

"That's what I'm here for. Noon's the long watch."

Lucy brought her feet to the floor. "Well, why don't you feed Owen, then?"

"Because I'm not his mother," Hudson said. He wished she were consistently unreliable. It was not the anniversary of Declan's death. She had given no signs of staying in bed today. "And I don't even know where he is."

"He's got to be in the yard somewhere."

"In the yard? Didn't you hear the alarm?"

Lucy gazed out the window. "I guess not."

"I'm running late," Hudson said. "I've only got a few more minutes before real noon starts."

She grabbed his hand and lightly jiggled his arm. "The new noon."

Hudson sighed and kissed Lucy on the head. There she was, the Belly of Boulder, the woman who had saved an entire city from specters simply by squatting in the fetal position, the last line of defense on the new frontier, in her nightgown at noon.

He went into the kitchen and opened the fridge. If he hid his face behind the door long enough, she might dress and do something. There was not enough time to make a proper meal and search the streets for his brother. He peeked above the refrigerator door. Lucy was still sitting on the bed with her head hanging down. Just as he was about to slam the door, he saw a plastic plate covered in tin foil. "Ah, empanadas," he said. "Thank you, Mrs. Benitez." He stuffed four in his pockets and one in his mouth, staring at Lucy while he ate it. She did not budge. Hudson looked at the large framed picture of his family above the television, wished in the general direction of heaven that his father was still alive, and walked out of the house, calling for Owen.

***

Lucy sat on the edge of her bed. The two-syllable pulses of Hudson's voice faded as he called for Owen deeper and deeper into the yard and then down the street. How had she lost track of so much time? She had learned by Owen's age how to fend for herself.

The tiny triangular hook on the back of the picture frame would not find the nail. Lucy brought her long, thin fingers along the wall while the last sliver of noonday sun slithered out of her bedroom. Household electricity was rationed for evening use; only the fridge was kept on.

She had wanted to look up and see Hudson in uniform and with a mouth full of food in the refrigerator light. She had been afraid, though, in the darkening cave of her little house, that she would see Declan instead, as he had been thirty years ago, in another memory, at the entrance to that ice cave in Antarctica, not glowing with love or lust or whatever had warmed them both at their excursion to the South Pole, but, just a week later, pale and terrified at what she had conjured from the Last Continent's broken crust of ice:

An ice sheet had recently calved close to shore, and drone footage revealed that one of the basal channels under an Antarctic glacier was now open directly to the sea. This was what Declan's team of graduate students would investigate—more incontrovertible evidence of global climate change. They had secured passage on a boat close enough to the new edge of the ice sheet and had sent another drone into the exposed basal channel. The rocky shore was just a few dozen feet past the wall of ice that cantilevered beyond it. They lost control of the drone, but the video it had taken showed the channel safe enough to enter.

As soon as the six geologists arrived, via rubber raft, at the hidden tongue of land no human had ever seen, they very quickly determined that this presumed basal channel, an under-glacier river heated by some source, had long been dead and was now a wadi of dry, palm-sized gravel. The gravel was hard to walk on, and its echo off the icy chamber walls did little to mute the occasional groans of ice above and around them.

Lucy collected rock samples for mineral testing with the others near the entrance to the channel while Declan went deeper to collect the drone. Once he found it, he mumbled something about it being broken and came back toward the lighted entrance to the cave. Lucy kept looking inward, where the high-vaulted channel continued to curve gently into the darkness. She glanced at the others, bent over their work, and looked again into the beckoning black. Lucy swung her bag over her shoulder and walked forward.

Though her lantern lit both sides of the ice cave, Lucy kept to the right-hand wall. It was not at all smooth, like she knew a river channel should be, and it had no horizontal striations to suggest seasons of flow. She walked forward, running her fingers along that rough-etched wall of ice. Eventually, the other wall curved out of the reach of her lantern light and into the pooling darkness. She had entered some immense cavern. She kept on, and the din of her colleagues' conversation faded away. Soon, all she heard was the crunch of the gravel beneath her feet, her own breath, and her heartbeat, solitary sounds that met no echo. Lucy stopped and waited. She watched her breath glow like a nebula in the lantern light. When the breath dissolved and the light faded, something else remained.

Two blue slivers like serpent's eyes looked at her from the other side of the darkness.

They had found her again, the shadows. They crept around her, blanketed her, stole her breath. Ice grew between her skin and her parka. Her throat ground against gravel when she swallowed. Her flinty face softened to rubber.

She should whimper like she used to as a girl. She should turn mouse so she could escape this again. But this was not her bed, and she was not half asleep. She was awake. Lucy did what she knew would rid her of the shadows. She turned off her lantern. If there was no light, there would be no shadows. The snake eyes disappeared.

Lucy waited for her heart to stop pounding against her skull and for the tide of tingles to wash down her spine. She shifted on her feet just to hear the real sound of grinding gravel. As she did, something hit the ground, as if a piece of rock or ice had fallen or been thrown at her feet. She gasped and felt unbound. The wheels of reason turned again. She relit her lantern. The two blue eyes she had seen were slivers of ice on the wall across from her.

A piece of rock unlike the others, white with flakes of dark blue, called up to her from the ground. She bent over and picked it up. Lucy would have studied the rock in the lantern light, but another curiosity beckoned her. Where the ice cavern beyond her had been completely dark before, a little light seeped through, ahead and to the right. She put the rock in her pocket and walked ahead.

She continued to cling to the wall at her right. The new light was coming from around the corner. It bounced against another wall. The other wall of the large cavern was closing in. This could be light from outside. The basal channel split at this large cavern, and Lucy was about to discover a second exit. All that fear was for nothing or was, at least, a small price to pay for discovery.

The light increased, and so did the noise. She had thought it was the echo of gravel and groaning ice but soon discerned the din of conversation. Lucy walked quickly and found her colleagues picking like crows over something on the ground.

Before she joined them, she studied the wall on her right. She had not removed herself from that wall for a moment. Upon returning to where she had begun her walk, it had become the wall originally on her left. This was physically impossible.

Lucy crept slowly toward her colleagues in case they were some strange copy the ice had made. Declan looked up at her and smiled.

"Come see what they've found," Declan said. "It's big and old, maybe a *Cryolophosaurus*. They're going to have to send in the paleontologists."

She bent over to look in, making herself interested, ready to pull back.

"You ran off again," Declan said quietly.

"I don't know why," she said. His tender rebuke and his crow's feet told her it was the real Declan. She squatted with the others, and the stone she had picked up pinched her stomach. She pulled it out from her jacket to put in her bag.

As she did, she heard Declan say, "Look everyone, Lu found something."

"It's just a pretty rock," she began but stopped short with everyone else, holding it out between her squatting legs.

The sides of the stone were cut smoothly and evenly, a cube of white marble the size of her palm, inlaid with perfectly made circles of lapis lazuli.

"Did you bring that in from outside?" Declan asked. His voice quavered.

"I picked it up inside the cavern down there," she replied.

"This isn't one of your pranks?" he said.

Lucy watched flakes of gold from the lapis glow in the lantern light. "Where would I get a piece of lapis this big? Or anyone on this Earth?"

The others looked on, making her turn the object in her hands. Each was afraid to touch it. As she turned the cube around, they discovered that, like a die, those circles overlapped to create the numbers one through six. One of the other students asked, "We're the first ones here, right? This isn't someone else's prank? Another team?"

"Not as far as I know," Declan said. "Look, Lu, maybe you want to lead us to where you found that?"

Lucy led them toward the large cavern the same way she had gone. All of them hugged the right-hand wall. "It opens soon into a large cavern," she announced. But it did not. As the wall curved around, they came up against a wall of ice.

"So this is it?" one of them asked.

"I swear it opened so large that my flashlight didn't hit the other walls," Lucy pleaded. She pressed and beat against the cave's new walls.

"This must be what the drone hit," Declan said. "Let's head back and get some more photos of the bone." The others went ahead while Declan paused for a moment. "I don't know what game you're playing, Lucy. We've got a real discovery on our hands with that bone. Let's just go and act professional."

Lucy stayed behind. Her lantern light shimmered off the blue walls of the ice cave. She waited until the others' voices disappeared to see if the wall of ice dissolved. It did not.

When she came back to the team, she found them arguing.

"We all saw the bone," one of them said. "We were looking at it for ten minutes. We pulled away the other rocks.

Who else is here with us? Who could have taken it? Don't we have pictures of it? My pictures just have gravel in them."

Declan looked at Lucy. Even in the dim light, she could see the terror in his eyes. He turned to the other students. "Enough with the pandemonium," he yelled.

It took a few seconds for his echo to wash up and down the corridor of ice. All were silent.

Lucy looked at the half dozen silhouettes of her colleagues. They all seemed to be waiting for her to give some answer. She hoped they had not entered the world she had always thought was her own private nightmare.

"It's time to go," Lucy said calmly. "This part is just the beginning."

Back in the present, back in New Norfolk, Lucy was clutching the picture frame she had so far failed to hang up again. She closed her eyes to feel for the picture hook better. The wall of her 3D-printed concrete house was cold. Once the picture was hung, she kissed the glass behind which Declan stood with his arm around her, his face forever frozen in a smile.

She turned and gazed at the large family portrait hanging above the television. The three men in that picture each had, in one way or another, known the comfort of her womb before it had dried up. So had a whole city. A knife of midday sun sliced across the glass. They had not been the first.

3

The sun fell behind some thin veil deep in the sky. The color it gave off jaundiced the muddy plain just a little, enough for Hudson to notice. It was still too early for the shadows to claim the ground. Without looking at his watch, he knew it was nearly four.

In the long silences of this second turn at the city gate today, Hudson had fixated on his watch. It had been his father's, an old-world twenty-four-hour model. Declan had died at an hour like this, at the breezy time of day, coming back from the slope with Lucy. That had been five years ago, when "they got him." That was the only description ever given. Hudson had seen what specters did. He had also seen his father's smile persevere through Lucy's rare but memorable tantrums and imagined he had held it to the end, through whatever the specters had done to him.

Hudson looked at the watch. It was 3:45. He could not remember if, in all the times he had stared at the hands, he had rewound it today. "Benny," he began when a certain slant of light caught his eye. He slammed shut the gate. The alarm soon sounded in double pulses.

From behind the closed gate, Hudson watched. For the second time today, he heard the scurrying of boots and mothers crying for their children to come in from their yards. He knew a mass of two dozen men and women was assembling behind him and along the inside of the fence, some with devonium Dreamcasters, some with old-fashioned bullets twitching inside barrels. When he let his eyes blur the diamond-shaped weave of the Faraday fence in front of his face, he saw more clearly the slinking glint of light fight against the darkening sun.

"Hudson," Benny whispered.

"Sh."

"I don't see it."

"It's coming up the slope, long and low. Just like before. But slow."

"That's a mile away."

The minutes passed. Hudson described what he saw to his commanding officer, who stood behind him. "It's slow and slinky, like a caterpillar on a leaf." The claims that other militia guardsmen made to be seeing the specter was what kept the sergeant, who could not see what Hudson saw, from canceling the alarm. Hudson could not hear the alarm anymore.

He did smell incense, though. The subdeacons were ready with blessed incense, which many claimed warded off the specters and drew in creepers, the souls of deceased humans. Hudson did not know if he believed this or not. The incense would have to prove or disprove whatever his eyes told him.

They soon did. Hudson stood straight and relaxed his gaze.

"I see heads, human forms. Creepers. About three dozen, single file. Still about a quarter mile away."

"Attitude?" his sergeant asked.

"Heads are down, I think. Permission to open the gate?" He looked at Benny, whose eyes tore back and forth between the terror of hell and the shame of human cowardice.

"You sure about this?" the sergeant said.

"I'm sure."

The gate closed behind Hudson and Benny. Hudson walked forward and twisted open the cage around the tip of his spear. The charge light showed five green bars.

The line of creepers slowed as they approached Hudson. He could not see the souls in front of him except where the crown of their heads bent the late afternoon light. The soul at the head of the line grew translucent and began to glow with what to Hudson felt like a mixture of anger and confusion. This person seemed to want something. Hudson smelled sweat, blood, wood, and salt water.

Once the line of creepers was within arm's reach, Hudson held up his hand. He planted his spear in the mud and held his hands in front of him, imitating a bound prisoner. The first in line imitated him, and it seemed that the more this disembodied soul moved, the opaquer it became. Hudson gently lowered his spear between the man's two outstretched hands. The spear met some resistance, and immediately, a long rope dropped to the ground. Sounds rang out from the line of creepers, cries of joy.

The sergeant walked forward with Benny, flanked by

two subdeacons swinging globes of incense. Benny led the procession of souls through the cloud of holy smoke. Hudson watched the once-invisible souls of thirty-two African bodies take color and strength inside that cloud, many of them wafting the blessed scent over themselves like they were splashing water for a bath. Some of the onlookers wiped away tears.

"Well done, MacDuff," the sergeant said, shaking. "It's four-fifteen. Go debrief. Get a drink. And somebody turn off this damned alarm."

***

Hudson ate dinner with Owen and a fellow guard named Eric at the Old Barracks. This had been the first building here fifteen years ago and, until the fence was complete, had housed the kind of soldier who wished he had not lived through the Great Eclipse. One of them, John Dungloe, Hazel's father, sat at his usual table with his usual companions. There were many men and women like them, who had no trouble with the day and no trouble with the night, but who could not watch the sun set upward, behind the moonshock, and who sat with a pint or two until the deep red twilight passed. Lucy, on the other hand, could not be wrenched from her widow's walk until Earth swam in darkness. Benny ate with his family every night. Hudson had taken out Owen to help him unwind after a two-alarm day.

Hudson had not come for praise for the day's action and sat facing the window so no one would think he had. Barb,

"Yeah." He looked out again over the sea. "I thought you were going to say something about my being in your womb during the Eclipse when you saved all of Boulder."

"You just did it for me."

"You've said it a thousand times already."

Lucy turned toward the *Eisenhower*. "Who knows? Maybe it was you who saved everyone from there." She looked down and tugged at her shirt. "Maybe a baby *can* save someone. Anyway, what's weird to us is when things are in between one state and another. We don't notice the spirits all around us when they're in their place. It's when they're coming and going that we get afraid. That's what every haunted house is, a place of transition."

"Is this world still in transition, or is it going to be like this forever?"

Lucy leaned low on the railing. "The ocean's still sinking. You know, in the ancient texts of some religions, the sea represented chaos. God was in a battle against the forces of chaos represented by the sea. That's what the world and humanity are born into, or born out of. The battle with chaos."

"You sound like Father Joseph when you say things like that."

Lucy looked up. Hudson's eyes drooped.

"I'm going to bed," he said. "Early watch." Hudson descended the ladder through the open hatch. With his head poking above the roof, he said, "Good night."

"But where there's chaos, isn't there room to expand or start again?"

"I don't know, Mom," he whispered. "Good night."

4

GE+28

Jody Conque hobbled down the stairs of the dormitorium. The concrete steps were painful but safer than the icy handicap ramp. There had been many scientific reasons given for holding sleepers underground—contact with circulating groundwater chief among them—yet the lines blurred more and more between data-driven rationalism and political expediency. It had become easier to rebuild when the weirdness was out of sight. Dormitoriums had become for sleepers what churches had become for religion: it was easier to deal with God and His watchers not as an everyday reality, but as monsters in a monolith. Even the great Hall of Watchers in St. Louis was treated like an Egyptian temple, visible from miles away but whose sanctuary was accessible only through a darkened labyrinth. This dormitorium, in downtown Denver, had a pleasant park on top.

Inside the dim charcoal-colored vestibule, Donna was at the desk. Jody could not see her face, of course, as it was hidden by a graphic novel. She always had one propped on the shelf of her bosom. This one was called Space Vulture. There was a stack of these under the desk somewhere. Humans still needed to imagine stranger things than what surrounded them. It made the return to reality more bearable. Jody coughed. Without looking up, Donna pressed a button to release the lock on the door.

The lights in the corridors had already dimmed to match the setting sun. Jody could have walked this route in darkness; he knew the steps and turns by heart.

A few cells down from Haleh, someone was muttering prayers in the corridor. Whoever it was did not have a key for that cell and was probably a member of one of the cults of the watchers. This person, or one of her friends, had a sleeper somewhere else in the building and had taken it upon herself to spend time with those without visitors. Jody had been trying to encourage this in the parish, not just because it was a good thing to do but also because it prevented people like this from making the subjects of their ministries into their own personal gods. There was no small number of people who offered oblations to the dormant as if they were a bridge to the divine.

"Hey, hon," Jody said as he entered Haleh's cell.

It was only seven o'clock, not bedtime yet, so he switched on the light beneath the slab. Translucent glass supported the sleeper above a river of groundwater redirected from the soil outside the dormitorium. Beneath the soft egg Haleh occupied and which her body had somehow made for itself, the dark silhouette of her skinny body was curled up like a baby. There had been a time when it had been hard to look at her, first when her skin had been puffy, then when she had been bloated but still breathing air, and again after the orifices had closed but her old mouth and eyelids still had floated on this billowing sac of skin. That first year had been difficult, and now, except for her old belly button, she slept in a smooth white sac. It was easy to love the chick and the egg but not what came in between.

Jody lay his cheek against the warm, soft egg she slept in and pulled back to speak. "I'm back from Siberia. We did it, sort of. We got Mort and Todd through to the other side. You'd be so proud of our little Claire Bear. She paved the way with those drones she and Danny have been working on. We got a good look at what's down there. If it's any consolation, you're no longer the weirdest thing about this world. Come on, let me tease you a little. It's all I can do now. God, Haleh, the Earth really is flipped inside out. I wish that was the worst of it."

He closed his eyes and let out a long breath.

"The whole thing is wrapped up by the Earth's old core. It's like a ball of string, metal string, if you can imagine. Maybe you see it where you are, in your dreams. But something, our enemy I guess, Doris still won't let me call it the devil, has built something down there. Cities. At least one. With humanoids. This is the bad news, hon. Our enemy sucked Todd into one of those cities. Mort says he went willingly. Maybe, maybe not. I don't know. I do know that Mort jumped. He grabbed one of Claire's probes and jumped. Then...here's the worst news. Or the best, perhaps." Jody felt his lips swelling and trembling. "I don't know how he did it. What God let him become to do this. But Billy saved them, Mort at least." He paused. "I can't say he's gone because he is somewhere. Like always, some place only he can understand."

Jody clicked off the under-slab light and lay his cheek

against her. Her heart beat slow and steady. She breathed the fluid around her body the same slow way the shore breathed the tide. He did not know what her body fed upon. No one knew what sugar sleepers licked off the air.

A shadow hovered behind the smoked glass door. When she shifted her weight, Jody knew it was Claire. He opened the door for her.

"Hey, Claire Bear. Why didn't you just come in?" He sat down again.

Claire put her hands on his shoulder. "I didn't want to spoil your moment."

"I was just giving her an update."

Claire caressed some stray hairs on her father's head back into place. "I wonder if she knows the battles we face."

"You guys making any more sense of the data Mortimer brought back?"

Claire sighed. "Is this a question about data or a question about Mortimer?"

Jody pulled his owl-head cane under his hands. "Yes."

"It's confusing."

"What's confusing? The data or Mortimer?"

Claire kissed the top of Jody's head. "Yes." She opened the door to Haleh's cell. "I'll leave you two alone now." She walked down the corridor.

Jody struggled upward and kissed Haleh. "I've got to go, hon. You know she'll punish me if I don't go after her. She is definitely your daughter."

He found Claire praying in front of another sleeper's chamber. "What's wrong, Claire Bear?"

"Nothing's wrong. And stop calling me that. I'm not a little girl anymore."

"Okay, then let a man take you out to dinner."

"He hasn't asked me."

"You won't let him."

"What do you know about it?" Claire turned and walked down the corridor.

Jody looked at the sleeper and raised his eyebrows.

Claire stopped and stared into another sleeper's chamber. "Do you think poor Todd is still down there, I mean, alive? How could he be?"

"How can your mother be asleep for twenty-eight years, feeding off the empty air? We've got to suspend our notions about the world for a little while longer. It's like people. We're never going to enjoy them or even love them without opening ourselves up to their faults and inconsistencies. And we're never going to love ourselves without knowing how to love someone else that way. Hm?" He kissed Claire on the head and walked away, pleased with his words. "Come on. Let your old man take you out to dinner."

Jody pretended to fumble with the door to the vestibule long enough for Claire to catch up and hook her arm around his.

When they walked through the vestibule, Donna was asleep in her chair.

***

Jody sat to dinner with Claire at Rolph's Steakhouse. He would normally not let himself indulge like this on a Tuesday night, but Claire was in town, and she needed consolation. Indulgence for the love in front of you was better than discipline for the perfection you imagined. Whether or not this was really about Mortimer, he could not tell. Claire's always-focused eyes drifted past Jody into the dark-wood floor and red-checker tablecloths of the nearly empty restaurant, or into some new place her heart was carving out for herself.

Their dishes arrived. Jody poured more wine.

"How can you even eat that?" Claire asked, referring to Jody's mastodon steak.

"You think it's gamey. I find it rich. Besides, Rolph has a nice marinade. Our ancestors thrived on this, you know. Ate it right up."

"Uncle Billy's ancestors, you mean. We were eating wooly mammoth." Claire's shoulders dropped, and she forked her salmon.

Jody stuffed another piece of meat into his mouth to keep himself from saying, I wish you weren't so smart, Claire. You might be happy for once.

"Where do you think Uncle Billy is?"

Jody gazed into his goblet of red wine. "I don't know. I…." He drank. "Whatever he did, only he could do. That was always his way. Is his way. For all we know, he's alive somehow." Jody sawed at the thick plank of meat, cooked to perfection: charred on the outside, bleeding on the inside. "Whatever he did, it saved Mortimer. Of that, I am sure." He filled his mouth with a juicy morsel. This bought him time for thinking.

Claire cut her asparagus and carefully brought thick and thin ends together on her fork. "Why would he do that for Mortimer? I mean, he could not even have known what was going on thirteen hundred miles away, let alone...never mind. He found them on Devils Tower before I could even reach him. I just...for what purpose? For information about the lower mantle?" Claire's eyes pleaded.

"Certainly, he acted on knowledge only he had, but, Claire, knowing the man, and everything else he's done, I can say with sincerity he did it because he loves you." Maybe Jody should not have said that. Claire would feel such pressure to love Mortimer because of what White Wolf had done. "Loves all of us, you know? Somehow, he knew that disappearing into the Earth would keep us all going."

Claire wiped tears from her cheek with her napkin folded into a thin finger. She drank her wine. If she drank, she would eat, and if she ate, she would be happy. When the world was taking everything else away, indulgence was the best discipline.

***

Jody pulled himself up the stairs of the rectory, helped by the hefty handrail he'd had installed. Sixteen ounces of grilled mastodon tugged him downward at every step, and two thirds of a bottle of wine sent his head swimming. Upstairs, he could focus on the framed image of Our Lady of Guadalupe filling the end of the long hallway. As he often did, he walked right to the image, leaned his cane in the corner, gripped the heavy frame of ornately carved wood, and contemplated her turquoise coat covered in constellations. Only her hands, feet, and face broke through the mountain of cloth she wore like an Aztec queen. The image itself was miraculous, down to the last detail, and Jody wondered most at her face. Her young Indian face carried sorrow with such sweetness. This was the secret of every people before the so-called enlightenment of their minds. Jody dared imagine this joy was creeping back into the faces of those who had survived the past twenty-eight years, the joy of a tribe at one before the unknown, where every sorrow was shared, and whose shared ignorance erased the sadness of the one who knew everything but was alone.

"Where's our Billy, Mary? Our Todd?" Jody prayed. He gently leaned his forehead against the glass. While he remained there, gripping the frame, his breath fogged the glass around her pregnant belly. No answer came. "Please look after them."

Jody released his hands and forehead and reached for his cane. The glass cracked. A sliver ran the length of the fog he had blown. His eyes darted while his brain searched for a reason for the break. Glass was expensive, especially at this size.

The image behind the glass seemed suddenly distant, like Jody were looking at the landscape from an airplane window. The contours of Mary's dress were like rolling hills and its decorations like foliage spreading across the land, like the lichens he had looked up to know something about Mort. Her turquoise cloak shimmered like the sea. The angel at her feet looked a bit like Lucy.

"I've had too much to—" Jody began, but a rush of heat told him to hold his words.

The crescent moon under her feet rocked gently forward and back, and, as soon as Jody realized it was like the motion of a baby's cradle, the pile of fabric at Mary's feet rustled. She was still bulging above with Jesus, but there was another baby at her feet.

"Who, Mary?" Jody asked, but his eyes fixed on the figure of an angelic Lucy lifting up that baby, her hair spread wide where angel's wings once had been.

"She's right, isn't she? He's still around. A mother's always right. Help us to find Hudson, good Mother, if he is the next link in the chain."

5

GE+19

Hudson lay on his bunk at the barracks, reading a magazine. Eric picked at a guitar. Benny polished his boots.

"What're you reading there, Hudson?" Benny asked.

"*Shelf Life* from last May."

"Sounds expired. Anything I missed?"

"You into the history of the old port of Dover?"

"No, not really."

"You want a chart of temperature readings of the Gulf Stream?"

"Not my thing."

"Then you didn't miss anything. Well, there's another version of the story of the discovery of flying carpets."

Benny sighed. "Let's hear it."

"Says here an old lady in Portugal is sweeping around the lab where they're leaving artifacts they discover on the littoral of the Azores, right, so she gets to this thing she thinks is a rug, looks all muddy and dirty, hangs it over a railing to beat it."

Eric interrupted, "This is a rug that, presumably, has survived mostly intact under the sea, in some Atlantean sepulcher, for ten thousand years, correct?"

Hudson folded down the magazine to look at his doubtful friend. "Correct." He hid behind the magazine again. "Anyway, she beats and scrapes and picks and gets all of this sort of metallic mud off of it, and underneath there is a beautiful, intricate rug to rival anything out of Persia. Mind you, she still thinks the archaeologists were using this thing to kneel on out there while they're scooping up ancient amphorae and whatnot."

"Is that a shellfish, amphorae?" Benny asked.

"Uh, maybe. I don't know," Hudson said. "Getting on with the story, unless you have better things to do. So this lady's all proud of her work, and, seeing that the rug is not too big or heavy, she picks it up to give it a few last flicks, you know, get the dust out before she takes the vacuum to it. And there it is, just floating in midair."

"Just because she flicked it?" Benny asked.

Eric stopped picking and said, "Her flicking gave waveform energy to it. The orichalcum metal woven into the wool picks up on graviton-volts stored in the atmosphere. Like a Tesla coil. Don't you guys read anything?"

"That must've been in the April issue," Benny said. "Hey, I thought you were the doubter here."

"I don't doubt the technology," Eric said. "Just its origin story. Orichalcum and devonium are effectively the same thing."

"So," Benny said, "if I wave my Dreamcaster around, can I fly on it like a witch's broom?"

Hudson pulled the magazine close and contemplated this image. Funny as it was, it must have felt familiar to Eric as well, for no one else spoke for a few seconds.

"I've got a true story for you," Eric said. "So you know how, in the old world, pre-eclipse, we used radio waves for everything, right? People would even open the doors of their cars with remote controls. Hell, they would even start them up while they were still getting dressed upstairs. Turns out that you could extend the range of a car remote by putting it to your jawbone and clicking the button.

"So a guy with the Ohio militia is out on patrol—and this is back in the early days, when people did stupid things like foot patrols—when a specter, whirlwind and all, comes blowing through. They're in a wide V formation, too wide to get spear points inside the circle and contain the thing. So this guy, in back of the V, sees his buddies in trouble and remembers about the car remotes. He puts the old-style devonium tip flat against the bottom of his jaw, pushes the button, and blasto. Specter's a pile of sparks and weird shapes, buddies are safe."

A second of silence ensued as Eric drew out the question.

"And the guy?" Benny asked.

"Roast beef," Eric said.

Hudson sat up and rolled the magazine in his hands. "I doubt this origin story. How would we know what the guy's thinking if he's dead?"

"It's all true, just like in *Shelf Life*," Eric said and strummed his guitar.

Hudson tossed the magazine at him and looked at Benny, who was not laughing with them but staring into space, boot on one hand and brush in the other, lost in whatever Eric had just said.

***

Atop Mammoth Tooth Hill, in front of the east gate of New Norfolk A-III, on watch again with Benny, Hudson gazed past the muddy ledge of North America, toward the Atlantic Ocean, in the general direction of the Azores. It was true that many archaeological discoveries had been made where the sinking sea had left those islands to merge again into a mini-continent. Governments would not confirm or deny that hover carpets and devonium had come from there, and they would always evade the question about Atlantis, saying only that they did not know what name the pre-historic civilization of the Azores had given itself.

Next to him, Benny was bouncing on his knees to keep blood flowing. He would not pace around in the mud like others did, not after shining his boots.

Hudson scanned the bare horizon. Gulls were hovering on the updraft of the Norfolk Canyon's steep shore. Nearby, a dog sniffed at a slop of muddy water.

Hudson could not stay here forever. He was young, and the world was always changing, but he saw so many people who had lost their early zeal for this place, pioneers on the continental shelf now numbed by constant danger. The young grew up quickly here, and some of the old had stopped aging. New Norfolk could become a version of hell for those who did not die.

Maybe these people would make a great civilization here someday. Hudson's own ancestors had done so, or partly so. Lucy's ancestors had fled a fledgling Europe and built the great mansions of Philadelphia. Declan's ancestors had carved a kingdom of coal into the mountains of West

Virginia. By the time the old world had ended, both families had become parodies of their own worst proclivities. The mountain poor possessed pride and insanity, the city rich, dignity and eccentricity. Both were just a generation removed, past and future, from making sucking sounds in the mud with their boots like Benny was doing now.

Hudson could go to college or flight school, even the Academy. But he had to stay here to protect Owen from his mother's degenerative sorrow. He was needed here. Maybe he could stay and build that great new city. He would start by paving the road leading through the gate. The government had spared this expense, anticipating the mass production of hover cars. That was yet to happen. In the meantime, two-legged humans had to stand tall on the muddy Earth.

The gulls flew inland. The dog pointed its nose upward. Before Hudson could spot what the animals had sensed, the alarm sounded in three quick pulses, then four. The specter was already here.

Benny was kicking the gate to unstick it. It would not close.

Hudson looked at his friend's harrowed eyes. Their duty had been drilled into them: fill the gap.

The two soldiers stood shoulder to shoulder, a wall of human nerves patching the Faraday fence.

"You switched on?" Benny said.

"I'm on."

Their breath fell down steps on its way out of their lungs.

The dog came running and tripped a few dozen yards ahead of them. It rose slowly, and Hudson knew this was not from pain or mud. It was a half second of lethargy, the last anemic act of life a creature would know while the specter studied it, surrounded it. Then its eyes bulged, its ribs burst, and blood billowed forth with one short keening yelp.

The specter could not have the dog's form for itself, but Hudson could see where the monster was now, a bend of light where the demon's erotic rage congealed. He fired his Dreamcaster, three short pulses from left to right. One of them hit.

Hudson watched the trail of sparks and bilious smoke run along the fence toward the canyon. It did not make it far. Two balls of blue light, shot from a turret above, pounded craters into the soft earth. When it stopped raining mud, Hudson could see a circle of Marines around one of the craters. The signal came: all clear.

Benny's shoulders bounced against Hudson's. He was able to finish closing the gate. Relief beat curiosity, and Hudson pulled himself inside. Benny powered down his spear and shook himself loose. Hudson looked at his own spear: one red power bar remained.

"You marked it," Benny said. He slapped Hudson on the shoulders and grinned. "Good job." Benny turned away, and Hudson thought he saw his lips pull down in jealous sadness.

"We filled the gap," Hudson said.

***

Hudson and Eric sat over clams and French fries while the band set up at the Old Barracks. Both men were a pint and a half in. Hudson wiped his fingers clean and fondled a 20mm metal cannon casing that stood on the table. Earlier in the day, it had been filled with balls of charged devonium. Its contents had carved one of the two craters currently being fingered by forensic scientists. This empty shell was a gift from the riflemen who had taken down the specter. Hudson drank deeply.

"Slow down, champ," Eric said. "It's gonna be a long night."

"Just filling the gap," Hudson said. "Can you imagine being hit by this? It's made to take down whole vehicles. Aircraft. In slow motion, you'd probably look like that dog today. Maybe that's all specters are. Slow-motion bullets. Filling a gap."

"You're a sore winner. If this is winning with you, I'd hate to see losing. Come on. Dance it off. Band's up soon. You'll dance with every girl tonight."

"Hope's not here."

"Forget about Hope."

"I wonder if that's what my dad looked like, that dog."

"Alright folks," came a voice through the microphone. "We're nearly ready to git started here, so while we're waiting, why don't y'all grab a pint, that's it, no, two for you, sir, you look like you need it, ha ha, alright. And you there, young lady, let's tryta behave tonight, eh? Alright. Well, folks, let's hear it for our Virginia Naval Militia!"

Hoots, hollers, shouts, and shrieks shot out from every corner of the hall. No one would be singled out for their action; they never were. But some nodded in the direction of Hudson, and he raised his pint a little higher, taking in the praise.

"Alright! Alright!" the bandleader continued. "The militia shows how it's done, dudnit?"

More cheers erupted.

"That's right, our guys and gals on the front line, standing in the mud 'n' the sun, showing ole Caspar the unfriendly ghost who's boss aroun' here. You know what? I gotta song abou' that. Wanna hear?"

The audience clamored.

"Well, alright, then. You fill your veins with the old eau-de-vie, and me 'n' my boys here, we'll fill your heart with pride. Let's hit it, boys!"

The six mustachioed, pot-bellied men on stage strummed their strings, plucked their banjos, and slapped their bass in frenetic and perfect unison. Their tempo was too fast for dancing, but some tried anyway, inventing new ways to balance beer and kick their boots in the air.

Hudson caught a face passing by the window sourer than his own. By the time Benny opened the door, though, he was all dimples.

Benny raised his arms in the air and hollered. Everyone in the Old Barracks cheered. Benny grabbed a half-drunken pint off someone's table, and while he chugged it, he pointed at Hudson.

Hudson could not resist a smile.

Benny then grabbed a full pint off a waitress's tray, set it on the stranger's table, tossed a coin on the tray, and winked. The beneficiary of Benny's theft-with-interest simply smiled and shook his head. Benny threw himself on the bench next to Hudson and Eric and picked up the cannon casing.

"Alright, folks, it's time to amass the continental army,"

the bandleader said. "Come on, rank and file, rank and file. Fill in the floor now, plen'y o' room. Hey there, sir, you're not so drunk you can't fix your feet whirr they belong. All y'all, young 'n' old, all can march with the army now. That's it, we all ready? You ready to march into battle? Yeah? Alright, let's hit it, boys!"

Hudson levered himself upward with the sturdy table. Arm in arm with Benny and Eric, he took his place on the dance floor.

On the steady beat of the bass drum, the crowd marched in place, raising knees left and right, left and right. Arms swung in rhythm, then the strings broke in, and at the instructions of the singer, they turned left in place and clapped, they turned forward, still clapping, and, back at the center, those who could kicked their right heels back to meet their left hands behind their butts. The stomping and clapping soon turned to sliding and twirling as the floorboard battlefield filled with music.

Song after song, Hudson forgot himself. The search for friendly female eyes wiped away the image of the dead dog. Beer after beer, he forgot what they were celebrating. Hudson was nothing more than a pair of arms waving in the air, a set of legs stomping on the wood, a body filling the gap, and this made him happy.

6

Hudson had danced off most of the beer, but not all of it, and while he walked home alone with the moonshock's marble of stars spinning above him, he slipped once or twice on the muddy streets of New Norfolk. He passed by the deli where Hope worked to catch a glimpse of her serving some militia-man a late-night dinner from steaming trays of fried chicken and dumplings, or better, to catch her alone, in which case he would pretend to be hungry and order whatever took her the longest to prepare. But the deli was closed, and the lights were out.

The door to his house was locked, and Hudson had to sweep his hand under the doormat for the key. Lucy rare-ly locked the door; they owned the same things everyone else owned, and a rapist would find death inside the Belly of Boulder as certainly as out on the specter-infested plain. She might still be in emergency mode. He opened the door and discovered this was the case.

Lucy's two eyes gleamed in the darkness, one above the other. She was lying on the couch with her alabaster knees tucked into her chest.

"Mom," he said. He rubbed her shoulder.

Only the slightest hum of human consciousness droned out of her.

"How long have you been like this, Mom? It's been hours, like, five or six hours, since the alarm."

A series of croaks squeaked from Lucy's throat, which Hudson eventually interpreted as, "I was waiting for you to come home."

Hudson's breath fell out of him. "God, I'm sorry, Mom." He levered her into an upright position, sat next to her, and let her fall against him. "I'm sorry. I, I don't know. I thought you'd come out to the Old Barracks. We all went straight there. The band came out and everything. Where's Owen?"

"Asleep."

Hudson let his bleary eyes rest against the near-perfect darkness of the living room. A ray of faint light from the *Eisenhower* stowed itself away inside the framed portrait of the family.

"It all went well today, Mom. Benny and I stood our ground."

"I heard them talking in the streets."

"It was ugly, what I saw."

"It always is."

Man and mother sat silently for a few minutes. Hudson wondered if he was always going to drink his way through the ugliness, like he saw many others doing. Or, when friends ran dry, he might take to sleeping through it like Lucy.

"Maybe we should move back to Boulder, Mom. I can go to college there."

Lucy pulled herself upright. "Your father was so proud of all this."

"I know, Mom. But only he had the personality to pull off being a pioneer hero. The rest of us are drunks and gamblers."

"You're not a drunk."

Hudson leaned forward. "No, but I might become one if this keeps up." He burst into sobs. "That poor dog, Mom. That stupid dog." Lucy rubbed his back. "I just can't help but think that that's what Dad looked like." He rocked back and forth, his mouth torn open in tears.

Lucy continued rubbing his back. "Sh sh shh…. Don't worry about what your father looked like when he died. It happened like that all the time in the old world. Car wrecks, cancer, you name it. Most of us just never saw it. Come on now, Huggy Baby." She pulled her arm around him and leaned her head against his trembling shoulder. "He was so beautiful while he lived. Don't let those beasties tell you how to see."

"Tell me something about Dad. Anything."

Lucy took Hudson's hand. "He made every other man look like a dingy little devil. He made me forget."

"Forget what?"

Lucy let go of Hudson's hand. "You have his mind. You look like my mother, especially with those droopy eyes of yours." She brushed a hair off his forehead. "But you think like him. You're smart, but you miss things."

"Tell me what I'm missing about Hope."

"You're not missing anything there, Hudson."

"You sound like everyone else. I don't get it. She's perfect to me. An angel."

"Take a woman as she is: blood and bile, milk and piss."

These words somehow turned Hudson's tears into laughter. "Father Joseph's poetical skills are rubbing off on you."

"Don't forget about Ladymouse. I'm a poet in my own right."

"You've never sung me one of your songs."

Lucy sang, "*I gave you all my plums, but you filled my arms with bruises.* You get it? Because they're both purple. I was sixteen. That's as good as it gets. You want to know who's the genius around here, it's Owen."

"I agree. But I don't know why he's still using the Speak & Spell."

"Because you used to use it. He looks up to you. He'll do everything you're doing."

"Then I should go to college."

"What's stopping you, Hudson? No one's stopping you from going to the Academy or Boulder or wherever you want to go."

Hudson sat back and twiddled his thumbs. "Who...?" he began but thought better of it.

"Who, Mr. Owl? Who's going to look after me and Owen, you mean?"

"There's a new program coming down from the Navy soon. Wind Scouts, they call it. They want militiamen patrolling the coast in hovercraft. That could be exciting. And safer, you know, off the ground."

"Hovercraft? I see."

"You see what?"

"The Navy wants the militia to give their new technology a test drive."

"They can't spare the airmen for it."

"So they tell you a step up from standing guard in the slop is riding a magic carpet over the horizon? I've seen these things. I know the program you're talking about. It's just like the government to sell certain death as excitement. I've been there before, and look where it's got us."

Hudson searched for his mother's face in the darkness. "Mom, you, like, saved an entire city because of what the government got you into. This entire complex is built around you curled up on the couch."

"So what are you worried about me and Owen for? Or you want to be the hero now?"

"No, Mom. I just—"

"You just think the world will stop spinning when you're not looking."

Hudson started to speak, stopped himself, then said, "Well, just look at the way you were when I got home. You're like that all the time."

"Oh, I see. I'm not a good mother. I get it."

"I'm not saying that," Hudson said then searched for a way around what he had said.

"No, no, no, you see poor little Owen running around like Huckleberry Finn while you stand sentry. But I can tell you that kid can sniff his way around danger just as well as you can see it."

"That doesn't mean he shouldn't be eating on a regular schedule."

A chill wind blew from Lucy's direction.

"And yet look at the way you were when you walked in here, smelly and drunk. That's what heroes become, champ. Drunks."

"So now I *am* a drunk?"

Lucy sprang up from the couch, stomped to her room, and slammed the door.

Hudson stared in the direction of the bedroom he shared with Owen, waiting for him to come out crying. Maybe Lucy was right. He should leave, and not just for himself but for everyone. The stars above would keep spinning.

PART TWO

WIND SCOUT

7

GE+19

Hudson stood with other onlookers from the militia before what the Navy recruiter called a Wind Scout. About fifteen feet long and five feet wide, it had an open, single-seat cockpit and rear bed. Benny declared out loud that it looked like an old Chevy El Camino and under his breath that it was a swamp raft. To Hudson, it was a rectangular boat he was told could fly. So far, he only understood that the woven rug that stretched between the two halves of the split hull underneath the cockpit and bed was somehow responsible for generating anti-gravitational lift.

Benny leaned on the gunwale into the cockpit. "Where's the engine?" he asked.

"Electric motor," said the Navy recruiter. "Under the hood in front. I'll open it up for you."

Underneath the front hood, a pile of wires and boxes met an array of wary eyes.

"The battery's in back, under the rear bed, to balance the weight," the recruiter said. "The motor moves the frame the carpet's attached to between the split hull down below. We call that carpet the wave runner. Adjusting motor speed changes sinusoidal frequency on the wave runner. A small flywheel feeds excess energy back into the battery for re-charging."

"Which leads to my next question," Benny said. Hudson caught some of the others smirking. "Your experimental aircraft is a single-seater. What happens if the system goes down?"

The recruiter visibly restrained his agitation. "If the systems fail or the pilot is hurt, this flying boat will float on water. I can assure you, ladies and gentlemen, that, contrary to rumor, the Navy is not asking the militia to feed bodies into testing. We are asking that you help the Navy provide a more precise patrol of the Atlantic coast by expanding your operations into hovercraft."

"More precise?" Eric said.

Hudson's friends were asking questions. He tried to think of something, but he had no frame of reference for this thing in front of him. He was missing something and did not know what it was.

"Slower," the recruiter said. "Jet and prop aircraft stall at the speeds we need to give us a better picture of activity on the ground. Plus, they suck up liquid fuel. Not so easy to come by these days. The Wind Scout is optimized for ten miles per hour at a four-hundred-foot altitude."

Benny's long snort opened the way for waves of groans from the militiamen.

"That doesn't sound exciting, perhaps," the recruiter said. "But think of it this way: at that speed, it's two hours north to Washington Canyon, two hours back. Your four-hour watch becomes a pleasure cruise."

This was not the most unpleasant thing Hudson could

think of after what he had seen last month, and he read the same consideration on the other faces. Benny's clenched brow was less convinced, and he let the recruiter see it.

"Oh, and there's one more thing," the recruiter said. "The Navy's already developing more advanced prototypes. Our aim is space travel without rockets. You get in on the ground floor with hover tech, and the sky's the limit."

Benny bent over, fiddled with a metal bar anchoring the wave runner at the bow, stood up, and slapped the hull a couple of times. "Alright. Count me in. Hudson? Let's do this thing."

Hudson lifted his shoulders and let his hands fall against his hips. This would be better than standing in the mud, at least until he retook his college entrance exams.

***

The image on the classroom projection screen made no sense to Hudson. He was reasonably smart, but here he was completely lost. This was a course in the history of flight, and there, above him, was some graph or series of overlaid graphs with blocks of color in between. The instructor, droning in monotone, pointed his laser pen at one empty corner of the image and spoke indecipherable words. Hudson caught his own head drooping.

He and Benny were in the US Navy now. Or so it seemed today. They had been lured, with a few others, into the Wind Scout program with the understanding that the Navy was supplying the militia with equipment in exchange for eyes in the air. The Wind Scout program then became, almost overnight, the Coastal Air Guard. Hudson had signed many papers and releases, had been ushered into many offices, and had had two different physicals. He had sworn an oath to support and defend the Constitution of the United States for the second time since his graduation from high school. After this, an officer had shaken hands with him and said, "Congratulations. You're in the Navy now."

Hudson, like a few others, had been too confused to be angry, and had only asked if he was committed to more than the year of duty he had promised the Virginia Naval Militia. "Don't you want to go into space?" was the only answer his new superior officer had given. He did, like anyone perhaps, and was becoming surer that the wilder the promise of glories in this world, the more certain he was to spend his evenings staring at a pint in the Old Barracks. But no one was offering anything else.

In the video now playing above him, Hudson watched a montage of old-world airplanes flying at steep angles, some of them too steep for some mechanism. Hudson understood that every machine had its limits, and this one had something to do with the graphs he had just seen. He had been lured into the Wind Scout program, now CAG, on the premise that he was to be driving a boat through the air, and yet it seemed he was in flight school.

This should have excited Benny, but he sat with eyes closed and mouth open, drooling onto his notebook. Then he began gently snoring.

Hudson poked Benny with his pen. He snored loudly and woke up. Snorts and giggles broke out across the darkened classroom.

"Benitez," the instructor called out.

"Sir," Benny replied.

"What are we looking at here?"

"The service envelope of an F/A-18F Super Hornet, sir."

Through the murky light, Hudson watched the instructor search the slide for this information and sensed, more than saw, the anger growing in the otherwise wooden man.

"Very good, Benitez. Moving on...."

With the instructor's head turned, Hudson gave Benny a fist bump.

***

Hudson and his training squadron hovered forty feet over the ocean, a mile from shore. On the new Atlantic coast, the continental slope fell steeply beneath the sea; ocean currents swelled upward and sometimes broke in white, toothy spray. This exercise was called "Lunch Break," and it was designed to make a body bear with seasickness. The magic carpet lifting the Wind Scout—now designated the SR-20 Manutara—worked by amplifying the gravitational waves rippling upward from Earth and sending them back down. The higher the Manutara hovered, the smoother the ride was over the choppy waves. Hovering at forty feet over five-to-ten-foot waves felt just a little easier than pointing a bow into them but not much easier. Hudson found that gazing at the horizon kept his spaghetti inside. Something pulled his attention downward, though, into the water.

Between the waves below him, Hudson noticed around a dozen black spots, places a shade darker than the blue-brown water. No one else could see what he saw, or they seemed not to care.

"Permission to ascend to one hundred feet, sir?" Benny asked Lieutenant Astley, their instructor, on Hudson's behalf. "We can maybe all see it up there."

Astley granted this request after their time had expired for the exercise.

Hudson saw the black spots more clearly from one hundred feet. At a thousand, near the operational limit of the Manutara, Astley himself acknowledged the contact.

One of the black spots began moving inland. Astley hovered alongside Hudson in the lead as Hudson followed it to the shore a few miles north of Norfolk Canyon. Birds began flying away, but no one knew if this was because of the hovering scouts or what lurked in the shallows. Astley sent up a two-part flare, and a single alarm sounded at New Norfolk Station. There would be no real harm on this unpopulated side of the canyon, and the specter that came to shore managed to disembowel only a hapless crane pecking at a crab before dissolving into the chaos from which it had emerged.

When they returned to where they had seen the other specters underwater, they found they had disappeared.

"That's his gift," Benny said to Astley and the others. "He can see things before others can."

The group stared at Hudson.

"Much good it's going to do all of us," Hudson said, turning toward the sea. "I can't scan the whole coast at once."

8

Cumulous clouds reigned over the sendoff for Hudson, Benny, and the four other scouts in line, ready to hover north on their longest training exercise to date. They would move north along the coast, camping along the way to Hudson's namesake river and New York City. Along their way, and on all their runs after this, scouts would use photography and lidar to map and remap the sinking coastline and ever-shifting rivers of the exposed continental shelf.

On the ground, Owen leaned into Hudson's Manutara, pointing at the various dials and gauges and asking questions Hudson was happy to answer.

Lucy walked up to Owen and ran her fingers through his hair. "Two weeks?" she asked.

"Two weeks, Mom," Hudson said. "Some of that is an intensive course on base in Hudson Canyon."

"This is what you want for yourself?" Lucy said.

"How does a person want anything?" Hudson said and looked ahead toward Benny. His brothers and sisters were surrounding his Manutara, and Benny made a game of yawing in place to shake them off.

Hazel walked by at that moment, cast her eye toward Benny and his scout, gave an approving nod, and walked away, pulling her hair behind her ear.

"Hm," Hudson said. "What'll it finally take for the two of them?"

Lucy leaned on the gunwale and whispered, "Benny's a coward. Don't let him keep holding you back."

Hudson brushed her away. "God, Mom. Way to spoil the mood. And don't say bad things about Benny. I'd hang my life on his any day."

"I'm just saying. You don't owe him or this place anything." She kissed Owen's head. "Come on, Owen. Let's let your brother go."

***

Patches of grass and groves of trees rose up where the extension of the Hudson River left orphaned oxbows and shallow marshes. The river explored new avenues on its way toward the canyon that now served as its oceanic gates. Hudson, hovering along the river, raised his eyes from the umbilical cord of nature's new birth to the vast sepulcher of civilization spreading out before him.

The long winter had already circled the globe once and was headed back to New York, which straddled the intermittent Arctic Circle. Years of groaning ice and howling wind had turned much of the low-lying boroughs into hummocks of brick, above which rose pre-modern municipal buildings. The same pattern held true for the city's taller specimens, and much of Manhattan had become a haunt of steel-and-glass skeletons clacking around the silent stone obelisks of a sturdier age. Those who still lived here, foraging from building to building for salable goods, were protected by sleepers and spirits in a city they claimed had always been as inwardly holy as it was outwardly hellish.

Astley took them underneath a triumphal arch and up Fifth Avenue, where they would start their exercise in producing accurate three-dimensional maps of the crumbling city. A mist that lapped inland provided an opportunity to navigate with lidar imaging. The mist also magnified the visible presence of human spirits, and Hudson was not alone in seeing the dead peering at them through windows and from street corners.

After several hours of this, as the sun drew toward the horizon, they hovered into a railroad tunnel. Hudson's world became outlines of orange on the heads-up display, and in the black, oily air, he made out tracks weaving in and out of each other between rows of steel columns. At one point, a tangle of orange lines swirled around itself. He glanced at the avatar of Astley's scout on the lidar screen and was about to shout for instructions when Benny jerked sideways.

"Shields up," Benny called.

Astley chuckled. "Rats, Benitez. The most famous rats in the world. Big enough to lift a car or at least snatch a slice of pizza from your hands." He laughed again. "This is their world. We humans are just passing through."

"Like I said, shields up," Benny continued. "I don't want any rats falling on me."

The others seemed to share Benny's fear, for the only sound that broke the breathy silence that ensued was the chirping of the rats. Hudson's skin tightened. He looked up toward the invisible ceiling and hunched forward in his seat.

Sighs of relief rose into wows of awe when the seven scouts passed through a gate into a massive cavern. The late evening sun poured through filthy arched windows high above them. The rail tunnel had somehow ended inside a building.

"What old-world magic is this?" Hudson muttered to himself.

"Grand Central Terminal," Astley said. "Come on. Let's head up into space."

The team hovered toward the sea-green ceiling, where each of them touched the painted constellations shining through the damp, moldy plaster.

"Maybe one day one of you will knock on the door to the stars," Astley said.

"And I'll open that door," Benny said. He knocked on Orion's belt. A bit of plaster fell onto his lap.

"If you reopen the door to outer space, Benitez, I'll be the first to follow you through. For now, let's get downtown. We've got a rooftop waiting where only King Kong can get us. We'll set down there for the night."

Hudson traced the lines of Pegasus above him and followed the others through one of the broken arched windows.

***

Hudson walked into his house in New Norfolk A-III and found Lucy diligently correcting student assignments at the kitchen table. She waved her hands in excitement, and before she could push the chair back and stand up, he came and held her to him. By the time her happy sniffles had ceased and she had stood up, a nervous knot in his stomach had pulled itself upward into an awkward smile.

"What?" she said, rubbing his cheek with her thumb.

He yanked back his head. "I stopped in Philly."

She crossed her arms loosely in front of her, and her eyelids fell softly toward the extra bag Hudson had brought home.

"I didn't know what kind of things you'd want from the house, so—"

"The house is still standing?" she asked.

"Very much so. More than the other houses on the block, but it looks like people are moving back in the neighborhood. Maybe someone is looking after your house to keep their own property values up. That's what Astley said, anyway."

"What do you say?"

Hudson shrugged and started to glance toward the family portrait. "It sort of felt like someone was still living there. Like a sleeper, maybe, but we didn't see anyone. You really haven't been back all this time?"

"Let's sit down."

On the couch, Hudson began pulling picture frames from the bag between his legs. "It's mostly you and Grandma, of course, but I brought some of Grandpa, too, you know, not knowing...."

Lucy hovered over a picture of herself with her parents, caressing the frame with her thumbs. "Yeah, no, I'm glad you did. I never had anything against him. I actually saw more of him after the moondark than I had since he left. We, uh, well, I'm not sure he talked to Mom, but..... These are in great shape." Lucy let her dark eyes fall somewhere else. After a few seconds, she perked up with childish glee and poked her chin at the bag. "What else is in there?"

"I really just went through your room. CDs of Lady-mouse, a UPenn sweatshirt, and these little guys." Hudson handed her the relics of girlhood and the stuffed animals he had found piled on the bed. He watched as Lucy hugged each one in a reunion that almost seemed rehearsed. "I'm sorry about this last one. I don't know what happened. It was all scraggly when I got there. Maybe the roof leaked at some point or an animal got to it, I don't know." He pulled out a clotted, filthy white tube of fabric that had once perhaps been a raccoon or a panda bear.

Lucy's eyes grew misty as she studied the wretched creature, and Hudson thought he heard the words "Peter Panda" choke her before she pressed it to her face. She sat that way for a while, convulsing with sobs, as if the stuffed animal had been a long-lost child. In light of the modest reaction her parents' picture had provoked, Peter Panda had clearly been a much more intimate companion.

All at once, Lucy stopped crying and pulled the sodden rag to her lap. "Is that all of them?"

"I scoured the place. That's it."

"No pink-and-purple dinosaur?"

"No pink-and-purple dinosaur."

Lucy's shoulders fell in studied disappointment. As if speaking to herself forty years earlier or to the spirit still haunting her old house, she muttered, "The adventure continues."

Hudson watched her fondle Peter Panda like it really were her own baby. Suddenly, she stopped.

"We have to talk about *your* adventures."

"What adventures?"

"Exactly."

"Not this again," Hudson said and went to the refrigerator. Owen sneaked up behind him and hugged him. "Hey, bud. You miss me or something?"

"Yeah," Owen said. He then went over to the couch and played with everything Hudson had brought home.

"One call to Miss Huntsman will get you into the Academy," Lucy said.

Hudson stuffed homemade cheese puffs into his mouth and made his muted reply: "Okay...." Crumbs fell out of his mouth and onto his uniform.

"Okay?"

"Okay, so what's wrong with going with the flow? You say I don't owe this place anything, but I'm not sure what else I'm supposed to do. You act like I'm supposed to have great dreams and desires. That's you old worlders. They drilled it into you: follow your dreams and all that. Have you seen New York City? That's what's become of your people's dreams." He chewed more cheese puffs and waited for Lucy's answer.

"Just set your sights higher, is all I'm saying. You're living on borrowed enthusiasm. Benny's excited about Wind Scouts because that's as high as he'll probably ever go."

Hudson huffed. "They're talking about shifting the program into space."

"Who cares about space? There's nothing up there. Are you going to be the one to get us past the moonshock?"

"That sounds pretty good to me. And besides, if I go to the Academy, I'm just borrowing your enthusiasm there, too."

"Magic carpet rides are not going to take us into the universe." Lucy turned back to Peter Panda on her lap. "Maybe you're right about enthusiasm. I just want you to want something a little beyond your reach."

He rolled up the paper bag of cheese puffs and set it on top of the refrigerator. "I don't know what that is, Mom. I'm not a scientist like you. I'm not one of these career soldiers around here. I get it. I do have a gift for seeing things before other people, and the Wind Scout's the best way to use that right now." Hudson licked his fingers.

Lucy played with Peter Panda's arms. "If you are given a gift, then hold onto it," she said. "But there are other things you should be fighting for, things you won't think are important until later."

"This is starting to sound like a different conversation," Hudson said, wiping his moistened fingers on his uniform.

Lucy did not answer. She was drifting into some long-lost world. Only Owen's persistent questions about the pictures Hudson had brought home carried her back.

9

Lucy lay in her bed in New Norfolk clutching Peter Panda.

Lucy's mother had once called him "Peter Pandemic" and thrown him into the washer and dryer, turning the plump pillow of his belly into a hard, misshapen lump. Lucy still loved him that way and perhaps all the more because he was ruined. Later on, her mother had ripped Peter Panda out of Lucy's fifteen-year-old lap and said, "Face it. You're a woman now."

In the winter after the Great Peter Panda Incident, she and her mother had been sitting on the couch, watching television into the night, like they always had. Lucy always had her homework done. She always earned good grades, so her mother would let her stay up late, next to her on the couch. They were watching reruns of *Gilmore Girls* until her mother began snoring, a second or third glass of wine clasped on her lap. At that point, Lucy gently removed the glass and walked upstairs to bed, letting the screen flicker on for company.

Lucy began her usual route to bed. As she turned to mount the staircase, she caught one last glimpse of her mother in the television's alien-blue light and looked upward, into the darkness.

Lucy knew every creak of the floor and stairs in the old townhouse, and as the din of the television grew quieter, she measured every step and every breath until she reached her room. There, on the bed, in the same place he always was, lay Peter Panda. The nightlight in the hallway reflected off the glossy black circles of his plastic eyes. Lucy used to think she glimpsed a secret life behind those eyes. Tonight, they told her to stay away. But Lucy was preparing for college and could no longer listen to him.

She woke up not long after falling asleep. The television was off. She closed her eyes again, telling herself the silence had been building up into a threat in her unconscious mind. It was too late. The shadows surrounded her.

Lucy unsheathed her eyes like weapons and gripped Peter Panda like a shield. Reason would take over, and fear would fold itself back into the shadows of the room she knew so well. Once her heart slowed and the tingles finished washing up and down her back, she would fall asleep again.

She knew the dark arms and fingers dancing across her window pane were the elm in the streetlamp. She knew the creaking of the wall was some adjustment to the wind. She knew the shadow in the corner of her room, by the closet, did not belong to nature and would disappear if she ignored it.

It did not disappear. She grew annoyed and almost cried out in frustration. Why could they not just leave her alone? What did they gain by creeping on her? She picked up Peter Panda to throw at the wall but chose another lesser bedfellow instead. From the way it felt, it was Amy Anklesore, a stuffed *Ankylosaurus*, pink with soft purple plastic plates on its back. From the way it hit the wall, it should have made a sound, but it did not. "Shit," she whispered. She shined the flashlight always ready by her bed at that corner of the wall. The light did not return to her.

Lucy took a hank of yarn from her desk with which she had tried to knit something for her father, a project abandoned. She tied the loose end of the yarn, still woven into a few inches of yellow-red scarf, to the post at the foot of her bed. Armed with her flashlight, she walked the yarn with her into the corner of the room. When she continued through the corner into some new void, she was not surprised or even fearful. It all somehow felt so natural. If she could not find her way back, the authorities would follow the yarn to her, and all would come to know this strange place in the corner of her room.

The creaking floor gave way to some kind of loose stone. The air grew very cold. She saw nothing, not even the dim light of her room behind her. The flashlight reflected off nothing. Some odor she did not recognize reached her nose. It was that weird smell all newborn babies had. *Fine*, she thought. *Whatever*. She continued walking, waiting for some new revelation.

She walked slowly for several minutes in total darkness. It grew colder but not by much. The yarn ran out, and she held its end behind her, looking all around. She wondered whether to continue on without her woolen guide or to return. This was just some blank, infinite darkness, she thought, and returned.

She began winding the yarn around her arm as she walked back to her room and felt the ground growing softer. It was somehow more like fine silt now, or sand. The air grew thicker, like she were walking through water. It grew difficult to walk like it did in dreams, and she began pulling herself by the yarn. Her feet would occasionally scrape the ground below her.

Not far into this, she felt herself begin to fall. She pulled her legs beneath her and waited, but she did not touch the bottom. She was floating in some breathable ether. Its chill filled her lungs with pain. Lucy winced with every breath. She fell faster and panicked. She pulled on the yarn, but it was too tight to wrap around her arm anymore. She hung by a thread above some abyss from which a slightly warmer current rose. She tried pulling herself upward but lacked the strength, and the yarn cut into her wrists. She tried again and failed. Lucy looked up and met no hope. She looked down and saw a little light, some golden glow below. *Okay*, she thought. *Okay*. She let go of the yarn and began falling gently toward that light.

The light grew, and she soon saw the silhouette of her own gangly frame below her, toes and feet, legs spread a little. It grew warmer, and her body came into view, still wrapped in cotton shirt and panties. The light took a form, a square or rectangle. Something was happening below it or behind it, the lapping of flames or the mingling of bodies. *Oh, no*, she thought. *Not me. Not this. No. No. No, no, no*, she continued, flailing her arms as if to swim upward. She kept falling, and she kept flailing with the window of golden flames now facing her. She made out its mullions. She knew its shape and size. She knew this window and began to scream.

Lucy finally heard her own scream. She screamed loudly and held her arms up by her face. The window grew no larger, but she felt its gaze grow menacing. The glass would break and tear her to pieces. That was what it wanted, to tear her to pieces. That was what she deserved. She screamed and tore at the air before her.

The window suddenly grew dark, as she felt something like a blanket wrap around her. She tore at this, but the blanket held her bound. "Lucy!" a voice said. "Lucy! Oh, God, dear," her mother said. "Sh-sh-shh.... Come on. Come on inside. Sh-sh-shh.... Come on, love. Come back inside. You're freezing out here in the snow. Come on in."

Lucy eventually saw where she was and walked up the steps into her mother's house, into the living room lit with the pulsing golden lights of a Christmas tree still not taken down. Her mother held her on the couch, rubbing her warm and rocking her.

When Lucy returned to her room in the morning, she found the yarn still tied to her bed, rolled into a skein in the corner. The pink-and-purple *Ankylosaurus* was nowhere to be found.

Lucy, remembering all this in New Norfolk A-III, clutched Peter Panda tightly. She heard Hudson and Owen snoring in the room next door, loosened her grip, and prayed: "Dear God, don't damn my boys to this half-life forever because of my sins."

tent, enigmatic, and mute. He should hate her for this unreliability because he hated God for the same reason, and yet he was overcome in her presence. He should try, like Lucy had once said, to show himself his own man.

"Oh, hey, Cici," Mort said. He then added two words he had never before spoken in his life: "*Quelle surprise.*"

She inhaled and said, "Hello, Mortimer," quickly ejecting her remaining breath. She had been rehearsing this, it seemed, and was here for someone else's sake. All the better for learning to hate her and, by hating her, to make her love him. "I was just passing by and thought I'd pass along Uncle Danny's invitation to dinner."

Uncle Danny had helped set up the lab. Mort had felt at home with him and Cynthia as fellow scientists. He had never been a nephew but had quickly submitted to what felt instinctively like family, open and immediate. Or this family in particular had made it easy. They were the people with whom he had connected through that travel poster of Iran, a long-lost family ready to welcome him.

"Thank you," Mort said. "I'll be there." He almost asked if she was coming as well but thought better of it and added, "Let me give you a tour. Something important is happening here." He stretched out his hand in the direction of a covered tray.

Without evincing any annoyance—or pleasure, for that matter—Claire sat on a metal stool and put her eyes against the glass window of the box.

"I didn't know the electronics stuff," Mort said, "so Danny devised a small antenna to generate radio waves inside each box. There's lead on the outside to keep them from leaking out. Inside, Claire, you are looking at a hitherto undiscovered species of lichen. I call it *Caloplaca theodori.*"

"It's all dark inside."

"Right. I'll turn on the light."

Mort nearly brushed Claire's fingers to switch on the viewing light and, as he pulled back, almost made to do so "accidentally."

She quietly studied the scene then said, "This is the stuff you found on your suit?"

"Yeah. All the covered trays here have it growing on different rocks I've found. Plenty of rocks around here, in Boulder. You get it?"

Claire's lips made the subtlest twitch.

No more dumb jokes, Mort.

"Anyway," he said, scratching his head, "it likes mantle xenoliths the most, stuff that's come up through volcanos. The deeper the better. But that's not the most exciting part."

Without removing her eyes from the viewing glass, Claire said, on cue, "What is, Mortimer?"

"Well, lichen normally only grows a few millimeters per year. *Caloplaca theodori* grows much faster. It seems to be feeding off high-intensity radio waves, like the kind Todd and I found down below. It spreads its wings like a bat out of hell."

Claire chuckled a little.

Mort inhaled proudly.

Claire pulled away and looked around the lab. "What's this one with the wires?"

"I'm trying to see if devonium will also make it grow. It only kills it."

"Do you have the right proportion of salt in the water?"

Neither salt nor water had ever figured into Mort's experiment. "Salt water?"

Claire rolled her eyes at Mort and gave a wry smile. "You do know that salt water counteracts devonium, right? Everyone knows that."

Mort, who had been awake in the new world for nine whole months, did not know that. A thought came, and the corners of Mort's mouth reached upward like the arms of a child to greet it. "Maybe you could show me, you know? The right proportion?"

***

Three months later, almost to the day Mort had woken from sleep, he ushered into his laboratory the head of the biology department along with Danny and Cynthia Shamshiri. Claire was already inside, flanked by Father Joseph and Doris Huntsman. The several small covered trays of their earlier experiments with Todd's Lichen were still there, but reigning over it all, at the far end of the lab, was a new world within a countertop, a diorama of mantle rock Claire had shaped into the seven continents, with a shallow salty sea surrounding them. She had fit it all inside an immense old fish tank. Once the audience was standing in place, Mort turned off the lab's overhead lights and switched on an amber darkroom bulb. With a theatrical flick of the wrist, he reached for his side of the lead curtain, Claire for hers. On the count of three, Mort and Claire pulled back the curtains.

No one spoke. Huntsman, Jody, Danny, and Cynthia

stared at the display, as if waiting to be told what they should be excited about.

The professor pulled his head from side to side. Under the red light, Todd's Lichen stood out clearly, light gray against black rock. "All this has grown in a few months?" the professor said.

"One month, in fact," Mort said. "Earlier iterations suffered an excess of scientific zeal. I'll explain that in a moment. In this scene, though, we populated some of the continents earlier than others to see if *Caloplaca theodori*, Todd's Lichen, would colonize across the water."

"Did it?"

"No."

"And the reason for the red light?"

"It does not light UV radiation. It feeds off radio waves. You can see how it spirals out from the antennas we drilled into the rock."

The professor made a mischievous smile. "Radio waves? So what do they like? Pop? Jazz?"

"Rock and roll, of course," Danny said.

Claire laughed at her uncle's joke, and so did the professor. Mort gently clapped his hands at his waist.

"It also likes devonium," Mort said. "What really supercharges growth are devonium electrodes in the water. But only in short bursts. And this differs from rock to rock. Each continent is made of a different kind of rock. We have peridotite, eclogite—"

"Uh huh," the professor said. "This looks great, Mort. I've seen the slides you sent me. Just write it up, and you'll have your doctorate."

Mort heard a few short gasps among the small audience, and it was as if the members of his makeshift family had sucked time itself into their lungs. In the dim amber light, he saw only their hovering faces and dark eyes fixed in admiration. Claire, too, her hands clasped at her chest, made a proud turn in his direction. In that little eternity, Mort studied the seven continents in the fish tank, creeping with lichen, Todd's Lichen. The work of the past few months, which had felt like a way to prove that Todd was still alive and speaking to him through the lichen, had suddenly become evidence only that Mort had ever known him at all, and that Todd was now somewhere very far away.

Father Joseph cleared his throat.

"What about Claire?" Mort said. "She deserves a great deal of credit."

"Oh, no," she said, waving her hands. "I'm just the window dresser here."

"Right," said the professor. "You'll have your page of acknowledgments, of course. Listen, I've got to run. Great job, Mort. I look forward to the defense. Good to see you all."

Mort watched the professor walk out of the lab.

"Congratulations, Mort," Cynthia said. "We're all so very proud."

"Yeah," Danny said.

Huntsman was staring at the diorama.

"He missed the best part," Claire said. "Shall we, Mortimer?"

"The best part?" Huntsman said.

Father Joseph had already seen what Mort was about to do and said, "You know, Doris, this is quite a thrilling moment for some of us. That we, for once, are about to surprise *you*."

Huntsman crossed her arms and dug her chin into her chest. "Alright. Let's see it."

Mort felt happy butterflies take flight within his stomach as he put his fingers on two switches, one to turn off the red light and one to turn on the devonium electrodes.

"Uncle Danny, could we get a drumroll, please?" Claire said.

Danny obliged. Huntsman huffed.

Mort turned off the red light, sending the room into total darkness. After a few seconds, he turned on the devonium electrodes.

The seven lichen-covered continents began to glow with spirals of blue, green, purple, and red. Huntsman's face shined with this fluorescent display. Her mouth fell open. "What is this?"

"Bioluminescence, Dr. Huntsman," Mort said. "Algae do it in the seas. A lichen, as we all know by now, is really two organisms, fungi and algae, living symbiotically. So here we are. Bioluminescent lichen."

"They look like galaxies," Cynthia said. "The way we do up our photos of deep space."

Huntsman almost pressed her face against the glass. She seemed mesmerized.

"I do have to turn it off soon," Mort said. "So as not to kill the lichen, you know."

Huntsman turned her head from one side of the splendid scene to another.

"Doris?" Father Joseph said.

"Galaxies," Huntsman finally said.

Mort turned off the devonium electrodes and switched on the red light.

Huntsman pulled her head back.

Mort looked at Father Joseph, who shrugged.

Claire pulled the lead curtains closed and turned on the overhead lights.

"What do you mean by galaxies?" Danny said. "I know what my wife means by galaxies, but I think you mean something different, Doris."

Huntsman pinched her brow. She made as if to speak but stopped.

"Come on, Doris," Father Joseph said. "You're in a safe space. You can speak an incomplete thought."

Huntsman side-eyed Father Joseph.

Mort caught Claire trying to hide her thrilled reaction to this.

"Mortimer," Huntsman said, "would it be possible for this lichen to grow under water, under the ocean?"

As always, there was something Huntsman knew the others did not, even in such a specialized subject matter as mycology.

"As I said during the presentation, it doesn't travel across the water."

"What if, I suppose, you laid a wire or a chain made of devonium across the little continents you made. Would it grow there?"

"It's easy enough to try," Mort said.

Father Joseph crossed his arms. "What is this about, Doris?"

Huntsman sat at a student desk. No one else joined her.

"This comes from the mantle, from all the way down there," she said. "But we once found something similar growing elsewhere."

"In the ocean?" Mort said. His lips briefly snarled in anger. Someone had scooped his doctorate. "So it got to the mantle through the sinking seas." He might still have something unique to publish.

Huntsman rested her chin on her hands. "It doesn't seem that simple."

"Simple's a good place to start," Danny said. "Secret to my success."

"What I mean is," she rolled her fingers on her thighs, "it may be a two-way street. You and Todd went under the Earth to help us look at what might be keeping us outside the moonshock. This lichen, Todd's Lichen, may be giving us a roadmap."

Claire looked at her father, who kept his arms crossed, as if to ask if she should say what was on her mind or keep silent and not encourage Huntsman to continue with whatever scheme she was devising. "To the galaxies?" Claire said.

"Maybe," Huntsman said. But that was a word Doris Huntsman never used. She was already convinced of something.

"Well," Mort said, "we have no way of getting back down into the mantle, if that's what you mean, to get into the moonshock from there, if that's also what you mean. The American and Russian boreholes are filled, and the Chinese are not having any luck. There's nowhere else to get through."

"That's not entirely accurate," Huntsman said.

Father Joseph closed his eyes. Claire crossed her arms. Danny spread his arms wide and let them fall. Cynthia thrust her chin forward.

Mort's belly trembled, and he worried he would black out and break the fish tank full of lichen. All he felt, instead, was searing anger at Huntsman for holding back this information, a burning urge to jump into a dervish and rescue Todd, and an old, familiar languidness at the prospect of sitting down under these conditions to write the thirty-page minimum his doctorate required.

"There's nothing we can do about it right now," Huntsman said. "Not until we find Hudson."

11

GE+19

This was what Hudson had wanted, somehow.

He stood at ease on the deck of the *Eisenhower* with seventy-one others, the first graduating class of the Coastal Air Guard. The speeches had been mercifully brief. Airman Hector Benitez, first in the alphabet, was approaching to receive a handshake and a certificate. They did not have the flag division or color guard of a Pass-in-Review like for normal Navy recruits since CAG had essentially been carved out of the naval militia. They had had neither the time nor the manpower to prepare for a grand ceremony, anyway. The Navy had accepted the six weeks of basic training the militia had given Hudson and the others and given them six more weeks in the Manutara. This special program came with a three-year commitment; Hudson would be twenty-one before he entered college and, if he went, twenty-five before he could apply for OCS or do anything else. Life had suddenly unrolled like a rug before him, all the way to the end. Or it looked like someone had dropped the rug on the stairs and watched it unfurl in a twisted heap. *He* had let the rug fall from his fingers. *He* had said to himself, as well as out loud, that he could not leave Lucy alone. He could have been in

Boulder soon, or Annapolis. He should have listened to his mother. Now that he could not have college, he wanted it desperately. Until then, his life would hang from a flying rug.

At the sound of his name, Hudson grimaced and stepped forward for his handshake.

***

CAG had chosen Hudson, Benny, and a few others for a special first mission in the middle of the Atlantic Ocean. Hudson had been near the top of their class academically, and Benny's technical proficiency was second to none. They were team leaders on a scouting trip in the Azores, where they would demonstrate the Navy's new technology for the Portuguese.

The Azores were holding great secrets, many said, none less than the lost city of Atlantis. If that were true, it would be many years before the sea gave them up again. Even though sea level had dropped almost six hundred feet in nineteen years, it would take centuries more to expose the rest of the Azores Plateau, a spill of lava over the otherwise well-zippered Mid-Atlantic Ridge.

At the end of a scanning run, Hudson landed at a small Portuguese naval base, near which he hoped to watch the sunset with a drink in his hand like he did nearly every night and then hang his face over a *cozido das Furnas*. Instead, he caught sight of an old family friend talking with a Navy officer. Hudson walked over and stood well behind the officer without interrupting their conversation, in line of sight so that Doris Huntsman would notice him.

Huntsman was clutching a black portfolio in her hands

and cast a quick glance at Hudson. She had not changed at all in the five years since he had last seen her at his father's funeral.

When, after a few minutes, the two started walking toward a hangar, Hudson called out, "Miss Huntsman."

"Sir," Hudson said, excusing himself before the officer.

"I'll see you inside," the officer said to Huntsman.

When he left, Hudson waited for her to recognize him. But he would have been thirteen, hardly pubescent, the last time she had seen him. "It's Hudson MacDuff, Lucy's son."

Her befuddled face broke open in bright surprise, and Hudson felt his shoulders fall to rest, especially when she unclasped her arm from the portfolio and reached out her hand, which he took. "Yes, it is," she said. Her head dropped a little to the side, and she picked it back up again. "I'm sorry for not recognizing you. It's been a few years, hasn't it?"

"A few, yeah."

Her eyes scanned him. She reached out her arm and let it drop. "And here you are, all grown up and in uniform."

Both were silent for a moment. He had been her height the last time he had stood before her, at a time in his life when every other adult was still taller. Hudson was not particularly tall—at five-foot-ten, he would never outgrow his mother—but now that he stood nearly a head above Huntsman, she seemed less like an adult and more like a woman.

"How is your mother doing?" Huntsman said.

"Fine, you know."

Huntsman nodded. She touched her ear.

Benny brushed up next to Hudson.

For the first time in their long friendship, Hudson was

not sure he was glad to see him. "Miss Huntsman, this is Airman Hector Benitez."

Benny gave Hudson a glance he did not understand as he shook Huntsman's hand. "Benny's fine, ma'am. That's what everyone calls me."

Huntsman pointed her eyes at Benny. "How did you earn that moniker, Airman Benitez?"

"It's from Benitez, ma'am. Even my brothers call me Benny. I guess my first name triggers some people. Rhymes with specter, you see."

"Why did your parents name you Hector at all, then?" Huntsman asked.

Benny pulled his head back. "It's a noble name, ma'am. Hector, the great warrior. Defender at the gates."

"Yes. Of course," Huntsman said.

"So," Benny said, "the OSS is conducting operations here as well?"

Benny did not need the gift of subtle sight that Hudson had. Everything Benny had ever seen, heard, or read was like an open file on the desk of his mind, accessible to him at once. Except on written tests. He must have seen Doris Huntsman's name written somewhere once as the Technical Director of the Office of Special Science.

"Benny, Miss Huntsman is an old family friend. She's worked a lot with my mo—"

"Yes," Huntsman interrupted. "We do have a little business here in the Azores." She gave Hudson what he could only construe as an instructive glance. "We are here studying the recent decline in seismic activity. The Earth's crust is very thin on the mid-Atlantic ridge."

All three stood silently.

"Well," Benny finally said. "Let me hit the showers before I lure some monster out of the ocean." As he turned, his eyes burned a line across Hudson's field of vision, and Hudson could still not decipher Benny's meaning.

"Me, too, I guess," Hudson said and reached out to shake Huntsman's hand. "But maybe we could catch up while we're both on the island."

Huntsman nodded. "Yes, that would be advantageous."

"Great," Hudson said.

Huntsman gripped her portfolio again and walked away.

As Hudson caught up to Benny, Benny said, "Yes, Miss Huntsman, that would be advantageous."

"Whatever you're saying, stop saying it. She's my mother's age."

"Not anymore."

***

Hudson had accepted Huntsman's invitation to dine at her project headquarters on the island. In one corner of a somewhat large and very clean hangar, a sumptuous table was set for ten. Hudson did not understand the seating arrangement: the highest-ranking officers were seated in the middle. Huntsman was near one end. Benny was with Hudson near the other end, where there was an empty seat.

Their two waiters were named, as well as Hudson and Benny could determine through consulting whispers, Izar and Lañoa. The language that the Portuguese officers spoke to them was not Portuguese, Benny insisted.

"You barely passed Spanish in high school," Hudson whispered.

"I learned enough to know what Portuguese sounds like."

Hudson caught Huntsman giving them both a slight, knowing smile. He looked back at Izar, who stood waiting for instructions as stiffly as if he was hanging from a hook. Something about the waiter's eyes bothered him. They were bright blue but were missing something, like the subtle twitching of a hundred small muscles. Hudson had the uncanny feeling this poor soul was trapped, like so many men in the new world, in the valley between life and death. Life must be tougher in the middle of the ocean than he had thought.

Conversation continued at the table about matters great and small. Airman MacDuff preferred listening to speaking in the presence of superior officers, but Benny's unusual reticence crept slowly into his own soul until he became aware of it all at once, like a man who had suddenly found himself alone in a forest or about to face a specter on the open plain.

Lañoa bent over stiffly to clear Hudson's salad plate. Their eyes were only inches apart, and, in the light of an overhead fixture, Hudson could see what had been bothering him. This man, whom he had thought had unnaturally dark eyes, was wearing contact lenses. Beneath them, his eyes were two different colors, blue and red. The whites had no blood vessels in them.

These were humanoids, and very advanced ones, the most lifelike Hudson had ever seen. Hudson jerked in his seat and had his hands gripped on the table to push away when he realized these humanoids had not been thrown at him by specters but had been trained by humans, and by Doris Huntsman, no less.

All eyes fixed on Hudson. He searched Huntsman, who very subtly pursed her lips as if to say, *Sh.*

"I'm sorry," Hudson said. "Thought I dropped my fork. Nope, here it is."

Conversation resumed. Huntsman hid a growing smile behind her wine glass. Hudson had never seen a woman exercise so much power by the shape of her lips.

Someone sat down in the empty seat, and before Hudson could turn to see who it was, he heard a man say, "Mr. MacDuff."

It was Father Joseph Conque. He had been at Hudson's high school graduation seven months ago.

"I didn't know you were here, too," Hudson said. "Miss Huntsman didn't say anything before. Good to see you, Father."

"How's your mother?"

"She's fine, you know...."

"I do know."

"What brings you to the Azores? I'm sorry—Father, to my right is Airman Hector Benitez. I don't know if you ever met."

The two men exchanged cordial greetings, and Father Joseph turned his attention back to Hudson. "What brings me here? The same thing I'm always doing for the OSS: keeping a steady hand or two on their assets. You've seen our new friends here waiting on us, which means you can see more than most people can."

"That may be a gift I have."

"It is," Benny said. "I've seen it."

"Your mother's mentioned it, too," Father Joseph said. "I wonder who else knows about it."

Hudson followed Father Joseph's eyes from Benny toward Huntsman. She tipped a wine glass into her mouth, hiding her face.

"It is curious that Dr. Huntsman forgot to tell you I was here," Father Joseph said. "There's so much to do. She must have been distracted."

***

That night, Hudson and Father Joseph walked along the seaside road that led away from the naval base. Streetlights glistened on the rippled water. Jupiter was making its way across the crystal ball of the moonshock—though it was only the diameter of the old moon when measured at its surface two hundred thousand miles above, when seen from Earth, some gravitational-lensing effect made its light fill the sky.

"Now *you* seem distracted, Hudson."

"This is a beautiful island. Mysterious."

Father Joseph inhaled sharply through his nose. "It's a dark place, and there are monsters in the depths you do not know how to handle."

Hudson had been trying to be poetic, to speak about the woman he had known his whole life now starting to claim some other place in his heart, as if she were this island revealing new secrets to him. But Father Joseph was a more practiced poet, using Hudson's own language to warn him about something Hudson could not see—about the woman or the island, he was not sure.

Hudson said, "I'm afraid of running aground on the shoals of this world." He held his head back and closed his eyes, pleased with the poet emerging within him.

"That's a bit maudlin, young Harold."

Hudson laughed, though he did not know the reference to Harold. It was enough to be compared to anything besides his grandmother for once, or even Declan.

Father Joseph put his hand on Hudson's shoulder. "You're at an age when you think a woman will break open the mysteries of the universe to you."

The old priest was onto Hudson.

With what she had done before the Great Eclipse, what she was doing here in the Azores, and what she was rumored to be doing in Yellowstone, Hudson thought Doris Huntsman was opening up the universe for everyone. "Is she at the center of all this?"

"No, but she is getting there," Father Joseph said. "The truth is, Hudson, if you do it right, a woman will open up great depths within yourself, an abyss you must draw on to love her."

This was the conversation Hudson had never had the chance to have with Declan.

Father Joseph continued, "I know that's what your mother did for your father, and he, in turn, became everything she needed."

"You just read my mind, Father. Mom always talked about seeing heaven in Dad's eyes."

Father Joseph pulled Hudson close. "She's not wrong

about that. What is heaven but love? And he loved her." Father Joseph took his arm away and wiped his eye.

The stars grew blurry for Hudson, too.

After a minute, Father Joseph said, "That's what all this is about, I think. The impenetrable moonshock, the infinite walled off from us. The cosmic order is like a person now, almost living, but a wounded person, shelled up inside."

"What does it take to open that shell?"

"Love, Hudson. Love. Always love. Our science will never get us there without it."

"But what about the humanoid waiters at dinner? Miss Huntsman is trying to use the science, I think. Are humanoids the next thing for us?"

"For the simple-minded, maybe. But Doris and I were trying to prove a different point."

"Because no one else could see them as humanoids. But why? I don't get it."

"You have a gift, but did even you see them at first? What we see goes right into a category in our minds. The officers were introduced to Basque waiters. And humanoid language is close enough to Basque to make it work. Add some contact lenses to cover their stereoscopic eyes, and voilà. The point is, Hudson, is that so much of reality, even our new reality, is covered over by our own expectations for it. The generals and admirals, along with most of humanity, see the humanoids as agents of destruction. But I think they are something else."

"What's that?"

"A warning. We didn't make them, you know that. Not

our generation, anyway. Your mother and I saw where they are built."

"A warning against what?"

"The night of the moondark, my mother and I were watching a show on television about artificial intelligence. A scientist was on there promoting her work, which was to summon spirits to teach her how to make more perfect robots, machines with a form capable of life. That woman was with us the day your mother and I visited the ancient humanoid factory in Antarctica. That's a state secret, by the way. I should not have told you. Anyhoo, a specter followed us out and sent a humanoid. It killed two people, including Uncle Billy's niece, Melanie. But, and now we're talking about the state of affairs in this world, when Doris and I drove by the site of our encounter on our way to Cheyenne Mountain, where you were born, Melanie was still there, very much alive, but in a way none of us would have dared imagine before, especially not this Catholic priest. She protected us. And I think that's what the Earth is doing, or better yet, what God is doing with the Earth. We were very close to letting demons into our homes, Hudson, and may get close again, soon. So take people like me and your mother, and Melanie and Uncle Billy: our special powers only work with other people and for other people. In love. If this new order of things should do anything, it should draw greater love from us. And God help us if we don't learn it soon. We'll be stuck in a world without oceans, where specters and humanoids run rampant, where we build cages around ourselves."

When, after a few seconds, Hudson felt Father Joseph

had finished, he said, "Who of us loves enough to break through the moonshock?"

"If you ask this Catholic priest, I would say God alone. But watch His love work great power in us. See where it takes you, Hudson."

Hudson found Jupiter again. That thick belly of a planet was making its slow march across the sky toward him. Winged Mercury was up there, too, speeding invisibly around the sun.

12

The next morning, Hudson and Benny had been reassigned. By midday, they were almost six hundred miles to the south of the Portuguese base they had been calling home, on a flat rock forty miles long and twenty miles wide called the Great Meteor Seamount. It was part of the Seewarte Seamounts, a line of submarine volcanos running south from the Azores. Once the receding sea had exposed it, the United States had taken control of this new island in the form of planting a flag and wrapping a small research base, population twelve, in Faraday fencing.

Hudson thought Huntsman had ordered the reassignment, fearful he or Benny would let word about her humanoid project slip.

Hudson also suspected that Father Joseph had something to do with it through his nephew, Commander Devon Conque, to keep him away from Huntsman.

Either way, there would be no mountainside from which to watch the sunset, and only beer in the kitchen. Hudson envied the birds, the only other living things to call this stillbirth of the sea their home. They could leave whenever they wanted. Hudson's Manutara would not take him far enough.

***

A few days into their mapping mission, Hudson and Benny sat on the hoods of their Manutaras, on a small hill near the east coast of the Great Meteor Seamount, eating lunch. A thick white mist, through which the seagulls seemed to swim more than fly, had enveloped the island.

"We are on exactly the thirtieth parallel north," Benny said.

Benny had already been taken in by the theories surrounding this place.

"Yep," Hudson said.

"Which just happens to be the same latitude as the pyramids in Giza."

"So is Tallahassee, Florida." Hudson had been finding ways to counter each so-called "coincidence."

"But we are also exactly sixty degrees longitude from Giza."

"Your point being?" Hudson knew the theory already, but he might catch Benny in a contradiction.

"My point is that it's not a coincidence. Look. You know the stuff they're digging up in the Azores is too much like what they're finding in the Bay of Biscay and even the Black Sea. There's too much for it all to be a coincidence. It's all connected."

Hudson bit into his tuna sandwich and waited to finish chewing before he replied. "Of course, it is. I don't see why this is a big deal. Obviously, human beings were all over the world by the end of the Ice Age. It was all flooded over, and now it's not. You guys are what Father Joseph calls 'archaeological gnostics.' You think you've got secret knowledge, but when it's finally revealed, it's not going to be that interesting in the end. It's like the moon and Mars. We got there, and all we found was dust and water."

"And what's the moon now? The portal to the rest of the universe or something? So maybe there's more to it all is what I'm saying."

Hudson tossed a scrap of bread as far as he could and lay back against the windshield, trying to guess from which direction a seagull would scoop it up. When nothing swooped in, he threw another. This time, a bird took the bait.

Benny picked up on what Hudson was doing, and soon they were taking turns tossing bits of their sandwiches into the mist. Hudson almost always won because he could see the birds through the mist before Benny could.

"I'm getting better at this," Benny said. "I've homing my instincts. Get it? Pigeons, homing?"

"First of all, Airman Benitez, these are seagulls, not homing pigeons. Second, it's called 'honing' your instincts. And there's nothing like home around here."

Benny stood up and brushed breadcrumbs off his uniform. "You, sir, are boring. You are making everything boring today. Even your game is boring. You're just mad you can't hang out with Doris Huntsman."

"I don't know what you're talking about. She's an old family friend."

"Tell your mother that."

Hudson slid off the hood of his Manutara and found his

fists already in tight balls, ready to dig into each of Benny's dimples. He knew what people had long been saying, that Huntsman was responsible for his mother's condition, if not everything that had happened to the world. But no one woman could have foreseen or controlled all, if any, of it. Hudson did not know all the reasons Huntsman had not visited since Declan's funeral, but he had never suspected Lucy of blaming her for anything. Benny was out of line.

The seagulls were circling in the distance, above Benny's head. "Let's get airborne. The birds are circling."

Benny mounted his Manutara quickly. Hudson followed, his stomach still quivering.

Hudson turned to see Benny pondering his control panel. Maybe he was angry, too. Benny turned to Hudson, and with a smirk on his face, his head jerked backward, and the Manutara disappeared into the mist.

Hudson huffed. "Now's not the time, Benny," he said to himself. Benny liked to perform the Bottle Rocket, the magic-carpet equivalent of burning rubber by overcharging the capacitors with the brake on and shooting forward like a firework.

But on Hudson's heads-up display, he could see Benny's location. He was going too fast, nearly sixty knots. It was always hard to tell when Benny was smirking or not. His friend may have been confused. His Manutara was malfunctioning.

"Benny, come in."

Benny did not answer.

Hudson unlocked his speed limiter, which would automatically send a distress signal, and took off after Benny, calling him through the laser-line radio. Benny did not answer.

Base station came on Hudson's radio, and he apprised them of the situation. Help was on the way.

Hudson followed the tunnel Benny was carving through the mist. He found himself clenching his teeth and storing up his breath. The mist was seeping into everything, and his hands began to slip on the wheel. Or that was his own sweat. A spectral encounter was usually over in seconds. It was already for a minute that Hudson had been chasing down Benny and his broken flying boat.

Based on his mapping, they were both over the water now. Hudson drew a deep breath and made his shoulders drop. Benny would run out of battery soon, the air would slow him down, and he would float on the water.

Benny's avatar turned red. He was below sea level. He was still making sixty knots. "One of these things is not right. It's got to be sea level. No one goes that fast below the water."

This incongruence calmed Hudson, the distraction of working on a puzzle while it stormed outside.

Benny began to slow, and after another minute, Hudson caught up. Benny was still showing below sea level, but this might mean his instruments were damaged. Hudson descended and reached sea level, according to his own instruments. The mist did not clear.

Hudson peered over the side of his Manutara. Waves should have been bashing against his hull. The Manutara hovered serenely.

Base station was not returning his calls.

His heads-up display was still showing Benny below him.

Hudson hovered downward.

At what should have been sea level, the mist broke. Where ocean water should have been, he breathed the open air. Above him, the mist held tight as a blanket of clouds. Below him, the ground was painted a murky gray.

"Alright, Hudson," he said, if just to pry his jaws apart. "This can make sense. Huntsman had said something about seismic activity. The sea's pulled away, that's all. Let's get Benny before it rolls back in."

Benny was now showing behind him.

Hudson yawed and then yelped.

The nearly vertical edge of the Great Meteor Seamount, a few miles away, was visible all the way to the ocean floor, or as it was now, the ground where the ocean had been. It was a wall in front of Hudson, thousands of feet tall. It glimmered white and gold near the top where the midday sun filtered through the mist. Below, it disappeared into a deep blue haze where, just barely, Hudson could see the ground sloping underneath and behind him, out toward the abyssal plain. It was a mesa in the desert where an underwater seamount should have been, painted with the colors of an iceberg, white floating on blue.

Some static on his radio snapped Hudson out of his mesmerized state.

Benny had landed on a small outcropping near the top of the seamount.

Hudson hovered alongside Benny and reached his hand across the two ships. Benny was unconscious but breathing.

His Manutara had shut down, and Hudson could not force a restart. After going so far, so fast, his ship had likely run out of battery and, just before it had, found the closest place to land. That place was a six-foot-wide and ten-foot-long ledge some five hundred feet below the top of the cliff. The front and rear of the Manutara hung over the edges.

"Alright, Benny. I'm here. Help is on its way."

The two Manutaras began to wobble, as if drawn by a strong wind or weak current.

"Nope. Now is the time to get you up. Before you fall off this cliff."

Hudson backed his Manutara against Benny's, bed to bed, so that he could drag his friend across. Tying them together risked sending Hudson's craft crashing down the cliff along with Benny's. He could, though, tie himself to his own flying boat while he walked across.

Skinny as he was, Hudson was strong enough to drag Benny's limp body. When he reached the rear end of Benny's Manutara, Hudson made the mistake of looking behind him, where the ground nearly disappeared into a deadly dusk over a thousand feet below. Hudson closed his eyes.

Benny groaned.

Hudson squeezed his arms tightly around Benny's sweaty chest. "Come on, you fat bastard. We've got one go at this."

Hudson waited for his wavering Manutara to hover a few inches closer. With another yelp muted by the thick air, he took one large step backward and thrust. Their two bodies fell backward onto the bed of Hudson's ship. They began to slip down through the gap between the ships. Hudson reached behind him for the roll bar and gripped it. With one hand quickly losing its grip on the thick chrome roll bar and the other letting Benny's sweaty body slip through, Hudson cried out. The rope he had tied around his waist was squeezing his rib cage.

"God, now."

The only thing that the tears filling Hudson's eyes would let him see was the stern of Benny's Manutara. Hudson lifted both of his thin legs and pressed his feet against it. When his Manutara drifted a little closer to Benny's, he pushed against it with his legs and pulled with his arm against the roll bar on his craft. This was enough, barely enough, to keep both bodies on board. Hudson wrapped his legs around Benny and pulled again with both hands. They were safe. Hudson could breathe again.

Hudson sat up and watched Benny's Manutara coast away from the force of his push. It drifted forward and sideways off the narrow ledge. It did not fall quickly, though, not as quickly as gravity would dictate but as if in slow motion. Hudson watched for several minutes until it hit the rocky ground on its side. From thousands of feet above, he could just barely make out the carpet and its chrome bars collapsing outward.

He turned back to Benny, who was still unconscious. He looked up at the cover of clouds.

A warning light on his console, which would normally have been red, pulsed black.

"One percent battery," Hudson read. "One percent battery? What…how…alright." He scrolled through the menu for estimated range. "Three miles horizontal, one hundred feet vertical." The cliff rose at least five hundred feet above him. He drew long, deep breaths and rubbed his face. "Quickly, Hudson."

Now, urged a word welling up from within him.

Those three letters told Hudson what to do.

He hovered over the narrow ledge where Benny's Manutara had landed. He hopped out and stood on it, holding onto the gunwale. The range now read ten miles or seven hundred feet upward. He nodded, reached over the gunwale, and tapped his way through the menu for the Homing function.

"Just like you said, Benny. You're going home."

The Manutara slid upward, across Hudson's hands. The wave runner sent a burning shower of static electricity against him as it passed. When it was too far above him to burn his eyes, he looked up and watched his Manutara lift through the mist and disappear. His eyes fell again, and he saw his new situation: he stood on a six-foot-wide ledge ten thousand feet above a darkening landscape. The sun had passed behind the seamount, whose shadow began to lurch across the ground. The same thick wind that had been moving around his Manutara was trying to topple him over, too. He sat down.

"Don't worry, Hudson. Help is on the way."

PART THREE

STILLBIRTH OF THE SEA

13

Hours passed, and no one arrived. There had been a brief flash of light above Hudson, at which he had waved his hands, but this had quickly disappeared again. The rescue team might not have thought to drop below the mist, which he was sure was still registering as sea level for them. But the sea had dropped. It had disappeared. Taking its place was humid air and a thickening darkness. The shadow of the seamount was merging, in the east, with a deep blue haze that hung in the air. The only light came through the cloud line above, which grew from gray to charcoal.

When Hudson thought the setting sun would paint the air the same deep red it always did, the clouds above simply turned black, and night fell like a stone sinking in the sea.

Hudson sat on the narrow ledge, five hundred feet below those clouds and ten thousand feet above the ground, in perfect darkness. His wristwatch, which had promised to glow even underwater, did so only dimly.

He had only been abandoned once in his life, when he was nine years old, on the *Eisenhower*. His parents had had meetings there, and he had been placed with other kids in some kind of play area somewhere below deck. His mother and father had each thought the other had taken him home, as apparently, they each had had different things to do after their meetings. Those had been the saddest hours of his life, being watched by some woman who was trying to be as pleasant as she could be, until Declan had shown up and showered him with kisses and stuffed him with ice cream.

That sadness welled upward now. There was no woman to watch over him. He might never be found.

There was one desperate thing he could do. He could turn on his emergency beacon. It did not work on line-of-sight laser, like all other wireless communications. It was an old-fashioned radio transmitter. Which meant that if human beings picked it up, so would specters, and it would be a race to see who could get to him first.

It had only been six hours. He decided to wait.

***

Lucy sat on the couch in her living room in New Norfolk. The streets were silent and covered in snow. Owen sat at the kitchen table, drawing cars and hovercraft. The sound of graphite on paper soothed her, much more than Owen's proclamations that the machines he was designing were sure to save Hudson. It had been six days since he had disappeared.

A pair of feet crunched through the snow outside. They grew closer, louder, and when they stopped at the door, Lucy stopped breathing.

Three knocks came at the door. It was not Hudson.

Owen might have asked Lucy if he should answer it, she

was not sure. Either way, a chill breeze blew inward. Owen's face glowed with snow-white light at the open door.

"Hey there, Owen," came Benny's voice, working too hard to sound natural. "How'ya doin'?"

Lucy's blood boiled upward like magma.

Owen shrugged and wiped his nose. "They haven't found Hudson yet."

"I know. Is, uh, your mom around?"

A grin almost stole its way onto Lucy's face, the kind a murderous madwoman might wear. She walked to the door.

Benny barely managed a glance upward. "Mrs. MacDuff, Owen, hello." He pinched his lower lip with his finger and thumb. "I'm here to say I'm sorry about what happened. For what it's worth, I know everyone says I was playing games with my Manutara, but I was not, and the Navy has confirmed that."

Lucy put her hands on Owen's shoulders.

"In any case, I've been grounded. For medical reasons, damage to my neck and whatnot, but you know that's another way of punishing me just to satisfy other people. I'm sorry. I shouldn't be saying all this. I'm just, you know...." He bounced and swayed on his knees. "I'm worried, too, but also not, if you can believe that."

He looked up, and Lucy saw a strange new confidence in his eyes.

"Too many things don't add up, Mrs. MacDuff. Where it says I was when Hudson saved me, below sea level. It's a strange place, and everything got really weird in the mist right before Hudson and I took off. I got angry at him for no good reason, like there was a bad vibe in the air."

Lucy buried her face in Owen's mop of hair, one of the many traits he had inherited from Declan.

"Don't fill me with false promises," she said and leaned her chin on Owen's head. "I've already lost one man in this world."

"That's not...," Benny began, and he pulled from under his arm a roll of magazines. "Anyway, these were Hudson's, old copies of *Shelf Life*. Not that I'm giving you his personal effects as if he were gone, just that I had them around. I've been reassigned, I'll probably be gone for a while. You want them, Owen?"

Owen took them and looked up at Lucy.

She nodded her approval and said, "Go on inside, Owen. You'll catch cold."

When Owen left, Lucy stepped outside. The snow on her door mat sent a welcome chill through her bare feet, a sign she was still alive to something that was not sorrow. She put her hands on Benny's shoulders.

She caught herself starting to grin again at the uncertain way he cast his eyes on her arms.

"I've been reassigned to El Jadida Nouvelle," he said, once again sounding unnaturally at ease. "Lots of folks moving to the Sahara. So...."

"Thank you, Benny." She kissed him on the forehead and met his eyes again. "You're going to live a long life, Benny. Don't get stuck behind anyone. And make sure no one else gets stuck behind you again."

Lucy quickly turned and stomped her way through her house, unsure if she had closed the door behind her, fell face first onto her bed, pulled Peter Panda's scrawny belly under her eyes, and drenched him with tears.

***

It had been almost eighteen hours by the dim light of Hudson's watch, but the sun had not risen again. He had not dared so much as standing up for fear of falling off the ledge. Pangs of hunger had kept him awake, along with the image of the ten-thousand-foot drop just past his outstretched legs. He was starting to shiver.

Confusion fought against the sadness of abandonment. The sea had vanished and not returned. The sun had vanished and not returned. His body ached for everything— food, warmth, movement, light, and sound—everything except water. He was not thirsty.

"Maybe now's the time," Hudson said out loud, his voice unnaturally muted. The cliff face did not release a single echo back to him. "I'm going to get hypothermia soon, before I starve. I'll take my odds against the specters."

He pressed his emergency beacon.

Hudson leaned forward and dug his hands into the soil on the ledge. It was cold as snow but soft in a different way, like the bottom of a lake, but made of fine powder. Even with his shivering, he began to drift into sleep.

Something appeared to him in fragments of dream life. A presence, deep down below him. It remained even when he thought he was awake. Or, he was neither really awake nor asleep anymore. He had a hard time telling when his eyes were closed without squeezing.

Eventually, though, he did wake up. He leaned against

the rock behind him. Something was in front of him, hiding behind six feet of black air. He did not need his sensitive eyes to see this.

A second presence arrived. If either presence had a shape, he could not see it. They made no noise. A bird would at least flap its wings, and a balloon would not hold so steady. A drone would whir.

What he did feel he might have called hatred, if there was a sad and mute kind.

The second presence crept forward. Without a sound, with no movement of the air around him at all, he could still feel this thing start to look him up and down. Its invisible eyes singed his skin, first on one side of his face and then the other, tracing the length of one leg and then the other.

Hudson's eyelids began to fall not from tiredness, but in submission to a gaze, a thing he had never known before. He forced himself to breathe slowly, but his breath still fell out in halting steps. Only his fingers worked freely, and he crawled them along the leg of his pants toward the pocket where he kept his knife.

The entity, as if noticing this, then seemed to sniff around his genitals.

Disgust crawled up Hudson's neck and pushed his lips into a snarl. He felt on himself the look he had seen on so many humans and animals right before specters thrust their way through them.

These were specters. This is what it felt like right before the end.

These formless vomits of life wanted to chew themselves out of chaos with his bones and blood. They would not succeed, but he would be dead, a pile of undigested tubes and teeth. He put his head down and closed his eyes, wishing it would end soon.

Something made Hudson snap in his seat. The specters sped away without a sound. He heard the long, deep groan of a bear or a moose resonate through the air. But there were no bears or moose or even dogs on this barren seamount and certainly not where the ocean had just been.

Whatever it was, it spooked the specters, and he was glad for it. It did not groan again, and Hudson felt alone in the icy dark.

"God, thank you." At those words, Hudson fell asleep.

He only knew he had fallen asleep from waking up again, twenty minutes later, to the first hint of pre-dawn twilight trickling downward from the clouds upon the old abyssal plain. There was no violet light of dawn, the kind he had always known on Earth and which the old worlders still found foreign. In its place, everything Hudson could see—the distant ground below, the wall of rock behind him, even his own hands—turned to indigo.

Hudson had not often seen indigo before. He had always been told there was a flash of it just before sunrise, and he had often pretended to notice it, too. This was no flash. It was a soaking in awesome sublimity.

God was right to hide this color from a fallen world, Hudson thought. He must have died, and this was God's smile. He had crashed with Benny or been torn apart by specters. Indigo saturated every surface, deeply and richly. The electricity of the angels began to course through his nerves, and each of his pains—empty stomach, frozen butt—became a treasure with which he would not part. This was what it meant to feel alive.

Hudson was alive. This indigo world radiated life, too, Hudson's own life. Nothing in this world could take life from him anymore. He was enthroned upon this rock. He could dive from the rock and swim through this new ether. He stood up.

Just as Hudson began to spread his arms wide, the indigo vanished. His world was brighter but monochrome, a gray moonscape. The feeling of power took longer to leave, though, and Hudson walked to the edge of the outcropping.

At the sight of the ten-thousand-foot drop, reality washed upward very quickly, and vertigo took over the angelic vibrations in Hudson's bones. He threw himself backward, against the rock, and fell on his butt.

Once again, confusion fought against the tears of frustration that wanted to pour out. He had seen a white line along the seamount's edge, what looked like a road, a hundred feet below. He crawled on his belly toward the edge and looked down.

The white line was still there and rose from left to right, north to south. It followed each crease and curve in the rock as if made by human hands for ascending from the abyssal plain to the mesa top of the seamount. Over the tens of miles of wall that he could see, it rose several thousand feet. If it continued this way around the southern tip of the seamount, it might bring him up to what was once sea level, or at least the part of the gently sloping top of the seamount that had still been submerged. The most promising way up was first to go down. But it was a long way down from the narrow ledge holding Hudson. He tucked his hands under his chin to think.

14

Hudson lay on his empty, aching belly, gazing down the face of the seamount for an hour, hoping his eyes would eventually make out some hidden steps or some ancient Atlantean rope left behind that could take him down to the road. He saw nothing but a smooth precipice. Nor did the road, if it was a road, come any closer. If he saw anything at all, it was a second road much farther down the face of the cliff. He could not tell how far down either one really was.

"Wait. Yes, I can."

He pulled himself backward and brushed the fine silt that had covered the ledge off his uniform. It fell very slowly to the ground.

"Almost too slowly," he said out loud.

He looked for a loose rock and found the largest one that would fit in his hand. He lay back down, and, peering over the edge, he dropped the rock. He counted six seconds for the rock to hit the road then drew the math in the silt next to him.

"That is not six hundred feet down."

He found another rock, very broad and flat. When he

dropped it, it did not fall straight but began to spin outward and away from the cliff face. He could not tell where it landed.

"Wind could do that, Hudson, but you know what would do that even more? Water."

Hudson pulled himself back so that he could lie down, facing up. The blanket of clouds above him, the mist through which he had first descended, which had not diminished at all and which did not even seem to be moving, was, however, very subtly undulating.

"Like waves on the surface," he said. He screamed. No echo came. "Just like screaming underwater."

He laughed and put his hands behind his head.

"You, Airman Hudson Bridgewater MacDuff, must contend with the fact that you are underwater. Breathing how, you do not know."

Lightning shot through his stomach at the thought that Benny had drowned. But Hudson had not, so neither had Benny.

"Okay, Hudson. This is why they are not finding you. The sea has not receded. Reality has. And your new reality tells you that you can fall as far as you want through water without getting hurt. You're a body. A buoy. You shouldn't even fall at all. In fact, you can swim upward."

He tried to do so. It did not work, though he fell slowly from his jump. He tried to climb the wall and slipped back down, though he did so, again, slowly.

Hudson sat, legs spread, on the narrow ledge. The vast, grayscale oceanscape below him began to look like a dungeon.

"Where is the indigo spirit? Ah. I know. It is within me." He stood up and toed the edge of the cliff. "I hereby summon the spirit of indigo." He spread his arms wide. Nothing happened.

He lay down on his belly and slowly brought his legs, bent forward like a lizard, over the side of the cliff. He hung from his hands over the edge. If Hudson was going to fall slowly, then scraping against the slightly angled seamount would slow his fall even more. "Dear God, this is not suicide. It's the only way I can think to live."

Hudson let go.

His body fell away from the cliff's edge. Some updraft of wind or water was pushing him away. His feet punched through some kind of slimy netting. He looked up; he had broken through the road, which was nothing more than a line of sea moss. He looked down; the second road was another layer of the thick vegetation, coming up fast.

"God, God, God."

Whether he did it, or God, Hudson did not know or care, but his body fell flat against the current rising against the seawall. A burst of adrenaline helped him manipulate the hundred small muscles it took to keep his body steered over the target, the second line of sea moss, a few hundred feet below the first one. He angled himself to follow the gently sagging line of moss to give himself more time to grab it.

Just before he did, a flurry of light blinded him. His arms scrambled outward to catch the moss, wherever it was, but his feet hit first, and they hit hard. Whatever his feet had hit his arms then grabbed, and Hudson hung from the slippery line of moss.

Hudson was clinging to something solid, though. The moss fell away where he was grabbing it. It was metal, this thing suspended along the seamount's edge. He pulled himself upward.

It was a chain. The links were each about three feet wide and four feet long, and fitted together like on a bicycle. Hudson sat on a crossmember. His feet began to burn. He looked down. Beneath him was ten thousand feet of gray air and the ocean floor.

Whether from the searing pain in his ankles or from vertigo, Hudson began to retch. He leaned forward to lie against the longitudinal members of the chain links. He closed his eyes, but the image of where he was grew into a nightmare. He pretended that the rectangular box the chain link formed was a television and below him, where his feet dangled, was a made-up world.

"In reality, Hudson, you have probably sprained or broken one or both ankles. It could be worse. It could have been your ribs that hit this thing first."

He looked ahead. Where the chain gently rose, bits of moss had broken off and were sparkling white stars slowly falling through the ether.

"You are where you want to be. You are a few hundred feet, maybe a thousand, below the clouds and old sea level. This chain is going upward. You now have to shuffle along this chain for many miles. But it is nicely lubricated with slimy moss. Thank you, God."

Hudson pulled one leg from the inside of the link to the outside, then the other leg. He could grip the outside of the chain with his legs. He lay face down and began to pull himself forward.

The metal edge of the chain dug into his thighs. He would have to crawl.

***

The day had become as long as the night for Hudson. Last night, he had spent twenty hours in shivering darkness; today he had determined to reach the southern point of the Great Meteor Seamount before the creeping sun cast its eastern edge in shadow.

He was no longer hungry. He had been eating the moss, which, despite its bitter taste, did not poison him. Hudson chewed his way along the chain. Eating, along with constant motion, reduced his shivering.

His feet, though, were flaming balloons he could only drag behind him.

After six hours of constant crawling along the moss-covered chain, he was just a few hundred feet away from a sharp turn in the wall. The terror of the ten-thousand-foot drop below him dissolved before the joy of making this next turn, one that would take him westward and upward. The chain was resting, up ahead, on a broad slab of rock. He would rest there, too.

Hudson had just barely reached the slab when a pillar of stone blocked his path. It was a small obelisk, ten feet high, with a triangular base, and richly decorated. The chain stopped at a thick metal ring at the base of the obelisk.

"Of course, there is an obelisk. What else would be pinning down this ancient chain?"

To his right, the chain continued from the obelisk like train tracks along a flat path carved through the rock.

"I'll take flat. At least it's not down."

Hudson used the obelisk to stand on his feet. He winced and puffed his breath in pain, quickly learning that his left foot was useless and was probably broken. His right was merely sprained.

While he waited for his feet to give him more information, he studied the decorations in the obelisk. Carved into the stone were a series of frames, arrayed vertically, and each frame featured symbols and small animals arranged on a bed of curling vines and branches.

"It's like something between hieroglyphs and painting."

He hobbled around the three sides and saw more of the same.

"There is some kind of pattern to this, Hudson, but you don't know what it is. Yet."

He looked around the flat road the Atlanteans, or whoever, had carved.

"I wish I could take this obelisk with me. I need something to keep me upright."

Hudson knelt back down and crawled the few hundred feet it took to reach the western end of the ledge.

The vista opened up. White rays of the setting sun broke through the sheet of clouds, casting the contours of the undulating ocean floor in three vivid dimensions. He could see, to the northwest, two smaller seamounts rising. The closer one, he knew from the study he had done on his flight to the Great Meteor Seamount a few days ago, was called Little Meteor Seamount. From its summit, another chain stretched to a point on the western wall of the Great Meteor Seamount, about eight or ten miles ahead.

"That's a thirty-mile chain, Hudson. They must have a sturdy obelisk holding all that weight back. Alright. Sun's about to set. We're safe here. Time to hunker down for the long night."

Crawling back to the gap in the rock, Hudson lay down.

"Dear God, why am I not dead yet?"

The sun set, the clouds turned charcoal, and, as if God had hit a light switch, the scene turned black.

Hudson kept his eyes open for a few more minutes, with only wispy thoughts of life at home—Lucy, Owen, Benny—slipping in and out of his mind. He had already spent the long day wondering what the chain was and where it went, and had arrived at no conclusion. He would have to follow it home.

15

GE+28

"I think she's finally taking to Mortimer, hon." Jody leaned his elbows on Haleh's glass bed and pressed his forehead to the pillow of her skin. "She's absorbing Mort's growing confidence. But she needs you to show her what to do now. And I need you to show me. Doris has got something up her sleeve. She got a little weird when Mort and Claire's lichens lit up. They really did, too, like a Christmas tree. You barely put up with Huntsman when you were awake. But I'll be honest, hon: I don't know where we'd be without her these days." He sighed. "When is 'Defcon-3 with a Smile' going to burst from her cozy womb and bring all this under control, like you used to do?"

A memory ushered itself into the theater of his mind:

He lay on the couch, one knee propped up, one leg across Haleh's lap. She was just beginning to show with Claire. Haleh rested her hands on Jody's leg while she texted on her phone. She had made it clear she barely tolerated the show they were watching. He had learned to suppress his judgment on her sitcoms, in which, to his mind, entertainment was nothing but mutual abuse. The two loners in this show, on the other hand, were much truer to life:

Mulder: *You put such faith in your science, Scully, but...from the things I've seen, science provides no place to start.*

Scully: *Nothing happens in contradiction to nature, only in contradiction to what we know of it. And that's a place to start. That's where the hope is.*

"Hm," Haleh said. She scrolled through her phone.

Jody ignored her.

"Think about it, babe." She was looking at the television now.

"She's quoting Saint Augustine. 'A miracle does not occur contrary to nature, but contrary to what is known of nature.' That's in the *City of God*. People like this quote it when they're looking for answers in some new dimension of this world instead of what's beyond it."

"Oh."

A commercial came on. "Think about what, hon?" Jody said.

"Don't the miracles tell us there is more out there?"

"There is more out there. It's waiting in heaven for those who are baptized."

Haleh put down her phone and pulled at the hairs on Jody's leg. "But what about this world? Can't this world become more? I mean, for instance, our little baby only knows my womb. That's her whole universe."

"She's a she?"

Haleh looked at Jody. "I'm sure. For now. Anyway, think of what kind of science babies in the womb would do. What would they make of our conversation? It would be like that background radiation at the edge of the universe. Then they're born, and they have to learn a whole new world. Imagine if all this is just one big womb, and one day we are all born into some greater world where everything makes more sense."

Jody restrained a smile. "Hon, that is literally the Christian faith that I have been trying to teach you. You know, heaven, the resurrection, the consummation of all things in Christ, et cetera."

She turned back to her phone. "Oh."

The show came back on. Jody sighed and turned to watch.

"Well, maybe if someone made a science out of it," Haleh said.

"You mean, a science of the voice of God speaking to us from outside the womb of the cosmos?" Jody said, raising his eyebrows.

Haleh raised her shoulder and snarled a little.

"It's called theology. We've been doing it for two thousand years. Except that God literally went into the womb to talk to us little fetus scientists to tell us what it's all like out there."

"Don't be gross. I was only trying to make an analogy."

"I'm not being gross, hon. That is what happened."

"Well, whatever. Watch your show."

Jody rubbed Haleh's arm with his bare toe.

"And clip your toenails, mister."

Jody leaned his forehead against Haleh's sleeper sac. "If you only knew, hon. If you only knew what birthing pains we've been in for almost thirty years. When is it going to be your turn to see the light again? You made it so easy for me the first time. Come back and make it easy for Claire.

"That reminds me. I've got a little something for you. I like this one. I tried writing a *ghazal*, but that's difficult. It did lead to some inspiration, though. Are you ready? Okay. I'll begin." He read:

May I remember always when
You fed your love to me in sighs
Upon each plate a broken breath
Well matched to after-dinner wine

May I remember always when
Our gaze cast down on growing moon
We gave our wine away to greet
Inebriations of the womb

May I remember always when
That chalice emptied of its mirth
We cast each other furtive glance
At tables messy with new birth

May I remember always when
Our sleep resumed its sober song
A nose to sip your scented air
A drink to last the whole night long

May I remember always how
The food my Haleh warmed for me
Became a share in God that filled
An empty soul with mystery

Jody leaned his head back and sighed. While flicking off the overhead light, he accidentally turned on the light inside the glass bed. "You'll be my nightlight." Haleh's cell filled with dim blue light. Jody's eyelids fell.

Something woke Jody. He cast a glance toward the smoked glass door, thinking Claire was waiting to come in. A shadow crawled through the dim light emanating from Haleh's bed. Jody looked carefully.

By her bent hips, there flowed a river of black. "No," he said. "No, no...." He wasted no more time and pressed the emergency call button. He heard nothing from the silent alarm and was not sure the evening guard was awake. He began to panic, wondering whether to tear open her sac himself or wait for the guard. "Help!" he called. "Help!"

At that moment, the guard burst around the corner. Donna, the guard, hurled her busty weight so fiercely he thought she meant to tackle him, and she nearly succeeded when she pushed him out of the way without a word. As Jody held onto the wall to keep from falling backward, Donna barked, "Come on! I'm going to cut, and when I do, you have to pull her out right away! Ready! Come on!"

Jody stood with his hands ready by her head, as if to catch a newborn forced from the womb. The guard quickly cut the sac with a short knife. Before she finished the line, fluid spilled out. Jody nervously reached in and grabbed

Haleh, catching one arm. She slipped out of his hands, and he began to panic again. Better to break a bone than leave her in there with her own poison, he thought, and grabbed her again by the neck and right arm. As he pulled, the guard pushed the sac away from her limp, red body. Jody sat her upright, and before he could form a thought, the guard already had a breath pump at her mouth. The guard took Jody's right hand and made him hold the pump to Haleh's mouth. The guard then pumped until Haleh began coughing.

The sleeper coughed out the fluid she had been breathing. Jody could not tell if the black fluid he saw on her chin had only accumulated around her body and had not come out from her lungs. The guard saw the streaks of black coming from Haleh's mouth. She looked at Jody with stern pity. "A doctor will be here soon," she said. "Keep holding her up. No. Let's get her out of this filth."

The sac of black bile that had filled her stomach was the appendix, which migrated through the digestive tract while the sleeper's skin billowed outward. The purpose of the appendix had finally been revealed to humans: it was for a transformation like this. It kept the stomach from shrinking during the years of sleep and kept the digestive system operating in the most minimal way. Upon waking, a burst sac would be evacuated through the colon or occasionally vomited. This was always painful. When the appendix burst while the sleeper was still in her skin, it was almost always fatal.

"Maybe it's not too late," Jody said. "I was here, I saw it before it spread."

He lifted Haleh by the arms while the guard pulled her sleeping sac from underneath her. Fluid poured into the floor drain below, swirling clear and black. Her legs now free, Jody took in, for the first time in nearly three decades, his wife's full figure. She was red and skinny, but he could still make out the familiar shape of her hips and fall of her breasts.

"She won't wake up just yet," the guard said, now more softly. Jody looked at her, covered in fluid from shoulder to shoe. "Can you carry her? We'll take her to the Waking Room. Hold on. It's too cold for her right now. I'll get you a blanket." The guard pulled open a drawer underneath the glass bed and took out a thick fleece blanket, deep red. Jody lifted Haleh again as the guard tucked it underneath her then pulled it over her arms and legs.

"Okay," Jody said, as with little effort, he lifted his almost weightless wife. Without asking the guard where the Waking Room was precisely, he walked toward the vestibule. The guard sped around him and opened the glass door then led him through a wooden door. Inside, where it was very warm, Jody saw leather couches and armchairs, tables adorned with books and flowers, and at one end, a small kitchenette. The waking process could take days or longer.

"On the armchair is best since she's still out," the guard said. Jody sat down with Haleh on his lap. He used one hand to pull the lever at its side, sending the chair back and Haleh lying on top of him. "That works, too, I guess. Here. Where should I put your cane?"

"My cane?"

The guard held it up. Jody had not walked farther than

the bathroom without a cane or a brace in thirty years. "Just there on the couch. Thank you." The guard tossed the cane on the couch. She did not look at Jody again before heading for the door. "Thank you," he repeated loudly.

"A doctor will be here soon," she said, but Jody feared her face said more.

16

GE+19

Hudson checked his watch, which illuminated only very faintly against the pitch-black oceanic sky. He had been asleep for ten hours.

He lay still, trying to sense if some presence had stirred him. Only the memory of the chain's clinking metal, made while he had crawled on it all those hours, echoed in his mind.

Between his feet, a dim light fell softly on the cloud line.

"Maybe search lights, Hudson. Hop to."

He checked his emergency beacon, which was still on.

"More small favors."

Hudson crawled from between the rocks, using the metal chain as a guide to keep from falling over the cliff's edge, which was hidden in darkness. It was no search light from above but some kind of light on the ocean floor. The light shined on the metal chain strung from the Great Meteor Seamount to the Little. There was some kind of knot or denser area in the chain right above the glittering circle of light.

"Well, you're awake. Let's go see what we can see."

***

Eight hours of crawling later, including breaks to rest, Hudson came to another obelisk. This one, he could tell by feeling, was much bigger at its base. He could see, from the light shining up from the ocean floor, that this was where the chain split off to cross the broad valley between the seamounts. He could not feel the chain continuing across the road cut into the rock face.

"But you'll worry about that in the morning. You've come pretty far in the dark."

Hudson leaned against the obelisk and picked off more moss to eat. The pool of light on the ocean floor was not much closer than it had been eight hours ago. It almost looked like a spiral galaxy.

"Is this what you people were into? Portals to another galaxy? Is this why God doth smote you, O people of Atlantis?"

He picked off more moss, stared into the starry abyss, and fell asleep.

***

Hudson woke up, only twenty minutes later, to the first hints of indigo dawn spreading across the clouds above him. The pain in his left foot was worsening. He did not dare untie his boots, which were the only thing keeping his bones and blood together.

The sparkling galaxy below began to fade in the encroaching sunlight. Soon, the whole scene was awash in indigo. Hudson could not summon any enthusiasm for it this time.

When the murky moon-gray color took over again, Hudson turned to study the chain system emanating from the large obelisk. But there was no system. The chain simply turned at this obelisk. It did not go up the side of the seamount. It only went across to the next one, thirty miles away, and deeper into the sea.

Hudson rubbed his face. "God...." He did not know what to say. His legs began to twitch, and he slapped the side of the obelisk behind him as if some primitive braid of neurons were telling him to flee. But there was no escape. There were only two directions: back the way he had come, where the chain might draw up to the top of the seamount somehow very far away; or across the abyss before him, even farther from base. He closed his eyes, clenched his teeth, and screamed.

"That's not very mature, Airman."

That was a female voice. Hudson's eyes flew open.

A woman was standing before him, on the edge of the road.

He pushed his feet against the ground to stand and thrust his back against the obelisk. Lightning shot through his leg and up his spine, and the pain nearly took his breakfast of sea moss up with it.

"What, what," he said, with more woof than whole words.

She looked a little familiar, and he squinted his eyes to see better.

"Yes, there are those puppy-dog eyes," she said.

She stood at ease in some kind of military uniform he did not recognize. In one hand was a tall pitchfork. No, a trident. This was some kind of Atlantean myth come to life. But Poseidon was male, if he remembered.

"Who are you?" Hudson said.

"The spirit of indigo," she said with a trace of sarcasm.

"Am I dead?"

She laughed. "Have you ever really felt alive?"

"I see. You're a product of my mind."

He turned over on his hands and knees, trying again to stand up. Neither foot would allow it.

Her two feet appeared before him, and then her hand. He took it. She was very strong. Once he was standing, she pushed the trident toward him.

"Here," she said. "There's lots of this junk lying around. I can get another one."

Hudson took the metal trident and leaned on it. Face to face with the woman, he could see her clearly. He knew her from the history books. "Lance Corporal Atalanta Bridge-water," he said.

"At your service." She bowed. "How do you know me?"

Hudson pulled his head back. Surely a sea goddess should know how she was known, especially one who was a product of his mind. "We all studied you in school. I'm even named after you. My middle name. But you know that, I'm sure. You know I'm an airman."

"Your name and rank are on your uniform, MacDuff. Along with a lot of dust and slime."

"What is this stuff, anyway?" Hudson picked at the sea moss smeared on his uniform.

"You've been eating it. You tell me. Not a scientist, here."

Hudson poked Bridgewater in the shoulder. She was flesh and blood.

She poked him back.

"Where did you come from?" he said. "You were at the moonshock when it sublimated."

"You just said more than I know about it. Again, not a scientist."

"What are you, then?"

"Force RECON. Eyes on the ground. What I know is how to get from one place to another."

Hudson nodded. She might be stuck in the same in-between state as he was. "Where's Rizzo the Rat?"

"Beats me. I think the only way I can go back and forth is that I was the only immortal soul to enter the moondark."

He gazed at her, and she let him. She did not take her eyes away, as if nothing about the encounter could be threatening or awkward.

"Back and forth?" Hudson asked.

"There." She pointed to the swirling pool of stars that had, by now, dimmed under gray daylight.

"Is that the way I have to go, too?"

"Yes, that would be advantageous."

"Those were Huntsman's words just a few days ago."

"Who's Huntsman?"

"Just a woman I know." Bridgewater might not be a product of his mind, after all.

"Great minds think alike."

"What is this place? How can I be here? How can you be here? How am I breathing under water?"

"How do your sleepers eat?"

"I don't know. No one knows."

"Then don't ask how. Why explains how."

"Why?"

"To get through there." She pointed in the direction of the glistening pit again.

"Again, why?"

"To live."

Bridgewater walked past Hudson to the edge of the road and looked over.

"How am I supposed to get down there? You see how bad my feet are."

She shrugged. "You got this far without your feet."

Bridgewater leapt. She did not sink but began swimming like a mermaid along the chain. After a mile or so, she disappeared into the murky gray light of early morning under the sea.

Tired of leaning on his new trident, Hudson sat down against the obelisk.

"Status update, Airman MacDuff. You have just received a visit from Lance Corporal Atalanta Bridgewater, who may or may not be a mermaid. Who swam to you from the moon. A moon-maid. A mer-moon. No, this place is the mer-moon. That explains the gray color and the low gravity, which is not a pleasant descent through water. You are holding an Atlantean trident in your hand, which by the color and feel, is devonium-slash-orichalcum. And which is not killing you because, as everyone knows, salt water neutralizes devonium. Which means you are in salt water. Whatever that means. You are not dead and maybe not yet fully alive. Like a baby in the womb. Yes, I get it. This is the dream of a baby in the womb. Imagining life as it must be, according to what he feels in the embryonic fluid. That's what you're breathing. And that swirl of stars down there is the birth canal. Thank God. This makes perfect sense now."

Hudson sat for a moment, staring at the chain. "My umbilical cord."

He slapped the ground of the seamount. "My mother, a dormant volcano."

He knocked on the obelisk behind him. "My fa—ew...."

Hudson struggled upward again and leaned on the trident. "Where are you, Dad, really?"

A favorite word of his father came into his mind, *druthers.*

"Yeah, Dad. If I had my druthers, what would I do? I'd say I'm a baby in the womb who can't hurt himself, whose mother is wrapped around him no matter which way he turns. She is a good mother, isn't she, Dad? Sad, but good. Sad for you, Dad. Sad for her world. A dormant volcano.

"Back to my druthers. I would swim like Bridgewater to that portal under the chain. But if I could swim, I'd go up to shore. And I know I can't swim through this air. So what of my druthers, then? I'd stop eating this bitter sea moss just to keep hunger away."

He leaned against the obelisk, favoring his broken ankle, and poked with the trident at the sea moss growing on the chain. The point of the trident kept slipping away, repulsed, as if trident and chain were identically poled magnets. Hudson went to his knees and held the trident over the chain. It hovered.

He shuffled sideways on his knees and drew the hovering trident along the chain. The trident spun along its shaft at each link. The magnetic poles were switching at each link of the chain. The shaft and center spike of the trident was neutral and kept the trident firmly in the center of the chain as it hovered forward and spun.

"You blessed people, you Atlanteans. You have made me a magnetic railway. No, you made it for yourselves first. And now it's mine."

Hudson sat on the trident and hovered over the chain but not far enough for his feet to dangle freely.

"Okay, Hudson. How do we do this? Where's Benny when I need him? Because I need some kind of bar to hang my legs up ahead of me. And if this trident-slash-ancient Wind Scout is going to spin around under my crotch, I need a seat, too. Bridgewater said there was a lot of junk lying around up here, but I don't see anything."

The answer came. Hudson saw an old memory in his mind, of being with his father on the widow's walk of their house in New Norfolk. Declan was pointing out the fleet in the distance. His father was wearing a white t-shirt, as he always was at home.

Hudson unzipped his flight uniform and took off his t-shirt. He cut off the lower hem with his knife and used the tough loop to tie his knees together. That makeshift rope would hold his thighs parallel with the shaft of the trident and let his calves and feet dangle freely. The rest of the t-shirt he folded into a seat.

The trident-slash-witch's-broom hovered over the chain but did not go forward.

"In fact, Hudson, you are going slowly backward."

Hudson turned the trident around so that its three spikes pointed forward. He drifted forward.

"Now, we're talking. Nice and slow."

He drifted to the edge of the road cut into the rock of the seamount. The dead volcano fell sharply away. Hudson slid back on the trident, which changed its angle against the chain and slowed him to a stop.

"Status update, Airman MacDuff. You are about to ride a prehistoric magna-rail over ten thousand feet of oceanic abyss, following the instructions of a Marine Corps mermaid, for the express purpose of dropping into a star-filled pit you are not entirely sure is a portal to another galaxy. And all this because it is the only way to live. Or at least to get out of this in-between. Amen to that. Eat your heart out, Indiana Jones."

Hudson looked up. "Again, Lord, not suicide."

He slid forward on the shaft of the trident and drifted over the edge. "Up, up, and away," he said with timid gusto and pushed forward. The ground plummeted away, his stomach flew upward, his head spun at the sight of certain death below him, but the trident followed the chain firmly. The sweat on his palms provided a lubricant against the shaft spinning in his hands.

The chain swayed in the submarine wind. The trident shook but held above the chain. Hudson stiffened. He slid back on the shaft to slow down. "Nice and slow," he said with more nervous chirp than words.

"Alright, Hudson. Do the math. This will help distract you. It's thirty miles from the western wall of the Great Meteor Seamount to the peak of the Little Meteor Seamount. You studied the map."

The chain swayed again. Hudson locked his elbows and closed his eyes. He could feel the trident locked in the center of the chain. It would rattle but not be shaken off. He opened his eyes again.

"The peak of the Little Meteor Seamount is seven hundred feet below sea level, nineteen years after the Great Eclipse. This chain was anchored to the Great Meteor around four hundred feet below sea level. The bottom of this chain's slight sag will be closer to the Little Meteor. You have just over fifteen miles. Maybe eighteen."

Forty minutes later, the circular void that had housed, by night, a swirling mass of stars spread wide and dark below Hudson's dangling feet. He guessed it was three miles across. And despite all the sunlight that diffused through the thin blanket of clouds above, this pit was deep blue.

"Midnight blue by day, noon-bright by night."

He neared the trough of the sagging funicular chain. It was not centered above the midnight-blue pit but ran along one edge. Up ahead, the chain split into a ring, like the kind that anchored it to the obelisks on land but much wider, about thirty feet in diameter. Hudson drifted to a stop when he reached the ring, whose floor was formed of metal mesh like the Faraday cages that wrapped cities on land. There was no guard rail. Hudson slid the trident from between his legs and lay down on the floor of the ring, looking down, through it, to the sinkhole below. The ring swayed in the current, and Hudson almost felt like a baby being rocked in the crib.

He turned his head to look back at the Great Meteor Seamount, which spread dark and wide across his field of vision.

More fascinating was the chain, whose mossy covering was glowing with iridescent colors. "Did I do that?"

Some of the slimy moss that clung to Hudson's uniform was also fluorescing.

"Bridgewater, you here?"

He turned his head to the other side.

A humanoid was standing on the other side of the ring, thirty feet away, staring at him. An owl was perched on its shoulder.

"Of course, there is," he said. He sighed, turned on his side to face the owl, and perched his head on his hand. "Well, Mr. Owl? Where do we go now?"

The owl did not move.

Hudson lay on his back. The western face of the Great Meteor Seamount was coming into full sunlight. His stomach grumbled. He looked at the owl.

"Probably not a good idea to eat glowing moss, right?"

The owl struck its wings out a little and brought them back in as if to fly or to adjust itself.

A slant of light moved upward on the other side of the mesh ring. A specter. The humanoid did not budge.

If this ring was what Hudson thought it was, he was protected. He grabbed the devonium trident and held it across his body. The noonday sun, polarized by the thin gray clouds, showed the specters clearly. They were rising all around him like gas fumes out of a stove. Hudson would light the burner. He extended the tip of the trident over the outer edge of the ring.

A few seconds later, a specter scraped it and burst into sparks. This did not seem to affect the other ones, who flew toward the Great Meteor. No more rose up around him.

Hudson looked toward where the specters were headed, the small Navy base. "Good luck, guys. Wish I could sound the alarm for you." He turned to the owl. "It's a red button on the gate at Great Meteor Base. You can poke it with your beak." The owl and the humanoid looked downward at the same time, into the pit. "Right."

The owl spread its immense wings and leapt downward, through the middle of the ring. The humanoid did not move.

Hudson sat up to follow the owl's trajectory. It sailed in a clockwise motion around the edge of the immense sinkhole, turning away right before it would have entered.

He turned the trident in his hand. "That's flight lesson number two this morning."

The humanoid started walking along the ring platform, toward Hudson.

Hudson stood up clumsily and painfully and leaned on the trident.

The humanoid kept coming toward him.

Hudson seethed. He could stab the machine, but the devonium would have no effect on it in the salt water, and it would crush Hudson's neck with its hands while Hudson tried to pull out the trident. Very few people had won fights with these killer robots at close range. In fact, only Father Joseph was rumored to have done so. Hudson could follow the owl into the portal, which seemed to be the bird's suggestion.

The humanoid had nearly reached him.

Hudson could not leap off his broken feet. Sharp breaths shot out of him. In one motion, he raised the heavy trident above his head with both hands and jerked it forward. The momentum carried him over the edge of the platform. His right foot buckled, his knees bent reflexively, and Hudson fell, head and hands first, into the abyss.

It took Hudson sixty seconds to reach the sinkhole. He fell as best he could in a clockwise motion, but without an owl's wings, he did all that he could just to keep on target. When he passed the ocean floor, the walls of the pit spread out wide, and he could no longer see them. He looked back up at the opening, which grew, for some reason, wider and wider, not narrower, not like a tunnel. The widening gray sky did not fill the pit with light but the contrary. The sinkhole, a well of midnight-blue ink from above, was blackening all around him.

Stars began to appear below. There were no brightest stars to pierce the darkness first, but a gray, diffuse glow emerged and then began to sparkle everywhere. A spiral galaxy took form. Either it was spinning or he was going more clockwise than he had thought, and each arm of the galaxy, as it turned toward him, began to look like a landing strip.

Sparks burst out at each end of the trident. He was scraping specters on his way down. They might not have been able to hurt him at this speed, anyway, unable to take that last half-second to sniff out their prey before penetrating.

Something banged against the shaft of the trident and burst into what felt like a flurry of snow or hail whipping Hudson's face. When he could open his eyes again, he saw that the galaxy was not growing bigger. He was trying to think about what had slowed him down when the swirling stars began to melt into each other, forming a milky soup. He was being drawn along one arm of the galaxy toward its bright middle. A flurry of snow or fine ice stung his face. The bright center of the galaxy turned into a bubbling stew of gray chunks. This gray center spread outward very quickly to fill his field of vision. It looked like a field of rocks.

The trident began to pull back, turning Hudson's body flat against his fall. When this rotation continued, threatening to put Hudson's feet first, he let go of the trident.

Suddenly, Hudson stopped falling a few feet above what was very clearly a field of ragged rocks. He put his arms in front of his face.

He resumed his fall and hit the ground. He could not breathe. The sharp rocks dug into his hands as he pushed himself up. Some instinct pushed him into a butt-up position, the way a baby sometimes sleeps. His diaphragm fought back, and he coughed up salt water. A long breath inward followed like a thousand knives in his throat, and he coughed up again.

Hudson, on all fours, looked around. There were no visible walls, only gray rocks that stretched dimly into darkness in every direction. Above him, the stars shined as if on the moonshock. He lay on his back. The shapes of the constellations above were strange. The air was very cold.

17

GE+28

Jody stared at the array of monitors standing sentry around him, around Haleh in his lap. The doctor was saying something.

"…but we have to monitor it closely. Even if she does wake, there is a good chance she becomes a severe diabetic."

Jody nodded and turned to Haleh. "Okay, I mean, that's a thing we can manage. Right, hon?" He kissed her forehead, which was covered in dried goo. Reflexively, he licked his lips. The fluid did not taste as sweet as it smelled.

"The sensor monitors here are connected directly to our nurse's station as well. We'll know immediately if there's any issue. You have the bottle and straw."

Jody lifted it from the table.

"Good. Just stay with her, then, as long as you can. Let her feel your arms around her." Jody squeezed a little. Haleh made a slight whimper. "See, already a good sign. We'll be back, Father Conque."

The door shut lightly, and silence wrapped heavily around Jody. He ran his thumb along the line of her short hair. The growing hair was a sign she had been ready to wake anyway. Jody was glad he had eaten too much at lunch.

He did not want to leave her now, not for a moment. He watched and waited, smiled and prayed. "Let her live, Lord. Please, let her live."

About four hours later, coming out of an involuntary nap, Jody saw Haleh's fingers move a little. Peering down, he saw her eyes opened halfway. He fondled her fingertips. She very weakly pulled up her head, just a little. Her dark eyes searched him above her red, blanket-wrinkled cheeks, just like Claire's had, once upon a time. He was not sure she saw him, but he smiled anyway. "Haleh! Honey!" he whispered and kissed her. "Uh…." he called out, looking toward the door. He saw the monitors and did not understand them. "They'll see this and come soon. Haleh, it's me, Jody. Your husband. You've been asleep for a long time."

She moved her mouth a little as if to speak, but no words came out.

"You're in Denver, love. I'm living at the cathedral with the bishop and the canons. I'm the rector, if you can believe that. You'll see Claire soon. She's all grown up. You've been asleep for a long time. Uncle Danny and Aunt Cynthia are here, too. They somehow managed to keep up that same house."

Haleh groaned.

"Oh, love, my radar love—you remember that? I've been your radar love now, taking my turn to feed on tears. It's a long story. A very long story. You just rest now. Keep waking up. Everything is just fine. It really is now."

She brought one leg up alongside him, weakly. Jody kissed her head again. He closed his eyes, laid his head back on the chair, and smiled.

***

Half an hour later, just as the nurses were laying Haleh in her own adjustable bed, Claire peered through the door. Danny and Cynthia pressed her into the room, and she leaned her hands on theirs like gymnast's rings.

"Come on, Claire," Jody said. "Come say hello to your mother." He stood and motioned for Claire to sit.

One of the nurses turned away, wiping a tear from her cheek.

Haleh managed enough strength to turn her head but could barely raise her arm. Jody took and pressed Haleh's palm to Claire's cheek. Claire held and caressed her hand there.

"Look at what a woman Claire's become, Haleh," Jody said.

"Beautiful," came Haleh's weak whisper with a faint smile.

Without relinquishing her grasp on her mother's arm, Claire reached forward and stroked Haleh's face.

"Claire has turned out as brilliantly as we thought she would," Jody said. "Danny and Cynthia have made her into quite the inventor. Drones into the deep earth, flying unicorns, you name it."

Haleh did not seem to receive these words.

Claire did not turn her eyes away from Haleh. "They only fly for a few feet at a time, Mom. Mom…." Claire buried her face in Haleh's hand and cried.

"A lot of cuts and scrapes come with her inventions," Danny said. "Hey. Come on. Let me see my little niece, too."

Jody had barely backed away before Danny walked forward and hovered over Claire. Danny leaned in but soon pulled back and lost his smile. "I think she's out again."

***

Two days later, Jody, Claire, Danny, and Helen were eating lunch in the Waking Room. The four of them had been taking turns at watch while Haleh came in and out of sleep. If Danny's recent attempt to lighten the mood had succeeded, it only showed in a short, shallow laugh from Claire:

What do you call a wandering caveman? Danny had asked. *A Meanderthal.* How did they get around? In their *Deniso-van.*

"Mort would be laughing," Danny said.

"Water."

Four heads turned toward Haleh. She held her head forward and was staring at her hands, which she moved freely.

"Her muscles have sprung," Jody said. "Finally. Thank God. She wants water."

He brought a cup and straw to her lips, but she brushed them away. "The water."

"This is water, hon."

Her eyes flicked upward and down again. Jody looked at the ceiling, but he knew there was no leak.

"The water...where, Haleh? You slept over a river of groundwater for ten years. Is that it?"

She grabbed his hand and brought it to her forehead.

Claire was standing on the other side of Haleh's bed. "Does she want you maybe to baptize her?"

Haleh gave a sharp breath as if of assent.

Jody ran both hands through his hair and held them

there, his gaze fixed on the two polished stones of obsidian and starlight Haleh's eyes had become. She knew she was about to die. "I need the ritual," he said and looked toward the door, hoping the doctors would burst through. "You want this, Haleh?"

"Jody," Danny said with unusual firmness.

"She's already said so," Claire said.

"Right," Jody said. He pulled the straw out of the cup of water. "Haleh Conque, I baptize you in the name of the Father, and of the Son, and of the Holy Spirit."

The water dripped down Haleh's face. Jody daubed it with a towel.

"The rivers," Haleh said. She arced her back a little as if to stretch or out of discomfort.

"What's wrong, Mom?" Claire asked.

Darkness drowned the starlight out of Haleh's eyes. Jody had seen this before. She was on her way toward somewhere else.

"Keep the rivers between us," Haleh said. "Between us and them."

The hairs on Jody's skin raised an electric shield around him.

"Make the rivers flow…where they need to go," Haleh said.

"Dad?" Claire whimpered, but Jody did not dare turn his head.

Haleh's voice grew weaker. "Wait for the light to grow…."

Haleh's head fell to the side. A monitor screeched. Jody's jaw trembled upward, and all became a blur. Bodies he imagined to be the nurses squeezed into the scene. Hands he imagined to be Danny's pulled him back or held him upright or both. A wail he took to be Claire's muffled into what he imagined to be Cynthia's shoulder. A strange silence filled the room. The monitor had stopped screeching. The nurses had vanished. For a brief moment, before he heard another muffled cry from Claire, Jody was alone with Haleh, the only two souls in the universe.

18

Mort sat next to Huntsman on stiff wooden chairs at the far end of the rectory living room. Father Joseph sat in an armchair, running his fingertips along a line of brass fabric tacks spiraling toward the center of each arm. Claire sat with Danny and Cynthia on a long couch. Commander Devon Conque, with his collar unbuttoned, tie untied, and second scotch in his hand, supplied most of the conversation.

"Where's Lucy?" Mort whispered to Huntsman.

"Mushrooms, right?" Devon said. He was looking at Mort.

"Sorry," Mort said. "I was just wondering if Lucy was going to make it."

"You study mushrooms?" Devon asked. The Naval officer looked earnest enough.

"I am a mycologist specializing in lichens, which are actually a hybrid organism of fungi and algae. Claire and I have seen some exciting stuff on that front recently."

Claire pressed her lips together.

"It's amazing," Devon said. "You poke your head out

like a turtle on the other side of the world and find the very thing you know about."

"Devon," Father Joseph said.

"No, I am genuinely amazed," Devon said. "I want to know how this works. I want to break through a barrier of my own, but so far, I've got no tools to do it with. I've shot everything I know how to shoot at the moonshock, and nothing gets through. So tell us, Mr. Sikorski. How'd you do it? How did you break the impenetrable barrier? The Russians are at it for decades. So is the OSS. You and the other guy show up, and suddenly, the golden passage opens? Tell us the secret." He formed his hand into a pistol, pointed it at Mort, and donned a villainous accent. "Tell us secret or die."

Mort looked at Father Joseph, who had retreated again, then at Claire. Mort finished his glass, chewed some ice, and shrugged. "I don't know. I guess Big Momma Earth likes me. She just opened up for us."

"What," Devon said, "like a virgin on her wedding night? Come on. Give me something scientific, biologist."

Danny chortled.

"Devon," Cynthia spat.

"Alright, sorry," Devon said. "But we could still use all the help we can get. The Navy's running short of brains."

Huntsman spoke, "Commander Conque, it's fair to say that the OSS would happily supply you with mission specialists once the Navy demonstrates it can sustain a stable orbit around the moonshock. We're just not going to throw bodies at a wall."

Devon flicked up his hand. "And yet isn't it fair to say

that you just literally dropped this guy into a hole in the ground?"

"Into a measured situation."

"Enough," Claire said. "We're here for Mom."

"And his buddy's still down there," Devon continued.

"Twenty-eight years," Father Joseph said. "When she woke up, it was like all that time just vanished. Like I had been sleeping, too."

Devon stared at Father Joseph's hands, which kept caressing the spiral shape on the armrest. "An entire universe sealed up behind a thin sheet of glass," Devon said softly without removing his eyes. "A snow-globe universe." He finished his glass and looked around. "Where's Chief Hoolahoop?"

The room erupted.

Claire stood up and stomped toward the kitchen.

Mort watched as Devon put up his palms in apologetic defense against pointed fingers and shielded his eyes in surrender.

Huntsman elbowed Mort and nodded toward the kitchen.

Mort found Claire gripping the edge of the sink. He put his hand next to hers and watched the tears drip onto her hands. Some rolled into the sink, others to the floor. She heaved broken breath. He did not know what else to do but hold his warm, steady body next to hers. If he spoke, he might startle her. Or offend her. Or just drive her away to wallow within herself.

She turned a little toward him.

"Devon's starting to apologize," he said.

Claire leaned toward him, and before Mort's brain could wonder what to do, his arms enclosed her. He felt her heaving into his chest.

"I miss him, too," he said. "I've never had a man take me under his wing like White Wolf did. And now your mother's gone."

She pulled back but brought a hand to his chest. "I don't know where you get your courage."

Every muscle fiber, every vein, every tender branch of Mort's lungs swelled with liquid bronze. Life itself assumed its throne within his towering frame. At the same moment, life made an exchange, and he watched a thousand tiny, tender muscles twitch around Claire's red eyes, within her cheeks, and around a mouth pulled down in a frown like a lost lamb around a shepherd's shoulders. She was vastly more beautiful in this moment of weakness than she had been in the demi-divine aura his mind had always wrapped around her.

"Looking at you," he said. He brought his hand to her cheek and ran his thumb through a trail of tears.

Claire brought her hands behind Mort's head, pulled herself upward, and kissed him.

Just as quickly, she buried her face in his chest.

Mort brought his nose to her neck and, gently swaying her in his arms, breathed in a garden full of flowers. The motor of his mind sputtered out. All that remained of the world was her skin, her scent, and her fingers finding grip on his back.

***

Lucy stood on the widow's walk. She held her hands on the rail and resisted curling up against the chill. She would grow bark, if she could, and stand exposed forever. A lone ray of sun found her, and she closed her eyes to welcome it.

Memories became daydreams. Declan was here with Lucy. She could almost feel him and imagined she had really caught his beard balm wafting into her nose.

Then he spoke.

"You should have seen you, Ladymouse."

Lucy heard these words with her ears. She dared not open her eyes. She risked seeing that he was not really there, that she was alone. Or she might see he really was there and come to doubt her sanity. So long as she kept her eyes closed, she and Declan could live together in their own world.

"I mean it," Declan said. "Your snow-white skin against that icy tundra."

Lucy's lips curled upward.

"All I could see of you were four points of a diamond, glinting red in the sun."

"Don't be dirty, Mister MacDuff."

"Excuse me. *Coruscating.*"

This really was Declan, in some way.

"It's as if you were daring me to trace your edges with my eyes, to find where the ice ended and you began."

"I never felt naked in your eyes. Or I always did, but never ashamed."

"And yet I'm not sure I ever reached the edge of your universe, not in all our years of marriage."

Lucy said nothing but breathed in the air that hid her lost husband.

"Listen now, Ladymouse. I need you to do something for me. Don't be afraid to let him go again."

"Again?"

Lucy's answer met silence. She opened her eyes. Declan was not there. She cleared her throat and ran her fingers along the rail's peeling paint. A flake peeled off to reveal dried, decaying wood below.

A trio in dark suits trudged through the street below. Lucy could tell Owen's gait, leading the way. He brought the others into the house below.

"Mom?" Owen called.

Without repeating himself, he walked upstairs, onto the widow's walk.

"Mom. Listen to me. You're not going to believe this. Mom." He grabbed her arms.

"What are you doing back from school?" Owen was the age Hudson had been when he had disappeared and looked just like Declan.

"They sent me to tell you. They've found Hudson."

"Who?"

Owen pulled his head back. "Your son. My brother."

"I mean, who found him?"

"The Army. You're never going to guess where. Mom, aren't you excited?"

Lucy knew Owen's words would mean nothing until she saw whatever he was talking about for herself. They had found Hudson.

"Can you believe it?" Owen said. "After nine years."

She nodded.

"Mom, he's alive."

Every reach of the visible sky conspired to send a swirling surge of soft, warm lightning through Lucy's ears, down her throat, and into her belly, where it danced.

"And you'll never guess where."

Lucy did not have to guess. She knew, somehow, what Owen was going to say next.

"Antarctica," Owen said.

Despite the golden glow of Owen's angelic news, Lucy winced at those last four syllables, which could only be crafted on human tongues by hammer and anvil.

"From the Azores to Antarctica. Nine years. The officers downstairs just want to talk to you, something about needing your help to get him out."

PART FOUR

DESERT OF THE DEAD

19

Hudson opened his eyes to a brilliant blue sky. He had slept on the jagged rocks under a foil blanket he kept in his flight suit. The same kind of chemical warming packet that had not worked when he was shivering under the sea had worked last night. The sea moss on his uniform had still been glowing when he had landed here, but its iridescent light had quickly turned to heat. So long as Hudson did not shift his body on the sharp rocks, they made as good a bed as any.

In the daylight, he could see the horizon. Nothing rose to interrupt the field of rocks, which ended at a thin white line in every direction.

"So much for your birth canal theory." Hudson tried to sit up, but his bruised ribs punched him back down. He had landed harder than he had thought. "Or this is the world's worst crib."

He checked his emergency beacon. It had run out of battery during the night and would not come on again this morning.

He could not feel his feet. "This is really bad, Hudson.

You could lose them. But where're you going to crawl to now, anyway?"

The naked sky revealed nothing. There was no secret there written in invisible ink that only his special eyes could see.

"Okay, God. Now what? I'm listening."

He felt around with his hands until he found a loose rock he could pick up. There was nothing particular about it, not even an embedded fossil.

"I'm the only thing alive around here. Won't be for long. Not this way."

Hudson tried to turn himself over and start crawling again. The pain in his ribs would not allow it. Without being able to stand up, he would not know where to go.

"I am Thor, and I summon my trident," he said, reaching out his hand. The trident did not obey. He was not sure it had made it into this realm with him. He was sure he did not know the name of Thor's hammer, anyway.

The swelling in his feet had reached his knees, which would not bend enough to let his legs push him one way or another.

"Not paralyzed but practically immobile."

He put his hands over his face and sighed.

"Okay, God, if this is the end, I'm sorry for my sins. For getting frustrated with my mother. For lusting after Hope and other girls. For all the other things I can't think of. Because I don't know what else to do. I'm out of ideas."

Minutes passed in silence. There was no wind, no birds, no chirping insects, nothing to break the silence except the gentle crinkling of the foil blanket and a slight wheeze in

Hudson's throat. His stomach growled. He had no provisions in his flight suit. Hudson fell asleep again.

***

Hudson woke up to see the thin horizon past his feet radiant with white light. This was not happening to his left or right. Behind him, the glow was more diffuse.

This changed, as the horizon between his feet began to lose its brilliance and the glow behind his head grew bigger and hovered toward him. It felt like sunrise, though the sky had already been blue, and the blob of white heat in the sky was much bigger than the sun.

Hudson squinted and barely managed to move his lips into a full sentence. "Alien sun, strange planet, or aliens on Earth. They've come to get me." He closed his eyes and lay still. The only thing he could do to alert anyone, human or alien, to his location would have been to wave his hands. But he was not sure he wanted to advertise his presence to this light.

In a few short minutes, the strange sun filled the entire sky with burning yellow-white light. The rocks glistened with it, but his foil blanket kept most of the hot rays away from his body, and he pulled it up over his face. His black boots were exposed, but his feet did not begin to boil inside them, as he had briefly expected. The field of light continued to pass over the sky, leaving behind a blue crescent shape behind his head as wide as the horizon. This sun, which was as big in the sky as he had been told it was during the Great Eclipse, eventually disappeared over the horizon past

Hudson's feet with no special sunset colors. The bright blue sky remained.

"Their sun is so big it's always day," he said. He was thirsty. "No matter what direction this planet is facing." He smacked his lips. He had coughed up seawater a few hours ago and had nothing fresh with which to replenish himself.

"It's always a spectacular sight, the great noon," came a male voice. There was a slight echo, and the last word, "noon," grew louder with each reverberation until it suddenly cut off.

"Who's there?" Hudson said.

"Aw, come on now, Huggy Baby. It hasn't been that long. You don't recognize my voice?"

This very well could be Declan MacDuff, Hudson's father. He did remember being called "Huggy Baby" but only by his mother. "Dad?"

"I'm here." Even softly spoken, the echo gave each word a sharp edge. But Hudson smiled and looked up at the blue sky. "The question is, kiddo, how did *you* get here?"

"Where am I? Where are you?" Hudson arced his head and saw no one.

"In a great desert. It's a special kind of space here. Easier for you to hear me when I'm farther away. But I tell you what. I'll move over so you can see me."

A small dark figure walked from behind Hudson's left boot to the space between his feet, a few dozen yards away. From that distance, it could have been anyone.

Hudson had always imagined leaping back into Declan's arms one day, when both were dead or both alive in the rebuilt world of the resurrection. It would not be like that today.

"You can't come any closer, Dad? Am I dead? Is this where the dead live?"

"Do you feel dead?"

"I'm numb. And thirsty. I could use some water."

"There's not too much of that around here, I'm sorry to say. But since you're not dead, and I am, there's a great gulf between us. Easier to talk this way. If I was closer, you couldn't hear me."

The echoes were like knives in Hudson's ears. But he would bear this for the sake of speaking with his father again.

"How've you been, boy? Look at you. All grown up and in uniform."

Hudson bounced his eyebrows. "That's what Miss Huntsman said. But I think she meant it in a different way than you, if you catch my drift."

Declan laughed and wagged a finger. "Better watch out for a woman like that, kiddo."

"You know me, Dad. I'm just talking. That's all I ever do."

"But you're young yet. We'll get you settled down with someone."

"You've got to get me out of this place first."

The figure crouched. "Well, now, we do need to talk about that, don't we? I can't figure how you got here in the first place."

"This desert of the dead?" Hudson asked.

Declan did not answer.

20

Jody walked back into the sanctuary of the Denver cathedral after the evening daily Mass. The altar servers were taking too long to straighten up. He could not carry much in his free hand, but he could put out the candles with the snuffer and hope this earned the servers' attention. When he turned from the altar to descend the steps after snuffing the candles, he caught a pair of green eyes he had known long ago glowing toward him from the back of the nave. He could not say why, but the promise of an intense conversation provided the most consolation he had felt since Haleh's death.

One of the younger servers walked out to finish clearing the credence table. Jody handed him the snuffer.

"But you already put out the candles, Father."

"And now I am handing you the snuffer."

The server took it, and Jody mussed the boy's hair.

Jody did not make it as far as the front row of pews before another familiar face manifested before him.

"Hello, Cassie," Jody said. In another world, Cassie would have been the prime audience for the apocalypse, a person who, because of her faith, beauty, and intelligence, expected the world to open every boulevard to her. With her talents frustrated in a low-level career or her beauty wasted in a dull marriage, her last hope for status on this Earth would have been to imagine herself some catcher in the rye for the children of God fleeing the blood-soaked sex dungeons of the antichrist. Now that she was actually living through the apocalypse, her concerns had become more pedestrian. "How may I help you?"

"Oh, it's just a little thing, but I thought you should know that lately, and maybe you've already noticed, but your left hand is falling a little lower than your right when you pray."

"I'm seventy years old, Cassie. Everything should be falling down. Instead, I get the promise of immortality without the joys of a youthful body."

"Well, things being as they are, you know. I mean, my husband had a stroke years before anyone noticed it, so...."

"Thank you for letting me know, Cassie." Jody laid the offending hand on her arm and smiled. "I will be more attentive to it."

Once free, Jody continued on his course. If Cassie had known who the man was sitting only a few pews behind her, she would have fainted for self-importance. Kai was bent over in prayer.

"Long time no see, Mr. Adamson," Jody said.

Kai rose from his knees and turned his green eyes toward Jody. He gazed at Jody for a moment in silence, as if retrieving a memory. Jody had not forgotten a word.

"It's been twenty-eight years," Jody said.

"The blink of an eye, for some of us," Kai said.

"To what do I owe the honor of a visit?"

"First, let me offer you my condolences on your loss of Haleh."

"Thank you," Jody said. "And you say *your* loss, knowing full well that she is heaven's gain, but it makes me wonder where you live, exactly, to disappear for so much time. Especially when we need your help."

Kai looked past Jody, toward the sanctuary. "You speak of my visit as an honor, Father Joseph. But why do so when there is such power in your hands?"

Jody turned his head a little. "Touché."

"This is the point," Kai said. "I can't make you understand my relationship to this bowl of clay we call Earth or what it means for me to wander through time on it. You have better images in your mind of living in time and in eternity than you ever could of the in-between realm I haunt. But let me put it simply: through my existence, like that of my father and mother, God has given shape to the clay. Just like your hands do. And it's time to put those hands to work in a special way again."

Jody's hands had felled a few humanoids over the past three decades and interrupted the circuit of more than a few specters. Apart from this and what he accomplished on the altar every day, he could not imagine what Kai meant.

"Is this about Antarctica? Doris wants me on a rescue mission for Lucy's son. But the military's capable now, and Claire needs me here. She's got a boyfriend now, thank God, and doesn't know what to do for him. Here again, Haleh is our loss."

"Bring Mort and Claire along. They might know how to see."

"See?" Jody said, as the lights in the cathedral dimmed.

The servers came out of the sacristy, and one of them stopped and formed a question mark with his posture. Jody motioned that it was alright to leave the lights off.

"How providential," Kai said. "This is a better way to see the beautiful."

"In the darkness?"

A winter wind howled outside.

Kai seemed to inhale it. "Isn't there a beauty in the winter? The gray light bending over soft waves of snow? Leafless branches giving eye onto the endless horizon?"

"It's beautiful in a picture or when you know you have a warm fireplace to get back to."

Kai stared off toward the sanctuary. "Yes, yes, exactly. Beauty is power made safe. Beauty is the edge of danger. Just look. How much farther can you see into that gilded stone sanctuary now that the light is dim? Beauty is the edge of darkness.

"You people think of the Greeks as in love with the sea, but they hated the sea, you know. They feared it. The sea is chaos, a place of death, 'a treacherous element, dark, misty, interminable, fishy, tempestuous—anything except beautiful to look at.' Only a people that is safe on the seas feels its beauty. And what pulls them in is being on the threshold— but only at the threshold—of darkness and danger."

Kai closed his eyes to continue. "When I was young, during a winter like this one, I went out alone one evening at dusk. My parents were practically trembling with anxiety. What to wear, what to eat, how to keep warm. Outside, I let my eyes rest on a solitary pine tree. There it was, just one tree, alone in the middle of a snow-covered field. I wondered at it. It had lived many winters out there. The biting wind, the heavy snow, the chill. The cold ate into my bones, and that tree stood tall, exposing a thousand tender fingers to it all. I wondered what it would take, what resolve, to stand as still as that tree in the cold.

"But God had dressed the tree to live that way. Not me. He had made me too sensitive. I would have to seek shelter. Found a civilization. Build a city wall to block the winter wind. To make the world as beautiful for everyone in safety as it had been for me in danger."

Kai turned to Jody. "In a well-lit room, you will see whatever is there. But where a single candle shines, what remains of darkness opens the way to infinity. You and Lucy and the others can see in the darkness. You can see more than what is there. I've tried to guide you as much as I could, to teach you how to become what I already am."

Jody leaned on his cane with both hands and let his eyes fall on Kai's well-traveled boots. "And what is that, exactly?"

Kai grabbed the sides of Jody's head with his hands and pressed their foreheads together. "Hands to reshape the world. There's nothing more exact to say than that, not while you still have decisions to make." Kai let go.

By the time Jody recovered from this intimate gesture, he raised his eyes to see the cathedral door falling closed.

***

Jody sat as far away from Vice President Philips as he could manage. It was evening, and only the small torches flanking the many sleeping bodies lit the Hall of Watchers.

The smell of incense wafted gently through the air, ostensibly to cover the newborn smell and insidiously to evoke a cult of adoration. The glass dome creaked under a heavy load of snow. Mortimer and Claire kept Jody company on a far bench.

Lucy, like Huntsman, had to stay near Philips. She was practically the star of the show. She had fixed her hair again into a smooth, glossy red veil. This alone, without news of her son, would have taken a decade off her age. The seeming agelessness of the new world, in which twenty-eight years had passed as if they had been five or ten, had been less kind to Lucy than to others, but so had the new world itself, taking her husband violently and her son mysteriously. How much effort redoing her hair had required, Jody did not know. But the smile that had not left her face these past two days seemed effortless.

After half an hour of silent watching by the dozen or so people around President Deborah Palmer's sleeping egg, Philips said, "Thank you, all of you. One learns so much about another person in silence. We must be joined in mind and heart. Rescuing Airman MacDuff, our dear Hudson, will not be effortless."

Jody checked himself from reacting to hearing Philips speak the word Jody had thought. It was likely a coincidence.

"Dr. Huntsman," Philips continued, "I sense that your team already knows each other intimately. I will not reach into your domain of expertise by suggesting that this can help us. Let me only say that it is a shame that Misters Farkas and DeSoto could not be with us, after all this time and given the greatness of their talent."

Huntsman cast an eye toward Mortimer then said to Philips, "Mr. Vice President, the OSS has lost many dedicated individuals over the years."

"Yes, yes, of course," Philips said. "And now that you have the full support of the military, we can better protect each other's assets."

The smarmy expression into which Philips's face then folded itself itched Jody like an allergen. For a brief moment, he reminded Jody of the dapper priest he had once met, encouraging him to embrace his strange new power like a god. Here at Palmer's bedside, Philips was doing much worse than making himself into a false god. He was making himself into its priest.

***

"Why is that worse?" Mortimer asked. He then stuffed a cheeseburger into his mouth. Five of them sat around a large table at a diner in St. Louis: Jody, Mortimer, Claire, Huntsman, and Lucy. Claire eyed the cheeseburger and the sauce dripping from Mortimer's chin. He had been gaining weight lately. While she muttered something to her boyfriend, Huntsman looked at Jody, anticipating his response as well.

"Because it's easy to ignore gods, real ones and false ones," Jody said. "But priests, they can demand your attention mercilessly. Especially when they're attached to political power."

"Like the Inquisition," Huntsman said.

If Jody could convince himself that he owned this statement first, it would not sting as much as it always did.

"Or the old Iranian clerics," Claire said.

"Young Iranians can be merciless, too, sometimes," Mortimer said.

Claire gave him side eye. Mortimer reached in for a kiss. Claire pushed him away, kissed her hand, and patted his cheek.

Lucy pulled her eyes away from wherever they had taken her, most likely the road ahead. "What did Philips mean by protecting each other's assets?" she asked. "Who else is involved in this?"

"I'm sure he just means the Marines coming with us," Jody said.

"They're only escorting us there," Huntsman said. "Army special forces are taking us in. The ones who found him. Locally based, apparently."

No one at the table replied to this. The logic was understood. Special forces already on the ground meant this project was more than plucking a long-bearded Hudson from some ice cave filled with nine years' worth of penguin bones. If there were special forces locally based in Antarctica, a fact revealed to them only now, on Huntsman's lips, then there was something Philips and the high priests of his cult of sleepers were protecting. Something Huntsman herself, relegated to digging holes and scouring the shores of the Azores for the past thirty years, did not know about, not if she had chosen to use the word "apparently" as carefully as she certainly had. The weight of Kai's words in the cathedral fell into Jody's hands, and he set down his sandwich. These five were going to have to see something no one else could, or should.

Across the table from him, the usually open page of Lucy's eyes filled with black ink, the same kind he had seen when he had first met her. Jody had known back then, the day he and Lucy had made their first remote visit to Antarctica, that he would have to protect her in a special way, and whatever secrets she kept. This was not going to be a remote viewing exercise, though. Whatever awaited them would grab them by all five senses, as well as the sixth sense they had developed, the most difficult sense to mute.

21

"Doris?" Lucy said. They were sharing a bunk bed at an Argentinian army base, on their way to Antarctica. Lucy was lying on the bottom bunk, Huntsman on the upper. Claire was across the room, asleep.

"Yes, Lucy?"

"How does Hudson get from the Azores to Antarctica?"

Huntsman took an audible breath. "The same way Jody crashes north of Boulder. The way Billy takes us to Siberia. The way Mort finds humanoids under the mantle and brings back fluorescent lichen. Something about where each of us started is bringing us forward, links on a chain."

Lucy lay with her hands on her belly. *This isn't where I started.* "You said 'us.' What about you, Doris? Where did you start?"

After a pause, Huntsman said, "I started in hell." Lucy thought she heard an abortive sob burst out of Huntsman. "Heaven help us if our chain leads back there."

Lucy reached her long arm to the sagging bulge above her and touched the metal links of the bunk with her finger.

"Could it be that bad, Doris, to open the world to everything you keep buttoned up inside you?"

Huntsman did not answer. This was really Lucy's question for herself, and Huntsman's silence proved it would not be easy to answer.

***

"Dad?" Hudson called.

Declan had been quiet for a minute or two and seemed distracted by something.

"I'm here, kiddo."

"What if you just come up closer? We don't have to talk. I'd like to see you again."

Pulling his head up to see his father, still standing at some distance between his feet, was straining Hudson's neck. More than once had he let his head fall back hard on the sharp rocks.

"'Cause I can't even get up," Hudson continued. "Can barely feel my legs, and my ribs might actually be broken, too."

"I'm sorry about that," Declan said. "I don't make the rules around here. Besides, you, uh, you know how I got it in the end. It's not a pretty sight."

Tears pooled in Hudson's eyes. As his breath began to heave, he heard his wheezing growing worse. "Is this hell, Dad? Did I get it from a specter, too?"

Declan made a couple of awkward-looking steps forward and stopped. "This is not hell. That I know. But you, I don't really know how you got here."

Hudson wiped his eyes. There still was not a cloud in

the sky. He still could see nothing except the thin white horizon surrounding him and Declan's dark figure, still standing far away, between his feet. If there were rules in this world, he was going to test them. That would mean testing Declan's knowledge, too.

"I don't know, Dad. I guess I just sort of fell through the water and landed here."

"Yes, I see." The echo on "see" had a slight hiss in it.

"How come you don't know everything? The dead know everything." As soon as Hudson said that, he remembered the African slaves who had come ashore, whom he had released. They had not known where they were or what was expected of them until Hudson had shown them. "Sorry. Maybe not."

"Tell me how your mother's doing."

"She's off and on. She misses you. A lot."

"And Owen?"

"He's a good kid. But, I don't know, I feel like Mom's neglecting him. I've got to step in now and then. And that's kept me from going off to college or the Academy, doing my own thing, I think."

"Well, while we're here and it's just the two of us, we can speak man to man," Declan said.

Hudson's wheezy chest swelled with the anesthetic of pride.

"You can see how your mom is, she's always been like that. With me, too. She pushes you away with one arm while pulling you in with the other."

"How'd you manage that?"

Declan did not answer. Hudson pulled his head up to see Declan squatting down.

"Dad?"

"I'm not sure I did. There are things you don't know about. But I committed to life on the shelf with her, new terrain. I couldn't convince her to stay in Boulder."

"She makes it out like it was all your idea."

"It was a thrill for her, I think. The edge of the sea. The risk of death every day. I couldn't make inroads."

"She says she's only stayed all this time because you loved it." This was what it might have been like to have a father around. To listen to each parent criticize the other at times. To have to defend one parent from the other. Hudson knew this from some of his friends' families and had never imagined it would happen in his own home. "She loves you."

"You, kiddo, I think I know how you got here."

This was the fourth time Declan had wondered how Hudson had reached this alien desert and the first time Hudson felt he might not be welcome. This Declan, whatever version of his father he was, did not respond to the word "love."

"And I love you, too, Dad."

Declan did not answer.

Hudson pulled a rock into each hand.

***

The sight of Antarctica from the air did not frighten Lucy like she had thought it would. The continent had not melted as much as others had said, nor could it have in one lifetime. As she flew in from a hot Argentine summer, she saw it all in order. Antarctic Peninsula had become an island. Ronne Ice Shelf was a tray of jagged ice cubes spilled onto the floor of the Weddell Sea. Thiel opened up to the Transantarctic Mountains. Streams trickled down their slopes and fed all manner of flora to the edge of the Ross Sea. That ice shelf had largely broken up and floated away. She wanted to see her old friends, Mounts Erebus, Terror, and Bird, but they were in the long winter; the South Pole was drifting eastward along the Antarctic Circle past the Ross Sea. But where they landed, Antarctica, the warrior that once had cast a stony gaze through a thick armor of ice, now looked like a skeletal old man shivering under a blanket.

Lucy walked down the stairs from the plane, and the humid air hugged her skin. Moisture orphaned from the icy ground, a refugee in the atmosphere, tugged down at her parka until it became too waterlogged to wear. She saw Mort taking off his as well.

"They told you not to wear it," Claire said to both of them.

Lucy was happy to be surprised at the transformation of this corner of the Earth after living for twenty years on the exposed continental shelf. "It's like Iceland now."

An Army officer approached. "It's been summer here for years in Queen Elizabeth Land. I'm Sergeant Major Darby. Welcome back."

"Well, this isn't so bad," Jody said to Lucy. "You always made it sound like a hellscape."

"Oh, it gets dangerous, sir," Darby said. "You don't want to be anywhere near an ice sheet when it collapses into the seabed or falls down a mountain. We travel from here in helicopters or hover tech."

Huntsman walked through the line of bodies toward Darby. "Hello. I'm Dr. Doris Huntsman."

Something like an involuntary twitch in Darby's lips nearly became a smile. "Yes, ma'am. You're the woman we've all been waiting for. It's a great pleasure to meet you. I'll, uh, let me take you, all of you, inside."

Jody limped after Huntsman, followed by Mort and Claire. Lucy took her time, absorbing, with the humidity, the strange new sight around her. The sickly old man she had seen from the air was becoming, from the ground, a quickening swell of earth.

22

The helicopter that took Mort with the team to the site hummed with pounding blades and swayed and bounced in every subtle draft of wind. This was not the Wind Scout. The more that flying in the air felt like dragging a wagon across the ground and less like swimming through the ocean, the more at home Mort felt. Jody and Claire seemed to disagree, as each clutched a vomit bag. Lucy gazed through the window, smiling serenely at the mountains that had trapped her son.

They landed on a level stretch of ice somewhere between the Whitmore and Thiel ranges. It was a great deal colder than near the coast, but Lucy seemed not to notice, bouncing out of the helicopter and uttering something.

"What was that?" Huntsman asked.

"Nunatak," Lucy said.

"Gesundheit," Jody said.

Claire laughed at her father's joke. Mort laughed, too.

"That's what these mountains are, or were," Lucy said, raising her arms. "When the ice cap was higher, we saw only the tops like pyramids. People thought all kinds of crazy things about them, vast conspiracies. But they're just mountaintops. Just ice-worn peaks poking through."

Jody tried to hide his doubtful expression, which Huntsman also seemed to be doing.

Mort breathed in Lucy's enthusiasm along with the crisp, icy air. He did not feel like he once had in this place as a doctoral student, nine years of conscious life ago. When he had been here before, it had been under the duress of a single-minded devotion to drive himself to the edge of existence and make a thesis out of it. That had failed. Once he had met a friend, falling to the edge of the Earth and back had become easy. He was with like-minded souls today. This would be an adventure. He raised his arms and yelled, "Nunatak."

Claire also raised her arms and yelled, "Nunatak."

Lucy smiled.

Jody and Huntsman gave Mort and Claire the same quizzical look they had just given Lucy.

***

An enclosed hover-tech transport took Mort, Lucy, Jody, Claire, and Huntsman to the side of the mountain. The melting snow and ice had carved a mess of winding channels for miles away from the mountainside. From a few hundred feet in the air, the Antarctic ice looked like a basket of snakes or an exposed brain. Their helicopter had landed on the closest smooth sheet of ice. The hover transport would take them up the mountain.

A series of concentric fences near the top of the mountain formed a familiar target. These fences were slightly different from those in Yellowstone and Siberia, though, and radiated from a large metal shed built against the side of the steeply sloped peak. The upper portion of the fence bent over to cover the shed like in a ballpark, behind home plate. A freestanding Quonset hut stood a little distance away and was likewise enclosed in a circular fence. Both of these, together, were enclosed in two more layers of fencing joined in a figure-eight shape. They landed near the door of the Quonset hut.

Mort had no sooner fixed his gaze westward, over the sinuous ice sheet, than the firm hand of a soldier in white camouflage pulled him forward.

"This way, sir," the soldier said. "This is no place to dawdle."

Once inside the hut, the same soldier took his overnight bag. Mort stood shoulder to shoulder with Jody, and both of them stood right behind Lucy, Huntsman, and Claire. A dozen storm-weathered faces welcomed them with closed mouths and cautious eyes. These were the kind of war-weary men and women Mort had seen in Yellowstone, though these were only men. They wore mesh armor Mort assumed was made of Faraday cage material.

Sergeant Major Darby stepped forward. "Gentlemen. This is Dr. Doris Huntsman, technical director of the OSS, and her team. They are here to help us contact and retrieve Airman MacDuff. Dr. Huntsman, this is the Steel Trap."

While Darby spoke on about the seriousness of his soldiers, Mort studied a plaque on the wall. They spelled their name "SThiel Trap."

"And don't you worry, Dr. Huntsman," Darby continued. "Our fence has lit up enough specters to light a city. Not a one has gotten through. And you, gentlemen, don't let the look of these civilians fool you. In addition to Dr. Huntsman, we have Joseph Conque, who opened the Bay Area Portal during the Great Eclipse. This is Mortimer Sowinski, who has seen the lower mantle with his own eyes. And last but not least is Lucy MacDuff, Hudson's mother. She built a Faraday fence around Boulder with her own body. Philips has finally sent us some real firepower."

Claire, who had no special powers, held her hands at her waist and dug her chin into her chest. Mort ran his hand along her back. She stepped forward. Mort let his arm fall at his side.

A short, stocky soldier with dark, fiery eyes stood up and reached out his hand to Huntsman, who took it. "My name is Sergeant Nogales. We are in awe of your powers. Welcome to the gates of hell. Let's get you some armor."

***

"Claire should not be here," Mort said. He slept on the upper bunk, with Father Joseph below.

"No, she should not," Jody said. "But what else could we do? She insisted. If we refused, I'd be disowned and you'd be dumped."

"I should not have come, then. You have these soldiers here."

"It's too late for all this now. You made a choice. We all made a choice. One way or another, God's will be done."

"You make it sound so easy."

"I sat by the bedside of my comatose wife for nearly thirty years, and then He took her. It's not easy. But it works."

"What's the point, then?"

"We're links in a chain, Mortimer, anchoring the ship to the abyss."

***

The next morning, Mort, grouped with Claire and Huntsman, followed Nogales and a squad of three soldiers out of the Quonset hut, through the concentric rings of Faraday fences, and toward the metal shed built against the mountainside. Jody and Lucy were ahead of him, surrounded by another squad led by Darby. The soldiers were impressive, but nothing, in Mort's mind, beat the look of Claire, Huntsman, and Lucy wearing almost form-fitting white uniforms with stitched-in diamond patterns of devonium thread. Father Joseph, in a white cassock of the same material, looked like the kind of pope the apocalypse should produce.

"The cassock covers my leg brace," Jody said after Mort had made his comment out loud. "No other ambitions."

When they arrived at the metal shed, Mort saw it was sealed only with a padlock, which Darby unlocked.

"This shed is just weather protection," Darby said.

The shed was barely lit inside. A control room wrapped in Faraday fencing took most of the space. Darby ushered Huntsman into the control room, where both would stay. One squad assumed positions on either side of a lead curtain, two standing, two kneeling, with long devonium bayonets aimed at whatever lay beneath. Mort, Jody, Lucy, and

Claire were pressed together, heaving their diaphragms into each other, sharing breath.

Nogales pressed a button, and the light disappeared completely except for whatever buttons glowed onto Huntsman's face in the booth. The sergeant then pressed another button, and the dark gray veil slowly parted.

In the dim orange light, Mort could see a shape emerge: a stone jamb, angled with the sloping mountainside, like a Gothic arch but much narrower. It was barely wider than a human body though a bit taller.

When the curtain motor stopped and the slight echo died down, Nogales turned his ear toward the portal. Mort hardly dared to breathe. After a full minute or more, Nogales waved Mort forward.

Mort moved his hand along the cut stone. It was rough under his fingertips, and he drew closer to see. "Is this something we carved?"

Nogales turned on a flashlight. There were decorations on the stone, carved birds and beasts, all nestled in a filigree of vines.

"The Army spares no expense," Mort said, trying to joke, hoping it were true.

"Should we be surprised by this now?" Jody said, also feeling the arched threshold. "When did *we* carve this?"

"I cannot say," Nogales said.

Mort turned. "Dr. Huntsman?"

She made no motion.

Mort turned to Lucy. Her eyes were blackened pools. Claire was practically clinging to her father.

"It is some kind of ancient utility shaft," Nogales said.

"How far down does it go?" Mort asked.

"Eleven thousand feet," Darby said from the control room. "And straight as an arrow all the way. The signal from Airman MacDuff's emergency beacon came up through here. Then his voice. In fragments."

"Fragments?" Lucy said.

"When we put them together, they make sense," Darby said.

Nogales took over and said, "Here's how we proceed. We take a hovering platform down the shaft. It fits all eleven of us. We will arrive in fifteen minutes at a large room. We do not need oxygen masks. You will not get off the platform until we have secured the room. If specters attack or you start going crazy, you press the up-arrow button on the control panel and you go back up. You do not wait for us or try to save us."

"Then what?" Mort asked. "I mean, if there's no problem down there."

"You will tell us. That's as far as we've gone."

"I'm guessing there is a mental block at depth, the kind only Todd and I could get through in the crust?" Mort asked.

"It is like that," Nogales said. "Good luck. Do not waste any time down there." He passed through the Gothic portal with the first squad of soldiers.

Mort leaned his hands on either side of the portal and looked through. Dim lights lined a few steep downward steps.

"It's okay," Nogales said.

Mort looked back at Huntsman, who gave a brief nod. He looked at Jody, Lucy, and Claire. Lucy swallowed and sighed. He tried to summon his old friend: *Todd, come in, Todd.* No wolves howled in the distance this time. Mort lowered a leg into the portal.

Four steel treads led him into a chamber somewhat bigger than the metal shed. Two soldiers stood on one side and one on the other. Jody clambered down in his leg brace with his arm on Claire. Lucy entered, and then the second squad.

"Ready, guys?" Nogales asked.

Jody put his arm around Claire. She leaned forward a bit, and her father let go.

Nogales pressed the down button.

After an initial jolt, the platform descended quickly. The square shaft rose at a slight angle above them, lit by dim floor strips on the platform. A breeze blew Lucy's hair upward. Claire's hair was tied tightly.

Jody began singing a medieval chant:

Dominus reget me et nihil mihi deerit. Nam et si ambulavero in medio umbrae mortis no timebo mala quoniam tu mecum es. Virga tua et baculus tuus ipsa me consolata sunt.

The shaft returned a polyphony of sounds back to the rescue team, but when Jody finished singing, a single low droning hum continued for a few seconds.

"We have accompaniment," Jody said.

"Yes, we do," Mort said. He raised his fingers to the shaft wall rising overhead and let the smooth stone rub his fingers warm.

"There's no information on our descent or anything,"

Lucy said. "We don't know how far we've gone or how far we have to go."

"Darby gave us the impression that this place has a way of distorting information," Claire said. "The less we know, the better."

None of the soldiers spoke.

"You guys are acting like you've never done this before," Mort said. The darkness hid a smile that stretched him open. Mort could finally make others marvel in his domain.

***

The platform eventually slowed then stopped inside a room with walls of ice glowing with veins of dark blue. A single black portal in the shape of a body stood on one wall, twenty feet in front of Mort.

The portal moved. It was a humanoid. The four civilian bodies jumped. Father Joseph had his hands out, ready to attack.

"Keith," Nogales said.

The humanoid stopped.

"Keith?" Lucy said, her voice trembling.

"His name is Akitho or something, but none of us can pronounce it right. Only when we just say Keith does he answer," Nogales said. "He's our canary in the coal mine. Looks like the coast is clear."

Mort stepped off the hovering platform onto fine gravel. The echo of twenty-two feet stepping on the gravel sounded like teeth chewing potato chips. The faint smell of frozen meat wafted into Mort's nose.

"Oh, God, Jody," Lucy said. "Do you smell that?"

"Yes," he said. "But we're all together now. With weapons."

"Okay," Nogales said. "There's a corridor behind where Keith was standing. It's shut right now. When it's open and we try to go through, it's like thick air, but mentally. Our brains stop our muscles. We can't push through."

Lucy walked ahead to the ice wall and felt it with her hands. "I know this drill." She pulled out of her jacket the white cube inlaid with circles of blue lapis lazuli she had once found in Antarctica and which she had been showing everyone since they had arrived. She pressed each face of the cube against the thin door of ice until, in a flash, it melted away. "Two. The side with two circles."

Mort took a deep breath. *Todd, come in, Todd.*

Lucy looked at the soldiers, none of whom moved. She took a step forward. Father Joseph's hand came down on her shoulder and pulled her back. He gestured to Nogales, who signaled for four men to lead the way.

The corridor began not much bigger than two bodies side by side and gradually grew wider. It curved gently to the right. The only light came from glowing blue veins in the ice. The crunching of gravel covered every other noise. The sound could not dispel the scent of frozen meat.

After a minute, Mort turned back to see how far they had come. Curving just out of sight was the door Lucy had unlocked and Keith, standing within the open doorway.

A breeze blew against the back of Mort's head. His eyes narrowed, his belly trembled, and by the time he faced forward again, sparks began to blow off the tips of the soldiers' devonium bayonets.

The scene went dark.

When Mort came to, bright electric lamps were lit. Three soldiers lay on the gravel, their blood pooling and mingling.

No one was speaking, or Mort heard no one. Everyone was staring at Father Joseph, bent over something.

Father Joseph's hands clung to some body that was writhing to break free. It looked more human than humanoid. It had a face full of fear and stared at Father Joseph, whispering some foreign word over and over.

"I think that's a man, a real man," one of the soldiers said.

Jody turned his head. His eyes glowed cyan blue. The veins on his hands glowed like the ice around them in the cave.

Claire yelped.

The man held in Jody's hands breathed one last heavy breath.

Lucy laid her fingers against the dead man's forehead. "This was a human being."

"Alright," Nogales said. "Alright. Status. Give me status."

One of the soldiers said, "Taylor and Vinson are down. Gupta's holding on."

"You others, you hurt?" When no one answered, Nogales continued, "Get them back up. Along with this body."

The other soldiers began carrying the bodies back.

"All of us?" Lucy said.

"Haven't you had enough fun for one day? And Conque needs some looking after, too, before he explodes. On top of that, the corridor's caving in."

The corridor had bulged inward in a nearly perfect circle around Mort's belly and broken into pieces of ice on the gravel. "Uh, I can explain that."

"Yes," Lucy said. "Can't you see? We can do this. I don't want my son down here another minute."

Nogales scanned the faces of the soldiers. When Father Joseph stood up, his eyes still glowing, Nogales lowered his head and put his hands on his hips.

"Keith," came the voice of one of the soldiers. "Stand aside."

"Mo-art," Keith said. "A-get dare-vits."

"He's always talking gibberish," Nogales said. "Keith, as-tand as-ide."

Keith raised one finger in the air. "Mo-art. Dare-vits."

Hot magma swelled upward from Mort's belly. He pounded one fist into a palm and heaved a ragged-edged war cry from his throat. When the echo subsided, he said, "Yes, Todd. I will get the dervish." He pounded his fist into his palm a few more times.

Lucy covered her mouth. Father Joseph's iridescent eyes sprang upward with his smile. Claire's face strained with calculation.

"Nogales," Mort said, with more bark than he had intended, "I'll take these bodies back to the surface. I'll meet you, Father Joseph, and Lucy, wherever you find Hudson. Claire? Staying or going?"

Claire looked at her father. He crossed his arms.

"Maybe it's best you go back, for now," Lucy said.

She nodded and walked past Mort toward Keith.

"How will you know where to find us?" Nogales said.

"Todd will tell me."

When Mort reached Keith, the humanoid stood aside. The soldiers loaded the dead and wounded bodies on the platform. Mort and Claire stepped onto it.

"Are you sure?" Mort said to Claire.

She looked at her father, who stood in the doorway Lucy had opened. His eyes still glowed, though more dimly. "I'm not sure about anything right now."

Mort pressed the up button. "That's the best way to meet what's coming."

***

When Mort and Claire arrived at the top of the shaft about fifteen minutes later, Huntsman and Darby were no longer in the control room. A silent alarm was flashing on the console, but the soldier asleep there did not notice it. Mort knocked on the glass.

The specialist woke with a start and reached for his gun before recognizing Mort. He hit a button on the panel.

Before Mort could say anything, a squad burst through the shed door and pulled him and Claire into the blinding daylight then into the Quonset hut.

"Talk to me, Mr. Sowinski," he heard Huntsman say.

"Are you hungry? Check their fluids," another said.

"I'm fine, totally fine," Mort said, blinking after a blinding eye exam. "Check Gupta instead. He got hit."

"Hit by what?" Darby said.

"Specters. Everyone else is still down there."

"There's an extra body here," a soldier called out. "Someone tell me who this is."

"He came with the specter," Mort said. He found Claire in the chaos. She was trying to explain to another medical technician that she was fine and did not need food or fluids. "We were down there maybe forty minutes," Mort said.

Huntsman grabbed Mort's shoulders and brought her dark eyes in to study his face. "You've been gone a week."

23

"I don't believe you're my real dad," Hudson said.

Speaking was as much movement as he could muster. His hands still held the rocks but felt pinned down by them.

"It doesn't matter," the fake Declan said.

"Then why bother?"

"Maybe just to pass the time while I figured out how you got here."

Hudson would give this devil no information now.

"Maybe just to make you wonder about other things."

Hudson would not enter into the devil's labyrinth of useless wonders by responding.

"You're right," the devil said. "Maybe Declan's not your real father."

Hudson closed his eyes, but he could not shut his ears to this.

"Your mother and that priest got awful close before the Great Eclipse."

Hudson slowly raised the rocks in his hands and banged them together above his chest.

"No coincidence you were born nine months after they started working together."

The rocks began to echo like the voice of the devil did. The echoes could not keep out all his words, though.

"I know why you're here," the devil said. "To sow new seed. Your body is a bloody bag of seed. All those wormy bacteria crawling inside you. You're here to die. To split open. To seed a desert planet. You maggot-filled men all want adventure. You want new shores and new stars. You don't realize that those thoughts are just a way to spread your disease. Your brains are run by viruses. Check your DNA. You'll see that I'm right. Your bodies are boats for bacteria. You have nothing of your own inside you. 'Be fruitful and multiply.' That's just a way for lazy Mother Earth to get you to do her dirty work for her, to dig her gardens and spread her shit across the continents. But here, in this desert, nothing grows, nothing lives, and nothing ever dies. This is the last clean corner on the moldy rug of Earth for real spirits to live. Your blood and crushed-up bones will drain through these rocks and never rise up again, not in any form. You tell that to whoever led you here."

Hudson banged the rocks and wondered if he should believe fake Declan, that he was still on Earth.

The devil walked forward between Hudson's feet and said, "Here, I will show you what I look like. What you look like to me."

Hudson closed his eyes and banged the rocks above his chest. The devil continued to hurl insults against Lucy, Father Joseph, and everyone Hudson knew. Contrary to what Devil Declan had claimed, his voice and footsteps did not grow quieter as he approached, but louder and with less echo.

When the devil was just a few steps away, he stopped. Hudson did not dare open his eyes and kept banging the rocks. Some other kind of noise, like rustling fabric, came toward Hudson from behind his head. Two warm hands held Hudson's hands together above his chest. He winced and squirmed as much as his broken body would allow, but he also heard running footsteps, as if the devil had been chased away. The two warm hands kept holding Hudson's together with great strength. A strangely scented breeze blew across his face, as if someone was blowing her breath on him.

"Hudson," came an old woman's voice.

He opened his eyes.

A young woman was sitting next to him on the rocks, holding his hands together with her own. Her arms covered her bare breasts, but he could not tell what was clothing the rest of her body. It was as if the light-filled air itself had folded up around her, like the way a wavy shower door lets light pass but not form. Her hair was long and red, like Lucy's. She did not otherwise look much like his mother, though, and yet she somehow felt very familiar, as if he had known her his whole life.

The old woman's voice could not have belonged to this girl. Hudson strained to peer backward. He could see only the top of the other woman's head; beneath a fur-lined parka hood and a forehead gently grained with the fine lines of age, two dark, severe, and protective eyes peered down at him.

The young woman leaned forward. Her red hair surrounded Hudson's face. She kissed his forehead, and he fell asleep.

***

After watching Mort and Claire ascend with a platform full of bleeding bodies, Lucy found Jody. His eyes were gradually dimming to their normal hue and brightness. "If only Dr. Doris Frankenstein could've seen that," she said.

"She'll have to get in the saddle herself one of these days," Jody said. His eyes were dimming again.

The image of Doris Huntsman on horseback sent a giggle through Lucy. She turned to Nogales. "It's up to you guys, if you want to go with us. I'm not stopping."

Nogales kicked some gravel over the pool of blood three of his men had filled. "Did that man do this? Is that what's riding the specters?"

"I don't know," Jody said. "It's usually humanoids that are sent through, if anything. But the first time I ever did this, at a bar in Illinois, something similar happened. Whatever I grabbed back then went from man to machine and disappeared. I bet the answers are down here."

Lucy stared down the dark corridor. Her belly trembled briefly, and she wondered if they should not wait for reinforcements.

Nogales said to his soldiers, "We follow these two in. No more waiting upstairs for spooks to come knocking."

Of the four remaining soldiers, two took up positions in front and two behind Lucy and Jody. They started walking forward

"It's no yellow brick road, is it?" Jody said, running a hand through his hair.

"We've been here before, Jody," Lucy said and hooked her arm through his.

The dark blue veins in the ice began to glow.

"The two of us, Lucy, make three legs and one set of eyes," Jody said.

Lucy took Jody's hand in hers and held them at her shoulder to make herself a tall cane for him.

A brighter blue light began to shine through the ice. It lit the gravel pathway before them.

"Well, this part is new," Lucy said.

Nogales turned his dark eyes toward Lucy and forward again.

24

Minutes became an hour on the gravel path in the curving ice corridor. The ice remained lit from inside even after Lucy had let go of Jody early on in their walk with the soldiers. For the past twenty minutes or so, she had been seeing columns of shadow ahead of her, inside the ice wall, which disappeared when she passed them. The others reported the same phenomenon. One of the soldiers explained it as an optical illusion.

"I'm not so sure," Jody said.

Those words fluttered like moths in Lucy's stomach.

"Here," Jody said. "We can mark where they appear ahead of us."

Nogales sent the other lead soldier ahead a few dozen feet to stand where all agreed a shadow stood inside the wall. He dug a line in the gravel with his heel.

When Lucy arrived, Nogales said, "Try your key again. The cube."

Lucy faced the wall with Jody next to her. "You get those hands warmed up and ready," she said.

"Like a defibrillator," said a soldier named Andrews.

Lucy and Jody tossed a look of scorn back at him.

Lucy pressed each face of the marble-and-lapis cube against the ice wall. Nothing happened.

"Maybe it really is nothing," she said.

"I'm not so sure," Jody said.

This time, Lucy heard only stubbornness.

"Stand back," Jody said.

Lucy stood behind Jody with her arms crossed while he pressed his hands to the ice.

The ice began to melt away very quickly and in the shape of a boat standing vertically.

"It's like the portal shape upstairs," Nogales said.

When the ice had melted away in the portal shape to a couple feet in depth, a darker, columnar shape remained in the center and would not melt away. The longer Jody held his hands at that spot in particular, the more the dark column took on a human shape. After several minutes of this, finer features came through, a nose and ears and an Adam's apple emerging from the sculpted ice.

"It's like Hans Solo in carbonite," Jody said.

"But it's just dark ice," Nogales said.

"Maybe it's imitating your shape," said Andrews.

"He might be right," Lucy said. She then made a gesture that, in other circumstances, would have been perfectly natural, but which she never would have dared while gigawatts of cosmic electricity were coursing through Jody's hands into one of his victims. She simply put her hand on his back as if to say, "Come on. Let's go."

Ice burst off the sculpted man in tiny fragments. A pale figure of flesh and bone appeared in its place and fell to his knees. Once on all fours, the man began drawing in deep breaths. He sat up and shot his wide eyes at each person standing in front of him. His breathing became quick and shallow.

"He's going into shock," Nogales said.

Lucy knelt down and wrapped her arms around him. His skin was soft but very cold. "Sh sh shh," she said and hummed to console him. He was shaking in her embrace. "Jody," she said, not sure what she wanted from him.

Jody stood behind him and put his hands on his shoulders.

The man stiffened, and Lucy pulled back to knock Jody's hands out of the way, but she saw some kind of relief softening the man's face.

"Keep doing that," she said.

The man struggled to stand and eventually succeeded. He was half a foot taller than Jody, who was already six-foot-two. Before Lucy could take his full measure, Nogales wrapped him in a foil blanket. His lips twitched for a brief smile while he studied the scene before him.

"What have we just done?" Lucy said to Jody.

"You, name," Nogales said. Putting his hand to his heart, he continued, "Me, Johnny." He pointed to the other lead man. "This, Brian."

"Lucy," Lucy said, bowing a little.

The others introduced themselves.

The man held his hands to his heart and said, "Phlege-thon."

"No kidding," Jody said. "He's named after one of the rivers of hell."

"Isn't that what this is?" Nogales said, hammering the toe of his boot against the gravel.

Lucy looked down the corridor. Shadow forms like Phlegethon's were still locked in the ice ahead of them. "My God. There are hundreds of these shadows. What is this place?"

"Thousands," Nogales said.

"It's someone's version of the Hall of Watchers," Jody said. "How long has this man been sleeping?"

Lucy remembered what White Wolf had recounted from his vision. Antarctica, he had been told, was the sight of an ancient sorcery far more sinister than what had sunk Atlantis. "Phlegethon," she said.

He was nibbling cautiously at an energy bar that someone had given him.

She spread her arms wide. "What this?"

Phlegethon, still shaking, shook his head gravely. It was clear he did not know either.

"Let's lay the puzzle pieces out," Jody said.

"Can we walk and talk? Hudson's down here. Omigod, Jody." She put her hands to her face and stomped a foot in the gravel. "He was pulled from Atlantis to Antarctica. Whatever this is…he could be one of these shadows in the ice."

"We should get moving," Nogales said. "That'll keep Phlegethon warm. The guy's barefoot and only wearing a foil blanket. It's gonna be hell for him either way we walk." He turned to the defrosted man and made walking signs with his fingers. "You, walk?"

"And I'll talk," Jody said.

The team started walking forward.

"First," Jody said, "Hudson's voice was coming through down here. He's not locked in shadow ice."

Lucy let out a stowed breath.

"Second, we've already met someone like Phlegethon on this mission. He came out of a specter. He's dead. Maybe because I held onto him for too long. Or Phlegethon survived because of the ice. All these shadows can be saved."

As they passed another shadow in the ice, Lucy let her fingers slide along the wall. Each of these once had been someone's baby and could be born again. She tried to lock arms with Phlegethon, but he resisted, making a kind of gesture that Lucy interpreted as prudish.

"That might not be allowed in his world, Lucy," Jody the priest said. "Only recently in our culture do we—"

"What's the next puzzle piece?" Lucy interrupted.

"Fine. Third, we heard Todd speaking through Keith. Or Mort interpreted it that way, and he's probably right. Fourth, it is usually humanoids that come out through spectral whirlwinds, not humans, but there have been exceptions, which leads me to point number five. The first specter I downed, in Illinois, as I recently mentioned, went from humanoid to human when I looked at him."

"I thought it was man to machine," Nogales said.

Jody inhaled sharply. "Either way. My point is this. Here's what I think is going on. Hold on. I have a sixth point. No, I'll save that for after."

Nogales turned his eyes back to Lucy again. She grimaced.

"Okay. Here it goes. Hold onto your seats," Jody said.

Lucy rubbed her palm along the icy wall as she passed another shadow.

Jody continued, "Human beings are trapped in the ice, in some kind of device, perhaps a hyperbolic chamber, like the kind Lucy and I walked into back on the Bonneville Salt Flats. Something, the devil maybe, but Huntsman won't let me use that word, is using its consciousness to control humanoids. Specter rips through here, sucks out a soul, sticks it in a robot, and voilà. Mass carnage.

"And here's my sixth point. That is exactly what Theodora Pandit was trying to do with artificial intelligence thirty years ago. Use spirits to tell her how to build a better humanoid. She almost got there, too. But someone had beaten her to it. Maybe the Nazis."

"You remember what White Wolf said," Lucy said. She could find no fault with Jody's logic. "All this evil long predates Atlantis. And the humanoids are from Atlantis. We think. Huntsman thinks."

"What the hell?" Nogales said.

"It's a perversion of the resurrection," Jody said.

"Hold on," a soldier said. "You've got more puzzle pieces to fit in. Like sleepers. And the moondark."

Andrews said, "If sleepers are protecting us, it's like the good witch version of the spell."

No one spoke for a moment, and only the sound of crunching gravel filled the curving corridor. Lucy's Hudson would be on the good spell side of things, like Jody's Haleh had been, whatever state her son was in now. Her hand was nearly frozen, and she stopped caressing the wall.

"Something tells me Vice President Philips should know nothing about this place," Jody said. "If he doesn't already."

***

The team fell into a few minutes of ponderous silence, in which Lucy wondered what Philips and his cult of sleeper-watchers would want with the terrible technology this ancient ice corridor represented. Then Phlegethon, his voice still quavering, started singing. Ladymouse, for all of her knowledge of music, could not place the culture from which his song came. Instead, it resembled the music of whatever culture to which she was comparing it at the moment: Crow songs White Wolf and Marigold had once sung; Sardinian shepherd's music; Georgian folk songs that some young women had made very popular on YouTube right before the moondark. Perhaps Phlegethon's songs predated all of it, like the man himself, parent to widely different cultures.

Lucy whispered to Jody, "This guy could be our great-great-great-grandpa, for all we know."

He did not answer, and she thought she saw his eyes filling with mist at the music.

A sound like bullets firing shot through the corridor. Everyone squatted, Phlegethon included.

"Five rounds," Nogales said. "Pop pop pop pop pop."

"Who would be firing at us down here?" one of the soldiers said.

"Maybe Mort brought soldiers in the dervish. They're rescuing Hudson," Lucy said.

The five-round discharge repeated.

"But Hudson's words have been reaching Thiel in fragments, right?" Jody said. "This could be one sound."

"One bullet?"

"One something."

"Let's keep going," Nogales said.

The team walked on for another hour. The corridor kept curving and widening. The five-part sound repeated regularly and was intermingled with fragments of a deep voice. The deeper they walked down the corridor, the closer those vocal fragments came together, until words formed in Lucy's ear.

She heard insults someone was speaking about her, Jody, and other people.

"Jody," she whispered.

"Just ignore it. All that hate simply means we're near our goal."

Running footsteps echoed toward them. Everyone squatted again, with devonium bayonets charged and ready.

A shadow preceded the running figure. Phlegethon covered his eyes. Lucy looked down just in case the ancient man had known already this would be a horrible sight. But she also wanted finally to face the figure hiding in the shadow of her bedroom all those years ago.

The figure stopped in front of Nogales and Brian, who were in the lead.

"Mom?" came Hudson's voice.

Lucy's belly leapt. Jody's hand came over her eyes. She nearly vomited.

"Mom? You're here. What's going on? Where am I?"

Lucy put her own hands over her eyes. Her thumbs would not reach to close her ears.

She could hear Jody standing up.

"Mom, what's Father Joseph doing? Mom, why are his hands out like a zombie? Mom, why is he grabbing me? Mom, help me. Mom, help me. Mom, Mom, Mom."

The voice stopped.

Jody walked back to Lucy. "It's okay. You can get up now. But don't touch me. My hands are hot."

Lucy slowly parted the veil of her sweaty fingers over her eyes. Nogales and the others were standing up.

"What the hell?" Nogales said.

"Exactly," Jody said.

There was no trace of the figure present.

"What was it?" Lucy said, verging on tears. But she knew the answer already.

"Come on," Nogales said. "There's natural light up ahead."

***

Jody could feel his eyes begin to smile. Sunlight washed across the curving corridor, which was now, after a little more than two hours, about twenty feet wide. The ice, until recently glowing with veins of cosmic blue, absorbed daylight's milky hue. He could no longer see the shadow figures through the white-washed ice. He and the team would only find them again, when it was time for a general rescue, in the darkness. Perhaps that was what Kai had meant.

The corridor ended a dozen yards ahead. Another Gothic-like portal stretched upward. Beyond it lay a large room filled with light.

"Here we go," Lucy said. She was beating her fingers against her hips.

The five-part sound had merged, like Jody had predicted, into a one-beat sound. Someone was beating rocks together.

"Keep doing it, Hudson," Jody said.

The team, still led by Nogales, walked through the portal. The room was not as bright as it had seemed from the corridor. It was circular, about three hundred feet across, with a tall dome. Five other portals opened onto the domed chamber. Light was coming through an oculus at the center of the dome. The oculus was about ten or twelve feet wide. On the whole, the chamber was in the same shape as the Pantheon in Rome.

"The room's empty," Nogales said. "And the noise has stopped."

Lucy's eyes were scanning the room. Jody was eventually able to make her look at him.

"There's probably more space here than we realize," he said. "Like in the Salt Flats."

She nodded. "That's a lot of ground to cover."

Jody hooked his arm out for her to take. "Don't get weirded out, guys. We're going small."

No one answered.

Jody turned to see Nogales and the men staring at a young red-haired woman, who was wearing some kind of light-bending cloth that made her look neither clothed nor naked.

"Jody, is that your sister?" Lucy said.

It was not Jody's sister. Long-dead Madeleine had come

to him and Haleh right after the Great Eclipse. During all the years since then, Jody had come to doubt it had been Madeleine accompanying Ethel Rede at the grocery store and Good Counsel Church in Walnut Creek. This girl looked, or rather gave off the presence, of that other redhead.

If this girl belonged to Lucy in some way, Jody the priest, Father Joseph, would not say it. He would not even think it. He had worried about protecting her secrets when coming here, the secrets that had made Lucy briefly hate the priest she had just met at the FBI conference room all those years ago.

Either way, this girl was going to lead them to Hudson. That might have been the reason she had been accompanying Ethel in the first place, twenty-nine years ago. It was not to console Jody during the moondark. It was to lead him to Hudson and make of Hudson whatever he must become. Jody remembered his vision in the cracked-glass copy of Our Lady of Guadalupe, with a version of Lucy holding up a baby he had thought was Hudson. Maybe it had not been Lucy in that image, but this girl. Maybe this really was the young Lucy he had seen the night of the moondark, next to the statue of the Blessed Mother in his parents' garden, and with Ethel Rede at the grocery store in Boulder. Whether the girl was going to be with Ethel Rede or the Blessed Mother, Jody did not know.

"Oh," Jody said. The chamber began to spin.

"Jody, are you okay?" Lucy asked. She held the back of her fingers to his forehead. "You're cold and clammy."

Jody put his hands out for his cane, but he had not

brought it. He had been wearing a brace instead. He wanted to lean on that cane.

"Your overwhelmed at seeing your sister again," she said.

Jody nodded to keep Lucy from knowing his real thoughts. "Let's go."

As the team followed the young woman toward the center of the chamber, Jody distracted himself from the excitement of the coming encounter by pointing out all the signs of hyperbolic space: the walls spread out wider, as did the oculus in the ceiling, until the oculus's walls lined the horizon in every direction. The gravel grew bigger until it became hard to walk across.

Then Jody saw Ethel Rede. His legs became noodles. She was wearing a white, full-length parka, with the fur-lined hood pulled over her head. Her head was bent slightly over Hudson, who lay underneath a foil blanket on the rocks. He was banging two rocks together across his chest. Jody could not hear that noise in this space.

The young woman sat next to Hudson and stilled his hands. She bent over to kiss him. Hudson let his arms fall.

Jody looked for Lucy, expecting her to run straight to Hudson. But something about the scene stopped her.

Ethel was gazing at Lucy, mouthing silent words.

After a long minute, Nogales yelled something.

Some immense machine, circular in form, began eclipsing the oculus. Jody knew it could only be ten or twelve feet in diameter, but, near the center of a hyperbolic void, it might as well have been a metal moon. This was Mort in the dervish.

Nogales gave rapid instructions on his laser-line radio.

Within seconds, the oculus-horizon filled with soldiers dropping from ropes. From Jody's angle, it looked like they were soaring across zip lines, but he knew they were coming in from right above him. Ethel Rede and the girl had disappeared. Nogales yelled something like, "Be careful with the artifact."

Before he knew it, Jody had been fastened to a line. As he was pulled upward, the circular wall of the oculus closed in quickly from the horizon, far more quickly than the ground fell away, like a mouth snapping closed to keep its prey inside. As he passed through the icy porthole that formed the oculus, though, it held open at ten or twelve feet in diameter, just like he had seen at the entrance to the chamber before walking into hyperbolic space.

A minute later, Jody was sitting across from Lucy in a helicopter. Hudson was strapped to a gurney with an IV drip in his arm. That was all Jody could see of him. Lucy's veil of glossy red hair covered Hudson's face as she bathed him with tears and kisses in her own private pietà.

PART FIVE

RETURN TO THE DARK CITY

25

Hudson opened his eyes, and this time it looked like he was going to stay awake. He was on a soft bed, in a warm room, covered with a thin blue blanket. He caressed the wall next to him with his fingertips: it was sheetrock, painted a cream color, meaning he was in an old-world building, not his 3D-printed concrete house in New Norfolk or a corrugated metal barracks somewhere. The early morning or late afternoon sun was sending thin blades of light through window blinds.

He turned toward that window. Below it was a small table and two chairs. On one chair was a duffel bag. It did not look like his own; perhaps someone had brought him a change of clothes.

Since the moment the young woman had kissed his forehead in a rocky desert, Hudson had known only brief glimpses of waking life: Lucy dripping tears on his face and Father Joseph anointing him with oil; an icy mountain range; an Army medical specialist shining a light in his eyes and asking questions Hudson was not sure he had answered; a very large and somewhat strange man staring at him on an airplane ride here whom White Wolf, sitting next to him, called Phlegethon and who interpreted what the man was saying:

"He says you are a river, Hudson. You led everyone to the dark place. Keeping flowing through the valley of death, and you will carry many with you."

If that was a day or a year ago, Hudson did not know. His left leg was in a cast, which meant it could not have been more than a month. His right leg was wrapped up, too. An IV was in his arm. His ribs hurt. He must have injured himself saving Benny and dreamt up his underwater journey and the devil posing as Declan.

Someone knocked at the door and opened it before Hudson could answer.

Standing at the foot of his bed was a young Declan Mac-Duff, minus the nappy beard. His eyes shined just like his father's had. This version of Declan looked Hudson's age and wore a midshipman's uniform, the Academy uniform Hudson should have been wearing. He had chosen to watch over Lucy and Owen instead. Hudson had worn the uniform of an enlisted airman and covered it in sea slime. Here was the devil again, coming to judge Hudson.

"There you are," said Devil Declan. That was Declan's voice, too, in a higher pitch to match his purported age.

Hudson began to seethe. He looked for another pair of rocks to bang together and found only the pillows beneath his head. He covered his face with these.

"It's Owen, Hudson. I'm sorry," came the being's voice, muted by pillows. "They said this would be hard for you, but I thought you'd recognize me right away. Mom's stuck in Antarctica, or she'd be the first person you'd see waking up."

When the thing posing as Owen stopped talking and seemed to be sitting down at the table, Hudson, still pressing the pillows to his face and ears, forced his breathing into a slower, calmer rhythm.

"Take your time, Hudson," strange Owen said. "It's already been...never mind."

Hudson would test this person posing as his brother. "How did I get here?"

"Okay, yeah. Special forces found you in Antarctica. For some reason, they needed Mom and Father Joseph to get you out, using their superpowers or whatever."

"Where am I now?"

"Walter Reed. They flew you direct."

"How did I get to Antarctica?"

"That, nobody knows, or they're not telling me. We were hoping you'd tell us."

"Where's Benny?"

"Old Norfolk. Married...uh, sorry. Just, in Norfolk."

"Married?"

Possibly real Owen cleared his throat. "It, uh, no one knows how to say this, Hudson. I don't, not without scaring you, but if you took the pillows away from your eyes, you'd see it was me, just older than you remember."

Hudson slowly lifted one pillow, unveiling human legs seated at a chair, then real human hands folded on a lap. The name tag said "MacDuff." The face was the same as Hudson had seen a few minutes ago: Declan, minus forty years, or Owen, plus ten.

"It's really me, Hudson," the young man said. "God, look at you. My brother. After all these years."

"How many years?" Hudson said, but he had already calculated that it had been at least ten for Owen to be at the Academy.

"Nine years," Owen said.

Those words inscribed themselves in Hudson's heart as dryly as marker on whiteboard. It might have been nine days for Hudson. He would test this version of Owen again. Hudson weakly lifted his hand for Owen to take. Owen had a firm grip.

"Look at *you*," Hudson said. His throat had become painfully dry. "Is there water?"

"Yeah," Owen said and sprung up to pull a bottle out of the duffel.

Hudson drank. Owen's smile would not descend. Hudson waved him forward and patted his cheek. "I love you, Owen."

Owen's face froze, like the dog Hudson had seen killed by specters, and flushed red and purple. Hudson waited for blood or demonic bile to burst out. Tears came instead. "I love you, too, Hudson. My brother. My brother," Owen repeated while he held Hudson's hand again.

While Owen's shoulders heaved, Hudson felt his own tears well up. This was his brother Owen. His brother Owen was eighteen years old. Hudson had been gone for nine years, somehow. He was home again. But he knew nothing of this world apart from these four cream-colored walls. If Hudson was a river, he had coursed underground for almost a decade. If he really had broken into the light of home again, Midshipman Owen MacDuff would have to serve as his ferryman.

***

Lucy gazed out a window at Thiel Station. Above the lines of Faraday fence enclosing the base, the storm Darby had warned was coming was already erecting an impenetrable barrier to her escape.

Jody took her hand. "He's safe now, Lucy. He's at Walter Reed."

Lucy turned and caught Claire glancing at Jody's hand. Claire leaned a little closer to Mort. Huntsman was talking with Darby, just out of earshot.

"What about that poor other man?" Lucy said.

"Phlegethon's in quarantine," Jody said.

"I know that, I mean, who's going to look after him? He has no one from his generation. He'll be all alone for as long as he lives."

Mort said, "Doris will find a place for him in one of her expeditions, among the rest of us loners and weirdos."

Claire scrunched her nose approvingly at what Mort had said.

Lucy did not like the coincidence that Doris Huntsman had been one of the last people to see Hudson before he had disappeared. She did not like the look of her scheming with Sergeant Major Darby right now. The two of them walked over. Huntsman was concealing a smile.

"Here's the situation," Darby said. "The weather's got us trapped for a few days, maybe a week."

"Why didn't we leave with Hudson?" Lucy said with more force than she had anticipated.

"Lucy, come on," Jody said. "Let him talk."

Lucy stared at the storm outside.

"While we're trapped...," Huntsman said.

Lucy grinned.

"...we might as well let Darby take advantage of our presence, our skill set."

Lucy faced Huntsman. "You love this. I just want to see my son again. How about this plan instead? We hover above the clouds, all the way to Argentina, and fly away from this hellscape. Then we stop digging up holes and humanoids and rebuild this world with our families, our own flesh and blood. How about we take advantage of that?"

Darby motioned to Nogales, who dragged over a whiteboard. On it was a map of the area: Thiel Mountain, from which a long arc ended at a small circle. This was the corridor they had discovered. From the small circle, five more dashed arcs emanated. The whole thing looked like a spiral galaxy.

"You walked a three-mile corridor," Darby said. "Based on your estimates, there's a body in the wall every thirty feet, on each wall. That's over a thousand people trapped in each corridor. Times six, as we're projecting, you do the math."

"We can save a lot of people here, Lucy," Huntsman said.

"They don't know the difference." Lucy crossed her arms. "It's been ten thousand years for each of them."

"Unless they really are the souls being sent out through the specters," Jody said. "And/or being used to animate the humanoids."

"We can't release all these people at once, of course," Huntsman said. "That would be irresponsible. The quarantine situation alone would be unmanageable. To say nothing of the chaos it would cause, the mere suggestion that we've been fighting ourselves this whole time."

Mort said, "Is that what this really is? One generation against another? Are we the 'other'?"

"I don't know," Huntsman said.

"That's right, you don't know," Lucy said. "You keep guessing and throwing our bodies into deep dark holes to make your discoveries for you."

Nogales cleared his throat and stuck out his chin.

Lucy huffed and released her arms. "I just want to spend time with my son again."

"The worry is," Darby said, "if we let you go, we might not get you back. We can't get into those corridors without Mort."

"And Todd," Mort said.

Darby cocked his head. "And Todd, and you and Mr. Conque—"

"Father Conque," Claire said.

"Father Conque," Darby continued, "seem to have the special recipe for freeing those people. Plus—" He glanced at Huntsman.

"Plus," Huntsman said, "we think there's a good chance, an excellent chance, that we've found the physical location of the city you and Jody once visited."

"You mean were taken to by witchcraft alien demons," Lucy said.

Mort chuckled.

Huntsman said, "If we can locate it precisely inside the hyperbolic chamber where we found Hudson, then we might find an easy way, or at least an easier way, to free all these people frozen in ice or at least keep them from being weaponized."

Darby said, "Just a few days, tops, while the weather's bad down below. You get us there, we zip in, take control. Hover tech won't work inside a hyperbolic bubble. Mort and Claire got us to the oculus from above last time, but Nogales had to point the way to you from below."

Lucy returned her gaze to the storm outside. She sighed. Darby and Huntsman were not being unreasonable. But visiting the dark city had killed two people last time. It would not be Hudson, though. He was far away from all this. It might be Lucy or one of these soldiers, but Hudson would not die. That was what she had negotiated with Ethel Rede.

26

Outside the window of the hover personnel carrier, snow-flakes flew by, frenzied in a wind that blew a hundred directions at once. They glowed as they whizzed by, lit by the interior light of the carrier, before disappearing into the steel-gray darkness of the storm. Each one of these snow-flakes had been forged for a brief moment of frozen solitude into a unique crystal falling from the clouds, whose form, whose distinct identity, would eventually melt away into water's basic molecule. A trillion of these took wings for their angelic exhibition, a blooming garden of life displayed by one of Earth's most basic elements, yet seen in their full number and in every detail by God alone.

"What are you thinking about, Lucy?" Jody asked.

"Hudson," she said without turning.

Jody waited.

Lucy continued, "His path. Take us, and Mort, others, too. Some first journey of ours led to a second. You and Mort each had your cross-country trip, then you opened up another dimension."

"And each one of us has opened the way for the next. Links on a chain."

She crossed her arms and leaned against the window. "He's got another journey, doesn't he?"

"What about you, Lucy? What was your first journey?"

"I made that years ago. When I was a girl."

"Hm."

Lucy knew that sound. Jody was not satisfied with her answer. It was all he would have for now.

Suddenly, brilliant white light flooded the window, and Lucy yelped in unison with everyone on board. She put on her sunglasses. The carrier had rounded Thiel Mountain, leaving the storm behind.

Through her polarizing lenses, the target was clear: three miles away, the smooth glacial plain gave way to an immense bowl, six hundred feet across and perfectly round. At its center was the ten-foot oculus through which Lucy had escaped with Hudson two days ago.

Why no one had seen this before the Great Eclipse, why it was not on online maps, Lucy did not know except to guess that whatever snow had fallen to cover this place in the thousands of years since it had been built had melted more quickly than the ice that remained, in the long Antarctic summers since the world had turned inside-out. She was not sure why Darby and his team had not seen it, either, and when she asked them, they only shrugged. Whether the bowl was shaped like a satellite dish for the purpose of receiving information or like the indentation in the Death Star for sending destruction, Lucy did not know, either. According to Jody, Hudson himself had blown off the snow and ice when he had passed through.

"No more speculation, Jody," Lucy said. "Just cold, hard facts."

"You sound like Doris now."

"Please."

The dervish Mort and Claire were flying pulled up near the personnel carrier. In the four weeks, surface time, that Lucy, Jody, and Nogales's team were in the corridor, Mort had managed to secure a dervish from the disused Yellowstone site. All he'd had to do was make Huntsman believe Todd had spoken to him through the humanoid named Keith. One phone call from Huntsman was enough to have the dervish flown down; one word of approval was enough for her to test Mort's reality and extend the reach of her influence down here.

Lucy said, "You know what, though, I realized that by doing this, I keep Hudson out of her hands."

"At least she's finally agreed not to send someone with a broken limb into the great unknown," Jody said.

Lucy looked at Jody's leg brace. Hudson was still in a cast and would be for weeks. After that would come weeks and months of rehab for a shattered foot, broken fibula, and two cracked ribs. Lucy would be in this icy death chamber for weeks or months, depending on what they discovered. This would buy Hudson time to heal and make something of his own way before Huntsman could convince him to make some other strange journey. Lucy and Jody were returning to the dark city to discover enough to keep Hudson from joining the ranks of monstrous scouts the members of Wepwawet Mountain West had become.

"Do you really think it's down there?" Lucy asked.

"It's worth a look," Jody said.

Mort came on the radio, approvals were given, and the dervish descended through the oculus. He and Claire were now the canaries in the coal mine. If anything was amiss, Todd would tell them, Mort said, though it was not clear how without a humanoid present.

"What happens if something goes wrong down there?" Nogales said. He had turned around to ask Jody and Lucy, though Huntsman was just one row ahead of him. "What does Mort do? What's his power?"

Jody looked at Lucy and shrugged.

"Dinosaurs," Lucy said, trying not to smirk. "Big toothy ones. That, or if he gets really mad, he'll just implode the chamber on all of us and call it a day."

"I don't know," Jody said. "It's a different world down here. I bet we get Taun Taun's, maybe a Wampa if things go south."

"Who are you people?" Nogales said with more earnestness than Lucy was used to hearing.

"Good question," Lucy said.

Jody muttered, "You should see the look on Doris's face right now."

Lucy leaned against the window and let herself smile. That smile fell away, though, as the carrier hovered over the broad bowl in the ice. Darby's team had quickly fabricated a gantry to surround the oculus, from which Lucy and Jody would be lowered into the chamber. They had not found

Hudson directly beneath the oculus, or at least not at its center. If there was a city down there, or a machine communicating through the oculus and the bowl, it would be directly beneath it.

The hover carrier settled just above the gantry platform. A blast of cool air came into the carrier; it was not humid on this side of the mountain. Nogales and one of his team hopped onto the mesh platform. Only Lucy and Jody would follow, for reasons of weight. The ice was only three feet thick at the oculus. Lucy stepped down and helped Jody descend.

She looked over the edge. If the chamber was a hundred feet tall, it was, because of hyperbolic space, also a thousand. Ten thousand, if they landed in its center like they had in the Bonneville Salt Flats. The dervish was built to carry a heavy drill head. They could easily have built a platform on which she could stand. But hover tech did not work in hyperbolic space. Mort and Claire could not follow them in all the way. Instead, Lucy and Jody would ride down in a devonium birdcage from the gantry.

"I suppose this is better than Dora Pandit's magic broomstick," Lucy said.

Jody spread his arms wide. "I summon the spirit of indigo."

Lucy pulled his arms down. "Stop making fun of my son. He was delirious when he said that."

"I'm not teasing. I'm envious. I'll set it to poetry someday."

Jody stepped into the birdcage, which sent it swinging

away from the edge of the platform. Lucy calculated its next approach and leapt. Jody grabbed her.

Lucy trained her eyes on the metal pole she was holding at the center of the cage. "You had your special word once upon a time."

"*Ma zad*," Jody said. He looked up. "You listening, Dad? *Tu m'écoutes?*"

Jody gave a thumbs-up to the specialist. The specialist swung the gantry arm over the center of the oculus. The ground swayed back and forth. Lucy looked ahead. The horizon rocked up and down like they were on a pirate ship ride at the state fair.

"I hope there's no dirty Declan down there, like that fake Hudson in the corridor," she said. "I don't think I could handle that."

The wall of the oculus rose past Jody's head. In the darkness, the veins of his eyes glowed bright blue. Lucy had almost made a comment about their both being widowed, about being in this together, but Jody was clearly becoming something else after all this time, something beyond her.

***

"Here we go again," Claire said.

She and Mort had just passed through the oculus.

Mort did not answer and instead counted the number of times he and Todd had shared the dervish. It was still more than the two times he had now penetrated this icy chamber with Claire. As the domed chamber spread out below them, a feeling began to grow in Mort's heart, and he could sympathize with what Lucy had said about Claire in Siberia. Just

INTO A HEARKENING SKY

like Claire had wanted someone to share her world with her, a world of inventions and natural adventures, Mort wanted to keep Todd's seat in the dervish sacred. He wanted to share much with Claire—everything, if he could—everything except the underworld, the domain of his friendship with Todd. But Claire *had* been there with them in the underworld with her probes, and besides, this was not the underworld. It was a sheet of ice piled up, miles thick, above the world, hell as a snow fortress. Claire belonged with Mort here as much as anywhere.

"I hope you believe me now," Mort said.

"I believed you before," Claire said. "Why else would I have gone with you to find Hudson?"

"I don't know, to maybe get away from a bloodbath."

"I can handle blood."

Two hundred feet above the hyperbolic zone, the dervish began to lose thrust. Mort steered toward the edge of the chamber, where he and Claire would circle until the rest of the team found what they were looking for.

"If that city is down here, we'll never see it," Mort said. "We'll never get close enough in this thing."

"But this thing helped us locate the oculus in the first place. Just think, Mort, you heard just a few obscure words from Keith and led us here. And now, all this discovery. You're like a prophet."

"'There is one Todd, and Mortimer is his prophet,'" Mort said. "Did you see Doris's face when your dad said that? Is she a Muslim or something?"

"Beats me. She keeps everything wrapped up tight. But I'm being serious. You want to know how religion works,

231

and this is it. You heard something you believed in and acted on it. You brought us here and proved it true."

"Maybe Todd's playing God to that spiral city we saw. I can think of lesser people to play God. Lord knows how he communicated through Keith all the way on the other side of the world."

"The same way Hudson gets here from the Azores. A communications portal."

The chamber fell into shadow. Mort looked up. The birdcage holding Lucy and Father Joseph was descending the oculus. Claire stared ahead.

"Now you look worried," Mort said. He rubbed Claire's hand.

Claire breathed in sharply and put on a smile.

"Your dad's been through this before. He's got power and knows how to handle a situation like this."

"Yeah, it's not...yeah."

"What? Lucy?"

Claire did not answer.

"I doubt it, Claire. Not with the way your dad watched over your mom all these years."

"Well, let's just say there's probably more than one reason Declan moved his wife and kids to the continental shelf." Her face fell. "And some reason my mom decided not to wake up."

Mort found he had been holding his shoulders tight, took a deep breath, and let them drop. He re-gripped the controls and said, "Well, I don't think your mom had much of a choice. And also, let's be honest. Your dad's not aging, but Lucy is."

"Meaning?"

"Meaning there are a number of factors at play." Mort looked up, hoping to change the subject. He saw the cable holding the birdcage extending from the oculus to some part of the rocky surface directly beneath it, but no birdcage. It had shrunk. "Looks like they're in the hyperbolic zone."

"At play where?"

Todd, come in, Todd. Todd could not help Mort with this conversation. He pressed the radio call button. "Sylvester, this is Tweety. We see the wire but no birdcage. Confirm status."

"Status nominal, Mort," Darby said. "Jody and Lucy are Tweety. You're just Mort. They have visual on the city."

Claire gasped.

"I thought we were the canary in the coal mine?" Mort said.

"Keep this channel clear of chatter, Mort," Darby said.

Mort released the radio button. "Well, fine, then."

"He's in the city," Claire said and began mouthing prayers.

Mort nodded and said by rote one of the prayers she had taught him.

27

It was not long before Lucy saw how far she and Jody would have to walk to reach the dark city. The mile-high obelisk was the first structure to stand out against the gravel floor of the chamber.

"Look, Jody. I can't believe it. We're really back here."

"Or a place like it. Cold, hard facts, remember?" Jody smirked, and before Lucy could find a repartee, he was on the hard-wire with the gantry operator, relearning his instructions on how to nudge them toward the obelisk.

Jody pressed a button, making the obelisk and its city erupt toward them like a fireworks display and Lucy's stomach open like a parachute. She clung to the pole with the constant feeling she was going to fall.

"Some nudge," she said.

Jody took a second to recover, too, and said, "And I probably only moved us an inch up top."

With a series of more subtle nudges, they reached the top of the obelisk and started descending alongside it.

"From this angle, it doesn't look like it's a mile high," Lucy said.

"That was a guesstimation before," Jody said. "Amplified by awe and wonder."

The cable stopped.

"How far are you guys from the ground?" came a voice on the wire.

"About a thousand feet," Jody said.

"Alright. We're out of cable. We'll have to pull you back toward the edge of the city so you can reach the ground."

Lucy looked up the length of the cable toward the wall of the oculus-turned-horizon. It bent the way a fishing line does in water.

"That'll send us walking for miles," Jody said. "How about we try the top of the obelisk?"

"Over my dead body," Lucy began to say when Jody started nudging the birdcage upward.

The side of the obelisk was smooth all the way down, but as they reached the top again, Lucy saw some decorative elements carved into the dark green stone like the kind she had seen on the jamb of the portal near the top of Thiel Mountain. They soon reached the base of the three-sided pyramid capping the obelisk. Each face was covered in gold.

Jody opened the door of the cage and began pushing his one good leg against the obelisk to nudge it to another face. On the next face of the pyramid was an opening.

"It's a door," Jody said on the wire. "Inset, with a balcony but no railing. The only one on the three faces of the pyramid." While they waited for instructions, Jody said, "This is technically a tetrahedron. Each face is an equilateral triangle. Four faces total. Three on top, one connecting to the shaft of the obelisk. The Great Pyramid actually has eight visible sides, set in just a little—"

"Here is how you are to proceed," Huntsman said through the wire.

Lucy was almost glad to hear Huntsman's voice interrupting Jody before he began another lecture.

"Set the cage on the balcony. Keep tethered to the pole. Knock on the door. If anything, *anything* at all responds, yell, 'Pull, pull, pull.'"

"And if not?" Lucy said.

"Then go inside if you can. Tie the cage down if you can. The other soldiers will use it as a guide to parachute in."

Lucy worked with Jody to position themselves on the balcony. "This is such a bad idea. People died the last time we were here."

"Yeah, but look at what Black Mare became." Jody turned to knock on the ornate bronze door and stopped.

"What, Jody? Bad feeling?"

"Black Mare. I don't know, a wisp of a thought, it just blew away. Anyhoo, ready? Here goes nothing."

"No. I knock. You get your death claws ready."

Lucy knocked. Her knuckles hardly made a sound.

Jody pounded. This was marginally louder. "Thick door. No handle. Nowhere to tie down. Dead end. We sit and wait. Watch the team parachute in."

***

Lucy stood with Jody in the birdcage, watching two dozen soldiers parachute from the oculus. This would have been suicide in a world governed by normal physics, as the oculus was only three hundred feet above the ground at the chamber's edge. But the soldiers had thousands of feet, maybe more, so long as they kept close to the cable. And they did. One by one, they landed on the street at the base of the obelisk and gathered in formation. Lucy and Jody could not follow them any farther. They had no parachute training. Mort and Claire, by accounts coming through the wire, were circling as close as they could to the city and reporting no trouble. Lucy and Jody's job had been to map the way in, and so they had.

Jody blessed the men from above as they started their march through the city.

The sun started its pass over the oculus. It was like a frothing yellow-white sea filling the sky. The inverse of the black disc of the Great Eclipse.

"What's the opposite of an eclipse?" she asked.

A warm breeze, scented with perfume, blew through Lucy's hair. She turned toward its source. Jody was already looking. The double doors to the obelisk had opened inward. Beyond them was a warmly lit room.

Their two faces turned toward each other, bearing the same question. Jody walked out of the cage, tethered to the center pole. Lucy reported the event on the wire. Jody's tether would only take him as far as the outside of the opening. The wall was a few feet thick. The doors' thickness was hidden by the construction of the jamb and hinge. Jody pulled the cage closer, with Lucy in it. This only took him halfway across the face of the open doors. He unclipped his tether and held it with his long, lanky arm to make up the distance.

Just as Lucy opened her mouth to order him to re-clip, her nose took in the odor of frozen flesh.

From around the door there appeared a well-dressed priest.

"Hello again, Pierre-Joseph," the dapper priest said.

While Jody froze, Haleh appeared behind the priest.

Jody turned to clip his tether back on and struggled with it. Haleh glanced at Lucy and opened her mouth.

The obelisk rushed away from Lucy, and she tumbled out of the cage. Her tether held her to the center pole as she dangled in midair. As she flew upward and the wall of the oculus closed in around her, she remembered seeing Jody fall forward as the tether ripped from his hand.

While the specialist helped Lucy onto the platform, Lucy said, "Who said 'pull'? He wasn't ready. Oh, God, my back. My back hurts."

"We heard you say it three times, 'Pull, pull, pull.'"

"I didn't say anything. I have to go back." Her knees buckled and hit hard against the platform's metal grating. Her spine felt like it had been ripped from her pelvis. "We have to go back."

"What happened?" Huntsman said. She was on the gantry platform.

"The devil happened," Lucy said. She lay on her belly, pounding the platform. Tears fell through the grating, followed by a thin trail of vomit caused by nausea. "Call it whatever you want, but that's who it is."

28

"The Navy does not recognize time portals."

This was the cipher for decoding all the decisions Hudson had heard regarding him over the past few weeks. He sat on a musty couch in the Ryddenhouse residence, Lucy's childhood home in Philadelphia. Though it was nowhere near the once famous Rittenhouse neighborhood, Lucy had always said she had never stopped her friends and professors from making the connection. He had passed through here just a couple of months ago, on his timeline. The US Navy, the official timekeepers of the new world, did not recognize his timeline. So it was nine years ago that he had last been here. The Internet had proved it. Hudson had found news articles describing his own disappearance and nine years' worth of earthly life since then.

Next to him, on the end table, was a box containing his Silver Star. The Navy had recognized his bravery in saving Benny by giving up his own Wind Scout. Below that, in a leather folder, was his certificate of honorable discharge. His three-year commitment had ended six years ago, Navy time.

With his shattered foot and implausible story about mermaids, owls, and portals, they would not let him reenlist.

Hudson had been advised not to return to New Norfolk yet. There was nothing in that town for him, anyway. Benny was in old Norfolk, and for some reason not free to visit Hudson. Owen was back in Annapolis. Lucy was in Antarctica.

Hudson was glad to hear from Owen how energetic Lucy had become while he was lost. That she had never lost hope in his return.

He stared at the black void of an early-twenty-first-century-model flat-screen television. Hudson had not become the spectacle some had said he would become. The Navy had downplayed his rediscovery. The world, for its part, had become distracted by the sudden appearance and disappearance of dinosaurs in Denver and reports about the underworld from Siberia.

Hudson looked down the length of the couch. While the rest of the world spun without him, he could lie down and dissolve into its mildewy cushions and no one would notice. He sympathized with how Lucy had felt after losing Declan. Maybe this feeling was inherited. Maybe it came with this house.

Grandma Ryddenhouse had left a lot of money in the bank for her eventual grandchildren before she had disappeared in the Great Eclipse. As far as Hudson knew, Lucy had not spent a dime to keep up this place. He could use it now, however much it was worth in the new world. By all rights, he could claim to be twenty-seven years old, eligible to receive his inheritance. The Navy had given him three years' back pay before discharging him; it felt like hush money. He could manage for a while until he found a job or withdrew his inheritance.

Hudson had no education, just a big empty house and a lot of money coming his way. He could live like the Great Gatsby, but no one in this or any neighborhood would live it up with him. Specters were as threatening now as they had ever been.

"Enough feeling sorry for yourself," he said and stood up. The pain in his left foot was lessening.

Hudson walked upstairs to his grandmother's bedroom. He would sleep there. There was a pink-and-purple dinosaur on the bed. "It was here the whole time, Mom. Sorry I missed it. *Ankle-saurus*. Not quite the bones I broke, but close enough."

A knock came at the front door.

"Owen's not free for another few days," Hudson said to himself. "He has a key, anyway. Maybe it's a neighbor with a housewarming pie."

Hudson studied the man at the door, whose freckled, light brown face was pierced with bright blue eyes. In civilian clothes, Hudson did not recognize him at first, then said, "Commander Conque, sir."

"You don't have to salute me anymore, Hudson. May I come in?"

Once inside, Devon Conque sniffed the mold-ridden air and cleared his throat. He had a long black case in his hand, whose size and shape suggested he had a keyboard with him.

"To what do I owe the honor, sir?"

"Don't speak about honor before you hear what I have to say."

Commander Devon Conque set down the long black keyboard case next to an armchair in the living room of Lucy's old home and sat. His bright eyes studied every detail in the townhouse, which no one but Hudson had touched in nearly thirty years. If he had come to bring bad news from Antarctica, he would have said it by now. Hudson had offered to hang his coat, but Conque insisted on keeping it draped over his arm.

"I've got some air fresheners in here for you," Conque said.

"Air fresheners, sir?" Hudson said.

Conque pulled out two cigars. "Here. You smoke?"

I do now, Hudson thought. "Uh, where are my manners? I'd offer you something to drink, but I just got here, and I'm not sure we should trust the tap water. My mother didn't exactly keep this place up."

"I figured. Got that covered, too. Just get some glasses out of the cabinet." Conque pulled a flask out of his coat and flicked it in his hand for Hudson to see.

Hudson sprang into the kitchen. From there, he could see Conque looking back at the large paned window opening onto the street.

"Yet this place is in decent shape, all things considered. No sleeper in the basement?"

Hudson walked into the living room with two glasses. "Just whatever ghosts kept Mom up at night."

Conque clipped the ends off the cigars. "Your mother's a good person. Probably the most realistic of all the people my uncle Jody got involved with. I'm surprised she followed your dad out to the continental shelf. Not everyone would've done that." He held out the flask for Hudson. "Pour."

While Conque lit the cigars, Hudson poured two glasses of whisky.

"So it was my dad's idea to go out to New Norfolk? 'Cause I've heard otherwise."

"Well, who knows." Conque puffed and handed Hudson a cigar. "Huntsman and that crew can be heavy-handed at times. All the time. Hell, I ran off to the Navy, too. Cheers."

"Cheers," Hudson said and drank. A smile stole its way onto his face as he swirled the whisky around in his glass. Commander Devon Conque had come all the way from Houston to talk to Hudson, to ply him with cigars and whisky. This could be good or bad. Either way, he might find a path of his own in a world that had passed him by.

"It's weird, huh?" Conque said. "Nine years, gone."

"Yes, it, uh…."

"*Flight of the Navigator*. You ever see that one?"

If that was a movie, Benny had never forced Hudson to watch it. "No, sir."

"Before my time, too. Uncle Jody got all excited when he found it at Cheyenne. Called it a cult classic. We were bored out of our minds back then, holed up in the mountain the first few years. Watched a lot of movies. This kid gets abducted by aliens, leapfrogs eight years into the future. His little brother is older than he is. Sound familiar?"

"All except the aliens part. What does the kid do?"

"He goes back in time at the end. Like nothing happened."

Hudson stared at his glass. Conque was about to propose something radical. Hudson puffed his cigar to play along. "Is that in the realm of possibility these days?"

Conque blew a smoke ring toward the ceiling. "I know you don't understand what happened to you. Nor do we, for the most part. But I tell you what, MacDuff: you led us down the yellow brick road, straight into Oz."

"You found Atlantis?"

"What's left of it is in a remarkable state of preservation. Almost as if it had just sunk under the sea yesterday."

"I came back with a trident from there. The Army has it."

Conque pointed his eyes at Hudson. "I know. One made of devonium. Or orichalcum, as they used to call it. But that's not the best thing we found when we went looking for you."

Hudson sipped, if only to shield himself from Conque's gaze. "What's that, sir?"

"Time."

"Time? That's the one thing I lost. Along with two metatarsals."

"You said you saw lights flashing above you when you were trying to help Benitez. How long did they flash for?"

"A few seconds, sir."

"And yet we were looking for you in that spot for days. You lost time under the ocean. The more time you spent on that chain, the more the world passed you by. It's a conductor of time. Somehow. To some degree. Going through the portal is what made you skip the most time."

Hudson puffed and tried, unsuccessfully, to make a

smoke ring. "Sir, what does this have to do with your work, trying to get through the moonshock?"

Conque dipped the butt of his cigar in his whisky. "Diving."

"Diving?"

"Diving. I would like you to come on as an independent contractor."

Hudson looked through the large paned window. It was lightly snowing outside. "I'm not a diver, sir."

"Neither am I. Neither are my people. But I tell you what, the moonshock has sent us an invitation into her house by your hand. Or by your foot, I guess. When you fell down the side of the seamount, you only broke your foot. Every bone in your body would have broken if it wasn't for one thing: you fell at the speed of the moon's gravity, not Earth's."

Hudson remembered dropping the stones down the side of the seamount. And how easy it had been to pull himself up the chain. "So you want me to help you find the portal again?"

"Not exactly."

"Then what, exactly?"

Conque leaned forward. "I've got a theory for you."

***

"I went through the moonshock?" Hudson said.

Devon Conque had just finished proposing his theory. The Navy commander had begun his presentation by claiming that the portal near the Great Meteor Seamount must have corollaries in other parts of the world, like under the Great Pyramid or, more likely, the Great Sphinx, which were exactly sixty degrees away from Hudson's portal and at the same latitude. When Hudson had protested that this sounded like the pseudo-archaeology Benny had been spouting the very day of their accident, Conque had replied that it was simply the logical place to start looking. When Hudson had asked why the portal had sent him to Antarctica, and not Giza, Conque had made his startling conclusion: the hypothetical portals do not connect to each other directly, but they go through the moonshock.

"Or along its edge, as it were," Conque said. "It could be that the arms of the galaxy you saw led to or from the other portals. You simply took the one to Antarctica."

"I was told that the Navy does not recognize time portals."

Conque leaned back in the armchair, puffed his cigar, and smiled. "It's liberating, isn't it? Not to be believed? Relieves you of the chain of command."

"I would've thought you to be the last person to believe in all this."

Conque pulled the long black case off the floor next to the armchair and set it on the coffee table. With his cigar pinched between his teeth, he opened the case. Hudson could not see what was inside until Conque pulled it out.

It was Hudson's devonium trident. Devon Conque was holding it in his bare hands.

"I thought the Army had that," Hudson said, not knowing what else to say.

Conque laughed, and with the cigar still pinched in his teeth, he said, "The Army? You just throw a little raw meat at them, and they'll give you anything."

"Raw meat?" Hudson said. "As in, my mother and Father Joseph?"

Conque set his cigar on the edge of the end table. "I was being, what's the word, facetious. The Army gets Antarctica. The Navy gets all of outer space." He held out the trident for Hudson.

"How are you holding that, sir?"

"Come on. It's heavy. Take it."

Hudson reached out a timid arm, like Adam toward God on the Sistine Chapel ceiling. Michelangelo's Adam looked lazy, reclining in nature before the sublime vision of God breaking through the heavens, but Hudson understood that laziness now, the laziness he used to see in Benny: it was an expression of fear. Hudson had once touched the stars on Grand Central Terminal's ceiling. The moment he touched this trident in the open air, not immersed in sea water, his path to the stars was all but certain. Hudson put a firm grip on the shaft between Conque's two thick hands.

Conque held on and shook the trident a little. "My uncle Jody's not the only one with a firm grip on the divine." He let go.

The heavy trident fell toward one end, and Hudson grabbed it with his other hand. It did not kill or hurt him; the devonium rod felt just like a piece of iron.

"It must run in the family," Conque said.

Hudson spun the trident in his hands. Conque's words brushed past Hudson like a stranger on the street, and, just like a brain takes a moment to process a familiar face in the crowd, Hudson felt Conque's full meaning. Conque was not talking about the power *he* shared with his uncle Jody, or about just those two alone. Hudson was somehow "in the family." Just like Devil Declan had suggested.

Conque must have seen the red anger rising in Hudson's cheeks before Hudson himself fully felt it and said, "I don't mean what you think I mean. Your dad's your dad. But us weirdos, we form a family, however much we, I, don't like to admit it at times. More than that, though, you were in your mother's womb when they were doing all their experiments. Uncle Jody walked inside your mother's mind. Some of what he got may have rubbed off on you. Looks like it did. And I bet something of your mom's ability rubbed off on him, too." He puffed his cigar. "But that remains to be seen."

29

Jody, flat on his belly, looked ahead. The double door closed quietly. Lucy had yelled to pull before Jody'd had a chance to clip back on his tether. He was trapped inside the room atop the obelisk with the dapper priest. If he lay here, perhaps the entity would not say anything else.

He should find a way to open the door. Lucy had been whisked away in the birdcage and would be back soon. Jody pushed himself onto all fours and looked for something with which to pull himself upward. The door was smooth, with not so much as a handle sticking out. To see any more of the room, to find something with which to pull himself up, Jody would have to turn around. He would have to see the dapper priest.

Jody's only other encounter with the dapper priest, a devilish version of what Jody had hated most about his fellow clergy, especially those of an earlier generation, had been strange but not unpleasant. This had been when Haleh first started falling asleep, at Danny and Cynthia's house in Boulder before the Great Eclipse. After his shameful reaction to her increasing weakness, he had slept on the couch and woken up to a grand vision of life across the generations. It was within this vision the dapper priest appeared, trying to tempt him into becoming some sort of *Übermensch* for the peoples gathered in Danny and Cynthia's backyard. That temptation, to great ambition, could only have been at the time a distraction from the memory of what he had tried to do to Haleh, a sin which he had long ago confessed but for which he had still felt ashamed. And just like the woman from the antique store in Walnut, another symbol of guilt, had accompanied the dapper priest the last time, a mockery of Haleh, another symbol of his shame, was here to lead him into temptation.

Still on all fours, Jody turned to see, in the center of the triangular room, a stone pedestal topped with a sphere. Behind that was a stone chair sculpted in a modern way. Resting one hand on the chair was the dapper priest. Like before, he wore gold cufflinks and a well-tailored clerical suit. His gray hair was perfectly coiffed. The expression on his face, with its fine features, was serene, almost stately. Jody did not see any other furniture in the room, which was about sixty feet along each of its three sides.

The dapper priest said nothing while Jody tried to push up with one leg. It should have been just like genuflecting, but Jody had not been strong enough to do that in years. He said a Hail Mary while he crawled toward the pedestal, toward this devilish entity.

"I suppose this pleases you," Jody said, once he was standing.

"Why should it?" the dapper priest said. "I'm only glad you are here, where you belong. Come, sit."

"Open the door, please."

"I cannot, I'm afraid."

"I will starve to death in here."

"If I could open the door, I would. But as it is, let us take advantage of this moment."

"Who opened the door, then?" Jody said.

"I wish I could say," the dapper priest said.

Jody's legs were tiring. The pedestal was an extruded hexagon about three feet tall. There was nothing on it except a sphere of green stone resting at its top like the ball of a pen. The chair was made of basalt. There were no special wires or buttons of any kind.

"Come," the dapper priest said, walking away from the chair. "You'll be more comfortable."

Jody sat.

The dapper priest stood on the other side of the pedestal, with the door behind him.

Haleh, or a fake Haleh, walked into view behind the entity. Before Jody could see too much of her, he closed his eyes. He did not want to ruin his memory with this mockery. He prayed another Hail Mary. Jody caught a scent of perfume, Haleh's perfume. He covered his face with his hands and plugged his ears with his thumbs. Soft, warm hands covered his. Haleh's hands had always been warm. She kissed the top of his head. No matter how much Jody winced and wriggled, Haleh stayed there.

Something would have to give. Jody could not shield himself against sight, sound, scent, and touch all at once. He pushed her hands away, stood up, and opened his eyes, ready to hate this mockery of his love.

Haleh stood behind the pedestal, in front of the dapper priest. She did not look grotesque or unnatural. In fact, she fidgeted like she used to.

"Is everything alright?" the dapper priest asked.

Jody was not sure the entity could see Haleh.

Haleh seemed to sense this, too, or knew it already. A devious smirk snuck onto her face, and she stood in front of the dapper priest. She opened her mouth, but the words she spoke felt like they came from inside Jody's skull: "Listen to what he is saying. You will know which word is a lie. He cannot see what is coming next. He cannot see past you."

Haleh walked behind Jody. He resisted following her with his eyes so as not to give away her presence.

The door banged loudly.

"Your friends are here," the dapper priest said. "I hope they do not ruin the door with their explosives. There's nothing magical to it. It's built like a bank vault. You might find you prefer to be able to close the door again, when you finally see you are at home in this place."

"I have a home," Jody said. Twenty-nine years ago, Claire had been the one to save him from the dapper priest, simply by showing up. She was circling the dark city with Mort right now; perhaps she could save him again.

"Yes, of course," the dapper priest said. "I see now how committed you have been to your daily duties: priestly ministry, wife…," he sniffed, "daughter. What you really wanted from the beginning were not grand adventures, exalted bearing, fame. That is what many from difficult families do want. I proposed those things to you where the Great Plains meet the mountains. Instead, you rolled up your sleeves and pointed your eyes in front of you. I would like to show you now that what I proposed back then is still yours, but in the way you would have it."

"What is this place?"

"A watchtower. Come, just bring those hands of yours to the device. You will see."

Jody searched his heart for a word from heaven, some indication of what to do. He heard nothing, which meant he would know when it was time to stop. He placed his hands on the green globe. It was glass, not stone.

The pyramidal chamber darkened, and Jody realized he had not seen any source of light within it before. He found himself on the streets of the city below, surrounded by Nogales's men. They were going from door to door, finding no way to open them. The vision around him felt like a holographic projection burning outward from his skull. His muscles softened, and his hands fell from the sphere. Warm lighting returned to the room, and the vision stopped.

"How do you feel?" the entity asked.

"Like I've been reading Hegel for three hours."

"But you should see the way you glow with ancient vigor. Take it in small steps."

"Like Dr. Morbius in *Forbidden Planet*. That's it, you want me to create monsters for you, chase everyone away from this place."

"Mm, not quite."

"Why don't you use this thing, then, for whatever you want with it?"

"It takes a certain intuition," the dapper priest said,

flicking his wrist. "A half-knowledge, one might say, which I do not possess."

"If you need a human mind, then bring someone like Dora Pandit here. A witch with her crystal ball."

"Who would believe her? Only a few, perverse and power-hungry. But you are a proven watchman."

Jody leaned on the hexagonal pedestal. He could still not fathom why the devil wanted him here. "What about those who built this place?"

"They are long gone. The world has been reordered since the river washed them away. But you are like them, are becoming like them."

These were like Kai's words in the cathedral a few days ago. "The river? Do you mean the Great Flood?"

"Do you know of anything but flowing water that floods?"

"This must be more than a watchtower," Jody said. "And you must want me to do more than watch."

"Touché," the dapper priest said. "One cannot see without being seen."

"You want me to be seen. Why? To distract the world from this murder machine?"

"It is no such thing."

"Then what is it, exactly?"

"I think you know by now that word 'exactly' seldom applies to the art of this world."

The entity was echoing one of Huntsman's many lessons. Jody said, "You say 'art,' but this looks like technology to me."

"Ah, but did God create from science or from art? For

the purpose of knowledge, or of love? Science is always catching up to art. When you people say 'the state of the science,' you are speaking of small increments and contingencies. But when you say 'the state of the art,' you are speaking of the most advanced thing, *n'est-ce pas*?"

"What art does this thing serve, then?"

"The art of life."

"It appears to me that this city, the chamber it's in, and the corridors that shoot out from it, are meant to send human souls into humanoids and make them into murder machines." Jody ran his fingers along the sphere. Nothing happened.

"There's always a bit of violence in cultivation," the dapper priest said. "Or, rather, let's call it a game. You are a computer scientist. You understand games. Children play games to become better adults. Adults play games, too."

"To become, what? Gods?"

The dapper priest, if he really breathed, drew in a deep breath of satisfaction.

Jody turned to one of the blank golden-colored walls. "I don't know how you're going to make machines into persons and those persons into gods when God had to breathe His own divine breath into the clay. Or are you going to borrow my breath?"

The entity said nothing.

Jody ran through the theories of artificial intelligence he knew, mathematical games of life, and biological evolution. Humanoids' servos were strange: inside kidney-shaped sacs of diluted honey were blue corals of calcium-orichal-cum composite that grew and took shape as they learned through imitation—the closest thing anyone had ever seen to real A.I. But their bodies were not organic. They were not shaped from the clay of the Earth itself.

"It's not so easy to make a thing live without evolving it from something simpler," Jody said. "A real being—"

"A material being, I think you mean to say."

Of course, Jody thought. The devil, as a spirit, would see himself as more real than a material being. But Jody could still not figure out what he wanted with material beings. "A material being, it needs time, struggle, renewal, to recode its DNA. To become something more. Something real."

The dapper priest's eyes burned with black fire. "It needs to kill in order to want to live. It needs to watch life leaving its victim's eyes and draw in the breath leaving its body. Every murder is a mirror. That's your process of evolution. It's not the transfer of carbon. It's the creation of a will."

Jody knit his brow. "And you think I'm going to watch your machines kill, or even make them kill?"

"I did not make these machines any more than I made the human souls trapped in the glacier around us, which would race to inhabit a humanoid just for the sake of freedom from this place. Like I said, I am an artist. Call it 'collage.'"

Jody resisted a smirk. "Well, whatever I do, I'd have to ask my bishop's permission first, of course."

The door banged loudly. Claire's muffled voice came through.

The dapper priest rolled his eyes in resignation. "Well. Time's up."

30

Mort stood in front of the heavy bronze double door blocking his girlfriend from his hopefully future father-in-law, and he would soon be dumped if he could not open it. Claire alternated between screaming at the doors and pounding on them and screaming at Mort and pounding on him. Huntsman, while trying to calm down Claire, took an arm to the eye. Lucy was being flown to base for an unspecified back injury. Nogales's explosives had not worked on the door, and no welding equipment smaller than a Detroit steel forge was going to melt through it. The humanoid Keith, who was standing in the birdcage, had not been strong enough, either, and Todd had said nothing through him.

Claire's yelling fell away as background noise, and Mort closed his eyes. He tried to summon the power in his belly that had, in Siberia, bent an aluminum trailer and broken through a hundred feet of ice surrounding the borehole. He tried to imagine the worst possible scenarios—Father Joseph being tempted and tortured by the evil Haleh Lucy had seen inside the chamber beyond this door, Claire running off with some other guy, a bundle of metallic mantle serpents crawling up the obelisk to eat him—but the engine of his anger would not turn again. All he saw, in his mind's eye, was Charlaine Jackson and a mother cougar and a wooly rhino watching him, waiting for him. He felt nothing but mild frustration. Against Claire's sensory onslaught and the dark reality of this obelisk and the city and corridors full of trapped souls that surrounded it, Mort's emotions shut down. Just like they had under pressure from his studies all those years ago.

Mort put his hands and forehead against the door. Claire might have stopped yelling, for he felt her hand on his back. Or that was Huntsman's. It could have been Keith's, for all he knew, imitating something the humanoid had seen someone else do once. That was what Mort would do now. He would imitate Todd. He would pray.

"Dear God, uh, we're in trouble. We have to get this door open, to save our friend. He's a priest, you know, if that counts." Mort rubbed the door, covered in a rough patina. "Come on, Mort. Make it real.

"Dear God, I'm at the end of my strength. You gave me something once, to survive, and I'm asking for it again. You gave me a friend and a girlfriend and a mission and a real reason to live, and I'm going to lose it all very very soon. I can't summon anything. No special powers. So please. I used to hate you for judging me, for looking at me, looking through me, for what I don't have, and so here I am, telling you it's true, I've got nothing and never have, and I don't care if you keep hating me for not being whatever I'm supposed to be, just don't hate these people."

Something like a fire did light in Mort's belly.

"Stop hating me. Stop hating me. You hated me through my despicable parents and my brick wall of a grandmother. But I love this family."

Mort slid his hands up the door to make his arms hide the tears pouring out. "I love this family. I love this family. I love this family."

The middle finger on each of Mort's hands reached some kind of decoration that was not firmly attached to the leaves of the door. While he repeated the words, "I love this family," he fondled those decorations. They almost felt like buttons.

Mort pushed one of them. It went in a little and sprung back. He pushed both at the same time. He felt a thud from inside the door, like the lifting of a bolt. He lowered his hands and pushed. The two leaves of the heavy double door slowly opened.

Warm light filled Mort's field of vision. Father Joseph sat serenely behind a globe on a stand. Haleh stood behind him. Claire ran to her father, who stood and held her. The two swayed back and forth in each other's embrace.

Haleh looked at Mort and opened her mouth, but the words came from inside Mort's head:

You look, my friend, to be a moved sort
At all that is displayed; be cheerful, Mort
Our reverie is ended; all you see
Will waft into cloud-capped memory

When she finished these lines, Haleh walked behind Father Joseph. Mort did not see her pass on the other side, and he stepped ahead to see where she might have gone. When he reached Father Joseph and Claire, he saw a shape slinking in the shadows where the sloped walls of the pyramid met the floor. Two green eyes turned toward him, the same eyes that had once warned Mort and Todd from the hedges at Todd's house to keep going. Haleh, in the form of a cougar, made the slightest meow, and disappeared into the shadows.

Someone rubbed Mort's back. Huntsman, with the first hints of a black eye, looked at Mort and smiled. "It was just the simplest thing to get this door open," she said. "Nothing magic."

"No, not magic in the end," Mort said. He looked at Claire, who was drying her eyes. "But it took a little magic to get here."

***

"He said the door was not magic," Father Joseph said. He was sitting in the stone chair again, facing the globe on its pedestal.

Mort stood with Claire, Huntsman, and pair of soldiers. Keith was brought in, but nothing about this room triggered any kind of code in his humanoid mind.

Huntsman was studying the empty room. "Where is light coming from? Not from this ball of stone."

"I don't know," Father Joseph said. "Maybe it's filtering through the gold sheeting outside. I do know that this glass ball is special. Here. Check this out."

Father Joseph put his hands on the ball. The room grew dark, and the image of Lucy strapped to a gurney filled the space. She turned to Father Joseph and knit her brow. He pulled his hands away quickly. "Um."

A look of awe Mort had never seen filled Huntsman's face. She touched the glass globe, but nothing happened.

"The dapper priest wanted me to stay here," Father Joseph said. "Like the Wizard of Oz or something. I'm not sure why."

"Well, obviously you're not going to," Claire said.

Huntsman, instantly restored to her normal disposition, cast a quick glance at Father Joseph.

Father Joseph stared at the globe.

"You are not staying here," Claire said.

Father Joseph said, "Here's the thing."

"What thing?" Claire said. "There's no thing. You are not going to do what the devil and some fake version of Mom tell you to do."

"Actually, I'm not sure she was fake," Father Joseph said.

"Me, neither," Mort said. "She seemed pretty legit when we walked in. I had a feeling about her like I had when I saw Charlaine."

Every head turned to Mort.

"You saw her?" Huntsman said. "I did not see her. Who else saw her?"

Claire had not. The soldiers shook their heads.

"Well, anyway," Mort said, "she recited poetry and then turned into a cougar. She might actually have been the cougar that warned me and Todd. I don't know. Actually, I do know. She was."

"When she was still asleep?" Father Joseph said. "Doris, is that what our sleepers are doing? Animating animals?"

Huntsman put up her hands. "All this...this is all new territory."

"Which is why I need to stay," Father Joseph said. "Stake our claim, so to speak."

"But shouldn't you do the opposite of what the devil wants?" Claire said.

"It's not about what he wants or doesn't want," Father Joseph said. "All that, I think, was a distraction. From what, I don't know. But this is about making a decision. Haleh told me he couldn't see what was coming next. He couldn't use this device. With some practice, I can." He looked around the room. "And with some furniture. Claire, I put you in charge of that."

"You are a priest, Dad. You have duties."

"I'll have to ask the bishop's permission, of course. But this is about me, Claire Bear, and I've got to trust this feeling now to do what I've always done: to keep my hands on the wheel. And besides, what's more priestly than this, to stand in the breach? If I don't do this, someone else will. And there is a lot of power here, Claire. More than most of us can handle."

"Maybe this is the distraction, Dad. To keep you from doing something else you need to do."

Father Joseph held his hands at his lap and stared at the green globe. He looked at Mort.

For the first time in his life, someone important was asking Mort for advice. Mort knew that there was exactly one right answer: to give Claire's father back to her. But Father Joseph was passing the dapper priest's temptation onto Mort, too, who could not resist the idea of a person watching over all of them, who could see ahead where they could not, of a god whose house they could visit and whom they could see in the flesh.

Mort heard some shuffling and murmuring behind him.

Darby, who had come down the birdcage, elbowed his way to the pedestal and set a tablet screen on it. "Maybe all this was a distraction."

***

The team huddled around the tablet and watched security camera footage taken at the Hall of Watchers in St. Louis a day ago, not long after the time Father Joseph had entered the obelisk in Antarctica, locally an hour ago.

The scene began as any typical day at the New White House, at a lunchtime meditation session over which Vice President Philips presided. Congressional suits and military brass sat in silence around Palmer's sleeper sac. They had not seen what was going on above, in the higher decks of the hall. Thin mantle snakes were slithering through the overflow drains of the sleeper beds. Unlike in Denver and most other cities, where the water that flowed beneath the beds came from and returned to the ground, the Hall of Watchers was fed by and flowed back to the Mississippi on the mystical pretext that the sleepers' protection would extend through its vast watershed. Mantle snakes had never surfaced, and the world had known of their existence only since Mort had reported them last year. They could have come in from the underworld via an ocean trench.

The snakes Mort had reported under Siberia were enormous, hundreds or thousands of feet long and as wide as they needed to be to swallow whole bodies. Those on the video today were small enough to fit through a three-inch pipe. Some of the snakes penetrated and deflated sleeper sacs. One of the women with Philips noticed this, and the whole group sprang up. Two guards ran in; one ran out again, presumably to call backup. Almost everyone in the group, about half a dozen watchers, walked out in an orderly fashion but clearly ill at ease. Philips stayed behind and seemed to be calculating how long he could wait before leaving. He pointed at Palmer's body, and the guard was either motioning to reassure him or to usher him out. There did not seem to be any specters at work.

While Philips waited, a pattern emerged above. The snakes were all slinking in a counterclockwise direction around the upper tier. When they dropped down the steps into a lower tier, they seemed to join together. The single serpent grew slower and fatter on its way down, like a river when it reaches the sea. Philips watched the whole thing happen.

Just as the snake reached the floor where Palmer was, armed men burst into the room. They fired what Mort assumed were devonium bullets at the beast. It split in two from its head to about twenty feet along its neck. Someone pulled Philips out of the way just as the two-headed monster made a quick lunge at Palmer's body. The two heads opened up and took Palmer's egg shape into themselves from either end. When they met at the middle, they fused.

"Now comes the strange part," Darby said. "Watch."

The snake, now in the shape of a needle's eye, moved toward the armed men. They had stopped firing. The soldier let go of Philips, and all stood as if in admiration of the serpent. The beast raised its needle-eye head before Philips like a cobra, with Palmer bulging horizontally on top. Everyone there looked mesmerized. Palmer's bulge moved down one side and into the joined stem. All at once, two arms thrust out just below the split, making an ankh shape.

Some kind of light flashed upon or pulsed from the silvery snake, the video filled with streaks and static, and the feed cut.

"That's all there is?" Mort said.

"I am told," Darby said, "that no one remembers anything after this. What anyone can piece together is that the snake split into a hundred pieces again and went back the way it came."

"Splitting Palmer's body, too?" Huntsman said.

"We don't know," Darby said. "Philips is genuinely shaken. I talked to him. He wants to know what you think of this, how it conforms to your experiences."

Mort rubbed his temples. "What I saw in Siberia was that we were attacked, but by something slow and somewhat confused."

"This is another level of intelligence," Father Joseph said. "Coordinated. It knew where our leader was."

"Now what?" Huntsman said.

"Now our leader wants to see us," Darby said. "Our new president."

PART SIX

ON THE ROAD OF LIGHT

31

Hudson hurried home to New Norfolk A-III as soon as he heard Lucy had arrived from Antarctica. He did not see her standing on the widow's walk. The door was unlocked, and he crept in quietly, in case she was asleep.

Lucy was asleep, on her bed, with the door ajar. She had not been given the full treatment Hudson had had at Walter Reed but had been treated at a local hospital in old Norfolk. As best Hudson knew, no surgery had been necessary on her spine, just time and heavy pain medication. He gently lifted Lucy's hand off her chest and set Amy Anklesore under it. Lucy did not stir.

Hudson walked to the refrigerator. Not much had changed in the house in the nine years he had been gone except for the addition of a lava lamp Lucy or Owen had bought from scavengers. The first thing to catch Hudson's eye in the fridge was an open box of baking soda. A streak of black marker told him it was the same one he had last seen nine years ago. He picked it up and said, "Hello, old friend."

Otherwise, there was an array of deli meat. Lucy had prepared for Hudson's arrival. He made a sandwich and sat down on the living room couch, gazing at Declan's happy face in the family photo, trying to wipe away all memory of the entity that had tried to pose as him in the rocky desert.

Halfway through his mountain of turkey, ham, and Swiss, Hudson heard Lucy whimper. He went to her room, sandwich in hand.

Lucy was holding the stuffed pink-and-purple dinosaur above her face, studying it.

"It was on Grandma's bed the whole time," Hudson said. "I didn't see it a few months ago when I went." He sat on the edge of the bed.

"Or it wasn't there," Lucy said. She rubbed his cheek. "Look at you. Walking again. My Huggy Baby."

"This is our first real conversation in person since before I disappeared," Hudson said. He bit into his sandwich. A few crumbs fell on Lucy's shoulder, and she brushed them away.

She said, "Oh, but you said lots of things as we got you onto the plane to the hospital. Stuff about owls and devils. Jody and Mort couldn't get enough of it. 'I summon the spirit of indigo' came out of your mouth several times."

Hudson took Amy Anklesore. "That actually happened. While I was under the ocean, of course. Breathing seawater will affect you like that."

"Do you know what this is?" Lucy said, poking the stuffed dinosaur.

"The doll you were missing."

"The other end of the thread."

"Now you're talking under the influence. Who's Mort?"

"It's been nine long years, Hudson. Mort's a person who

made a trip like you, only much deeper down. He's actually dating Claire now, if you can believe that."

Lucy must have seen jealousy stiffen Hudson's jaw before even he felt it, for she said, "If you even call it dating. She hardly lets him touch her."

"I don't know him, but knowing Claire, I can believe that. I *can* believe, though, that someone wanted to date her." Hudson had always kept a crush on her growing up. "But she's the kind of person who pulls you in with one arm while pushing you away with the other."

Lucy knit her brow. "Where did you hear that expression?" She laid her head back.

"Uh, maybe when you and Dad were arguing once. I don't know."

"Not *your* father." Lucy winced in pain.

No matter how much Hudson wanted to forget his encounter with that entity in Antarctica, he would have to remember what it had said to him, so he would never repeat it. But in this way, too, the devil would keep influencing everything.

"How long are you laid up for?" Hudson said.

Lucy let out a stowed breath. "As long as it takes to get me out of this business."

"Sleepers are waking up, though. That thing in St. Louis has got sleepers waking up everywhere. You sure you want to be out of it?"

"You see Benny yet?"

Hudson put Amy Anklesore on the bed. "That's next on the agenda."

"And Hope?"

Hudson had not thought of her in a month. "It's weird now, you know? She'd be older than I am."

Lucy poked Hudson in the stomach. "And more desperate."

"Gee, thanks."

"Give yourself time, Hudson. You'll be at your best-looking in ten or fifteen years. Then you'll have your pick."

Hudson dropped his head. "Hm."

Lucy narrowed her eyes at Hudson. "Benny told me you flirted with Huntsman."

Hudson tried to hide his smile behind what remained of his sandwich. "I can neither confirm nor deny an event of that nature." He took a bite.

"And Devon Conque saw you."

"He did?"

"Did he not visit you in Philly?"

Hudson had thought Conque had seen him with Huntsman nine years ago. "Right. Of course."

"And?"

Hudson picked up Amy Anklesore again. "What did you mean, this is the other end of the thread?"

Lucy put her hand to her forehead and sighed. "They've already got something lined up for you, don't they? This is how it always goes."

"I have choices. I've been discharged. Maybe I'll become a priest like Father Joseph. Same as waiting ten or fifteen years for the right woman."

"You're not even Catholic."

"I'll be a wrinkly old man by then, the way this world treats people."

"What did Devon say to you?"

"It's strictly confidential. I could tell you, but then I'd have to kill you."

"Okay, Maverick."

Apparently, this was a movie everyone had seen before the Great Eclipse, not just Benny's family.

"You know what he does for a living," Hudson said. "Let's just say he thinks I've already been there."

Lucy took the stuffed pink-and-purple dinosaur from Hudson's hand and pressed it against his chest. "Let me rest for a while. There's a lot to do." She put his hand over Amy Anklesore to gesture for him to keep it and closed her eyes.

***

Chief Warrant Officer Hector Benitez had one of his staff members pick up Hudson and Lucy in a hover car from the vehicle pool. Hudson was as mesmerized by the advances in hover tech over the past nine years as he was amazed by Benny having a staff. When he mentioned this to Lucy, she said, "Yeah, but ask yourself why he invited me, too."

Hudson knew what she meant. Benny, though he commanded a few men, was still a coward. "Way to spoil the mood, Mom."

When they arrived in a cozy neighborhood of old Norfolk thirty minutes later, the staff seaman knocked on the door of a house and opened it without waiting for anyone to answer. He waved Hudson and Lucy inside.

"You're shaking," Lucy said.

Hudson had not noticed, and before he could distract himself with the Christmas decorations still hanging in the living room two months after the holiday, Hazel Dungloe appeared. At her warm embrace and moistened eyes, Hudson felt himself at ease.

"Look at you," she said, fanning tears off her face. "All these years."

Hudson wanted to say that she had not changed a bit in nine years, that she looked just the same, but she did not, exactly. It was not that she looked much older; she was only twenty-eight years old. She had not gained or lost weight, either. "You look just the same as I remember," Hudson said. "And yet wiser."

"Thank you," she said. "Taking care of four kids and one Hector Benitez will do that to you."

Hudson looked around the living room. He counted the four children; a baby was in the arms of the oldest. Hazel introduced them, in descending order, as Virginia, age eight, Lucien, six, Victoria, four, and Julien, ten months.

"You have such a lovely family," Lucy said.

Hudson wondered if Lucien was named for Lucy and why they had named no one after him. "And where is the man himself?"

"Dad's in the garage," Lucien said.

"Maybe I should go out there," Hudson said.

Hazel nodded her reluctant agreement and signaled to Lucien, who showed Hudson the way.

"Dad?" Lucien called once they reached the garage.

"Yo," came Benny's voice.

It had been less than two months since Hudson had seen Benny and nine years since Benny had seen Hudson. They had never been apart more than six waking hours since

Hudson had moved to New Norfolk as a child. In the nine years he had skipped, New Norfolk had expanded. New technologies filled the seas and skies. But nothing, not even seeing Hope as briefly as he had yesterday, had foisted the weight of nine years upon Hudson like seeing Benny's four children. In just a few minutes, Benny had become long lost to Hudson, too. He was also lost somewhere in this garage.

"Dad, Mr. MacDuff is here."

"Mr. MacDuff? Who...damn. Is it four o'clock already? Alright. Uh, I'll be out there soon." Benny's voice was coming from underneath the empty shell of an old car.

"No, Dad, he's right here."

"Benny," Hudson said.

After a second or two of silence, Hudson heard Benny slowly make his way upwards. He emerged from underneath the rear of the car with a wrench in his hand, which he rubbed with a cloth. Lucien took some subtle clue from his father and went back into the house. Benny gazed at Hudson, wrench and rag in hand. He was thicker in every dimension: belly, chest, shoulders, neck, and face, and another decade of life in this dangerous world had worn much of the youth off his face and filled in his dimples a bit. It had not dimmed the light in his eyes. He stood there, frozen, and it seemed like if Benny took a step forward, he would shatter like dry clay.

Hudson looked at the workbench behind Benny. The array of wrenches, hammers, saws, and screwdrivers was so meticulously arranged and sparkling clean that if it were not for the obvious use Benny was making of them, one would think the man was a mere collector. "You still polishing your own boots?" Hudson said.

Benny pulled his head back. "There are certain things a man must take pride in."

"And this family of yours, too. You've got quite the noble brood."

"Look at you," Benny began, pointing the wrench at Hudson. He brought his wrist to his eye. "This isn't real. This can't be real."

"Listen, Benny, I feel the same way. But here we are." Hudson now felt like walking forward to hug his old friend would seem like a threat. "What's this you're working on?"

Benny put down the wrench. "This, my friend, is a 1957 Cadillac Eldorado Brougham. It was in excellent condition before the Eclipse, then mold grew in the interior. What you see is original bodywork. Under the hood it's all new: four graviton flywheels, extra battery, you name it. I'm just waiting on the canopy and seats from the upholsterer."

"It's a beauty. Everything you've got here is beautiful. Your house, your family, everything."

"Thanks." Benny leaned on the rear fin. "I mean, you know, I owe this to you. I told your mom that on the phone. Anytime you say, I'll quit the Navy. We can go into business together."

"Hey. All I did was pull your heavy ass onto my Wind Scout. You did the rest for yourself."

Benny nodded. "You seen Hope?"

"Yep," Hudson said. He had seen her at the Old Barracks last night. "It seems Hope feeds well on the present."

A short laugh burst out of Benny, his head tucked into

his shoulders, and his face swelled red. When Hudson saw tears begin to fall, he walked forward and put his hand on Benny's shoulder. He then did as he thought he should do and put his arms around him. No matter how deep an impression the instantaneous change to Hudson's world had made on him, time had dug more deeply into Benny and everyone else.

32

Time had made no impression on Dr. Doris Huntsman.
Hudson sat on a stone bench in the Hall of Watchers, looking at her. She looked the same as she had nine years ago—
even younger, if it were possible—and Hudson wondered if
she had not slipped through some portal with him.

The slab that had housed former President Palmer was
empty, as were many of the spaces sleepers had occupied
until just a week ago. Armed guards patrolled the steps of the
small arena. Hudson imagined one of those metal serpents
slithering by his feet and twitched with disgust. Huntsman
gripped the edge of the bench. Devon Conque stared at
something a thousand miles away. Dr. Mortimer Sowinski,
the only other person on Earth to have encountered mantle
snakes, sat with his hands on his hips and one foot in front
of the other, as if ready to spring upward at a moment's notice. But President Philips had wanted to meet here. Philips
sat with his eyes closed, almost serenely.

Huntsman had arrived on her own. Conque had briefed
Hudson and Mort before their arrival. Claire was in Boul-

der, preparing a care package to be sent to Father Joseph, who was stuck in Antarctica for some reason.

After an eternity, Philips opened his eyes and gazed at the empty slab at the center of the floor. "It would not be easy for an angel to become human, would it?"

Hudson had heard about Philips's quasi-mystical musings before. "Sir?"

"An angel can see everything as it is, black and white, true and false. Humans learn by experience, contact, trials, errors. There are humans for whom this kind of contact with the world, learning by feeling, is difficult. They are born with an almost angelic level of intelligence and have little understanding of what it takes for most other humans to learn, to engage the world on a normal level. Angelic intelligence can deceive the person navigating this world, though. It is as much a disability to them as it is a source of admiration for others. A real angel would be lost as a human, unless he had forgotten everything he knew about heaven and had to start over."

Hudson tried to read Huntsman's face. But Hudson had also heard about the stone wall she had learned to put up in the presence of Philips and his followers. When Hudson had said hello to her a few minutes ago, she had already been chiseled marble.

"What do I mean?" Philips said, crossing his arms and looking up at the skylight. "I'm not a politician. I have not learned to lead the way our beloved Deborah Palmer did, through compromise and persuasion. I was a man of ideas, of insight, a close advisor to presidents before her. She was more like a queen. A queen is flesh and blood." He laughed.

"And she had a lot of both. That's what a leader needs to be. Flesh and blood. Not angelic insight."

Philips closed his eyes again. A few seconds later, he opened his eyes, sighed, and looked at Huntsman. "What is your plan, Dr. Huntsman?"

She brought her hands together at her lap. "It is time for us to regroup, Mr. President. Some of our team members were injured in Antarctica. Mr. MacDuff, too, still needs some time to recuperate fully from his wounds and surgeries. And that is to say nothing of unpacking the vast discoveries to which MacDuff has led us."

"And then?" Philips said.

"And then, Mr. President, we will search for more portals, if they can be found."

"With our dear Hudson, I presume."

Hudson looked at Conque, who made the subtlest shake of his head. The Navy commander had not yet made known his plans to bring Hudson back to the moonshock. With his talking of diving, and with Doris Huntsman here, Hudson did not know in which direction Conque had planned to send him: directly through space or through the supposed portals.

"MacDuff is a civilian now. He can do as he chooses," Huntsman said.

Huntsman let her eyes linger on Hudson half a second longer than she needed to, or Hudson imagined she did. She was not pure stone, after all.

"It looks like you have some decisions to make, young man," Philips said. "You can plumb the depths or shoot for the stars. The world is your oyster, Hudson, and she has opened up for you her pearl. The question is, through which abyss do you see that pearl shining?"

Philips fixed his dark eyes on Hudson. This was not, apparently, a rhetorical question.

Huntsman and Conque were staring each other down. Hudson glanced at Mort, the only person who had not said anything so far. Mort's mouth was tight; he looked angry.

Hudson did have a choice to make. Philips, with the vision of angelic intellect, seemed already to know Conque and Huntsman each wanted Hudson for their projects. Huntsman might have another borehole somewhere—Mort had alluded earlier to something she had said at Mort's doctoral presentation. Conque was diving near Hudson's portal to turn humans into time machines capable of breaching the moonshock. But Mort, too, had experienced a time dilation at the Earth's mantle. This no longer seemed like a dilemma for Hudson. The pearl shining for him on the ocean floor was the moonshock itself, or a reflection of it, which had sent him to Antarctica. Conque had already said so. Philips did not want Hudson to decide between two paths. He wanted him to show everyone here how it was one path.

"Mr. President, in my experience, it seems like the search for portals is a search for the way through the moonshock. It is one pearl and one abyss, sir."

Philips's face, which had been full of patient expectation, took on a look of supreme satisfaction without a single muscle moving, the way a bare winter landscape becomes an enclosed garden by simple bud of leaf and bloom of flower. "There it is. My point is proven. The human mind can see what angels never will because it creates as it sees. Well done, Hudson. And welcome home, if I have not already said so." He cast his eyes at Huntsman and Conque. "Between the three of you, I know you'll find my own son, too. His name is Tyne."

***

Walking outside, away from the Hall of Watchers, Hudson struggled to keep up with his three companions. Mort was far in the lead. Huntsman and Conque followed, twenty feet apart from each other. They were all angry. Hudson knew Conque and Huntsman did not always agree and that he had perhaps gone too far in suggesting, however indirectly he had, that they work together. He could not fathom why Mort was so upset.

The late afternoon sun reflected off the Gateway Arch. "I'm glad to see they finished fixing the Gateway Arch these past nine years," Hudson said. He would try to lighten the conversation however he could.

"They still haven't fixed it," Huntsman and Conque said, almost in unison and without looking up.

Mort thrust an angry finger toward the completed arch above him.

Huntsman stopped. "Just a few weeks ago, it looked like it did twenty-eight years ago, after the earthquakes of the Great Eclipse."

Hudson caught up to her. "So they finished it."

"No," Mort said, still walking. "That's a problem. That thing is a big problem."

***

The next morning, Hudson stood next to Doris Huntsman on the widow's walk of Lucy's house. Huntsman had come to check on Lucy, who was lying in her bedroom downstairs. Since then, she had told Hudson in more detail about the adventures of Mort and Todd and of the team that had found him in Antarctica.

"This is a stark place," Huntsman said. "Even after fourteen years."

Fresh snow covered the city, a rarity for Virginia, especially when the long winter was on the other side of the world.

"We do it to survive," Hudson said.

"You are saying more than you realize. People aren't here just because they have to be, to support the Navy, be the tip of the spear. People come to a place like this to come alive."

Those had not been Hudson's thoughts when he had started going on watch after high school. "That feeling can only last so long. As far as I can tell from being back a few days, most of these people still just drink through the sunset."

"Not everyone has it in them to keep going."

"How do you keep going after thirty years?"

"Remembering where I came from," Huntsman said. "And knowing that kind of hell can always creep back into our world."

Hudson leaned on the railing to face her, eye to eye. The black eye Claire had given her was healing. "Tell me about it."

"That's a story for another time." She gazed over the snowy city.

"You think you've been through a worse hell than any of us now? That we can't handle your story?"

She turned her dark brown eyes toward him. "Because of all this, Mr. MacDuff, human beings are at peace with each other. I'll take a fight with an unknown entity over one with my own flesh and blood anytime. You and Lucy and Jody keep calling all this the devil, but look what it's done for humanity. I've seen the gates of hell in my own city." She looked down at her hands, which were clutching the wooden railing.

Hudson turned away. "But all this is making devils out of some of us. All that talk about angelic intellects—"

Huntsman put her hand on Hudson's. He lost his train of thought. She pulled her hand away.

She smiled and turned away from something in the city below. Spies, perhaps. "So you understand that we have to find our own way forward. We have to get there before anyone else does."

"Is that why Father Joseph stayed in Antarctica? What was with the note he left my mother about being an antenna?"

"That's what he is. That's why his hands connect to that glass ball. The more he learns to see through it, the more the other will learn they are watched."

"Now you're being cryptic," Hudson said. He felt ten years older when he spoke to her, maybe fifteen.

She stared at the deck of the widow's walk.

"Is everything alright?" he said.

"Billy's not here. He would have some instinct about what to do next."

"Maybe so, but it seems you do, too. Father Joseph knows where he needs to be. Todd followed some instinct of his into that spiral city. Mort's maybe still figuring it out. My mother is doing her thing, watching and waiting. And the way you react to Philips, Miss Huntsman, you've got an instinct, too. You draw it out of people. That's what my mom always said. Maybe that's how I survived Benny's accident. Seeing you first."

Those last three words echoed more strongly in Hudson's mind than they had felt when saying them. He hoped she did not draw another meaning from them, unless she liked that meaning. Hudson was not sure whatever attraction he felt for her—as the enigma she had always been to him as a child, as the woman he saw here, and as the heroine she might become—had made him say, "Seeing you first."

Huntsman, still staring at the deck of the widow's walk, brought her hands together in a strange way: her knuckles came together as she pointed at her chest. It was as if she recognized, like Hudson had insinuated, that everything was converging on her. "I have a plan," she said.

***

After Huntsman had left, Hudson helped Lucy up the steep pull-down stair to the widow's walk. She leaned, stiff-armed, on the railing. This had always been a place of bittersweet feeling for Lucy, Hudson knew, but he did not know if the physical pain it took to reach it would make her hate it or love it all the more.

"Tell me about Benny," she said through pursed lips.

"He wrote me an email. Says he owes me his life. That

he'll quit the Navy and set up shop with me and his father-in-law, Mr. Dungloe, turning old-wheeled cars into hover cars. That was it, like three or four grammatically incomprehensible lines, followed by dozens of pictures of classic cars he's worked on."

"Can you see it now?" Lucy said. "You were never going to belong to your generation. I need to sit."

Hudson helped Lucy sit on a lawn chair. When Lucy's face stopped twitching with pain, he said, "You sound like Philips, with his angelic intellect. Maybe he had an ambitious mother, too." But Hudson could see what she had been trying to say to him all through high school and after. The people around here, for all the pioneering spirit they had once had, were not going anywhere.

"I'm a realist, Hudson. And reality tells me God put you and Philips face to face for a reason. He's afraid of you, afraid of Huntsman, and afraid of all of us."

"Why?"

"Because we don't answer to the gods he's constructed. It's the oldest story there is."

"His gods are dead. Eaten by mantle snakes. Mort thinks he uses the Hall of Watchers to read our minds."

"Mort would know."

"And that the Gateway Arch is where the mantle snakes went. That he's under their control now."

"That is speculation."

"Is that little city in Antarctica really the same place you and Father Joseph went during the moondark?"

Lucy nodded. "It all comes back around."

"But that means we're never going to find portals by

looking for them. You guys made one in the desert that disappeared, then I fell into one that no one can find now."

"It found you. What were you doing when it found
you?"

"Saving Benny."

"No. You had already done that. What were you doing?"

"Looking for a way out. Trying to survive."

Hudson watched his mother's face contort with pain.
He went downstairs, into the house, and brought back up
Peter Panda. He set it on her belly, which shook with each
halted breath.

"Mom?"

Lucy, her eyes still closed, knit her brow and mouthed,
"What?"

"Who were the young girl and the old lady I saw?"

She did not answer. A tear streamed down her face.

Hudson waited and watched her face twitch with some
new pain. Many children were raised to fight their parents'
battles. Perhaps that was what the girl and the old woman
were.

Hudson leaned on the wooden railing and looked out
on the landscape of his battle. During his absence, New
Norfolk had expanded in all directions. The coastline had
dropped another hundred feet. The bony finger of land on
which New Norfolk sat pointed ever deeper into the North
Atlantic Ocean.

Perhaps Lucy was right. He had no generation of his
own in this world. Like Phlegethon, the man Father Joseph
had pulled from the ice, had said during the flight from Antarctica, he was a river, flowing from valley to valley, abyss

to abyss. What tests the Army was conducting on that poor man torn from his generation, Hudson did not know. Why he had seen White Wolf, who had disappeared in Siberia over a year ago, with Phlegethon, Hudson did not know. Where Hudson would flow next, what plan had come to Huntsman, what she was devising with Conque, Hudson did not know, either.

A three-pulse alarm sounded in New Norfolk. Hudson grabbed his old Dreamcaster from the wall next to the front door and ran to the city gate. He was too late, as was the specter's victim: someone Hudson did not know, lying on her back, chest torn open and heart exposed, still beating its last. Hudson looked up at Lucy's widow's walk and saw her sitting just as he had left her a minute ago. Hudson hoped it would not be as painful or deadly for Lucy to open her heart, if that was where her battle lay.

33

Mort stood on the back deck of Danny and Cynthia's house in Boulder, beer in hand, while Danny grilled giant sloth steaks for lunch on a balmy February afternoon far from the long winter. Sir Bear sniffed around the edges of the lawn. Mort and Danny were swapping puns to the tortured amusement of Cynthia and Claire. But this could not keep a question out of Mort's mind as he watched an ancient and revived creature sizzle on the grill: if Haleh had animated the cougar he and Todd had seen, it was possible that a sleeper had done the same for this giant sloth and all the other ancient megafauna populating the plains. It almost felt like cannibalism.

Doris Huntsman sat with them and played along with the bad jokes, but Mort could tell she was concerned about something, too. He'd had no doubt, since she had arrived this morning from New Norfolk, that she had come to share in a little "R and R" with them after their big adventure in Antarctica. She had even let her hair down, literally; Mort had never seen it except in a tight bun. Huntsman, as much as she was here to relax, would soon burst if she could not unlock the next step of her plan. But Danny and Cynthia, self-declared "lord and lady of the manor," had declared a moratorium on business.

The growl of distant motorcycles overcame the sound of sizzling meat. Mort had heard about the biker gangs who were prowling the American countryside, their Harleys covered in devonium mesh Mad-Max-style, looking for specters to send back to hell. This was a pair of bikes, and they came closer until they stopped somewhere near the Shamshiri residence.

Mort puzzled at the knowing look Danny and Cynthia were giving each other. Huntsman's face was in her hands. Mort looked at Claire and said, "Am I missing something?"

She shrugged.

The doorbell rang.

Cynthia gazed at Huntsman as she walked into the house to answer the door.

"What am I missing?" Mort said to Danny.

"You'll see."

Murmurs of welcome came from inside the house.

Huntsman stood up and straightened her flannel vest.

Following Cynthia through the French door were two men, each as tall as Phlegethon and endowed with a bearing Mort would have called "princely" if not for the terrifying glow of their green eyes.

"Everyone," Cynthia said, "this is Kai, whom we met years ago, and his brother, Av."

Mort did not know Kai or Av and had never heard of them, but Sir Bear sprang happily to Av.

Kai said, "We're sorry to intrude like this on your family

get-together. But time is of the essence. Dorsina, how are you after all these years?"

Mort looked at Huntsman, who had adopted the round eyes, velveteen pose, and thin, permanent smile of a teddy bear.

"What, no hug for your uncle Kai?"

Mort and, to his knowledge, everyone else in the world, had only known about the Huntsmans of Chevy Chase, Maryland.

Huntsman searched everyone's eyes as if for permission, and Mort discovered it was too late to keep his head from pulling back in surprise. She straightened her flannel vest again, and Kai held her head to his breastbone. Mort could hear and feel everyone's reaction; he dared not look away from Huntsman's girlish face, squished against the man's jacket. When Huntsman looked up and leaned her chin against his chest, Mort looked at Claire, whose eyes were frozen wide.

"What are you doing here?" Huntsman asked, hugging Av a bit more formally.

Av kissed Huntsman's forehead. "All in good time. First, I wanted to meet the people of whom Kai spoke so highly when he was here last." He bowed slightly to Danny and Cynthia. "Especially Claire, who reminds him so much of another young woman who once carried her people to safety."

Claire now pulled back her own head in surprise.

"And to shake hands with Mortimer Sowinski."

Mort wiped the condensation from the beer bottle off his hand and reached out.

"Thank you for bringing Todd as far as you have," Av said.

Mort pinched his mouth to keep a sudden gush of tears from spilling out then said, "How is he? Where is he?"

Av's eyes grew somber. "At the mouth of the ram's horn. Waiting."

"Waiting for what?" Mort said.

"For the essential time."

"Speaking of," Danny said, "lunch is ready. Would you care to join us?"

***

After lunch, in which Kai and Av revealed little of themselves except as vegetarians, the party of seven sat on sofas in the living room. Huntsman had apparently not seen her uncles since the moondark and shared with them all that she had been doing: studying humanoids in the Azores, sending humans into holes she had dug, and discovering dark secrets in Antarctica.

"No moss grows under your feet," Kai said. "But it does grow under the sea, as I've come to learn."

Mort cleared his throat and waited for Kai, Av, or Huntsman to tell him to speak. Av turned, and Mort felt the man's eyes saying, *This had better be deep and true.*

"It is because the lichen growing on the chain is a new species, *Calaplaca theodori*. It thrives in moist, hypoxic environments and gorges on small doses of electric current."

"Don't we all?" Av said.

Mort stuck out his chin, trying to resist turning away from Av and his seemingly dismissive comment. Av had wanted to shake hands with Mort before; now he seemed distant.

"What Mortimer means," Huntsman said, "is that Todd's Lichen, as we like to call it, glowed underwater, deep underwater, on an Atlantean chain. This is what led us to Hudson MacDuff. Or what led him into the portal to Antarctica. Maybe you have some insight into how all that works, Uncle Kai or Uncle Av?"

Kai said, "You have a biologist to tell you how lichens live. Ask God, Dorsina, why He gave you one just when you needed it. Then you'll understand how portals work."

Huntsman stared at the floor in front of her for answers.

"If there was ever a specialist in portals," Mort said, "it was White Wolf. He practically became one."

Av leaned back against the couch and let his face repose in the look of a teacher satisfied his student was about to stumble into something brilliant.

Mort did not know what to say next.

"But he's gone," Huntsman said. "He would have some intuition about all this. Something I could test."

"I think you missed what Mortimer just said," Kai said. "How often did Billy serve as a bridge for others? So let him draw out your intuition now, Dorsina."

Huntsman sighed.

Av rubbed Huntsman's back. "Something's on your heart, Dorsina. Lay your burden on us."

She sighed again. "All this is coming together in a strange way, and I'm not sure.... What I mean is, I have a plan, and I'm not certain it's the right one."

Danny leaned forward. "You've got some pretty smart people here. Let's hear it."

"It's not from me, really," Huntsman said. "Hudson said it yesterday. But he got it from Devon Conque, I think, and Philips really liked the idea, so I'm not sure how to evaluate it. It's this: just like the moondark before it, the moonshock has been eliciting new realities from Earth, from us. It's not just a physical reordering. That's why Mort and Todd were able to reach the outer limits of all this; they had something—"

"Have," Mort corrected.

"Have," Huntsman continued, "something within them...."

Mort breathed in sharply.

"Between them," Huntsman said. She smiled, and her lips quivered for a brief moment. "That's it. The portal appears where we need it to. Between us."

Sir Bear barked outside. Mort's belly quivered, and a fountain of insight gushed upward. "Oh." He laughed at how simple and almost silly it sounded. "That's why White Wolf isn't here for him."

Claire broke through a few seconds of awkward silence. "What does Uncle Billy have to do with this?"

Mort looked at Av for help; Av continued to return nothing but a happily expectant expression. "Uh, how do I say it? They're the same. What White Wolf was for going down, he is for going up?"

"He who?" Claire said.

"Hudson," Huntsman said. "Hudson actually saw Billy on his plane ride from Antarctica."

Claire crossed her arms on her lap and let her head fall.

"Hudson's the way up," Mort said. "So you're right, Doris. Someone has to go down. That's what Hudson was getting at in the Hall of Watchers. It all seems too easy."

"I am grotesquely confused," Claire said. "Who said anything about going down again?"

Huntsman fixed her eyes on Mort. "I was thinking it."

"You said it at my defense," Mort said, though he was not sure he had not read her mind just now. "We go down. Hudson goes up. Like an arrow on a string."

"Down where?" Claire said. "Miss Huntsman was allusive before."

"Where is this borehole?" Mort said, rubbing his hands. "I'm ready."

Huntsman pulled back her hair. "It's not a borehole, Dr. Sowinski. It is a natural cavity in the Earth, one that has torn wide open since the Great Eclipse and the inversion of the Earth. It is also the site of the most intense spectral activity on planet Earth, a place marked by constant, violent attacks, where we recorded the first spectral activity after the moondark, and which nearly led to a third world war back then: Kashmir."

Danny took in a long draft of air and exhaled sharply. "That sounds intense."

"It is," Huntsman said. "We would never get permission to bring OSS or military equipment there. It's a no-go zone. Especially with sleepers waking all over the Earth. Spectral activity is at a peak right now."

"Who would go anyway?" Cynthia said. "Who has a

special connection to Hudson, like Mort has to Todd and Jody to Lucy?"

The only person Mort could think of was Lucy herself, the mother who had kept hope alive and believed, against all evidence, that her son would return and save everyone. But he saw what everyone else in the room seemed to be avoiding: Doris Huntsman, with her head down and hair covering her face, twiddling her fingers at her lap.

Kai cleared his throat and said, "Well, let's be scientific about it, shall we? Widen the net a little? Send everyone? Claire, does your father still have the car Av and I gave him?"

"Do you mean the white Trans Am?" She eyed Kai warily. "Yes...."

Huntsman said, "Uncle Kai, for all your ancient technology, that car doesn't have enough firepower to get through Kashmir."

"It has no firepower," Claire said. "Please tell me it has no actual weapons."

"No, I was suggesting you would use it to hover in. It seats four."

Mort stood up and spread his arms. It was the only way to handle the burst of energy in his belly, the place where the idea he was about to express seemed to originate. "Let's widen the net even further. We don't need firepower. We need horsepower."

"Horsepower?" Huntsman said, but her face fell as if she understood Mort's meaning.

"Horsepower," Mort said. "And I know exactly where to get it."

***

The four-hundred-mile trip to Marigold's house in Crow Country took three hours, nearly three times as long as it should have. Claire drove her father's car much more cautiously than Mort had seen her ride the unicorn she had made. Huntsman sat in the back seat with Sir Bear and said little.

After Mort's suggestion to speak with Black Mare, Kai had stood up, imitated Mort in stretching his arms, and said, "It looks like our work here is finished." He and Av had each kissed Huntsman on the top of her head, thanked Cynthia for her hospitality, and left on their motorcycles.

Av had intervened only to keep Huntsman from asking how Black Mare could possibly help them. This was the same question Marigold now posed to Mort.

"She comes and she goes as she wills," Marigold said. "She is with the Spirit. She is like the wind."

"You don't have a way of calling her?" Huntsman said.

"If I did, Doris, I'd tie her up and never let her leave. She came for Mort last time. Let's see if she really likes him. Who gave you a black eye?"

Everyone looked at Claire.

"Were you fighting with Claire over Mort?"

"What? No."

"I'm just saying. He's filling out nicely." Marigold winked.

So much for dear old Grandma Marigold, Mort thought.

Mort led the way to the stables. He ran his hand along some of the tall grass. After his adventures under the Earth, he had confined himself to a lab to earn his doctorate and to work with Claire. He had both now, though he was not sure how much Claire really felt for him and how much she was dating him just because it seemed right. The tall grass, big sky, and wide-open adventure before him let Mort see past this doubt for the moment. He was not sure how to call Black Mare. She had come to him last time.

Black Mare was not in the stable.

Mort led the way to the tipi, where he had seen Black Mare trotting across the valley one morning last year. She did not come. She was not in the forest, either, where she had held up a snail for Mort to see. From there, Claire took Mort, Huntsman, and Marigold in the hovering Trans Am to the Wolf Mountains, where White Wolf had made his vision. Black Mare did not appear.

"I told you," Marigold said.

When they arrived at Marigold's house again, Joe Curly, Jr., and Grey Swan were waiting on the porch.

"Any luck?" Joe asked.

"How do you know what we're looking for?" Mort said.

Joe said, "We see you going to all the places you saw her before. It's only logical. We want to see her, too."

Mort turned to Marigold. "What if, maybe, you lit a candle in front of her picture, you know?"

"She's not a god or even a saint, Mortimer. I'll not treat her that way. If she's too good to help her grandma's friends, that's up to her." Marigold started walking up the steps of the porch.

A horse's snort came from somewhere. Black Mare walked from around the corner of the house.

Everyone clapped and cheered. "She listens to her grandma," Marigold said and nearly tripped as she hurried back down the steps to see Black Mare. But Black Mare walked directly to Huntsman.

Huntsman put a timid hand to Black Mare's nose, rubbed a little, and pulled her hand away. "That's...I'm sorry, you're a person."

Black Mare walked forward, pushing Huntsman a little to the side, and stopped where Huntsman was at her flank.

"She wants you to ride her," Grey Swan said.

Huntsman laid a less timid hand on Black Mare's side. "I'm not going to ride a person."

"I did," Mort said.

"Not knowing who she was," Huntsman said.

"She knew who I was."

"Black Mare, Melanie," Huntsman said, "it's a simple matter of Mort's thinking you can help us in some way."

Black Mare turned her head and snorted.

"Speak her language," Marigold said. "Get on and ride."

"I don't know how to ride a horse. There's no saddle or reins. And I'm too short to get on."

"I'll help," Joe Curly, Jr., and Grey Swan said in unison. The two men stood on each side of Huntsman. Grey Swan made a step out of his hands, and Joe held out his hand for Huntsman to take.

Huntsman put her hand to her face. "What am I doing? Alright." She stepped up on Grey Swan's hand. Once on Black Mare's back, she said, "Alright. Easy now."

Black Mare sauntered in a circle in front of Marigold's house. As she made a second pass, the circle grew wider. Huntsman, who had been leaning on her hands at the base of Black Mare's neck, sat straight up, let her hands go, and waved.

Black Mare began to trot, and Huntsman grabbed Black Mare's neck again. The circle grew wider, and Black Mare ran faster. Mort almost felt sorry for Doris Huntsman, whose face had become terror sculpted in stone, but he knew what Melanie De Soto was doing for her. It was what she had once done for him: to prepare her for traveling to a new place, and perhaps to make her love herself a little better.

Black Mare lifted her hoofs off the ground, and they did not return to it. She and Huntsman were flying.

Sounds of awe echoed out from everyone and most loudly from Marigold, who was weeping.

Black Mare lifted Huntsman forty feet in the air before descending. When they landed, Mort was the one to help Huntsman off. Before Mort could say anything, Huntsman grabbed Black Mare's neck, buried her face in her long mane, and wept for several minutes.

Mort saw what Black Mare was saying: they did not need to open the net so wide, to send everyone down. Exactly one person needed to plumb the depths of Earth to help Hudson open the skies.

34

"What is this plan of hers?" Lucy said. She was having dinner with Hudson at home, with food he had brought from Hope's deli. Her elbows dug hard into the kitchen table to keep weight off her back. Spoon in hand, she stared down at foil tray of paella. She took a mouthful of food and chewed slowly, waiting for a bout of nausea to pass so she could swallow.

"I don't know, or I should say, she would only tell me half of it, which, knowing her, means there's even more to it. Maybe she's still formulating it, but she seemed really determined."

Hudson was eating his food less like he used to—stuffing heaps into a mouth still half full of un-swallowed food—and more like a grown man. But Hudson was eating chicken tenders and French fries—not an adult-level dish, exactly.

"So you're to work with Devon Conque?"

"I could leave in a few days. But if you're not well...."

"I'll be fine."

Lucy took another bite and forced herself to swallow. It

might kill her, but she would not show her son how much pain she was in. She would not hold him back again.

"It's just the Azores, anyway," Hudson said. "It's a diving program. Not Houston. Down, not up. It'll be years, I'm sure, before anything big happens."

"You'll see your brother before you go."

"Of course, I will," Hudson said. "But you know I'll be back and forth."

"Sleepers are waking up," Lucy said. She was avoiding a third bite. Nausea did not pair well with seafood, whose odors, lurking upward with the slightest threat of poisonous putrescence, were already shutting down her appetite. "Things could be locked down anytime."

"Our fences are sturdy here. When's the last time anything got through?"

"That's not the point." Lucy forced a spoonful.

"What is?" Hudson said. "You want mine instead?"

Lucy nodded. Hudson hated seafood. This was another sign he was growing up. They switched plates.

"The point is, they'll use this crisis as an opportunity."

"Well, what if it is the end, and Conque can't send me up, down, or in any direction? Then it doesn't matter."

Lucy found it easier to eat the French fries. "You found Amy Anklesore."

"Give me a break, Mom. I just missed it last time."

Lucy pounded the table. "It wasn't there last time."

Hudson did not say anything but kept eating.

Lucy bit into a chicken tender. She had no way of telling her son what Ethel Rede had said to her in Antarctica. "Your dad came to me. Right before Owen did, to tell me they'd found you. You know what he said to me?"

"What, Mom?"

Lucy waited for tears, but none came. "Don't be afraid to let him go again."

"You sure it was Dad?"

"A woman knows."

Hudson sat back and shrugged. "Alright, then, here we are. You tell me to stay and to go in the same breath. A stuffed animal and Dad's ghost tell you I'm supposed to go, but you're telling me to watch out for the people I'm going to."

"That's all I'm saying."

"Then do as Dad says, and don't be afraid to let me go."

"Oh, it's so easy for you to say. You were gone nine years. Nine years, Hudson. Which felt like four days to you, but which were an eternity for me."

"You think it's so easy to come back to a world I don't belong to? Huh? All my friends are old, they've moved on. The Navy dumped me, won't have anything to do with me. No one even wants to experiment on me. The only woman…." Hudson stuffed his mouth with paella and winced.

Lucy smirked. "The only woman, what?"

Hudson pulled his arm around the bowl like he had done as a child.

"The only woman who what, Hudson? Don't be fooled. That's her trick. She's roped more than one man into her little spider web with that cool demeanor and toothy little mouth. Now she's got you, too. Hook, line, and sinker."

Hudson did not look up but said, "Well, she's come up

with a lot of big fish. It's not about her, anyway. Devon Con-que is the one who wants to work with me."

Lucy bit into a wad of fries. "In the same place Doris Huntsman, excuse me, Miss Huntsman, has been digging up robots and magic carpets for the past thirty years. What are you diving for, exactly?"

Hudson pointed his eyes at Lucy. "Time."

"Time?"

"That's all he said."

***

A few days later, Lucy's sendoff for her son came much more easily than anticipated. As she held him at the door of her house in New Norfolk, she felt in his muscular body more than the sum of the parts she had given him. She held his shoulders and looked at his strong but incomplete face. Whatever adventures awaited him would chisel its finishing strokes. His eyes, though, her mother's eyes, lay like lazy old cats on the back of a sofa. Lucy hated those eyes, even as she knew that, like a cat's, they were taking in everything and would spring to life at the first twitch of a mouse's whisker in the shadows. An urge welled up inside Lucy, and she gave it free reign. She slapped him across the face.

Those eyes sprang open.

Lucy grabbed the scruff of Hudson's shirt. "I don't know where you're going next, Hudson. But if you catch yourself hesitating, looking back, don't. Owen and I will be fine. This world will keep spinning. Just keep going. Go all the way."

35

Hover technology had not advanced as much as everyone had been claiming. The C-2A Greyhound, retrofitted with graviton motors, and in whose cargo hold Hudson was strapped, felt like it had been falling for six hours. The pilots assured Hudson they did not feel this same sensation. But they were facing forward, with an expansive view of the North Atlantic rolling underneath them. Hudson was facing backward, with only a carpet of clouds, visible through a single portal window near the tail, falling upward and away. The problem was one of hybridization: the Navy had thought it could save energy, that is, money, by maintaining lift from the wings. The graviton motors fought against the wings and the rear stabilizers, and they did so inside Hudson's stomach. Wherever the Navy saved money, it usually came at the expense of someone's body.

Near the end of his flight, the plane banked, and Hudson could see the Great Meteor Seamount rising from the sea. That was where they would land. Nine years after Hudson's disappearance, with the sea having receded another hundred feet, the abortive volcano had grown outward and upward like a scab and looked just as hard, bare, and for-bidding.

The naval base had grown, however, into a small town. In its center was a vast warehouse, into which Hudson was ushered. Objects of stone, clay, metal, and petrified wood sat on tables in marked areas of the concrete floor. This was all the "junk" about which Bridgewater had spoken. For all that Hudson had seen during his journey under the sea—metal chains, sea moss, and obelisks—he had not seen anything resembling a city. But these objects were organized according to where they had been found: Atlantis Ring 1 NW, Atlantis Ring 2 SE, and so on.

"Funny, isn't it?" came the voice of Commander Devon Conque from behind him.

"Sir," Hudson said.

"Your eyes were opened to something no one else can see. And blinded to something else. Where you saw a portal to another time and place, we found the city itself."

"Not at the Azores? The terrain doesn't fit the descrip-tion."

Conque slapped Hudson on the back. "Take Plato for what it's worth. You were gone nine years. The story of this place had to survive nine thousand years." Conque's heavy hand, still on Hudson shoulder, turned him toward a deco-rated stone plaque. "Can you read this?"

Hudson looked at vines, leaves, fruits, and animals ar-ranged on the rectangular surface as neatly as a tossed salad. "I'm afraid not, sir."

Conque whistled and uttered two incomprehensible

syllables. A humanoid walked briskly toward them. "Ree-duh fiss," Conque said to the machine.

The humanoid spoke in its programmed language, then translated, "Fah-resh fah-lesh, war-muh mih-luk, sof-tuh beh-duh."

"You get it?" Conque said.

"Fresh flesh, warm milk…soft bed?"

Conque raised his eyebrows.

"Atlantean hotel?"

Conque patted Hudson's cheek. "You've never been at sea for months at a time. Some languages can only be learned by experience. This is your work for now."

***

Hudson spent several weeks cleaning and cataloguing the artifacts that Navy divers had brought up in submersibles from the sea floor while he trained for deep diving. Evidence grew stronger every day that the ancient city tucked between the Great and the Little Meteor Seamounts and covered in a blanket of steel-colored ocean almost two miles deep had been made of thickly plastered mud brick, with stone serving to frame doors and windows, raise obelisks, and pave important areas. No statues had been found. Heavy timbers had held up ceilings and roofs.

That divers were finding these artifacts relatively intact at a depth of nine thousand feet after eleven thousand years confirmed the hypothesis about the portal: it froze time, and, where time froze, space formed a singularity. When the divers entered the city from above, time slowed to a near stop. The minutes they spent below became months above.

That could be the only explanation anyone could give for why the humanoids were still functioning after all this time.

"Functioning" was a loose term. Humanoid behavior became more erratic as the weeks wore on. The only correlation was confirmed reports of sleepers waking en masse.

***

"What were the Atlanteans up to with all this?" Hudson asked. He was having drinks with a few of the divers at a hilltop bar near base, watching the sunset.

"Space travel," said one, named Elgin Marson. "Instantaneous. No rockets, no worries about the time it takes to get anywhere."

Hudson nodded. This seemed plausible. It was, after all, what modern humans were trying to do with the discovery.

"I would say it was more of a personal transformation," said Lewis "Dock Stud" Studdock. "Trans-humanism. Go in the portal a human being, come out something else. I bet that's what these humanoids are, experiments gone wrong, poor Atlantean folks who got their brain buzzed by whatever all this is."

"They were made in factories," Hudson said. "People I know have seen them."

"And where are these factories?" Studdock said.

"Antarctica," Hudson said.

"Right," Studdock said. "Your people—I know the story—they saw what they were meant to see. No, we got too close, just like Atlantis got too close. God shut the trap, sunk the city."

"Too close to what?" Marson asked.

"To God," Studdock said. "Just like in the Garden of Eden. We grabbed the fruit, got too close to God, got kicked out. Atlantis gets too close, gets kicked out. Hell, I bet that's the same story as Noah's flood. Only they don't say it in the Bible because if they said what really got God mad, then people would go for it again."

Hudson said, "But according to your theory, here we are again."

"It's inevitable. We always want to become more than we are. It's basic human ambition."

Marson said, "But don't religions teach us to become like God?"

"Aha," Studdock said. He drank his glass and raised his finger. "No. Religion is a handy barrier, a fence between God and humans. See a little bit through but come no farther. Get God in bite-sized pieces."

"Well," Hudson said, "maybe that's the best way. After all, we don't want our brains buzzed, right?"

"You guys are ignoring an obvious problem, though," Marson said. "The specters. The metal snakes below the mantle. There's a whole 'nother world out there. Maybe that fits into it. Maybe that's why God shut the trap. Keep the snakes out."

"That hasn't worked," Studdock said. "Look where we are. Wearing mesh underwear." He adjusted his crotch. "As good a chastity belt as anything." He shook the ice in his empty glass. "*Senhorita, outra bebida, por favor. Obrigado.* You guys want another round?"

"Why not," Hudson said. "After all, it is my nineteenth birthday tomorrow. According to my calendar."

"Why didn't you say so?" Studdock said. "Let's make this a proper celebration."

"Nineteen?" Marson said. "You don't look a day over twenty-nine."

As Hudson's lips curled upward, he felt his muscles loosen. These guys could joke with him about lost time; each of them had lost years of surface time by diving into the sunken city. They were his generation.

"How many years have you missed because of your dives?" Hudson asked.

"Five here," Marson said.

"Seven for heaven," Studdock said. "Been at it since soon after you disappeared and made the chain glow."

"Maybe that's what this is all about," Hudson said. "Heaven. Maybe it's not a trap at all, but the inverted Earth is itself the springboard. Think about it. Everything we're doing, scrounging around Atlantis, saving up time, the moonshock, it's like God has just piled up all our massive mistakes over the years, mixed them together, flipped the whole thing inside out, and said, 'Here. Now figure out what you can do with this.'"

"What *are* we doing?" Marson said.

The three men sat quietly, pondering this. The sun bent its last red rays around the moonshock. Hudson held up his glass and caught the sunlight in the amber of his beer.

"Cheers, gentlemen," Hudson said. "May we never be men who turn our backs on the sunset, no matter how frightening a form it takes."

***

A few months later, Hudson emerged from the single-seat submersible in which he had started training. He
had dived to a depth of ninety-six hundred feet, his deepest
yet. Such a dive of a few hours would have meant months
away for men like Marson and Studdock, but it had meant
just thirteen hours for Hudson, for whom time in the sunk-
en city of New Atlantis A-III—this had been Hudson's name
for it, since he did not believe it to be the true site of the
mythical city—was the same as time on the surface. Passing
through the portal had given him some kind of immunity to
slippages of time. This meant something to Hudson today:
it was the date of his birthday, making it his official twen-
ty-eighth birthday, according to Earth calendars.

When the hover personnel carrier that took him from
ship reached base, Conque was waiting for him next to a
white Trans Am.

"Shower up, son," Conque said. "You've got ten minutes."

Hudson peered through the windshield. "Who's that in
the back seat?"

"Nine minutes and fifty-five seconds."

Hudson ran to his quarters, changed into civilian
clothes, and splashed cologne on his face. The submersible
was always cold, and Hudson did not sweat when diving.
Even after a watch on shore at New Norfolk A-III, Hudson
would forget to shower, sitting down to eat first, instead.
Lucy had sometimes hinted at this neglect with a heavy sniff
and sometimes ordered his "stinking armpits" off her couch.
Hudson would have no one to impress today except Conque, who always smelled like cigar smoke.

Hudson ran back to the car and saw Conque inside, at the driver's seat. Hudson opened the passenger side door, sat down, and turned around. Doris Huntsman was in the back seat. Hudson wished very much that he had showered.

***

The hovering Trans Am made the six-hundred-mile trip from Great Meteor Seamount Naval Research Station to the Azores in less than an hour. Conque drove no higher than twenty feet above the water, which whipped so quickly past Hudson's eyes it began to resemble the mist that had taken the place of Earth's atmosphere when he had gone missing. Huntsman said very little, mentioning only that, after doing a little horseback riding back home, she was here to coordinate her work with Conque. After four months, Hudson still had no idea what her side of the plan looked like. Once near the Azores, Conque took the Trans Am out of sight of ports and cities. He found a steep mountainside, flew upward alongside it, and landed the car's rubber tires on a road. From there, it was a slow, pleasant drive to a restaurant.

Lucy was already at the restaurant. Hudson held her, but she seemed distant, like coming here was a formality, or that Lucy had already said goodbye in her heart with that slap.

The sun set, dinner came out in many courses, and just when Hudson could fit nothing more in his stomach, waiters arrived with a cake lit with sparklers. The cake was in the shape of a volcano. The waiters set down the cake, one of them pressed a button, and molten chocolate spilled over the top. "I had the guys rig this up," Conque said. "Fitting for the son of a vulcanologist."

Lucy leaned her head against Hudson's shoulder. She had said almost nothing during dinner, but after the waiters set the sparkling cake on the table, she said, "Make a wish, Huggy Baby."

Hudson watched the sparklers' golden lights dance across the muddy slope of chocolate. He thought of how far he had come in the year since he had graduated from Norfolk Canyon High School. These people, his mother's people, had risked everything to find him in Antarctica. This had led them to believe he was their way forward. He hoped they were not stuck in the same gambler's paradox as the pioneers of the continental shelf, committed to the risks they had already taken. Those risks had killed his father and sent his mother into depression. But searching for Hudson had brought her back to life and, indirectly, given Owen a fighting chance. Hudson wished that, whatever these people had planned for him, it gave life. He blew out the sparklers before they could fade away.

***

Later that night, Hudson left the hotel where Lucy was staying and walked through the garden, sauntering slowly so as to take the warm summer breeze into his head, which was still swimming with wine. Just off the path, leaning against a railing and looking over the shimmering ocean, was Doris Huntsman. She wore a pink night robe over her blouse and skirt. She turned to see who it was. Hudson let himself imagine her eyes were sparkling for him. He was not sure what he could expect from an older woman, or from her in particular. If nothing else, he might enjoy having a real conversation with a woman, and Huntsman always provided that. He stood in front of the railing and put his hands on the finials. Just a foot or two separated their bodies.

"Thank you for taking care of my mother all these years. I guess I really did think I was the only one who could do it. Now, I'm out here, on my own, getting ready to rocket through the moonshock."

"I would like to tell you a story," Huntsman said. "Something to take up with you."

"I'm all ears."

She breathed in and nodded. "When I was a girl, old enough to know what was going on and too young to do anything about it, that's when Kai and Av found me. You've heard the members of Wepwawet talk about them."

"Yes, the mystery men of antiquity."

"Well, I was sitting on the steps of my cousin's house in my native Tuzla, reading a book. These two men stand right in front of the sun, so I look up. The rest of them are in silhouette, but I can see those green eyes, gazing at me. At the time I didn't understand the look. I only knew that they were not the Blue Helmets and they were not, how should one say, the kind of men who would visit my cousin's house."

"What book were you reading?"

"That's what opened up the conversation. It was *Coco Besucht die Sterne*. 'Curious George Visits the Stars.' Kai says, 'How does a little Bosniak girl know enough German to navigate the universe?' I explained that, of course, my father had taught me German and my mother had taught me French. 'And where are they now?' he asked me, in fluent French." Huntsman looked out over the sea. "'*Parmi les étoiles*,' I told him. Those were terrible days."

"So they took you in after that?"

"Little by little. They came by my cousin's brothel the next morning and found me lying on a filthy Styrofoam mattress, practically starving. My little frame has never caught up to Slavic standards. The rest isn't so clear, and I think my cousin thought they were trying to buy me or something—she had her limits—but they put me with some nuns in Switzerland, where I was told to learn English. I did, of course. Then it was life with the Huntsmans of Chevy Chase, Maryland. They were nice people, older, but there was only so much they could do with me. I graduated high school at sixteen. Then it was Princeton, and the rest you can read on the Internet."

Hudson looked at her, waiting for more, but she kept staring up at the stars.

"What's the secret, then?" he asked. "Why not tell anyone this? All these people who work with you, they're like you in some way."

"I suppose I never wanted them to frame their experiences by comparison to mine. If I could just be no one to them, then they could open up to me, give me their honesty."

"It takes longer to earn trust that way."

"But it's earned on better terms."

"That's how Kai and Av earned your trust. What made them stop and talk to you, take you in?"

"They never said why. They never claimed to have a motive more than basic humanitarianism. They only said that everything I had done so far, every move I'd freely made, confirmed what they had first seen in me. Then, 'Maybe you help us all find a home among the stars.' I don't know what's going to happen to you up there, if you ever go. But take my story with you, for whatever it's worth, and remember I helped someone reach the stars."

She kissed him on the cheek and walked away.

Hudson gazed at the sea, shimmering with the stars above. He understood the water now. All it wanted was to hold the light it gave back, to possess it forever. For the first time, he yearned for a day in which sea and stars would become one. But that could not happen yet. So long as sea and stars kept a chaste and distant gaze, they built a road of light between them for people like Hudson to follow.

36

Mort sat on the front deck of Marigold's house, holding a cup of coffee. Sir Bear lay next to him. He could see the horse trailer Huntsman had ordered rounding the farthest hill on the horizon and put the coffee mug to his lips to hide his schoolboy smile. Their plan had been to take a subtle approach, following Black Mare alone in Jody's car. Like Black Mare had done for Huntsman and Father Joseph on their way across the Utah desert twenty-nine years ago, she would carve a path through the specters streaming out of the cave in Kashmir where Huntsman and Mort would go underground again. This was the plan on which Huntsman had been working for four months. Three days ago, she had left for the Azores to coordinate with Devon Conque.

Since then, Black Mare had been revealing that what she had done for Huntsman, riding in the sky, should be taken quite literally. Claire had been the first to understand this. Mort was giddy, waiting for Huntsman to see what Melanie De Soto and Claire Conque had waiting for her behind Marigold's house.

The horse trailer bounced and swayed in the many ruts

and potholes in Marigold's driveway. Huntsman's black car hovered smoothly in front of it. They came to a stop. Sir Bear sat up and yawned. Huntsman walked up, wearing boots, jeans, and a knit vest over a white shirt. He had never seen her so relaxed.

She pet Sir Bear and said, "Why are you smirking, Mort?"

"How was your trip?"

"Productive."

Mort stood and stretched. "We've been productive, too. Come."

Mort led Huntsman through the house and onto the back porch. He heard Huntsman gasp.

Filling the grassy plain were, as of his last count, ninety-six horses. Their riders were camped in tents in a patch of wood nearby.

Huntsman held her hands to her head. "I thought we agreed on a subtle approach. Slip through undetected. I've chartered flights, Mortimer. The Kashmiri authorities are expecting—"

"Black Mare had a different idea."

"Melanie can explain to us, then, how she expects us to transport a hundred horses across the ocean."

"I'll let Claire explain that part." Mort whistled.

Claire poked her head up from behind a dapple-gray horse. From eighty yards away, Mort could tell she was not pleased at his whistle. He waved. She raised her eyebrows in rebuke.

"Okay, fine," Mort said to Huntsman. "I'll have to apologize for that one later. Anyhow, let me explain. After you left, Claire decided, in so many words, that Black Mare was telling all of us to fly like unicorns. But maybe that's a little professional envy. I'll let Dr. Doris Huntsman, Doctor of Psychology, decide that."

Huntsman fingered the hair on her nape and raised her own eyebrows.

"So," Mort said, "she finds the first horse she sees, mounts it bareback, and rides alongside Black Mare, who takes her on a chase. The next thing you know, whoop, up they go. Joe Curly and Grey Swan get in on the act. The rest is history. Everyone within riding distance starts showing up. They all want in on the Battle of Armageddon."

Huntsman leaned on the porch railing. "All this in three days. I had it timed perfectly with Commander Conque. The flight, everything. Once he's in space, swirling around the moonshock, we'll only be in laser comms for minutes at a time. I'll have to call. Reorganize everything. How many trailers will this take, do you think?"

Mort made a megaphone with his hands and called out, "Claire."

She leaned on her dapple gray.

Mort pointed to Huntsman then made a swirling motion with his hand.

Claire mounted and found Black Mare, and the two began trotting in a clockwise motion. One by one, the other horses followed. Their riders watched on as, after a minute, when all the horses were circling together in one glistening current, they rose into the air.

"I think that solves our transportation issue," Mort said.

***

Jody sat in the stone chair facing the globe and pedestal in the upper room of the Antarctic obelisk, sipping brandy and reading. Claire had sent the brandy, along with extra volumes of his breviary and other books, at his own cost. Major Darby had suggested this, citing the amount of time it would have taken to receive approval for costs associated with civilian contractors, et cetera. Darby had provided some Army-issue furniture and food rations. This stone chair was more comfortable. Jody sipped sparingly, not knowing when he could acquire another bottle.

The cables on the makeshift funicular Darby had installed began to move. Jody turned back to his reading of Saint-Exupéry. A few minutes later, two soldiers he recognized appeared in the birdcage followed by two soldiers he did not. Behind these were two older priests he did not know—no, they were bishops, he could tell, by the gold chain running from their collar to the jacket pocket where they had tucked their pectoral crosses. Coming out of the gray light of the dark city and the icy pantheon surrounding it and into the warm light of the obelisk room, Jody recognized one of the men as his own bishop. Jody had sent a letter with Claire asking permission to remain here until a secure situation could be arranged. It was obvious, with the bishop's arrival, that he did not approve and was here to escort Jody home.

Jody set down his book and brandy, grabbed his owl-head cane, and stood up.

"Joseph," the bishop said, walking in front of the other bishop, "I received your letter. This is a peculiar situation you put us in. Given its gravity, I asked the Holy Father's advice on what to do with you. All these years, I've tolerated your research with the OSS because it's promised some level of security to us. Whether that's true or not, I don't know. But to have you sit here and play Saruman with some occult device...let's just say I had letters ready to have you dismissed from the clerical state. The Holy Father, though, in his wisdom, has had another idea."

Jody's bishop stood to the side while another one walked forward. Jody held his head down and leaned on his cane. This was it for him: no more priesthood, no more wife, he would become a prisoner in this God-forsaken place.

"Pierre-Joseph," came the other bishop's voice, rich with African French.

Jody knew that voice. He looked up. Standing before him, in a black clerical suit, was Pope Sylvester III. Jody had seen his familiar face among the other bishop and four soldiers but would never have matched it to the pope without the white cassock.

"Your Holiness," Jody said, hobbling around the pedestal to kiss the Ring of the Fisherman.

"I want to see this device," Pope Sylvester said. "Place your hands on it."

Jody obeyed. An image came up of the fields surrounding Marigold's house, where Jody had last been looking. Horses were circling in the air, led by his daughter, Claire.

"Enough," the pope said. "I've long been sympathetic to your work and these strange realities. You've been a bridge for others and might even have saved many during the Great

Eclipse. But this is too much like playing God. As far as you know, there is no one else who can activate it?"

"No, your Holiness."

"Then we are all safer if no one is here at all. You are here because no one else should be. But you are standing at the devil's throne. I will not risk your soul for this. You will come to Rome and work at the Vatican Observatory. We will need you and your knowledge close at hand for what is coming. But you will never touch this crystal ball again."

***

Mort stood next to the horse Joe Curly had found for him, waiting. While he waited, he calculated the route again. The shortest path from Crow Country to Kashmir would take this team directly over the old North Pole and was seven thousand miles. That was over water, and so they would travel through Beringia, the ancient land bridge that had brought mankind to the Americas long ago, exposed again by the sinking seas. That was a longer route. A modern horse could walk at four miles per hour twenty or even thirty miles in a day. Without incident, this trip would take eight months. But a horse gifted with flight, such as were the one hundred and forty-one horses so far assembled for this journey, had already shown they could travel ten times as fast. They would make Kashmir in just over three weeks at forty miles per hour, eight hours per day. Mort remembered his week in the Wind Scout with Todd. No one here was used to traveling like this. Everyone was filled with more excitement than sense. But they lived in a world too full of excitement from specters. Perhaps it was finally time to push back.

Mort adjusted the crotch of his devonium-mesh suit, the same one he had worn in Antarctica.

Grey Swan, in war paint, feathers, and little else, hummed a critical note.

"It's going to get cold up in Alaska," Mort said.

"I'll wear a blanket."

"You're not afraid of specters here, but what about up there?"

Grey Swan looked directly at Mort and said, "Jesus fought the devil wearing nothing but a loincloth. I will do the same."

Before Mort could respond, he saw Grey Swan's eyes grow wide and heard cheers erupt from the gathered crowd.

Huntsman and Claire emerged from Marigold's house. Claire wore the white devonium-mesh uniform she had worn in Antarctica. She had painted white wings around her eyes. The only thing that kept Mort's legs from turning into noodles was the sight of Doris Huntsman: she wore a black devonium-mesh uniform, whose coat ran nearly to the ground, and had black wings trimmed in gold painted around her eyes. Claire was arrayed like the queen of Mort's heart that she was, but Huntsman was taking her seat on a throne in some dark kingdom long hidden in the man's primordial mind.

"Good God," Grey Swan said and ran his thumb across his flabby chest.

"You have any more war paint?" Mort said.

There were no speeches. Huntsman mounted Black Mare. Mort and Claire mounted their horses on each side of her, and, without a word, walked through the assembled regiment. A number of OSS specialists rode horses as well, and two drove the Trans Am with Sir Bear in the back seat. After a quarter mile, when the rest of the cavalry was lined up behind them and Marigold's ululations were thickening the air, Black Mare took her newly minted unicorns into the sky on their long march northward to the other side of the world.

PART SEVEN

○

STRANGE NEW SKY

37

It was midnight when Hudson MacDuff and eleven divers were woken and whisked without a spoken word in a hover personnel carrier to the top of a mountain in the Azores, which they reached in a few hours. Hand on the shoulder of the man in front of them, the team walked in silence on a grassy path, in the black of night, into a station without exterior lights, and which none of them had known existed. Once the exterior door closed behind them, hall lights came on and they released their hands. The door was a sealed hatch. The hallway was constructed of metal. This was a bunker in the mountain.

A commander named Thomas led them into what almost looked like the ready room of an aircraft carrier but whose seats rose out of low-walled pods with open glass canopies. Hudson counted twelve pods, six on each side of a narrow aisle. In the front of the room, on one side of a narrow, unmarked door, was a small counter with coffee and fresh pastries. "Relax, gentlemen," Thomas said.

Hudson sat in the narrow-cushioned pod chair reserved for him up front and ate his breakfast.

Marson pulled a lever in his chair, and a footrest sprang up. "Nice," he said.

Studdock, not to be outdone, pulled the lever on his chair. The footrest sprang into a horizontal position, and the back fell flat, sending him backwards and spilling hot coffee all over him.

While Studdock cursed heaven, hell, and everything in between, Hudson stood and looked at the room.

Above him, in the front of the room, a few stars shined through gasket windows. The entire rear wall seemed to be a loading ramp.

Devon Conque walked through the unmarked door next to Hudson into the room. He wore the uniform of a rear admiral.

"At ease, gentlemen. Take a seat," Conque said. He lowered his gaze at Studdock. "It's not bedtime yet, son.

"Listen up. As you know, a few months ago, mantle serpents penetrated the Hall of Watchers by coming through the muddy waters of the Mississippi. Many smaller attacks have taken place at sleeper centers across the world. No one knows if sleepers are waking up because of this, or if the snakes are attracted to waking sleepers. It's a chicken-and-egg thing, no pun intended.

"Anyhow, sonar shows massive movement across the sea floor from several distinct points across the globe: one near Easter Island, one near New Zealand, and one right here in the Azores. Our honey-brained humanoid friends have been making noises that seem to keep the serpents at bay, but caution tells us this will not last, as one by one they

succumb to some kind of reprogramming or outright shut-
down."

This is what Hudson had been experiencing with the
humanoids. He had begun to steer clear of them.

"We've been able to save some. We have two dozen
healthy humanoids stored on the deck below."

Someone groaned.

"The situation is dire. Philips and the OSS on our side,
as well as military intelligence across the world, have every
reason to believe a massive attack is imminent. The clock is
ticking down. I won't beat around the bush. This might see
a significant reduction in allied forces. We don't know what
these creatures are or what they're capable of. They seem
to do everything metal can do and more, from penetrating
steel hulls to swallowing presidents.

"The reason we're here right now is simple. This is the
only time we're likely ever going to get to send you men into
the moonshock. Look around. You might be humanity's last
hope, making contact with whatever lies beyond.

"As you have discovered, these seats fold down into
beds. This is where you'll sleep. This is where you'll eat. This
is your world until we reach a new one. Welcome to the *USS
Moonbright II* or what I call the *Dawn Shredder*. You are in
a US Navy spacecraft, and we are about to ride the biggest
wave of all time."

As those words danced around Hudson's ears, and as
he stared upward, through the windows, into the stars, the
only thought that came to him was of Lucy, sitting at home
in pain.

"We leave this volcanic crater and Earth behind at precisely o-five hundred, one hour from now. Commander Thomas will take your questions and give you the grand tour. Get to know this place like you know your own body."

Hudson stood and saluted with the others, as Conque walked through the hatch back into the cockpit.

Commander Thomas stood in front of a projector screen coming down from the ceiling. "Any questions, gentlemen?"

"Sir," Studdock said. "We understand the urgency, but are we mission-ready? Doing this kind of science during wartime—"

"This is not a science experiment, Studdock. You are all scouts. The *Dawn Shredder* has already breached what's become of the outer Van Allen belt. Everything about this mission is a known entity except what's going to happen to your bodies at the moonshock."

No one moved a muscle inside the ready room. A bird perched on the window, startling Hudson.

"Sir," Marson said, "why are none of the female divers with us? If we are going to another world, maybe we should, you know...."

"They may follow separately, Marson. The choice of this crew was made at the highest levels. The twelve of you are the pioneers. You have the humanoids to help. If there are no other questions, let's go through some protocol."

Hudson sat down with the others. After a year of sublime adventures in New Norfolk, New York, the Azores, Atlantis, Antarctica, and the Great Meteor Seamount, he would spend what was likely the last days of his life stuffed in a sardine can with killer robots.

***

Lucy lay on her side, on the couch in New Norfolk A-III. Her back was feeling better, but not completely. Perhaps this was why Huntsman had not invited her to ride horseback for seven thousand miles and send Mort into the Himalayas. She should not feel so bad; Jody had been summoned to Rome, confined to quarters at the Vatican Observatory. At least he had a garden nearby. All Lucy had was concrete and mud.

A Naval officer had come a few minutes ago to tell her, in all secrecy, that Hudson had launched into space with Devon Conque, who had been appointed Rear Admiral just hours before. Lucy wanted to have said more at Hudson's surprise birthday party in the Azores. But she had nothing more to say. She had nothing more to give this world. Declan was long dead. Owen was making his own way, doing well at the Academy. Lucy was not ageless, as were Jody and Huntsman, Danny and Cynthia, White Wolf and Marigold. Who knew where they kept their private picture of Dorian Gray—maybe it was a humanoid, hidden away somewhere. Lucy would live forever in her two children. Three. And Lucy would keep that first one frozen in her private picture frame and do like all mothers do, like every flower that blossoms and sends her pollen upon the wind: shrivel up and die.

She pulled Peter Panda close to her breast. "It's just you and me, kid. Like old times."

Lucy remembered her first meeting with Wepwawet Mountain West, a lifetime ago:

Lucy had come into the conference room at the FBI office in Denver, her fingers still tingling with Declan's last caress. None of the agents looked up at her, busy scrolling through their phones or talking in pairs. Dr. Huntsman showed her to her seat and drew everyone's attention. White Wolf kept staring off into space, and Melanie Black Mare waved her hand in front of his face, saying "Yoo-hoo" or something similar.

"Everyone," Huntsman began, "this is Dr. Lucy Mac-Duff, née Ryddenhouse, Professor of Geology at UC Boulder."

A few barely audible groans of acknowledgment told Lucy they already knew her better than she would have liked.

"Lucy is fine," she said.

"Professor MacDuff, you certainly are aware of the serious nature of the events occurring near the Earth right now."

Lucy looked at Huntsman, who had stopped talking and was obviously looking for a response. Lucy nodded and shrugged. Who did not know about the moondark?

"Right. And so, please understand that our continued interest in your case is for the benefit of all our understanding. For the good of mankind, perhaps. You are not in any trouble here. We are simply gathering information."

Lucy looked at her again then at White Wolf.

"For the record," Eric Lees asked, "would you recount the events of January 20, 2016?"

Lucy leaned forward. "We were collecting data on the mineral content of water in the basal channels. An opening to the channel had appeared when an ice shelf fell. I went in and got lost. When I tried to lead the others to where I had been, it was blocked off again."

Lees flipped through some papers in a file. "Everyone there attests to some other phenomena as well. Dinosaur bones that appeared and disappeared. And you stated before that you found an artificial rock, some kind of crafted cube of marble and lapis lazuli. Do you still have it?"

"It's at home. I didn't know I needed it now."

"You don't. That's fine. No, what we're interested in knowing is what you experienced when you found that rock. What you saw or felt."

She thought a moment. "Hate," Lucy said. "No, not hate. That's not the right word. I've felt hate before. This was, um, frustration. Intense frustration. Terror. Like a prisoner on death row or something. Looking at me in the darkness."

"Did you speak to this, oh, I don't know, thing, this entity?" he asked.

"I never do," Lucy said, turning her head sharply in regret.

"I'm sorry," Lees replied. "What does that mean, 'I never do'?"

White Wolf cleared his throat. The others gave him the floor. She looked at him and felt at once at home in his deep eyes.

"Lucy, this is not the first time you've experienced something of this nature, is it?"

She looked down.

"Lucy, you'll find you're in sympathetic company here. This is the kind of thing we want to know."

She felt her arms, hands, and fingers begin to frost over.

"Let me tell you what I see, then. You had a traumatic experience, and still you went on to complete your masters and doctorate in geology. You're terrified here, too, and something still gives you the strength. You're like a taut wire, a guitar string pulled too tight. That won't last, Lucy. Those strings snap. So the more you open up to us about your fears now, even though we're strangers, the more we all can relax before what we're facing. Because, believe it or not, I believe that what you've been facing on your own your whole life the whole world is soon going to face all together. And so, we just need your experience to help us. Teach us your fear, Lucy."

Twenty-nine years later, alone on her couch, Lucy replied to White Wolf, "Why, Billy? What good would it do?"

***

Hudson strapped into his seat. He had already found a nook for Amy Anklesore in his cubicle. It had been on top of his ready bag at the barracks, and, in the blur of being woken up three hours after going to bed, he had never questioned taking the pink-and-purple dinosaur with him. In ten minutes, though, he would be heading into space, and Lucy's old companion with him.

Commander Thomas was in the cockpit with Conque and a crew of three. While the divers waited, they watched a video in which Thomas explained the route they would take to the moonshock.

Our trajectory assumes the condition that the Earth is physically wrapped around the moonshock.

A cutaway diagram appeared, in which the moonshock occupied most of the space that the inside-out Earth had enclosed.

We take a spiraling course out of Earth's atmosphere until we reach the outer Van Allen belt. This is not our most energy-efficient trajectory, but it is the only way through the Van Allen, which has become a massive gravity cliff. Going straight at it would be like taking an ocean wave sideways. Once we cross this wave, which has been lensing light from the moonshock, making it look bigger, outer space will open up to us again. We'll head to the edge of the moonshock from there.

The animated spaceship, the first glimpse Hudson had had of the craft he was in, took a spiraling course inside the Earth toward the center. After it crossed the dashed line representing the Van Allen belt, the blue circle representing the moonshock grew very small.

Hudson looked at Marson, next to him. His eyes were cartoon spirals of incomprehension.

"How long is all this going to take?" Hudson whispered.

Our estimated travel time to the gravity cliff is two days. After that, it will be four days to the moonshock.

After reviewing a few more nuts and bolts, the video ended and the projector screen withdrew into the ceiling.

Hudson checked his watch. Less than one minute remained.

Thomas's voice came over the speaker. "Strap in."

A deep hum tested the rivets and welds of the *Dawn Shredder.* Hudson gripped his armrests. The hum drilled deep into Hudson's bones and circled around his eye sockets. The machine jerked quickly left and right.

Marson's wide eyes met Hudson's. "It's going to be that kind of trip, huh?"

A green light came on between the windows.

Hudson's stomach sank into his pelvis.

After misting the windows briefly, the clouds broke away before the first violet traces of dawn. The ship was ascending in a horizontal position. Hudson would not see the Earth fall away. He could not say goodbye.

A few minutes later, the violet in the windows gave way to white haze and then a rippled silver-blue.

"That is the ocean," Studdock said from across the aisle.

"How...?" Hudson began. The Earth was curving upward, before him. The waves that had just been below their ship rose around them in all directions. Hudson looked for the black of space, but the windows showed only ocean until, finally, the east coast of North America, distant and hazy, fell downward across the windows.

In half a second, Hudson saw the wide wash of mud that was the continental shelf and located the Virginia coast. Lucy was down there. Maybe someone had told her to look up from her widow's walk and wave.

The land continued to fall toward the front of the window. In a few minutes, the Appalachian Mountains appeared.

Rear Admiral Conque's voice came over the loudspeaker. "We're over Norfolk now. Wave goodbye."

Abyssus abyssum invocat

It was the middle of a mild summer in the hills above Anchorage, Alaska. Mort, Claire, and Huntsman had been leading their ever-growing army for two thousand miles. It had been five ten-hour days. Some of their number had turned back, not because riding a horse was hard—galloping on a cushion of air had been as hard on horse and human as driving down a paved road on rubber tires—but because, one by one, horse or human had suddenly grown fearful. It was not natural to fly. Claire had known this from her experiments with winged unicorns. Horse and human needed to feel the ground.

They had followed the Continental Divide, keeping far from peering eyes, but reports kept finding strange activity along the sea coasts. Mort and Claire had insisted they go as directly as possible to Kashmir, which would have been across northern Alaska. Doris Huntsman, ever vigilant, had suggested they gallop by Juneau and Anchorage, for reasons of global security. That the Pacific Coast was ten to fifteen degrees warmer than the interior had nothing to do with it, she had insisted.

Two hundred and twelve horsemen hid behind a large

hill; Claire was with the horses. Mort, Huntsman, Joe Curly, and Grey Swan lay on the ground with four OSS specialists, surveying the scene. The inlet from the ocean had drained almost thirty years ago, during the Great Eclipse, and the city connected to the sea via the Knik River. Something had used that conduit to make landfall. The humans on the hill could not see it. Ten humanoids, assembled in a pattern of paired hexagons on the river's edge, could see it. They were pointing and speaking.

"That's not the language I heard," Mort whispered.

"Nor the language with which we've learned to communicate with them," Huntsman said.

"I think they're just talking really fast," Joe Curly said.

"Faster than we could understand unless we recorded and replayed it slowly," Huntsman said. She took out a device of some kind.

"Don't," Mort said. "You can't see without being seen, remember? We're not here for this."

"Since when did you become an expedition leader?" Huntsman said.

"Since you dropped me and Todd into a hole in the ground without help."

Mort thought he caught Huntsman snarling as she turned away. The water stirred. Mort looked through the binoculars. As soon as the first glimmer of nickel-iron broke the surface, he lay the binoculars aside. He could see from afar what was coming next.

A mantle serpent raised its faceless head like a cobra ready to strike. The head split into six, and each new head hovered above a humanoid. Two more humanoids walked forward. The six-headed serpent seemed to be confused: it was looking for a hexagonal pattern in the standing humanoids, but since they formed two hexagons joined along one segment, the serpent could not decide which hexagon to engorge. The two other humanoids appeared to be directing the mantle serpent, but it grew more confused, fused its six heads into two, and swallowed the two free-standing humanoids.

A full minute after it retreated into the river, a few human beings in Native parkas emerged from a building. They gave directions to the ten humanoids still standing in the pattern of paired hexagons. The humanoids followed the humans back into the building.

"Is that an OSS technique?" Mort said.

"Not exactly," Huntsman said.

"That's Native intelligence," Grey Swan said.

"Let's go talk to them," Huntsman said.

"No," Mort said. "We're on flying horses. They've got humanoids. We don't want to threaten these people, theirs or ours, any further, you know?"

"I think Mort's right," Joe Curly said. "We've got our mission."

***

Hudson had hardly slept in two days. It was not the excitement of the mission or even being in space for the first time. It was the strobe lights the windows of the *Dawn Shredder* had become. Land, sea, light, and dark rushed toward the men in marbled streaks. The craft was completing a circuit of the Earth's circumference every twenty minutes. They were racing toward the Van Allen belt at nearly one hundred thousand miles per hour. Whenever Hudson had managed to close his eyes, a ten-minute day throbbed through the ready room. No one had thought to bring sleeping masks. Conque kept assuring the men this was the hardest part of the trip to the moonshock.

"And here comes the best part," came Conque's voice through the intercom. "We're about to sail off the gravity cliff. Seats upright. Strap in. Y'all are about to be tripping balls."

Hudson looked at Marson. He was baggy-eyed and slack-jawed, too exhausted for any excitement.

Thirty seconds to Van Allen.

Studdock was tapping his fingers on the armrest.

Hudson held his hands at his stomach. He almost reached out for Amy Anklesore.

Ready.

The starry sphere of the moonshock soared up and away. Hudson's stomach tried to follow it through his throat. The blurry streaks of Earth raced forward and hid behind a blanket of darkness. Hudson's feet floated up. Someone's vomit coalesced into a floating ball.

"Sorry," Marson said. "Could someone catch that?"

We're through.

"What just happened?" Hudson said.

"Get up," Conque said. "Float to the windows. You'll see."

Hudson unbuckled his belt and pulled himself with his hands toward the windows ahead.

He could see the other side of the Earth.

Far away, no bigger than the sun had been in the sky, was

the moonshock, black and shimmering with stars. Beyond it was planet Earth, lit up by the sun somehow held within the moonshock's tiny ball. He saw the vast blue Pacific Ocean. As the *Dawn Shredder* rounded the moonshock, it entered into the daytime the Pacific was enjoying. But Hudson could see North America already cloaked in night. Sacramento, Phoenix, Salt Lake City, and Denver each glowed like constellations. The *Dawn Shredder* passed into that night. The moonshock was a ball of stars again.

Hudson watched with the other divers for an hour. With each pass across the Earth, it was clear they were still lifting upward from its surface. But the moonshock did not grow bigger as it came closer.

"Why is that?" Hudson said.

Conque said, "This, gentlemen, is how you fit four hundred thousand miles of space, the old distance to the moon and back, inside the diameter of Earth. The Van Allen belt had magnified the moonshock before. Now, we see where we're really going: to the center of a vortex, hyperbolic space, the black hole hiding the rest of the universe from us."

"It's so small," Marson said.

"That's how big the moon looked in the sky before all this," Conque said. "It'll get bigger again, eventually. We'll make our turn toward it soon. Watch it fill up the windows over the next four days. Watch the moon become your world again."

***

At the end of two weeks, Mort, Claire, Huntsman and their army neared the site of the Siberian borehole that Mort and Todd had once taken to hell and back. They had in-

341

creased to a two hundred and fifty-one riders, skirting the edge of winter encroaching from Europe, camping as they went on what used to be islands in the Arctic Ocean.

A skeleton crew of Russian scientists and security personnel welcomed Mort, Huntsman, and their team. The Russians had been planning to pump the mud out of the borehole. The second dervish they'd had on site last year was ready for use. Mort tried on the extra space suit once made for him. It was a bit tight now. He held up the one meant for Todd. Todd might still be wearing the other one, for all he knew.

Mort took up his old bed in the trailer he had shared with Todd last year. Todd would not be in the upper bunk this time. Joe Curly and Grey Swan had been good companions on this long trek, but none of this could measure up to the adventure he had shared with Todd, an adventure that had made him into the man he was now, a year after waking up from the long sleep his life had always been. The seven-thousand-mile journey on horseback Mort was making simply felt like a march into battle.

These had been Claire's feelings as well. As Mort had learned over the past few months of dating her, she had spent a lot of time in situations like this. She had grown up in the shadow of Cheyenne Mountain, ready to run from specters at a moment's notice. Once the Faraday fences started going up, first in Denver and Boulder and then everywhere else, she had found ways to break free. Huntsman had first come back from the Azores with a magic carpet of wool and orichalcum over twenty years ago; within weeks of that find from the ancient world, her scientists had drawn the connections from it to what made Father Joseph's car, the white Trans Am Kai and Av had given him to replace the blue one, hover. Claire had not been far behind, weaving the material into wings for her horses. While Father Joseph had been reciting poetry to his sleeping wife, Claire had been developing ways to master the new world with Danny and Cynthia.

If this trek on hovering horseback was to be life-changing for anyone, it might be for Huntsman the most. She had not said much in these two weeks. She was far out of her element. There was nothing to measure, no one to lead into a strange new world except herself. She'd had intuitions about Jody and Lucy, Mort and Todd, and many others over the years. Some special knowledge she had about Hudson was leading her and hundreds of men and women on horseback seven thousand miles into certain danger and uncertain rewards.

As Mort was about to fall asleep, words welled upward on the wave of a memory. He had been speaking with White Wolf one day about the special powers some people were manifesting in this strange new world:

"*Abyssus abyssum invocat,*" White Wolf had said.

"Okay," Mort said.

"A person is an infinite well. That's where your power comes from. From one person to another. Everything I can do comes out of love for my sister, Lola."

Mort let himself absorb these words again. Todd had said something similar once, that the inverted universe, with its hyperbolic space, was like the person White Wolf was describing, an infinite well. Maybe Huntsman did have some deep connection with Hudson and that was what had been driving her intuition about him. Doris Huntsman had been pairing people together over the years, each a conductor of special power, and watching divine electricity arc between them. Now, she, herself, had been held close to someone, Hudson MacDuff, and sparks of some kind had flown between them, even if they had only seen each other briefly every few years. This was what Kai and Av had ridden to Danny and Cynthia's house to make her see. Black Mare had seen it in her own special way and had told Huntsman so. Huntsman was no longer here to stand back and measure. She was a conducting wire of supernatural power, as ignorant of the God supplying her patients with cosmic energy as she was of herself as Zeus's lightning rod. A devonium lightning rod.

Just as Mort's mind settled on the conclusion that devonium, also known as orichalcum, was a literal conductor for divine power, he fell asleep.

***

Hudson used to watch the sun set as a child, standing with Lucy and Declan on the widow's walk. He remembered now one such occasion, when Lucy had been round with Owen. He used to kiss her belly every day, counting down the months and weeks and days until his little brother was born. "You don't notice it happening," Declan had said, "then it comes all at once. Just like you did. Just like this sunset. You can't see how fast the sun moves across the sky until it's near the horizon. Then, just like that, it's gone."

Six days to the moonshock had become four and then three, at which point Devon Conque began measuring in hours. They had finally come close enough for the moon-shock to poke its star-stubbled chin below the top of the windows. If, on Earth, the moonshock had been the mag-nified face of a mother hovering just above her baby, a face that smiled upon his whole world, the moonshock was, in the depths of space, the stern gaze of a father, urging his son into the unknown.

All the lights were out in the ready room, where Hud-son and the others sat. They circled the moonshock in silence. Hudson stared through the windows. He was here to see something the others could not, a pathway through the moonshock. If he could not see anything special, they would return to Earth. He and Marson and Studdock and the rest of this crew would enter the fray, the frenzied battle mounting on Earth's shores. In the end, it might mean very little to break through the moonshock. But if hope was food for the journey forward, it must be made out of the stuff of the present. For the first time since he had been alone in the darkness of another abyss, falling down the side of the Great Meteor Seamount, Hudson prayed.

"Dear God, if it's You who've given everyone else confi-dence in me, prove them right. Show me what You want me to see."

39

Lucy stood on the widow's walk, gazing at a canyon in the clouds, through which a river of stars coursed. Hudson would pass by soon. The same Naval officer who had told her Hudson had launched with Devon Conque had told her that the Van Allen belt would magnify their ship just like it did the moonshock and everything inside it. Lucy had seen his shooting star pass by several times, the *Dawn Shredder* lit by the graviton motors that pushed it away from Earth on its steeply curving path around the moonshock.

She had set on the railing the white-and-blue cube of stone someone had once tossed at her in Antarctica, and which she had used to open the corridor that had led her to Hudson. But Mort and Claire had also found another way through, the way Todd had shown, the way Hudson had opened, the oculus above the chamber where he had lain. Lucy had needed to lead the others on her path—Mort never would have led the team to the right place from above if she and Jody had not been standing there, if Nogales had not radioed, if Ethel and that girl had not led them there first.

That girl. Lucy knew exactly who she looked like, someone long gone, someone Declan's bright blue eyes had burned away from her memory.

Someone was climbing the steps to the widow's walk.

"Mrs. MacDuff?"

It was Benny.

"What are you doing here?" Lucy said.

"You sent for me." Benny reached the rooftop and brushed imagined dust off his pants.

"I sent for Hazel."

"She's not coming out in this."

The four-pulse alarm had rung for an hour earlier today before someone had shut it off. This had not meant the coast was clear. Another series of pulses would sound when that declaration was made.

"I thought they would've sent you back to Norfolk," Lucy said. She knew Benny was on leave for a few days.

"We're locked down until secure transport comes. So what did you want Hazel for?"

Lucy picked up the cube of marble and lapis lazuli. "This is for her."

"What is it?"

"It opens doors."

Benny sighed. "Wouldn't you want to give your weird woo-woo stuff to Hudson?"

"This is for mothers and daughters."

"We're not people like you, Mrs. MacDuff. We don't have powers."

"Look at me, Benny. I don't have powers, either. Can't you see how I'm aging, where they're not? I'm a person they use, they look through. It wasn't me who saved Boulder. It was Hudson. He was in my belly at the time. Now he's up there. He leapt into the ocean once to save you. Now he'll save all of us."

"What are you saying? Our fences are handling specters. How bad is this gonna get? Are we all going to die here?"

Lucy closed Benny's hands over the cube. "Not with you and Hazel out there at the gates." She pulled up his chin with her finger as if he were a child crying about something.

Benny looked up. The *Dawn Shredder* slipped across the canyon in the clouds.

***

It was a clear day in Kashmir. Mort stood with Huntsman and Claire, Joe Curly and Grey Swan, and four hundred men and women on horseback, above the snow line of a mountain called Nanga Parbat overlooking a broad valley in the Himalayas. With them were a group of Pandits, guardians of this part of Kashmir. Also with them were Danny and Cynthia, who had joined them, via a trip to Iran, at camp in Tajikistan and whose function today Mort could not imagine.

Huntsman was gazing upward. Hudson MacDuff and Devon Conque were up there; everyone could see the *Dawn Shredder* streaking across the moonshock at night.

"Doris?" Mort said.

She was standing next to Black Mare.

"Doris?" Claire echoed and rubbed her arm.

"Let's give them eyes," Huntsman said. She mounted Black Mare.

"Doris," Mort said. He made knowing eyes at Claire. "Claire will lead the horses with Black Mare."

Huntsman knit her brow. "Who's in charge of this mission, anyway?"

"You are, Doris, which is why you need to go inside with me. You're the one this time."

Huntsman looked out over the valley. "Who will ride Black Mare?"

Claire said, "One of the specialists. She'll lead the charge. I'll follow. Joe Curly and Grey Swan will flank me."

"Come on," Mort said. "We're burning daylight here. And the *Dawn Shredder*'s burning up battery. They're waiting on us."

Huntsman dismounted Black Mare and kissed her. Mort opened the door of the white Trans Am. The calvary cheered. Claire mounted her dapple gray, and the others followed. Mort sat in the driver's seat of the car. In the rearview mirror, sitting on either side of Sir Bear, were Danny and Cynthia.

Before Mort could ask what they were doing, Danny said, "It's simple: if this fails, and we lose Claire, there's nothing else this world needs us for. And besides, you could use our help to lay laser-line hubs on your way in. Fewer distractions."

"That's not everything," Cynthia said. "Tell him about Shush."

Danny turned toward the window.

"We stopped in Iran on our way here. In Danny's old town, where he was born, we made a little homage at the tomb of the prophet Daniel," Cynthia said. "He spoke to Danny."

"What'd he say?" Mort said.

"To go all the way," Cynthia said.

"In so many words," Danny said. "Come on. Let's go."

Mort looked forward. He gave Claire the thumbs-up. She blew him a kiss. Happy courage filled Mort's veins like fire. His first instinct about Claire had been right: she was a genius and an Amazonian goddess. He had helped bring it out of her. He would not stop until she was queen of the universe.

Black Mare started forward. War cries and ululations filled the air inside the arrow the horses had formed, with Black Mare and Claire at the tip. Mort was in the center, the head of the shaft. "You ready, Doris?"

She did not answer. Her eyes, set again like pearls in black painted wings, looked straight ahead.

Black Mare led the horses across the saddle of the mountain in the arrow formation. When she disappeared over the edge, Claire followed her. Mort's stomach leapt upward. Joe Curly and Grey Swan were next, shouting as they went over. Mort watched two hundred pairs of horse rumps and jubilant riders gallop over the mountainside. Like on a rollercoaster, the chain of bodies fell faster as more of them made their descent, and Mort had no time to ponder the edge of the steep mountain slope before he pushed the Trans Am over it. The sight of the broad and seemingly bottomless valley sucked the air out of his lungs. The only way to grab it back was with a war cry.

The snow line rushed quickly beneath Mort, and he was

racing over treetops at three hundred miles per hour. Not a horse ahead had stumbled, and no rider had fallen. It took thirty seconds to reach the valley floor at this speed.

But Black Mare was slowing down.

"Why...?" Huntsman began when it became clear to everyone.

A thick woven cord of specters and mantle snakes was streaming out of the mountain, and when it seemed they noticed Black Mare, the glinting mass of them turned toward her as one serpentine body. Mort had expected something like this. What he had not expected was that, when Black Mare slowed down, the air in front of her and the other horses would fold like the wake behind a boat. She was turning speed into power.

When they slowed to forty miles per hour, Black Mare began kicking her hoofs more rapidly. The other horses imitated her. She touched down on the ground. Mort had thought she might lead the horses above the stream of specters-and-snakes, but Black Mare was building a battering ram. The earth quaked with the pounding of sixteen hundred hoofs. In the bent light of the wake of air shielding the horses, Mort could see the evil serpent splinter into a thousand pieces. Each of those pieces burst into sparks against the arrow of bent air until a wall of electric fire filled his field of vision.

Through it all, Mort saw the entrance to the cave ahead. He knew that once he was shrouded in darkness, no specter could touch him. Claire was still following Black Mare. Within a few feet of the cave, Claire went right and Black Mare went left. The wall of spectral fire opened liked a cat's eye. He slipped the car through the cat's eye, and, safe inside the cave, he slowed down. He expected to exhale a long-stowed breath, but found he had been breathing normally.

A lidar map came up on a screen propped on the dashboard.

"Is it over yet?" Cynthia said.

"You missed the best part," Danny said. Cynthia had shut her eyes at some point.

"You ain't seen nothin' yet," Mort said. "You either, Doris."

Huntsman, eyes wide open, said nothing.

***

A proud smile rose on Lucy's lips. She stood on the steps of the Old Barracks, a full head above the crowd in front of her. John Dungloe, Hazel's father, was giving a rousing speech. The Faraday fence had repulsed a constant stream of specters from the sea all day. This was a lull, but it would not last. Reports from Wind Scouts showed concentrations of spectral forces underwater all along the coast. *This is the first of our last great battles*, Dungloe had said. Lucy knew why: the sea had sunk below the line of its old mesopelagic zone, the so-called "Twilight Zone" of the ocean, where no light had reached in almost twelve thousand years, six hundred and sixty feet below sea level in the old world. This was where the beast had been hiding all this time, and now he was exposed.

A gauntlet stood ready at the city gate, two double rows of men and women, many of them volunteers. Benny took his place in a front row, a body or two from the Old Barracks. Two more sets of interior gates on either side of the Old Barracks blocked the way to the rest of town. If those gates fell, everyone would be on their own.

Lucy saw specters rise like a wave out of the sea. They flowed together across the muddy surface of the ground and formed one thick, slow, heavy serpent around which mantle snakes spiraled. Cannons pounded balls of charged devonium against it. No human budged when sparks, blown over the wall, singed their armor. The composite serpent split, reformed, and continued, fed by an endless surge from the sea. The heavy devonium gates of the city burned copper-red and bent inward.

This was Lucy's final moment. She would spend herself and save another city.

The serpent breached the gates, which melted off their hinges. The crowd was silent as the serpent slithered into the city square. It did not strike. Men and women shot at it with devonium bullets and sliced it with orichalcum spears. Sparks flew, and the many faceless heads of the heavy serpent of bent light stopped. Its long body continued to emerge from the sea. Everyone backed away as it coiled around itself in the city square. Its outer coils pressed the people against the concrete buildings surrounding the square. Some yelled to open the inner gates and others prevented them. Everyone shot and slashed at the monstrous specter. So did Benny. He was pressed against Lucy. Everyone would soon suffocate, pressed against each other. Most snakes suffocated their prey by coiling around them. This one suffocated by squeezing human bodies against each other, against their own city.

It was time. Lucy squatted into the fetal position and prayed. Nothing happened.

She rocked back and forth. Nothing stirred inside her. Nothing trembled. Hudson had been inside her before. No one was there now. Hudson was up in space. Owen was in Annapolis. Lucy had no one to protect, no one whose salvation demanded tearing open the universe. She could not summon enough love for New Norfolk to stop this invasion, not even enough for herself.

"Declan, my love," Lucy began, when words welled up through her. "Benny," she yelled.

He turned.

"Your name is Hector."

The slight cock of Benny's head and the deepening of his dimples meant he understood.

Benny turned, put the bayonet of his rifle against his chin, and charged the devonium rod.

Benny was already in the air when Lucy regained her sight from the blast. His eyes glowed blue like Jody's had after killing the man who had emerged from the ice. The specter-serpent raised its head toward him. The higher Benny hovered, the higher the serpent went, coiling around itself for support. It was a writhing pillar, an obelisk of bent light. Benny turned his rifle around to face the ground. As if by simply willing it, he thrust himself to Earth.

Lucy woke up a second or a minute later, she did not know. All was silent except for the melted city gate creaking on its hinges. Something was burning, but Lucy saw no flames. Sparks had torn holes in her dress, the dress she had worn because Declan had loved it and because she could squat easily in it.

The serpent was gone. In its place, lying at the center of the city square, was Benny. Smoke rose from his charred body. Hazel ran to him. One by one, men and women who had filled the city square struggled upward. Many did not stand up again.

Lucy knelt next to Benny, across from Hazel. The cube of marble and lapis lazuli was tied in a kind of sling around Benny's waist. Lucy untied it and pressed it into Hazel's hand. Hazel gripped it though she kept looking at Benny, her eyes and mouth wide with pain but muted by wonder.

Lucy stood up, looked at the crowd and at Benny, and turned toward the ocean. It would not be long before they were attacked again. Lucy let her dress fall to her ankles. A breeze caressed her naked body. She walked along the narrow finger of land on which New Norfolk was built, toward the sea.

40

Mort steered the Trans Am very slowly through a narrow crevice that was miles deep. This was not a neat borehole. It was a tear between mountain and valley. Lidar imaging promised ever deeper access to crust and mantle but not without constant turning and doubling back. The lidar map provided by local intelligence—Pandits crawling in the darkness with laser pointers—had been as useful as a Renaissance map of the New World.

"Here be dragons," Mort said.

"Not so much a myth anymore, are they?" Danny said.

"There's a blue light down there," Huntsman said. It was the first she had spoken in twenty minutes.

Mort knew what a blue light meant. But they were a thousand miles or more from the underside of the mantle. To shine through that strongly, especially where the crust was thicker—

"Mort, watch out!" Huntsman said.

He jerked the wheel, narrowly missing a thick stalactite.

"I thought we were going straight down," Mort said. "What's that hanging from?"

No one answered.

"Are we losing our sense of gravity already?"

"I'm about to lose my mind," Cynthia said. "We should not have come here."

"You're the one who suggested it," Danny said. "You felt all cooped up at home."

"And what about what the prophet Daniel said?" she said.

Danny took her hand. "He knows what makes for a happy marriage."

Mort made a mental note, as he had been doing of everything regarding Danny and Cynthia, the only happily married couple he knew.

"He was single," Huntsman said.

Danny bounced his eyebrows as if to say, *Way to spoil the moment.*

"That's how he was able to see the things he did," Huntsman continued.

Mort did not know if this was true or not. Maybe it had been true of Mort and Todd, but not Jody and Lucy. Huntsman was probably talking about herself. Or Hudson.

"I see your blue light," Mort said. There was a narrow slit in the rock ahead. He steered the Trans Am slowly through. The rear tires bounced the car off the bottom edge of the opening, and just as the rear spoiler was about to hit the top edge, Mort accelerated forward and missed it. Lidar showed a massive chamber ahead. Mort breathed. "I think this goes all the way. Uh, so once again, you guys aren't worried about your mental state when we pass one thirty-three?"

"What's this about mental states?" Cynthia said.

"We're not worried," Huntsman said. "Todd is still down here."

"Meaning?" Cynthia said.

"Meaning we're in my world now," Mort said. "Forget I said anything."

"Do you know what they're talking about?" Cynthia asked Danny.

"Beats me," Danny said.

"Then let's go," Mort said. "Gravity will get us down there in a few minutes. Hold on to your lunch."

In a few minutes, the Trans Am fell past the gravity well, and Mort thrust downward. "Down is the new up," he said.

"I'm going to throw up," Danny said.

"We'll be stable soon. I hope."

Huntsman pushed a slight puff of air through pursed lips.

"What?" Mort said. "Hope is a strong word. It's based on certain knowledge. Claire's been teaching me."

"Watch the road," Huntsman said.

There was no road. The slice of rock through which Mort had breached the Himalayan mountainside had broadened into a canyon and was now a valley of its own a thousand miles deep.

"It's almost like the Earth is breaking apart," Mort said. "Imagine that. What's even holding it together now, all turned inside out?"

"Is this how you get through a journey into hell?" Cynthia said.

Mort rubbed his hands against the steering wheel. "Todd and I had a good sense of humor about all this, you know?" Mort eyed Danny in the rearview mirror. Danny was as serious as Mort had ever seen him. Danny's sense of humor had stopped at the Earth's surface. "Maybe that's what helped."

No one spoke while the Trans Am fell upward through the mantle. The blue light was reflecting off the strands of metal that made up the old core of the Earth and which now comprised its strange new sky. Where those strands still glowed hot red, the blue light blended with it to make a purple hue.

"We're about to break through," Mort said. "I'm going to flatten out the car to give us more control."

Mort turned the nose down, and the force of the car's thrust drifted from his back to his butt. He did so just in time.

Gasps broke out from Huntsman, Danny, and Cynthia. Even Mort was surprised. The underside of the mantle was covered with blue spiral cities, like the one he had seen under Siberia. They dotted the spongy surface of the rock as far as the new horizon would let them see.

"Maybe this is where everyone went," Huntsman said.

"Each of those cities fits a lot of land inside it. Mini continents, almost."

"We're not here for those," Huntsman said. "But we are definitely coming back."

Mort heard sniffling in the back. It was Danny.

"All these people," Danny said. He slapped his thighs and pounded Mort's headrest.

Mort knew Danny's brother, Sunny, Sunny's wife, Leila, and their son, Cyrus, had been missing since the Great

Eclipse. "Right, so, where do you think this portal'd be?" Mort said.

Huntsman swiped at the lidar map. An orange star floated not far from where they were, just a few hundred miles away, disconnected from the three-dimensional map they had thus far made.

"Why'd you put it there?" Mort said.

"It's a hunch. Hudson fell through his portal exactly sixty degrees west of the pyramids of Giza, on the exact same line of latitude, thirty degrees north. Given the spectral activity coming out of Nanga Parbat nearby, which is almost sixty degrees east, I thought, 'Why not try?'"

"I'd buy that," Danny said.

"You and your alien shows," Cynthia said.

"Look around, honey," Danny said. "I'm not saying it's aliens, but...."

"This is not aliens," Mort said with more force than he had intended and yet as much as the response required.

"Why aren't the mantle snakes coming after us?" Cynthia said. "I thought we'd be dodging them."

Mort looked at the Firebird emblem on the hood of the Trans Am. It had been glowing blue since they had passed the gravity well. "Simple biology. Snakes are afraid of birds."

"They are not real snakes, biologically speaking," Cynthia said. "Right?"

"Try telling them that," Huntsman said.

"What does that mean?" Danny said.

"It means," Mort said, "it's not just that we make the other, our enemy, into the things we fear. It's making itself into those things, too, and even it can't tell the difference. This evil runs deep. It runs back on itself."

***

Hovering at just under the speed of sound, they reached the presumed location of the portal. There were no blue spiral cities of ice around. There was some atmosphere, enough for Todd's Lichen to grow.

"Now what?" Danny said.

"Now we go down," Mort said. He slowed the car at just a few feet above the surface and tried to look over the side, through the closed window. "This would have been easier in the dervish."

"But we'd still be trudging through the mountain in that thing," Huntsman said.

"Glad we have this car, then," Mort said.

"Thank Uncle Kai and Uncle Av."

Mort rolled the car so he could see the surface. There was a faint glow from the ground. Todd's Lichen had responded to direct touch from devonium before. The graviton discharge from the Trans Am's hover coils was not enough to make them fluoresce, at least at this distance. Mort landed.

Huntsman turned her head sharply in rebuke.

Mort drove ahead and looked through the rearview mirror. He was right. The lichen glowed.

Huntsman twisted back, saw the glowing lichen, and faced forward. "It will take forever like this."

"Doris," Cynthia said, "can we stop and assess for a moment? We're driving a hovering muscle car across the Earth's mantle, a thousand miles below the surface, making the world's most impossible organism glow so that we can locate a portal that will open up the moon for a crew of deep-sea divers to voyage into the universe. Give it a few minutes."

"Well, look who's the sudden convert," Danny said.

Mort drove on, grinning from ear to ear.

Danny continued, "Next you're going to concede my point that Kai and Av are Cain and Abel."

Huntsman breathed in sharply.

"See? Doris knows that."

"I do not concede that point. That is myth," Cynthia said.

Huntsman put her face in her hands.

"Come on. *Kai N. Adamson*? *Av L. Adamson*? Read their names in Hebrew. Sounds the same."

Huntsman cleared her throat and pulled her hands away from her face. "In all the years I've known them, that thought has never once occurred to me."

"Really?" Mort said.

"Why should that be obvious?" Huntsman said.

"Those brilliant green eyes," Danny said.

"That's not in the Bible," Cynthia said. "Neither is any of this."

"And yet," Mort said. He lifted the car into the dark, thin air of the underworld. Lichen glowed green, pink, and purple in a swirling pattern around a black center. Lichen did not grow on one part of the black circle so that the whole looked like a solar eclipse right before the moon lined up fully. "I think we've found our way."

***

"I think I see our way," Hudson said. He had been lying in his cubicle for hours while the moonshock passed above him in regular blurred patterns. Something had made him sit up; boredom, perhaps. What he saw was not on the moonshock at all but on the surface of the Earth: a thin black line stretching mostly across the open ocean, from the shores of Pakistan on the Indian Ocean, through the Strait of Magellan between South American and Antarctica, across the Pacific Ocean to the Russian Kamchatka Peninsula. "Does anything else explain that line? A structure inside the moonshock?"

"Hold that thought," came Conque's voice.

While Hudson waited for Conque's response, he watched the black line expand outward in wispy clouds like ink leaking through wet paper.

"But it only spills out on one side," Marson said. "On the whole, it looks like a solar eclipse right before the moon centers on the sun."

Conque came on the intercom. "That is the longest straight line through the ocean on Earth."

The screen lowered, and the *Dawn Shredder*'s motion-tracking software appeared. Hudson and the others could see the line mapped on the screen.

"Sir," Marson said. "On a hunch, sir, what is the longest straight line across the ground?"

The line came up on the screen. It ran from Sierra Leone to southeastern China, right through the pyramids of Egypt.

"I'll be damned," Conque said. "They intersect right

where Huntsman is, in the Himalayas." Someone zoomed in on the map. "Nanga Parbat."

Hudson had no idea what Huntsman was doing in the Himalayas when Earth was under attack from spectral forces and the *Dawn Shredder* was seeking a way through the moonshock.

As if reading Hudson's mind, Conque said, "She's down there looking for a portal to light our path. Looks like she's done it."

Before Hudson could process the words Conque had just said, Conque continued, "Listen up. Commander Thomas is going to align us with the black line, the sea path. MacDuff, you saw this first. You're going to look up as we're aligning and tell us if we've got a highway to the stars or not."

Hudson lay down again. His heart raced. It took an hour to align the *Dawn Shredder* with the thin black line. He calmed down during that time until, as the ship matched its path with the newly christened Great Oceanic Arc, Hudson could see what they were facing as clearly as he had once seen through the ocean. The thin black line on Earth was a canyon in the moonshock, a canyon formed by a subtle difference in the light, nothing more than a specter would produce on Earth. The canyon was narrow, but it was deep.

"I see our way," Hudson said.

"Suit up, gentlemen," Conque said. "We're going in."

Hudson put on his diving suit. The suit he had tested in the pressures of the deep ocean and the time dilation present near the Great Meteor Seamount was the same suit he would wear through the moonshock. If the *Dawn Shredder* broke apart, his pod would hold together. If his pod broke apart, his suit would keep him alive, at least for a little while, long enough to send a report, long enough to contemplate the beauty of the cosmos, before he suffocated.

Hudson lay back down. The glass cover of his cubicle closed. The rear door opened, and, as the divers had drilled several times a day on their way to the moonshock, the pods drifted backward until they formed one long chain with the pods in which the humanoids were kept. The only logic Hudson had heard for this had come from Conque: "Longer the chain, better the odds."

The *Dawn Shredder* accelerated. Pressure increased on Hudson's spine. The smell of blood rose into his nose. The moonshock became a blur. All Hudson knew of the world outside his body was the face of Rear Admiral Devon Conque on the heads-up video in his helmet. The man seemed calm.

Hudson's eyes sagged from the strain as they accelerated toward a few percentage points of light speed and into the canyon he had identified. Conque grimaced. Static came through the radio. Commander Thomas said it was like fine sand hitting the ship. Hudson knew it was ice, like he had fallen through into Antarctica. Maybe that was where they were headed. Conque had grabbed the controls. Through the static, Hudson made out the words, "I once drove a flimsy RV through two thousand miles of specter-infested wasteland. I can do this, too."

Conque's eyes and veins glowed blue. It must run in the family, Hudson thought. Conque was making the whole ship into a devonium spear, a battering ram. Maybe the whole moonshock would burst into sparks like a specter, the specter looming over Earth for a generation.

Something rocked the *Dawn Shredder*. The feed cut. Hudson's pod slammed sideways. Another pod flew past Hudson's. Then a body in a diving suit. Hudson's pod was sliding on something. Ice. That was what he saw in place of the shell of the ship: the interior of a vast globe of ice. He was inside a snow globe. Ice all around and blackness in between. No stars. No sun. No planets. He hit something else and spun for a few seconds, but the friction of the ice righted him. He did not know how fast he was going. His pod vibrated. The vibrations grew stronger, and the glass shattered. Hudson was in midair. It was white ice all around him. He hit the ice and slid, head first, face down. His body grew hot from the friction. Something was in the ice. It took a minute until he slowed enough to see the blurry blobs in the ice below. They were people, frozen in the ice. They seemed calm. Maybe they were dead. Maybe he would join them soon.

Hudson stopped sliding. There was a body in the ice below him, much deeper than the others. He thought it might be moving, but that could have been a trick of the light bouncing through the thick ice. He turned around and faced the interior of this inverted globe of ice. Where light came from, he could not see. Far away, on the line his body had traced along the ice, he could see black dots. Those might be the others. They might be alive. Hudson checked his vitals. His suit was intact. He had three hours of oxygen.

He put his hands to the visor of his helmet, sighed, and prayed.

***

Mort started taking the Trans Am back toward the surface, but new laser scanning contradicted the map they had made coming in.

"I don't see those cities, either," Cynthia said.

While Huntsman, Danny, and Cynthia pressed their faces to the windows to look for familiar landmarks, Mort looked straight ahead toward a spiraling column of red, silver, and blue. Nickel-iron mantle snakes were heating a pillar of ice, which had probably drained from the Indian Ocean and which was now flooding the underworld.

"We're being locked out," Mort said. "Like Todd and I were last time. There's only one way out."

"The portal did not open for us," Huntsman said.

"It's time to make a leap of faith, Doris."

Sir Bear woofed.

"See, even Sir Bear says so."

Danny and Cynthia held hands. Mort took Huntsman's hand. She did not let go. He sped back to the portal. Mantle snakes, dozens of miles long and glowing red and silver, were descending from the sky of metal coil in a spiral pattern around the portal, drawn to Todd's Lichen. Water from the many melting pillars of ice Mort had seen on the way was oozing in thick, semi-frozen chunks into the portal between the snakes.

"This is the way you want to go?" Danny said.

"Done this before," Mort said. He let go of Huntsman's hand, angled the car sideways to slip between two snakes, and aimed for the center of the portal. The whirlpool of water that should have formed a tunnel on their way down fell away to form the horizon of this hyperbolic bubble. The Trans Am shut down. Mort had no control. He did not know if he was falling or sitting still until he felt the front tires make a gentle thud against something.

"We are stopped," Mort said.

"Omigod," Cynthia said. "We're stuck in a singularity."

"What's that ahead?" Huntsman said.

Mort squinted his eyes to see an L-shaped slice of light. He moved his head back and forth to make sure it was not just a reflection on the windshield.

"It looks like a door," Danny said. "See, no singularity, dear."

Mort tried the ignition. The car was dead. "Well...."

Huntsman opened her door.

"The vacuum of space," Danny began to say, but warm, mildewy air poured into the car. "Well, anyway, Doris, at least grab the flashlight I put in the glove box."

Mort, Danny, Cynthia, and Sir Bear followed Doris Huntsman up a flight of stone steps to the door. It was a modern metal door that opened after a few hard shoulder thrusts from Mort.

"Easier than at the obelisk."

The light that had been slipping through the door and jamb was from an exterior floodlight. The night air was dusty, and the ground was hard and dry.

"We're somewhere," Huntsman said.

Mort walked ahead and turned around. Rising above a low platform was the rear end of the Great Sphinx. Sir Bear barked at the ancient cat.

41

Lucy sat, shoulder-deep, in the brackish water at the mouth of Norfolk Canyon. Some frogs had already found a place to play here. Her body trembled, but not with power she had hoped to conjure. She was shivering.

"It's not working, is it?" came a voice.

Lucy stood and looked around. No one was there. "Declan?"

"It's Jody, Lucy."

She crouched under the water again. "I thought the pope told you not to touch that crystal ball."

"What the pope doesn't know can't hurt him."

"How did you get here? Why are you here? How are you even talking to me?"

"Call it an urge, Lucy. A sense about a friend."

"Whatever you're doing, stop. I'm naked."

"You dropped your dress at the city gate, and now you're embarrassed? I've seen more of you than this, Lucy. I've been inside your head. We all have."

Lucy saw her face reflected dully on the water's surface. She blew ripples. "You haven't seen everything."

"What did you see when you looked up at the sky a few minutes ago?"

Lucy laid her chin on her knees and stared out to sea. "A faint streak of orange flames. The *Dawn Shredder* in a million pieces. It's over, Jody. I just have to pretend I'm not a mother again." Lucy made a false start of tears. "Why won't the monsters come and tear me to pieces? Why didn't they ever just do that for me?"

"*Parce que la mer te couvre*, Lucy. Besides, you don't know Hudson's fate."

"A mother knows. He's not in this world anymore."

"I lost a nephew up there. But you have another son. And I have a daughter."

The sea began to stir.

"Here we go, Jody. The monsters are coming. I'm ready. Hear my confession."

"You're not even Catholic. There's nothing I can do for you. Let them hear it, instead."

"Who?"

Clear figures walked out of the sea, visible only from their dripping water. They seemed human. As water ran off and evaporated, the figures began to disappear again, though Lucy could see their footprints in the mud.

"What," Lucy began to say when she felt two hands on her knees. It was the red-haired girl. Lucy tried to pull back, but an equal and opposite force within her pinned her to the ground. The girl looked at Lucy with somber and confident eyes. Lucy stuck out her chin. "Jody, it's your sister."

"That's not Madeleine, Lucy."

Lucy grabbed fistfuls of mud. "Where's Ethel, then?"

"You're on your own this time. What did Ethel say to you back in Antarctica when she was standing over Hudson?"

Lucy washed her hands of mud and put them on top of the girl's hands, which were still on Lucy's knees. Tears did come this time, and Lucy buried her face against the pile of hands. Through halting breath, Lucy said, "She said, 'I'll make you a trade.'"

The girl put her forehead against Lucy's. The girl's red hair, its ends wet and heavy, fell forward and completed the enclosure.

Jody did not answer, and Lucy knew she was alone with the girl. A curtain of red hair would be her confessional.

"I," Lucy began when the girl shushed her.

"Let's play a game," the girl said.

"Okay," Lucy said. A smile flashed across her face. "What kind of game?"

"We'll sing a song, Ladymouse."

Lucy tried to remember one of the songs she had written as Ladymouse. None of them were appropriate, not "Dirty Band-Aid on the Floor," "Strawberry Bullets," or even "Don't Assume Seamus Amuses."

"I know," the girl said. "I say a word, and you make a line out of it."

"Okay," Lucy said.

Within the recording booth their tent of red hair had become, Lucy and the girl sang:

Hail hits hard on hollow homes
Hallowed womb or harrowed tomb
Not a very merry choice

"I know what you're doing, my love," Lucy said. "Let me finish it my way."

The girl smiled, and Lucy sang:

Grace is sown in aggregate
Earth is full of ripened fruit
Cleaving, leaving seed for birds

Plucking, tucking into beaks
Flicking up in skyward streaks
Mothers feed off each other

Eve arrives with shriven flesh, and
Makes this Earth her wedding dress
Grooms a sea that belches death
Tames it with each blessed breath

Lucy grew tired and said, "What's your name?"

The girl took Lucy's hands and pulled her forward. They plunged into the water. The girl pulled Lucy deeper. Her eyes smiled now, lit by rays of the sun slanting through the waves. With those eyes, or some other organ Lucy could not see, the girl answered Lucy, *Ryddenhouse.* That was their name. That was what they would do together.

Where? Lucy asked.

You mean when?

While she processed this answer, Lucy looked about. Mantle snakes were slinking up to shore. *What about them?*

My friends will take care of them. The ones I came with.

You made a trade, remember? The world has my friends, and
now I have you.

Lucy turned and saw the mantle snakes writhing at
the feet of the transparent people who had walked ashore;
they were unable to slither forward. Sparks burst above the
surface of the water, a line of fireworks as far as the water
would let her see. She faced forward again and saw the girl
swimming freely. Lucy was falling downward in her wake.

They swam deeper and deeper for several minutes this
way, and Lucy saw the edges of the hidden river the Chesapeake had carved into the ocean floor over the millennia.
The light faded. There was a moment of complete darkness,
and Lucy thought the girl had abandoned her, lured her
into the death she deserved, or at least craved. She had not
breathed in many minutes. But the girl reappeared in silhouette. Below her, something glowed. The sea itself turned
indigo. Spiral arms of starry light appeared from behind the
girl's body. Then a whole galaxy. This was where Lucy was
going. She was not going to die. Wherever this portal took
her, or whenever, as the girl had said, Lucy would live.

Just as she smiled at this and started kicking forward
with her feet, her belly pulsed with lightning.

***

Hudson jumped in near-sleep, the way a body does
when dreaming of a fall. He had one hour of oxygen left.
Trying to reach the others had been pointless; the shell of
ice on which he lay, in which he was trapped, was the size
of the moon, and the others were scattered across hundreds
of miles of its surface. There was nowhere to walk, so he

stopped and uttered prayers as dry as the ice surrounding him.

They had made it through the moonshock. An empty shell was all that had waited for them. The rest of the universe had been an illusion, a projection made by some great entity on the outer wall of the moonshock or the remnant of the great lie nature had always been telling and in which, for the past thirty years, it had been caught.

But Hudson and his body and the bodies of his friends were real. He was breathing real breath, the last he would take. Perhaps his soul would join those of the others trapped in the ice below him. He held up Amy Anklesore, which he had tucked into his belt. "Looks like the end of the road for us."

A humanoid appeared above him.

Hudson sprang to his feet and slipped on the ice.

The ice shifted. A crack extended between his legs. That was what had woken him a minute ago.

He turned around. Liquid water was not far below the surface. The ice would melt soon, and he would fall in. It made no difference if he died up here or down there. But there was a promise, at least, in something new.

A body swam deep in the dark water. He hoped it was his mermaid, Lance Corporal Atalanta Bridgewater. The swimmer drew near the surface. It was her.

Hudson knelt on all fours, heaving laughs and happy tears that dripped onto the visor of his helmet. Here was another way forward. He would live.

Bridgewater floated just below the ice, pointing at Hudson. The ice was melting and, with an hour's worth of oxygen, he could wait.

The radio in Hudson's helmet screeched. The humanoid was talking.

Hudson looked past the humanoid. The whole of this icy sphere had been visible to him before, but now a mist began to rise from it. "*Muito obrigado, Senhor Roboto.* But I've seen this before. The sky will become the mist and the ice will melt away into sky and Bridgewater will carry us to safety."

The mist thickened and a warning light came on in Hudson's helmet. He tapped the control panel on his arm to see what was the matter. He felt tapping at his feet. Bridgewater was knocking on the ice. Hudson found the problem. The mist was not registering as water vapor. It was showing as gaseous oxygen and hydrogen. "That's not water," Hudson said. "That's—"

A bright orange flash appeared in the corner of his eye. It was growing bigger. The world was on fire.

Hudson made a hammer from his joined fists and pounded the ice. It did not crack any more than it already had. He stood and jumped, but his feet did no better, and pain from his previous injury shot up his left leg.

The humanoid imitated him. It pounded the ice with some hideous strength, tearing away at its own rubbery skin and woven muscles until a skeleton of devonium alloy finished chipping away at a hole big enough for Hudson to slip through. But not big enough for his helmet.

Bridgewater pointed to her head. Hudson mimicked her, tapping his helmet. Taking that off meant certain death.

Almost certain death: he would have less than a minute in the vacuum of space to make his way through. And then he would have to hold his breath for however long it took to swim with Bridgewater wherever she led him. Unless he breathed the ocean again, like he had with her before.

He looked up, spread his arms, and said, "It's all I've got, God."

Hudson knelt. He held his breath and unfastened his helmet. The vacuum inside the shell of the moonshock scraped at his face with icy fingernails, and he felt like that dog had looked so many months ago, ribs and eye sockets ready to burst and billow out blood. He squeezed through the narrow, inflexible hole the humanoid had made.

Bridgewater grabbed his hands, set her feet against the ice on either side of the small hole Hudson had made, and pulled him through.

He could not see, but he felt certain that the edges of the ice had scraped off his diving suit. The water was not breathable, but it was not as cold as he had thought it would be. Bridgewater pulled; she was somehow swimming backward. The water rushed by more slowly and seemed to be thickening. Hudson could see nothing. His body quaked for breath, but he would not let his lungs take in the thickening stuff around him. As Bridgewater continued to drag him through the mud, he was passing the limit of his brief training as a diver. Fighting not to take a poisoned breath was to teach his body hope.

The mud became gritty. Change was good. Something tickled his neck. Flowing water. A sound filled his ears. Waves gently breaking. Hudson opened his eyes. Sparkling sand between his fingers. A gentle breeze along his body. He took a gaping breath. He did not know where he was, but he was alive.

Another sound: someone coughing. Hudson turned and saw another person crawling onto shore. He was not alone. Hudson heard rustling ahead of him and looked into a grove of ferns and palm trees. An animal of some kind looked at him; it was indescribably strange at first, a bundle of eyes, horns, and fur, until it coalesced into something familiar, a sheep, and yet it was not completely like the sheep he knew.

Hudson sat down, facing the sea from which he had crawled. It was a turquoise color up close where it was shallow and deep blue toward the horizon. It was almost the color of a tropical sea on Earth. The same was true of the color of the sky, the trees, and the sand; it was all a little different. Hudson looked right to see the other person who had come out of the sea. The young man was sitting down, like him, taking in the strange new scene. Past the young man, on the horizon, a moon rose. Hudson looked left: another moon was setting, and another person was crawling out of the water. Hudson pulled Amy Anklesore from between his belt and what remained of his diving suit—she had become a sodden, muddy mess of a stuffed animal, more turtle than mighty *Ankylosaurus*. Holding her in both hands, he knew Lucy had somehow made this journey possible for him and understood how glad she had been to see her old companion, Peter Panda, again. As mute as both ragged balls of cotton were, they were a sign, even a promise, that life was never lost.

Someone cleared his throat behind him. Hudson stood

and turned around. Next to the alien sheep was Uncle Billy, William De Soto White Wolf. He looked younger physically, but his eyes and his bearing kept all the wisdom and poise of old age. "It's about time, Hudson. Welcome to our new world."

42

Mort sat on a makeshift stage underneath the Gateway Arch in St. Louis. It was midmorning, and the arch's long shadow slunk ahead of him, to the west, climbing up and down the sun-bleached walls of the New White House and Hall of Watchers. He was as certain now as he had been months ago that no human had repaired the Gateway Arch overnight. He was in the shadow of a giant mantle snake and whatever entity controlled it.

But this was an occasion for joy and celebration. Almost every sleeper on Earth had woken. Specters and their carriers, the mantle snakes, were held in check at the ocean's edge by some mysterious force. The world's thirty-year exodus through the desert was over, and human beings could reclaim their promised land. President Philips could have given Mort, Claire, and above all, Huntsman, commendations for their efforts in his private office. But this, and the many ceremonies to come, was a way to tell the world all was well.

Under the shadow of the arch, Mort could not shake the feeling that, though the exodus was over, a Babylonian exile had begun. He sat next to Claire and Huntsman, Joe Curly, Jr., and Grey Swan, and a number of those who had ridden with them to Kashmir and back. Black Mare had run off on their return to Marigold's house. Marigold, herself, could not be bothered with an event like this.

The president was honoring them not for helping send the *Dawn Shredder* through the moonshock, a project that seemed to have failed—and which, to their work, no logical connection could be made—but for discovering a horde of underworld cities that a special joint operation of American and local forces would investigate. Mort did not know if they would call on him or not, if anyone else besides Huntsman and the OSS believed he and Todd had ever possessed particular powers for penetrating the mantle. Mortimer Sowinski, Ph.D. had other things he could be working on, especially life with a woman who had not rejected him yet. He took Claire's hand.

The band finished their brassy song, and President Philips took the podium. Before he spoke, a murmur rolled through the crowd. Mort heard footsteps on the wooden platform behind him and the chuff of a large cat. Philips turned to look, and Mort followed his gaze.

Standing on the stage, for lack of a chair, was Melanie De Soto Black Mare. She wore a long black sequin dress that sparkled in the morning sun, but the light seemed most pleased to dance around her long black hair and sculpted form. Two saber-toothed cats sat on either side of her. By some violent glint in their eyes, Mort could tell the ancient *Smilodons* were docile to her alone.

Grey Swan leapt from his chair and gave it to Black

Mare. An usher arrived with another chair for Grey Swan. Grey Swan ignored him and gawked at her while she sat and nodded to Philips, inviting him to start his speech.

Philips faced forward again with reluctance and cleared his throat. "My fellow Americans, and people of a new world, welcome. We are here to honor a work that has, these past twenty-nine years, largely gone unseen."

Mort was not so sure about that. Many had cheered when Huntsman had taken the stage.

"But we need to recognize here, today, the invaluable work of the Office of Special Science, and in particular, its technical director, Dr. Doris Huntsman."

Cheers erupted. Mort was right. He let go of Claire's hand to applaud.

"Her work began in Navy intelligence, investigating the links between activity in deep space and the deep sea. What emerged from her efforts and that of her team was evidence of the transformation the moondark and the new cosmos has had on our very bodies and souls. We have some miracles walking among us, much rumored about all these years. Some are even on stage with us now. Would you please stand?"

Huntsman nodded to Mort, Claire, and the others, and they stood. As Mort scanned the crowd, he saw Kai clapping. Kai leaned over to the woman next to him, and she whistled.

Philips continued, shaking a proud fist. "You, Dr. Huntsman, have been masterminding this work from the beginning. We should never have doubted what your patience has produced. Like a queen on the chessboard—"

"Queen Doris," the woman in the crowd called out.

Philips froze. None of the military brass or senatorial suits on his side dared twitch a muscle.

"Queen Doris," a man echoed, and the phrase bounced from mouth to mouth until, in unison, it formed a tsunami wave rushing toward the stage.

Huntsman locked her hands at her waist and let her head hang. She looked at Mort with what seemed like the first expression of helplessness Mort had ever seen on her.

Claire's face was frozen in a smile, and she hammered each clap together.

Before Mort could fully formulate a question in his mind about Claire's reaction, he fixed on Philips. The president's eyes were knives of polished silver, and he wore a triumphant smile that told Mort that, with a crowd squeezed between a mountain of triumph and a cliff of madness, Philips wanted Huntsman for a queen just as he had wanted Deborah Palmer before her.

***

Jody was in position for Huntsman's arrival. His legs were propped upon a pedestal that housed another green globe. He held a book in one hand, a glass of brandy in the other. He ignored the book and sipped the brandy while he listened for footsteps coming down the hallway.

The porter knocked, Jody replied, and Doris Huntsman walked into his office at the Vatican Observatory.

"Queen Doris," Jody said. "Please excuse me while I try to set my legs down." Jody set down his book and his brandy and made a pretense of pulling his legs off the pedestal.

"I see you've grown comfortable in your new role."

"We shall enjoy it."

"We?"

Jody sat back waved his hand. "The royal 'we.' And you, your majesty?"

Huntsman clasped her hands at her waist. "Jody, I am the American delegate and founding chairperson of the International Office of Special Science. Nothing more."

"And nothing less. How does it feel to be a queen?"

Huntsman leaned on the pedestal. "How does it feel to be a god?"

"So far, the only problem with being an all-seeing god is that you can't see yourself as others see you. You can't see yourself through the eyes of your adoring fans. That's the genius of the one true God: in the Son of God, the Father can see Himself as He is seen. He knows the joys of His own existence. And those will be our joys in heaven, too: to see ourselves with God's own loving eyes, to know how we are loved. Until then, it's merely comfortable, especially with a little brandy."

She tapped his feet. "You're maybe a little too comfortable with a device like this. They've let you build a new one?"

"What, Doris? This *palantir*? It's a bowling ball on a birdbath. Go ahead. Put your hands on it."

"I do not possess your powers."

Jody adopted an epic tone and said, "See if the *orbuculum* shares its power with you."

"Move your feet off it first."

Jody pretended to try to move his legs again, and Huntsman helped him, lifting his feet and pulling them aside.

When Jody had his feet beneath him, he nodded. Huntsman smirked and laid her hands on the green ball.

The office darkened and filled with an image, that of the *Dawn Shredder* breaking apart against the moonshock. Huntsman pulled away her hands.

"How did I do that?" she said.

"Let's look at the science," Jody said. He pulled the ball off the pedestal and handed it to Huntsman.

"This really is a bowling ball," she said, putting her fingers into its holes. "Jody, what's going on here?"

"Doris, come on. You, yourself, got it right years ago."

Her eyes narrowed and fixed on him. "You're the antenna, Jody."

A smile tugged timidly against the hem of Jody's cheek. Like a parent reeling from some hidden pain, he cast stern but sympathetic eyes down to the bowling ball. He replayed the crash of the *Dawn Shredder* in the long canyon of the moonshock.

"I've gone over this a thousand times, Doris. Not all of the pieces are accounted for. Many of the divers' pods made it through."

Huntsman held the bowling ball at her belly as if it were a baby in her womb.

"You did it, Doris. The path he followed matches the line of lichen you saw."

"How, Jody? How did it work?"

Jody leaned forward. "Dr. Doris Huntsman, you of all people should know. You went into the bowels of the Earth on a hunch. One formed by a certain connection, one you might even call, I don't know, love."

She put the ball back on the pedestal.

"But the Greeks have many words for love," Jody said.

"Exactly," Huntsman said. "For instance, you've never had sight like this on your own. Only when you've made connections. So tell us, Jody, where are your eyes? Where's Lucy? She disappeared in the chaos at New Norfolk."

"Tell *us*, Doris?"

She flicked her wrist. "The royal 'us.'"

"Of course, your majesty. And where are my manners? Do you want some brandy?"

"I do, actually."

Jody stood and poured. While Huntsman took her glass, he motioned an invitation to a large window overlooking the garden. A thin blanket of gray clouds filtered the sunlight, deepening the garden's greens, which practically dripped off the grass and hedges with the mid-August humidity.

"What's your next move, Doris?"

"To do what I've always done. To measure the givens."

"And what are the givens?"

"There are thousands of souls trapped in the ice at Thiel, and so far, only you and Lucy have been able to free them safely."

"Safely," Jody muttered, realizing Huntsman, or at least Darby, had tried again. "How's our Phlegethon doing?"

"We've hit a language barrier. A conceptual barrier. Or, more than that, I should say. A totally different way of relating to this world." Huntsman sipped her brandy.

Jody continued, "Let me offer another suggestion, then: the humanoids, Doris. They're not really effective assassins, are they? That's a lie the government's been telling for thirty years. One you and I know better than to believe but one we've helped perpetrate to keep people away from them. Haleh, when I saw her in the obelisk, told me the dapper priest would hide a lie in what he was saying. He made himself out to be the *artiste* of this whole thing, sending souls into humanoids, and these into specters, et cetera. And that had been my theory, too. But I don't think he sent the humanoids."

"Who did, then? God? Ethel Rede?"

"Yes. You and Lees and Billy were always so careful not to name our enemy, not to give it a form to hide behind. And the devil, excuse me, I mean the *other*, seemed happy enough to make us think we were fighting humanoids. But it's always been bare specters who've done the most damage, those entities looking to occupy some form of life or another. I think the humanoids filled the gap, as it were. Were sent into the breach."

"You want me to believe that this Ethel Rede has been orchestrating a massive ruse, one that has been supplying the human race with the very thing you think led God to cause the moondark in the first place, AI so advanced it could be possessed by demons? That's your theory now? To what end?"

"They're like dinosaurs were for Mort and Todd. Something to help our imagination, something measurable to train against for the bigger battles ahead. The more these machine-men are woven into our daily lives, the more human we're going to have to be, which means, from my perspective, living more like God."

Huntsman sipped her brandy. "Your friend Ethel, then,

would have to have gone way back in time to send them to us. You know where they come from. Or *when*, I should say."

"Well, who knows? Maybe there's someone working for us from before the Flood. Someone who's already proven he can communicate through humanoids. Someone, as your dear uncles said, who is at the mouth of the ram's horn."

Huntsman crossed her arms, held her brandy snifter to her forehead, and closed her eyes.

"You get it now, Doris. You and I and the members of Wepwawet, we're pieces on a four-dimensional chessboard. When it's time, Lucy and I will free those souls trapped in the ice." Jody sipped his brandy, letting the thick spirits deep in the glass dance inside his nose. "After all, we'll going to need a bigger army."

"For what, some final battle between good and evil? Across all the generations?"

"It's shaping up that way."

Huntsman looked back toward the green ball on the pedestal.

"With him, too, Doris. But like Haleh said before she died, he is wherever he is to keep the other away. And when our river runs back to us, he'll arrive with the host of those people I sent away during the Great Eclipse." He grinned and nodded at Doris. "*Parmi les étoiles.*"

Caeli enarrent gloriam Dei

Hudson sat around a fire the night of his arrival with the others who had come ashore. They were twelve in total, with several humanoids, and the story of their lives on Earth had somehow intersected. Hudson had known Tyne Philips, the president's son, by sight. He had also heard a little about Jordan Conque, Father Joseph's nephew. With them was Niles Jackson, who had wept openly at the story about his mother, Charlaine, which Mort had shared with Hudson. Among the eight others, Hudson knew only William White Wolf. No one from the *Dawn Shredder* had come through.

"Not here, anyway," White Wolf said. "It's possible they're on other worlds."

The men argued about why they had been transported, where they were, and what Hudson and White Wolf had told them about the world after the Great Eclipse. None of the others had spent any time on Earth after those three days but had come straight here. White Wolf tried to explain that Hudson had opened the gate for them.

"And where are the women?" Niles said. "Are we here to populate a new planet, or what?"

A pair of green eyes, glowing through the darkness,

hovered toward them on a dark silhouette, as if the eyes had been borrowed from the reflection of the stars on the turquoise water and the silhouette taken from the dark sea itself. "Good evening, gentlemen," came an accented voice from the silhouetted figure. He walked forward, and the light of the fire, more than reflecting off the strange man, seemed to give him skin and bones. "You no doubt have many questions."

Hudson turned to White Wolf, who did not seem to recognize the man.

White Wolf said, "What is your name, sir? You look like two others I know."

"My great uncles have carried you well," the man said. "My named is Henoch. I was taken up to visit you and give you insight."

Jordan Conque said, "What do you mean, you were taken up to visit us? Didn't you live thousands of years ago?"

"Look up at the stars," Henoch said. "How long would it take to travel to any one of them, even at the so-called speed of light? Thousands, millions of years, you would say. But you would feel it instantaneously, like a photon does. And if you could travel instantaneously, how could you accomplish that? Only with a thought. And your thought would be based on the sight of things as they were when you left. You would arrive at a time that their light is showing you here, now. Just like you did from Earth."

Hudson watched the other men's faces contort as they pondered Henoch's words. White Wolf matched his gaze and shrugged.

"I will speak in your terms, then," Henoch said. "You are

four hundred light-years from Earth. If the light from Earth could reach you, you would see it as it was, four hundred years ago."

"So," Tyne Philips said, "if we wanted to go back to our time on Earth, we'd have to wait four hundred years on this planet?"

"Which is how much time you have, my friends," Henoch said.

"To do what?" Hudson said.

"To receive the light of the new Earth. It wraps around this whole universe. It is like what your people on Earth used to identify as the cosmic background radiation. When that light arrives, you will have needed to make these people ready."

White Wolf cleared his throat. "What people?"

"You are not alone here."

"Oh, good," Niles said, speaking Hudson's thought.

"Yes, it is good for you to be here," Henoch said. "And the twelve thousand other cohorts like yours spread across the universe. But your life will not be as you think. Not as you had hoped it would be. You are to take nothing from this world for yourself. You are a chain, holding this world back until it is ready and helping it forward when it is. These people have been here for a long time, much longer than thirty years."

"How long?" Hudson said.

"Long enough to forget where they are from and what that light is that is returning to them from the edge of the cosmos."

* * *